NANO

NANO

JOHN ROBERT MARLOW

A TOM DOHERTY ASSOCIATES BOOK
NEW YORK

This is a work of fiction. All the characters and events portrayed in this novel either are fictitious or are used fictitiously.

NANO

This book is printed on acid-free paper.

Book design by Milenda Nan Ok Lee

Edited by James Frenkel

A Forge Book
Published by Tom Doherty Associates, LLC
175 Fifth Avenue
New York, NY 10010

www.tor.com

Forge® is a registered trademark of Tom Doherty Associates, LLC.

Library of Congress Cataloging-in-Publication Data

Marlow, John Robert.
　　Nano / John Robert Marlow.—1st ed.
　　　　p.　cm.
　　"A Tom Doherty Associates book."
　　ISBN 0-765-30129-6 (acid-free paper)
　　1. San Francisco (Calif.)—Fiction.　2. Nanotechnology—Fiction.
　3. Inventors—Fiction.　4. Disasters—Fiction.　I. Title.

PS3613.A766N36 2004
813'.6—dc22

　　　　　　　　　　　　　　　　　　　　　　　　　　　2003061748

Printed in the United States of America

0　9　8　7　6　5　4　3　2

for my mother,
and the world

ACKNOWLEDGMENTS

Few books make it to publication without help; the present volume being no exception, the author would like to thank Kenneth Atchity of Atchity Entertainment International (AEI), for taking on the project and for editorial suggestions which improved both novel and subsequent screenplay, for presenting the book and its author to Jim Frenkel and to Colden-McKuin-Frankel, and for being a helluva guy in general; Joseph Austin of Forge Books for his remarkable forbearance; Tom Doherty, publisher; Greg Beal, for talking me up all over Hollywood and for his tireless efforts on behalf of all writers entering the Nicholl Fellowships In Screenwriting of the Academy of Motion Picture Arts & Sciences, which program he oversees; James Frenkel of Forge Books, for editorial patience and suggestions which improved the novel and the script that followed—and who can wear sandals anytime he pleases; Jeffrey Frankel, Joel McKuin and David Colden of Colden, McKuin & Frankel for changing the numbers; Peter Hauck, for building my first real computer and for putting up with annoying technical questions relating thereto for far too long; Jacqueline, my darling and *mein schatz,* for suggestions on the screenplay that were so good, I went back and incorporated them into the novel—and for so many other things that mere words cannot suffice as thanks; Mark Kasdan of Kasdan Pictures, for *Silverado* and for sticking with me through several pitches and biting on the *Nano* script just when I thought I'd never hear from him again—thereby aiding and abetting my avoidance of a first-rate hangin'; Seth Lerner of St. Martin's Press, for coming up with the cool cover design; Todd Lieberman, of Mandeville Film & Television for questions about nanotech and suggestions on the screenplay, which caused me both to add material and to realize that existing material in novel and screenplay would benefit from clarification; Janis Lonnquist, for making it possible for me to meet the King of the World; Don Madderra, for giving me the time; John Matthews, for indirectly providing the aforementioned first real computer; Captain Donald P. Savage (retired, he likes to think), for service above and beyond the call of duty, a desperately needed refuge from all things politically correct, and the occasional turkey sandwich; Chi-Li Wong of Atchity Editorial/Entertainment International (AEI), for editorial suggestions so eerily similar to my own line of thought that I immediately recognized her innate brilliance; Eliezer S. Yudlowsky, co-founder and director of the Singularity Institute for Artificial Intelligence, for answering numerous questions; the people who provided the benefit of their expertise in scientific and other matters, and who—for various reasons—would probably prefer to remain anonymous; the guys and gals (especially Jason, Louise, Dominique, Jeremy, and Mike) at Godfather's Pizza on Truxel, who kept me fed with my favorite during dinner buffets; and, last and least, those literary agents and agencies which "passed" on my various works—*Nano* included—at various times, ultimately leaving me free to find representation with Ken. The fault for any technical errors contained herein lies solely with the author.

*Any sufficiently advanced technology is
indistinguishable from magic.*

—Arthur C. Clarke

Man will be his own destruction.

—Mraxis, A.D. 132

NOTE TO THE READER

Nothing portrayed in this novel is impossible. Nanotechnology is real. The United States Army, Air Force, and Navy are currently working to develop nano capability for use as a weapon. More on this in the afterword and on the author's Web site at www.john robertmarlow.com.

PORTENT

[Nanotechnology] is a development which I think cannot be avoided.

—Richard Feynman
Nobel laureate, 1959

When the richest man in the world calls a press conference to announce the most important discovery in the history of the human race, a crowd can be expected. When the man calling that conference is also the head of the largest computer technology firm on the planet, Jennifer Rayne will be in attendance.

At twenty-eight, Jen no longer passed for young in the techno-geek community which she covered for *TEK* magazine—but by any standard, she did pass for beautiful, and that quite easily. Black-haired and emerald-eyed, her features spoke of intelligence and culture, with a dash of the rebellious. This impression was not misleading.

Jennifer Rayne was not, however, at the press conference. The reason was a rodent.

A blinding white flash rent the darkness, illuminating and then obliterating the desert landscape. The air became red-orange with gamma-heat spreading outward at the speed of light. The earth trembled with the seismic shock wave—on its heels the crushing blast wave which left no thing behind. Next came the mind-shattering roar of detonation, and the demon-howl of supersonic winds. Last of all, the blinding whiteness faded to the mere scintillating brilliance of a rising thermonuclear fireball.

John Marrek would not see the cloud which followed—given its distinctive mushroom shape by the greater drag of the atmosphere at the cloud's expanding edges—because his eyes melted from their sockets even as his body turned to vapor, leaving only a shadow on the ground where once had stood a man.

John awakened with a jolt, eyes haunted by the nightmare fireball—a familiar afterimage burned into his vision as surely as the genes of his ancestors were encoded in his DNA.

"Jesus."

Disturbed by the sudden motion, three pizza boxes fell from their perch on the running desktop to the floor. Rubbing tired eyes, John stared at the framed photograph on the desk before him. "Your nightmare, not mine," he said, and pointed at the picture. "And it's over."

Ten of the thirty-three computer monitors occupying the fifty-foot-long, wall-hugging desktop and the shelf above it flashed to life, displaying the words IT'S SHOWTIME as a particularly annoying rendition of Sousa's "Stars and Stripes Forever" blasted over speakers hung from the walls.

Shaking his head to clear it, John reached past a stack of *Nano-Technology Magazine* back issues to kill the alarm clock program. Checking his watch, he rose from his chair and moved to the refrigerator. The photo on the desk peered after him with eyes more haunted than his own.

John Marrek's thoughts were not the thoughts of an ordinary man, and never had been. Ordinary men debated the relative merits of cubic-inch displacement vs. horsepower, sports team performance, next Friday's hot date. John Marrek pondered the hazards of benevolent dictatorship vs. technotyranny, the probable nature of a technological God, and the undeserved fates of extinct species. And he knew, better than anyone else, that the ranks of the latter might soon include Man. That was the nightmare, in one of its infinite permutations.

Arguably not the worst.

John speculated often upon the mechanisms by which intelligent life might have spread itself throughout the universe. He possessed a fervent hope, almost religious in its intensity, that intelligent life did exist elsewhere; that Man was not alone in the cosmos. And each time he examined his fellow-travelers upon the small and fragile jewel-in-the-void which was earth, this hope grew more fervent. The reason was simple.

He longed for better company.

Guiding a rented Lincoln Navigator along a wooded two-lane blacktop on her way to the press conference, Jen checked her look in the mirror, then her watch, and then the curving road ahead—where four sets of startled skunk eyes stared back at her.

She jerked the wheel hard left. The truck swerved violently, turning on two wheels and flying over the ditch at the side of the road. Crashing nose first into a tree, the Navigator fell to earth.

Punched in the face by the forward air bag, Jen took a moment to wiggle fingers and toes and, convinced no major damage had been done, wrestled the deflating air bag out of the way. She checked her look in the mirror again: hair flattened, makeup ruined, nose bleeding.

"Good move, Jen."

Gazing through the open side window, Jen spotted her cell phone on the ground outside. Forcing open the crumpled driver's side door, she stepped from the vehicle. Immediately, a cloying cloud of skunk stench wafted over her. Looking to the road, she saw the mother skunk and her babies looking back at her. *"You stinkers!"* she yelled.

John's current home was a living-room-like corner situated on the second story of a battered Los Angeles warehouse. He slept here, ate here, and worked a few feet away during every waking hour. It had been that way for longer than he cared to remember.

Opening the refrigerator, he withdrew a bottle of absurdly expensive champagne and a chilled crystal glass—both of which had been waiting five years for this moment. He then made his way to an old leather lounge chair before an oversized Microtron digital television. Beside the chair was a small table, atop which was a telephone. In a few moments, simply by dialing the words NEW WORLD, John would create one. He smiled—a thing he did too seldom.

Popping the cork on the champagne, he poured a full glass and settled in to watch the media frenzy of the approaching press conference with the self-satisfied expression of a man who knows he is one of only two living humans to know already what the world is about to learn.

The other being Mitchell Swain.

The centerpiece of the sprawling Microtron Global Headquarters Complex was the "Black Pyramid," an imposing dark glass pyramid thirty stories high. The great glass panels reflected the sky overhead in darker hues, turning the brightest of days into omens of foreboding. The symbolism was appropriate, for when it came to computer technology, Microtron ruled the world, and its founding CEO—Mitchell Swain—was Pharaoh.

One mile distant from the pyramid, a cab screeched to a halt in the parking area. Jen climbed from the back, thrusting money at the driver.

"Keep it," he said, holding his nose and speeding off with the windows down.

Spotting Jen, Microtron press liaison Bernie Jensen hurried over. "Miss Rayne."

"Sorry I'm late."

Bernie stopped, then retreated a step at the smell. "We're, uh, about to begin," he coughed. Hurrying to keep ahead of the skunk scent, he led Jen to one of several walk-through scanning devices.

"If you'll just step through here, we'll be on our way." Walking through himself, he turned and waited for Jen. Several nearby security men became suddenly interested in the scanner's display screen. More interested, thought Jen, than they should have been.

"How much detail does this scanner show?" she asked.

"Uhmm, let's just say it's anatomically correct," said Bernie.

Jen cut him a look.

"Right. *Madge!*"

A heavyset security woman appeared, shooed away the men, and took over at the monitor. Jen hurried through, getting a thumbs-up from Madge, who clamped her nose shut with the fingers of her other hand.

"Right this way," said Bernie from the driver's seat of an open-air shuttle. Taking a seat in the back, Jen began her pilgrimage to the center of Microtron's domain.

The van band came first; satellite trucks with their oversized dish antennae atop telescoping poles, poised to beam the press conference to the world at the speed of light. The trucks—several of them semis containing portable television studios—formed a single, thin line so that each might have an unobstructed view of the proceedings via telescopic lenses large enough to be bazookas.

Stationed beside each truck and constantly patrolling the grounds were well-dressed, efficient-looking Microtron security men. Moving beyond the line of vans, Jen's shuttle approached the lawn.

Microtron's front yard was the size of a football stadium, and packed to capacity. Jen passed through what seemed a mile-deep ocean of reporters and news crews from around the globe. The print reporters were seated, while video journalists and newscasters addressed their cameras in English, Japanese, German, French, Russian, Spanish, Farsi, and a dozen other languages she couldn't identify. Rising above the crowd on both sides were camera platforms topped by still and video photographers. Portable, cottage-like rest room facilities were tucked discreetly out of site on the far sides of these.

The shuttle pulled to a stop just before the seating area. Bernie hopped out to show Jen to her seat. "Right this way, Miss Rayne."

Jen walked along one of two paved roads normally used to ferry Microtron employees from the parking lot to the complex and back again. The walk was a long one. The only reason she could think of for making this journey on foot was that Mitchell Swain wanted to make a point. And as always where Swain was concerned, the point was hard to miss: This was the biggest press conference in history.

Oddly, an area fully the size of the great Black Pyramid itself had been roped off on the open ground to the audience's left. Improbably, a single, gleaming pay phone stood at the center of this grassy tract.

The stage was massive, overshadowed only by the sheer enormity of the pyramid behind it. Arriving at her front-row seat—just before and to the right of the black marble podium with gold Microtron logo—Bernie removed the *TEK* placard from the lone empty chair and checked off Jen's name on his guest list. The list was, of course, stored in a wireless networked palmtop computer built by Microtron and running Microtron software.

As the press liaison departed, Jen noted that a small leather pouch hung from a clip on the back of her seat. Gazing about, she saw small, identical-looking devices perched in the hands of other journalists. Lifting the pouch from the chair, Jen opened it as she took her seat. Nearby journalists leaned away from her in an effort to escape the skunk smell.

Removing the sleek black palmtop computer inside, Jen found a small card reading: "Compliments of Mitchell Swain." Beside the gold-inlaid, pyramidal corporate logo was the name *MicroTek III*. Its predecessor was still the best-selling palmtop in history—and here Mitchell was, trumping his own product before obsolescence. It was the kind of signature move which distinguished the man from his lesser corporate brethren, and largely spared him the unending vitriol heaped upon them daily by both consumers and the press.

Estimating the size of the crowd and the probable cost of manufacturing the five-hundred-dollar device, Jen used the palmtop itself to calculate what it had cost Microtron to give one of the things away to every invited member of the press. The figure was impressive—but less than a moment's pocket change to Swain and Microtron. The release of the product had not even been announced.

Whatever this conference was about, it was going to be shattering. Only Mitchell Swain, earth's first trillionaire, could schedule a press conference without telling anyone what it was about—and have the entire world show up to find out.

Unsmiling security men in thousand-dollar suits ringed the elevated stage, scanning the crowd with predatory eyes. A veteran of several Microtron press conferences, Jen had expected to see these men—but something about them still made her flesh crawl. The impersonal gaze which passed over and through her each time one of them looked her way brought to mind a well-attired raptor sizing up its next dinner opportunity.

The fact that they showed zero reaction to her beauty or to her perfectly tailored ruby red dress didn't score them any points, either.

One man in particular caught Jen's attention. Older and harder-looking than the rest and with colder eyes, he moved among the others like a lord among vassals. It wasn't so much the man's own mannerisms which drew Jen's attention; rather, it was the manner in which the others reacted when he passed by, or looked their way—a combination of respect and awe.

Standing at the rear of the elevated stage, Mattman surveyed the crowd and the area beyond through twenty-power binoculars. The view did not waver in his steady hands. At fifty-two, Mattman's face was as hard as his mind. A former Army Ranger, Secret Service agent, and Kennedy Space Center security chief, Mattman was the highest-paid security specialist on the planet. His eyes, and his network, missed little. He'd advised Swain against making this appearance, recommending instead a more limited, indoor appearance with a live feed to the media. Large events made Mattman nervous because they rendered complete security impossible—and a man of Mitchell Swain's influence attracted enemies like blood drew sharks.

Because of the resources at their disposal and their record of success, there was a tendency among Swain's security force—dubbed the SS by the media, for Swain's Security—to veer toward an invincibility complex. Mattman fought that constantly, disciplining or firing anyone who fell below his own standard of vigilance. The standard he set for others, that is; no one could be expected to match his own, personal standard.

Mattman did not worry about the lone lunatics who sometimes took out presidents or pop stars; Swain's actual, in-person public exposure was minimal, and Mattman's security was second to none. Celebrities and politicians were required to make frequent public appearances; Swain was not. No, what concerned Mattman was the fact that, with each passing year, other companies, other nations which had once hoped to dominate Microtron or the United States in computer technologies saw themselves slipping further behind. That, and the possibility that an enemy of vast resources—a nation, perhaps, or a large corporation—might one day take it into its collective head to better its own position, or to alter the course of world affairs, by taking out Mitchell Swain. For though Microtron was a brain drain on the rest of the world's high-technology companies, Swain was, largely, still the brains of the operation. And though Microtron would not fall with Swain, it might be sufficiently weakened to provide rival companies or nations an economic advantage not otherwise attainable. A bit paranoid, Mattman thought, at times—but then, his was a profession of paranoia.

Lowering the binocs, he listened through a flesh-colored earpiece as his seventieth perimeter scout reported in with his all-clear code. "Scout Seventy. Code: Rhino. Clear."

The man beside Mattman checked the only printed list of scouts and code words, confirming that the man was using his assigned clear-code; use of any other word would trigger an immediate security scramble. "Two more and we're clear," said Mattman's companion.

Mattman's eyes scanned the crowd. "Run the dogs through the parking lot again," he said. The seventy-first perimeter scout checked in as Mattman turned and headed down the steps behind the stage. Pausing before a steel door with a camera above it, he tried the handle; locked, as it should be. A gunport slid aside in the door, revealing the muzzle of an integrally silenced, MP7SD3 submachine gun. An eye blinked behind the iron sights. The door opened as the last perimeter scout checked in. As the first door was closed and locked behind him, Mattman approached a second, which was featureless. A ceiling-mounted camera turned to track him.

"Mattman," he said to no one. A hidden microphone picked up his voice, which was matched with a recording made earlier that day. Once his identity was confirmed by the camera, the microphone, and the guard in the hall via radio, the second door opened.

Mattman stepped through into a combination command center and high-tech office located beneath the stage. Corporate assistants worked phones and computers as stern-faced security men took radio reports and monitored surveillance devices. Unlike many corporate honchos, Swain was at ease with heavy security; to him, it was just one more cost of doing business. Mattman had quit more than one gig in the past because of the principal's "I'm-not-going-to-let-security-change-my-life" attitude; those who wanted to have a life, adapted.

Glancing toward the chief executive, Mattman made his way to the monitoring station.

Across the room, before a clean desk bearing three laptops connected to a satellite dish, sat Mitchell Swain. Tall and a shade too thin, Swain was intense—but just a tad too geekish to be considered handsome. He worked the three laptops simultaneously while speaking into a headset.

"Uh-huh," he said. "Say this: If they'll give us an exemption on property taxes and defer corporate taxes for three years, I'll put up a billion-dollar complex and hire six thousand people in six months. Full benefits. Ten days to decide."

Swain cut the call as his lead attorney approached, laying a contract on the desk. "The BrightStar acquisition," he explained. Swain clicked into another call as he glanced through the pages, which concerned themselves with the purchase of the world's third-largest private satellite network. Under his guidance, it would quickly become the largest.

"Swain," he said into the microphone. Picking up a pen, he signed the document and nodded to the attorney, who departed with the contract. "No, I won't do business with his country. Tell him I might reconsider if he starts treating people like human beings and stops pirating my software. Also tell him I laughed when you asked."

He hung up. One of the two security men in charge of Swain's food appeared with crystal glass in one hand and Cherry Coke in the other. Setting down the glass, he opened the bottle and poured. "Your drink, sir."

"Thank you."

"Sir," said Swain's communications assistant, "I have the prime minister on five."

Swain turned to look at her. "Which prime minister?" He checked his watch. "Never mind. Tell him I'll get back to him after the press conference."

"Yes Mr. Swain."

"Some privacy, please," announced Swain. The room emptied in moments. Mattman was the last to leave, eyes scanning the room before closing the door behind him. Shifting his attention to the center laptop on the table before him, Swain spoke. "Prometheus."

After confirming Swain's voiceprint, the computer began to dial.

On the table beside John Marrek, a notebook computer beeped. John glanced at the monitor screen, which displayed the words SECURE CALL in gold letters. "Caller?" he inquired.

Gold letters appeared from left to right: CRASSUS

"Accept."

The face of Mitchell Swain appeared on the screen. "Behold," he began, "we say 'Let the world be born anew,' and it shall be so."

John smiled.

"You should be here."

"Not my style," said John.

Swain gazed downward. "Everything I've ever done . . . Next to this . . ." He looked up, meeting John's eyes. ". . . it's nothing. Thank you."

John nodded.

"Soon the world will be thanking you."

"We'll see," said John.

Swain grinned. A sharp knock sounded on the door behind him. "Showtime," he announced, a bit nervously.

"Knock 'em dead."

Standing, Swain nodded, then cut the connection.

Returning his gaze to the television, John raised his glass in toast. "To a new world," he said softly.

Moving to the steel door, Swain checked the video feed from the hall beyond before pulling it open. After four years with Mattman, the security man's penchant for caution was becoming second nature to him as well. The hall, of course, was filled with security men.

"All clear, sir," announced Mattman.

Swain stepped from the room.

Two thousand miles away, a laptop computer rested atop an antique desk in a dimly lit office. A leather chair creaked as its occupant swiveled around to face the computer. On the monitor screen was an image of the Black Pyramid and the stage before it. Across the bottom of the screen, in flashing red letters, were the words: GUN READY.

A manicured hand moved to grasp the joystick beside the computer. The hand bore a ring depicting a dragon. Using joystick and keyboard, the hand manipulated the image on the screen via satellite, bringing the stage into sharper focus. The hand moved again, aligning crosshairs on the Microtron logo affixed to the podium.

From her front-row seat before the podium, Jen checked her recorder and went over her notes for the interview she'd wrangled with Swain immediately following the mysterious press conference. A few well-placed questions had elicited from Microtron's public relations coordinator the flattering revelation that Swain had read every article she'd written for the past three years. From there it had been a short step to securing an interview.

She suspected, but was not quite certain, that the interview had been Swain's idea and not hers—and that she had been deftly maneuvered into seeking it. No matter. Still, despite her knowledge of the industry, it was difficult to structure interview questions without knowing in advance what the primary topic would be.

On the stage, Joseph Jennings—the man who'd arranged Jen's interview—approached the podium, tapping the microphone a few times for attention. The crowd quieted.

Jen switched on her Microtron digital recorder, checked for the RECORDING light, and dropped the device in her purse. Opening a small notebook, she sat with Fisher Space Pen poised over write-anywhere paper. An apostle of high-tech Jen might be—but when it came to interviews and press conferences, she'd learned the hard way not to place her faith in high-tech gadgets.

"Ladies and gentlemen," said Jennings from the podium, "president, founder, and CEO of Microtron—*Mitchell Swain.*"

Leaving a group of security men, the richest man in the world by a factor of ten took the podium wearing white sneakers, tan chinos, and a white turtleneck with the pyramidal Microtron logo sewn into the collar. A forthright and idealistic-looking man in his mid-forties, Mitchell Swain stood six-foot-two. Though not quite handsome, he was an impressive speaker.

Taking a deep breath, Swain surveyed the massive crowd gathered before him. "Good morning," he began. "I'm sure you're all wondering why we're here. . . ."

The scene on the laptop moved upward, focusing on Swain from chest to head.

Swain paused, sniffing the air for the source of the skunk odor which suddenly assailed his nostrils. His gaze fell upon Jen. She felt like cringing, but flashed her most devastating smile instead. Swain smiled in return, and continued.

"You know that I am not a man given to overstatement. Nevertheless, I am here today to tell you that the world, as we know it, is about to end. In its place will be a *new* world, unlike *anything* we can imagine . . ."

Jen wrote "NEW WORLD" on her pad.

The image on the laptop moved upward again, focusing on Swain's face.

"I've summoned you here today, to announce the *ultimate* technological breakthrough. An achievement that is without doubt *the most important development in the history of the human race . . .* "

Jen gazed up at him, wondering what came next. Swain's normally placid features seemed possessed; ecstatic—as though in the throes of religious revelation.

The laptop display zoomed closer, until Swain's face filled the screen and the crosshairs settled on a point over the bridge of his nose. The hand bearing the dragon ring left the joystick and moved to hover over a gray button.

"The development of a radically *new* technology which will forever *alter,* the *destiny,* of Mankind—and perhaps the very *universe* itself."

Brain matter spattered Jen's face and clothing as Mitchell Swain's head exploded before her. The deafening thunder of a distant rifle shot rent the air an instant later. Jen leapt up, at once startled and horrified—dropping pen and notepad to the grass.

Before her, Mitchell Swain pitched forward onto the podium, then slid lifeless to the stage.

Security men rushed toward the body with guns drawn and radios at their lips. Mattman looked at Swain, then moved to the front of the stage and raised his binoculars, as if daring the shooter to take his life as well. Others radioed for a medical team—but Swain was beyond help. Shot through the *medulla oblongata,* he was dead before the .50 caliber, depleted-uranium-core bullet left his skull.

Recovering from the initial shock, Jen whirled around. Standing on her chair, she strained to see past the shouting, screaming crowd around her—looking for an impossibly distant sniper who was already gone.

Seated in the warehouse before the television, John lowered the glass from his lips to the table beside him. His hand trembled so badly the glass fell to the floor and shattered. A single tear coursed downward over solemn features.

Man had just taken one giant leap toward extinction.

There was, John now knew, at least one other living person who knew what Mitchell Swain had been about to say. And if that person knew of and could locate John, what happened to Mitchell would happen to him.

The nightmare, he realized, was not over after all.

It was only beginning.

(2)

Two days earlier . . .

It was the accident which drove home the nature of the thing he had created. More than anything, it was that. It was one thing to understand the technology on an intellectual level; he as well as others had done that for years. But to actually *see* it in action—that was quite a different thing, indeed.

He'd planned to use the OMNI batch in a controlled experiment later in the day, and had removed it from the lab's secure storage area, placing it on a countertop. Three minutes later, as if planned in advance, the old building had trembled in a moderate earthquake. The quake itself was not serious; it was the cabinet falling off the wall that was serious.

The vacuum jar containing the OMNI batch exploded with the impact, spewing its contents over the counter as John leaped back in surprise. The effect was instantaneous, and despite knowing better, despite the years of preparation and the sheer, emotional terror the event should have inspired in him—John could not help but stand motionless for an instant, fascinated by the sight of it.

In that instant the thing became almost incalculably more dangerous. And then he found his voice and spoke the word.

"Safe," he said, hardly recognizing his own voice. In five seconds every room in the building was flooded with submicroscopic antagonists delivered through a kind of souped-up fire-suppression system John had had installed five years before. Neither the OMNIs nor their antagonists had existed at that time, but he had known they one day would. And that this safety system might be needed— for no fire on earth could match the all-consuming ferocity of the OMNIs. Holding his breath, he backed farther away, watching as the antagonist agents did their work.

When it was over, counter, cabinet, and interior wall were gone, and there was a hole in the floor some ten feet in diameter. Stepping cautiously forward, John peered down through the hole to the floor below.

"Have to make the next lab earthquake-proof," he muttered, making a mental note to add this to his list of safety enhancements—for, in the field he had chosen, few lessons indeed could be learned the hard way.

Fishing through her purse, Jen moved the cell phone aside and withdrew a fresh digital tape. Dropping it into place, she closed the tape bay and turned the camera on the ship below. She watched through the color flipsreen as Sergei Valenkov stepped from his red Mercedes SLK320 and walked up the gangplank into the sea-lift container ship *Titan*. Jen's position in a corner office of the dockside warehouse afforded her an excellent view of the big ship's pilothouse.

Sergei had come to her attention three months before, when she'd caught a glimpse of him in the alleyway behind the corporate headquarters of a high-profile Silicon Valley start-up called Orion. She'd been on her way to interview the company's CIO. Missing the entrance to the proper parking lot, she'd used the alley to turn around. Sergei's deep-set eyes had given her a quick, appraising glance before turning away without a second look.

Jen had always harbored a profound suspicion of men who failed to give her a second look.

And Sergei had seemed familiar. His dark, angular face had remained with her for the next two weeks. It had come together, in that odd way in which the mind works, when she'd seen someone place a bottle of Stolichnaya on the counter at the supermarket: Sergei Valenkov, former Soviet missile guidance systems engineer turned freelance software pirate in the wake of the Soviet Union's economic collapse.

Because of his rumored sideline as freelance missile guidance systems engineer, half a dozen intelligence agencies and the FBI had been looking for Sergei—without success—for ten years. What was more surprising was that Microtron had been looking for five years—ever since he'd pirated them out of some three hundred million with very convincing counterfeit high-end server software—and that they, too, had failed to find him.

The fact that the company in whose back alley Jen had caught sight of the man happened to produce missile guidance components for a major U.S. defense contractor had struck her as something more than coincidence. Calling the police then and there had never occurred to her.

Instead, she'd called *TEK*'s resident *uberhacker* Paul Gigner. With his help, she'd gotten a line on Sergei's after-hours phone calls to the company's founding president and begun tracking his movements. Which had eventually led to the seldom-used Berth 46 at the Port of Los Angeles—where Sergei stood now beneath a late-afternoon sun taking delivery, from the Chinese ship's captain, of two suitcases filled with money. Sergei was quick-counting the bills now, and it all came out beautifully in Jen's viewfinder. But then, the image processor was Microtron's.

Crossing the boards which now covered the hole in the floor, John seated himself before a monitor and composed a simple message. He then instructed the on-site parallel computer to encrypt the message to the best of its ability, afterward forwarding the message to another, larger computer which would peel away the initial layer of encryption and then reencrypt the message to the best of its own, considerably more substantial abilities.

By the time this simple message reached its intended recipient—who alone held the decryption algorithm—it would be the single most securely encrypted email on the face of the planet.

Twenty minutes later, the wealthiest man on earth checked his vibrating prototype MicroTek III PDA and tapped the SCREEN ON button to read the incoming message:

YOU HAVE MAIL
FROM PROMETHEUS

Mitchell Swain grinned at the absurdity of the notice, excused himself from the virtual board meeting in the conference room of his home, and headed for his office.

At the other end of the continent, inside a high-security office just north of the nation's capital, another man's eyes perused the message meant for Mitchell. Vincent Raster was a dark and intimidating man of fifty-four. He had the face of a man who knew too much, and was no stranger to death. To those unaccustomed to his manner, his gaze made their flesh crawl.

Raster checked the hall monitor on his desk when the pressure sensors under the hall carpet sounded a bell inside his locked office. He buzzed the door before the man in the hall could knock.

Michael Janz entered the office, closing the door behind him. It locked automatically. Raster's office was a place of perpetual darkness and gloom, as if the room itself somehow reflected the thoughts and deeds of its occupant. Janz, who had grown accustomed to Raster's ways years before, still felt uncomfortable when entering it, and when those piercing gray eyes turned his way, as they did now.

Janz was thirty-six, and weary of the pressure and the weight, the worry over the implications if they managed to develop this thing themselves—much less what might happen if someone else managed the feat. He'd have been happier not knowing anything, like the rest of the world. Or like the rest of the world had been until that loudmouth Bill Joy had started screaming that the sky was falling.

The trouble was, he'd been right.

Janz would have requested a transfer to some other spook haven had he not feared that Raster would have him killed as a potential leak. That was the way Raster's mind worked. The man was unquestionably brilliant—his IQ was so high it was classified—but dark and emotionless. The latter were both things Janz had been accused of himself—but he couldn't hold a dark candle to Raster.

Vincent Raster's eyes were even colder than usual. "Swain received an encrypted message today," he informed Janz.

"What did it say?"

"Two-fifty-six encryption."

Janz's jaw dropped. "We can't decrypt it . . ."

Raster nodded once, solemnly. Short of an implementation error—which seemed unlikely at best—whatever information Swain's message contained seemed safe from prying eyes, including Raster's. He doubted the encryption could be broken in any meaningful time frame.

"Ten minutes after receiving this message," Raster continued, "Swain canceled tomorrow's trade meeting with the British prime minister."

Janz stared at him. "You don't think . . ." He left the dreaded words unspoken.

"I don't know. I want the SIGINT stepped up immediately; I want to know about cancellations, changes in his schedule. Anything out of the ordinary. All of it. And I want to know immediately."

Leaning forward, Raster spoke in his most menacing tone. *"With-out de-lay."*

Nodding hurriedly, Janz left the room, pausing in the hall as his eyes readjusted to normal light levels. The steel door swung shut automatically, startling him as the bolt locked behind him.

Raster turned back to the monitor on his desktop, staring at the endless string of encryption code which flowed across it. In the lower-right-hand corner of the screen was a status indicator showing the progress of the agency's supercomputers in decrypting Swain's email. It read:

JOB .0000000001% COMPLETE
ESTIMATED TIME TO DECRYPT:
6 YEARS, 7 MONTHS, 10 DAYS
5 HOURS, 15 MINUTES, 27 SECONDS

Raster tapped the fingers of one hand impatiently on the antique desktop, dragon ring clacking against the wood.

As afternoon stretched into evening, Sergei departed the pier, returning again some twenty minutes later with a flatbed semi-truck behind him. The truck was promptly relieved of its forty-foot cargo container, which was loaded aboard the ship with an overhead crane. Men armed with submachine guns occasionally stepped into view on the ship's deck, scanning pier and harbor with binoculars. The camera in Jen's hands whirred softly, duly recording all. During the activity on deck, Sergei had disappeared somewhere below. She'd pick him up again when he returned for his Mercedes.

It took her a moment to realize that the faint *click* in her ear was not the digital tape reaching its end. Eyes tracking to the right, over the camera, she saw the ugly, Teflon-coated black steel of a Benchmade Armed Forces Only switchblade.

Above it: Sergei.

"А что у нас тут?" he asked in Russian: *And what have we here?*

Jen jumped to her feet and leaped back, wielding the camera like a club. Sergei smiled, revealing his trademark steel incisor. The smile faded at the sound of a submachine gun bolt *snakking* closed behind him.

"One dead Russian asshole," said a voice from the doorway.

Jen's eyes darted to the doorway—and LAPD Lieutenant Steve Price, who had a fondness for MP5s. Sergei kept his hands out to the sides, dropping the knife to clatter on the floor, as if surrendering. He turned his head to the left to look toward the doorway.

"He has a gun," said Jen, spotting the Makarov in the front of Sergei's waistband—where Price couldn't see it.

"Is that a fact?" asked Price conversationally, depressing the switch on his Sure-Fire laser sight to place a red dot on the side of Sergei's inquiring nose.

"Сука" muttered Sergei: *Bitch.*

"He says thank you for pointing that out," Price mistranslated, adding, "Good thing you didn't call any later."

"Da. Vohnderful," added Sergei, raising his hands.

"He's ditched everything," said Janz, proffering a stack of papers. Raster stared at him with worried eyes as Janz handed over the report. "As far as Harrington can tell, he's canceled everything for the next two months."

Raster flipped through the document. This was not good, he knew. Swain was busier than the president, and had meetings with five heads of state and dozens of billionaires slated for the next three weeks alone. This was so not good he felt a sudden surge of adrenaline pulse through his system. It seemed to settle in his temples, which throbbed almost painfully. "I have to know what that communication was," he said.

"But—"

"I *have* to know," Raster repeated, voice edging toward panic. The sensation was unfamiliar to him.

"We don't have that kind of muscle." *Muscle* was the term they used when referring to computing power.

Raster's mind raced. He needed this piece of information. More than anything. Going outside the agency was unthinkable; the potential for leakage, unacceptable. But this would not wait. Could not wait. He dared not make a move without confirmation. To act on his suspicion—and be proven wrong—would mean the end of everything. The program, the secrecy, his life.

But if his suspicion was correct . . .

The most powerful computers in the world were not equal to the task of swiftly decoding the encryption used on the message. The only alternative, Raster quickly concluded, was to task multiple supercomputers to the effort. To maintain some semblance of secrecy, some control over the process, the computers would need to be together, located in the same place. That way, if control proved impossible, they could be destroyed. That ruled out foreign computers.

The three largest supercomputer consumers in the world were all in the United States: Microtron, Industrial Light & Magic—a Hollywood special effects house—and NASA. The choice was not difficult. "Get Richard Tripp on the phone," he said, referring to the space agency's director.

"So what are we gonna find when we open up that trailer?" asked Lieutenant Price as the SWAT team led Sergei away in handcuffs. LAPD officers now swarmed over the pier and the ship below.

"Valenkov cut a deal with Mallory," explained Jen.

"Orion's president."

"Right. Sergei designed the new missile guidance system they're selling to the Pentagon. Orion gets the patent, and the profits. The Pentagon gets the guidance system."

"So what's in it for our boy Serge?"

"Can't you guess?"

Price looked at her. "No way," he said after a moment. "No fucking way."

Jen nodded. "Twenty new guidance systems for Sergei to sell to the highest bidder—China, apparently. Not only can they use them to guide their own missiles, or redesign their own guidance systems—they can analyze them for weaknesses and learn to defeat *our* missiles. Fifty million in Sergei's pocket is my best guess. The suitcases are a tip."

"Je-sus. We'll be picking feds out of our teeth for the next six months."

"I told you it was big."

"Where do you *get* this shit?"

"Sorry. That's classified."

Price eyed Jen's camera. "You know I'm gonna have to take the camera and tapes into evidence."

"Yeahyeah."

"You don't have any other tapes? Or copies of these tapes. Do you . . . ?"

"Of course not. You think I ran them down to the post office with the Red Army out there?" Jen indicated the view out the window.

"I guess not," said Price, frowning suspiciously.

"You should look happier; you'll make captain out of this."

Price grinned. "Could be. Thanks for the lieutenant spot, by the way," he said, referring to an earlier high-profile, high-tech bust that hadn't hurt his career and which had also been called in—to him, personally—beyond-the-last-minute by Jen.

Immediately afterward, he'd been promoted out of the SWAT unit to tech crimes. He'd been slipping her information on the high-tech crime scene ever since, knowing that if he didn't, she'd find someone else who would—a someone else who, in Jen's good graces, might become a competitor for advancement within the tech crimes division. After all, no law said she had to call *him* the next time. Most of the information he sent her way, he suspected—correctly—she already knew. Some of the hacking offenses, he also suspected—also correctly—didn't count in her book as crimes.

He indicated the equipment on the desktop beside them, which had been connected to the shipping office's computer. "What's this?"

"Playback deck. I wanted to make sure it came out."

"Thought of everything, huh?"

"You bet," Jen answered sincerely.

Richard Tripp stood on the third tier of Firing Room One in the Launch Control Center at NASA's John F. Kennedy Space Center, in Florida. A mission-control conversion test was scheduled for the day after next, for which he'd have to be present. This would entail the reprogramming of all launch control computers in the firing room to assume mission control capabilities as part of the emergency mission control center, or EMCC, plan. By having such a capability on standby, in-progress missions could be controlled from Kennedy in the event LBJ Mission Control Center in Houston—which assumed control of all shuttle flights the moment the Bird cleared the launch tower at Kennedy—became nonfunctional.

On the other end of the phone in Tripp's hand was Vincent Raster.

"You know," Tripp said, "there's a reason we have all these computers, Vince. Do you have any idea of the kind of capacity it takes to calculate stellar burn rates and supernova criticality thresholds?"

"Is the fucking thing going to blow up tomorrow?"

A pause. "Not for a few billion years, no."

Raster forcibly collected himself. He couldn't remember the last time he'd reacted like that, speaking before thinking. It was a dangerous habit. He'd seen people killed for it. He'd *had* people killed for it. Nevertheless, the slip served to convey the urgency of the matter to Tripp. And Tripp owed him.

At the time when President Miller had been considering candidates to fill NASA's top slot, Raster had been instrumental in publicly destroying Tripp's only real competition for the job. He hadn't done this out of any fondness for Tripp; he hadn't even known the man. Rather, he'd done it because Tripp's rival had despised the intelligence community upon whose assets Raster relied for much of his information. And NASA's director was in an excellent position to delay or cripple the deployment of space-based intelligence assets. Tripp's appointment, and the destruction of his rival, had scored Raster important points within that community—assuring him of even greater access to their assets in the future.

And Raster had seen to it that the new director was made aware of his own role in his appointment. The man owed him. Or thought he did—which was just as good. The president knew nothing of these maneuverings.

"I have a situation here," said Raster. "And it needs to be resolved immediately. My hardware doesn't have the muscle. Yours does."

Tripp exhaled heavily. "What are we talking about here?"

"Two-fifty-six-bit encryption." He could hear the director's breath whooshing out of him over the phone line. "I'm hoping to get lucky," he added.

"This is on the level?"

"I'm not calling for my health."

"And it's not ours?"

"No." Raster preferred to remain vague; let him think it belonged to some foreign power plotting against the United States. Tripp had been an Air Force colonel; let his imagination run with that.

"This is gonna shut us down completely."

Raster remained silent. He needed this, and he couldn't force the issue without going to the president, which meant *telling* the bastard everything and explaining why he'd told him nothing for years. He didn't even want to think about where that road led. The guy was a Boy Scout; squeaky-clean with no handles for leverage. How someone like that could become president Raster didn't know. Thankfully, it was an aberration.

At any rate, if Swain was eccentric enough to be using 256-bit encryption to scramble a conversation about blueberry muffin recipes, or the next Dodgers game, or even Microtron trade secrets, Raster's worries would be over—and he wouldn't have to tell that self-righteous sonofabitch in the White House a goddamned thing.

"Bring it in," said Tripp.

"I'll be there in two hours."

"I've got people in orbit; something goes wrong, they need me on-line. I can't shut down until they land."

"When?"

"Tomorrow, if the weather holds."

"The weather," repeated Raster.

"You don't land a billion-plus-dollar spacecraft in bad weather."

At the mercy of the goddamned weather, thought Raster. *Unbelievable.* "I'll be in tomorrow morning," he said.

"I'll see you then," replied Tripp.

John stood before the fridge for a moment, realizing he was out of cheese pizzas and regarding the crystal glass and Krug champagne which had been chilling for five years, awaiting the moment which would soon come.

Technically, everything was in place. He was ready to move. A final meeting with Mitchell to fine-tune the details of "The Presentation," as they'd come to call it, and the world would be forced over the brink of FTF—the final technological frontier. This was the Last Big Breakthrough, and the genesis of all things that would follow. The alpha would become the omega, and the omega the alpha.

Or, as he'd said to Swain—the world would begin anew.

Shaking his head to clear away such grandiose thoughts, John grabbed a Cherry Coke and closed the door. Moving across the room, he paused before the black-and-white photograph he'd come to know so well. In it, a man stood before a blackboard covered with equations. The man himself was older, his face drawn. Physically, he appeared harmless. This was deceptive; it was the *mind* which was dangerous. The eyes were haunted, as if by some terrible knowledge or unimaginable burden—windows to a tortured soul.

Raising the Coke in silent salute, John drank.

Gregory Brandt hung up the phone in Los Angeles. At forty-seven, Brandt was chief operating officer of the Parallax Corporation. His duties were not those of a typical chief operating officer, as Parallax's definition of "operations" differed somewhat from that of the typical corporation. Few people had heard of Parallax, fewer still of Brandt—which was how he, Parallax, and the corporation's clients preferred it.

"Jee-sus Christ," he said on hanging up.

"What?" asked Adams, his deputy.

"That was Raster."

"Raster . . . Haven't heard from him since he left Spook City. What does he want?"

Brandt leaned back in his chair and frowned deeply. "He wants us to surveil Mitchell Swain."

"Jesus Christ."

Brandt nodded. "What Raster wants, Raster gets." He tossed his pen on the desk.

"That's like trying to follow the fuckin' president. Worse."

Brandt nodded. "I want eighty men on the ground, another fifty on standby in the field. In place by oh three hundred. The usual equipment. Preference to people who've worked the Portland area. See if you can find out who runs Swain's operation. Find out who's on it. Could be useful." Rising, he headed for the door. "Meet me at the airfield in two hours."

"Give me ten this time," said John to the pizza shop proprietor.

"Ten. You gonna get fat."

"Fat chance."

"You gonna clog you arteries shut."

"You know, I think you're right. Maybe I should switch to alfalfa sandwiches."

The man looked at him in alarm. John let him worry for a moment before smiling.

"All the same?"

John nodded. "Double cheese and triple sauce. One hot; the rest go in the freezer."

"Got a little party planned, eh?" said the man, washing his hands behind the counter.

"Yeah," said John without humor. "Like the world ends tomorrow."

Leather bag on a strap over one shoulder, Jen moved down the brightly lit second-floor hall of the *TEK* building which had been her virtual home for the past five years. It was well after midnight.

TEK was the world's leading source of breaking news on leading-edge information technologies. No self-respecting geek, CEO, Silicon Valley start-up, or high-tech venture capitalist would dare be caught dead without having read the latest issue within twenty-four hours of its release. Though available on newsstands, by subscription, and free on the Web, the truly technophilic paid what anyone else would consider an exorbitant fee to access the contents via the Web one week prior to the publication's general release. And paid gladly.

TEK was the best-paying information technology publication on the planet—which, in combination with its unrivaled quality—accounted for Jen's presence on its staff. She all but lived in her office.

There was very little, Jen had discovered, which could not be accomplished from a properly equipped, leading-edge office—research, grocery shopping and delivery arrangement, videoconferenced interviews—and the list of things which could not be so accomplished grew smaller with each passing day. Jen's influence,

TEK's growing budget, and Paul's ceaseless upgrade efforts saw to that.

Interviewing Mitchell Swain would be an exception; *that* she wanted to do in person. One reason was that no one had been granted such an interview in over four years as Swain, too, saw advantages in leading-edge offices. Using them to conduct virtual interviews, for instance.

Just ahead, down the hall, was a door marked: SYSOP.

The company SYSOP was and always had been Paul "Gig" Gigner. Like Jen, he had signed on early and taken payment in stock options. Unlike Jen, who saw technology as a means to an end—Paul regarded technology as an end in itself. He did live in his office, most of the time, and looked forward to the day when he would upload his personality into an artificial body which required no food or sleep, and would thus be free to pursue technological perfection twenty-four hours a day. Perhaps more, with parallel processing.

In what had been a spacious office prior to his occupation, Paul divided his attention between the five glowing monitor screens which provided the cramped room's only illumination—and a half-eaten carton of Ben & Jerry's Cherry Garcia ice cream. Paul referred to this activity as multitasking. The door opened, flooding the room with bright white light from the hall. Paul threw an arm across his face like a vampire at dawn.

"*Aaggh . . .*"

"You live like a mushroom," said Jen, moving inside and closing the door. Paul lowered his hand.

"Oh—hey Jen." At twenty-nine, with blond hair past his shoulders, gold-rimmed glasses, a lanky frame and, indeed, the complexion of a mushroom, Paul was the quintessential aging hacker. The room in which he spent the majority of his time was crammed with computers, storage media, printouts, and dog-eared software manuals from floor to ceiling and wall to wall.

"Hi. I—" Jen stopped in midsentence, staring at an eerie blue monitor screen displaying an Air Force seal, engineering drawings, and the words:

UNITED STATES AIR FORCE
CLASSIFIED DOCUMENT
PROJECT SNOWBIRD
ABOVE TOP SECRET

ACCESS APPROVED

"What's that?" she asked, looking at the screen.

"Some new spy plane. Keeping the world safe for tyranny." Reaching over to the mouse in front of the monitor, he clicked on DOWNLOAD. Jen flicked on the lights. Paul squinted.

"Where's my video?"

Paul punched up displays on a bank of monitors. "Got a rough edit with the high points right here. Five-, three-, and one-minute versions for the time-challenged."

Jen scanned the monitors as Paul, in typical multitasking mode, ran all three versions of the dockside Sergei video simultaneously. "With *TEK* logo and your name prominently displayed in each frame, of course," Paul added.

"Of course."

"The cops know you have this shit?"

"Yeah. Right."

"So what did you tell 'em?"

"I told them I didn't have a copy of the tape."

"We wouldn't want to *lie*, would we?"

"I did *not* lie. I have a very high standard of journalistic integrity . . . I evaded. There's a difference which is obviously beyond you."

Paul paused in his color adjustments to look up at her. "You told them you didn't have a copy, right?"

"Wrong. You're not listening. I told them *I* didn't have a copy of the *tape*. Is it *my* fault they didn't realize I was feeding the video to you? That they didn't ask the right question? Couldn't grasp the distinction . . . ?"

Paul turned back to the monitor. "You lied," he repeated.

Jen rolled her eyes. It was quite possible Lieutenant Price had realized what she'd done and simply asked the most convenient question for both of them—making it unnecessary for her to lie while at the same time covering himself with the department. She had after all made it plain, albeit in a very oblique and charming manner, that there was no shortage of other L.A. cops bucking for promotion to or within the tech division. She preferred Price because he was ambitious, intelligent, and discreet—a rare combination in a cop. She and Price might discuss the nuances of who-knew-what-and-when one day after his retirement, but for now such matters were best left to speculation.

"The second they see this they're gonna say, 'That lying bitch,' " said Paul.

"Yeahyeah. I care."

Shortly before dawn, Mitchell Swain sat behind the bulletproof desk in his bulletproof office, gazing out the bulletproof window at the forested hills surrounding his estate. Swain smiled; he enjoyed sunrises. He didn't like the city, and never had. His "home office" cost more than most corporate headquarters buildings. Or so the IRS complained.

Someone punched a code into the box outside the office, causing a brief music file to be played over the room's speakers—in this case, the drumbeats from *The Terminator: BA-dum-dum-DA-dum.* That would be Mattman, Swain's head of security. Like most counterterrorist types, Mattman had a dead look about the eyes which reminded Swain of the Terminator—hence the tune he'd assigned Mattman's code. His chief tax advisor's code played the *Imperial March*—Vader's Theme from *Star Wars.*

Swain touched a button on his desk, displaying real-time video of the bulletproof hall beyond the bulletproof door. Seeing Mattman, he tapped another button to unlock the door.

"We're drawing a crowd," said Mattman, stepping inside and closing the door behind him. Swain watched as Mattman tugged unconsciously on the knob before releasing it, to be sure it was locked. The door, the design for which had been approved by Mattman, had been built to lock automatically upon closing. Which it did without fail. Still, Mattman double-checked. He was like that.

"Oh?"

Mattman nodded. "The house is under surveillance. They're not amateurs."

Mitchell's brows arched upward in inquiry.

"Possibly government, but I doubt it. Too smooth." Seeing Mitchell's brows contract at this, Mattman explained. "The feds never learned finesse because they never had to. . . . We picked these guys up on thermal scans and seismic sensors. Few radio emissions; encrypted, burst, and freq-hopping. The longer they hang around the more we'll know. Their behavior indicates surveillance only, but we have to assume they're armed. We'll confirm that shortly with millimeter-wave detection. . . ."

He paused. "You want us to move on them?" he asked. "Could get nasty, but they're likely here illegally, in which case, feds or no—their hard luck."

Turning, Swain gazed out through the bulletproof window which formed the entire eastern wall of his office, fingers of his right hand tap-tap-tapping on the desktop beside him. Most armored windows were bullet-resistant. Swain's were bulletproof. "No . . ." he said after a moment. "In fact," he continued, turning back to Mattman, "I don't want them to know we know."

Mattman frowned. "That's complicated, and dangerous."

Swain smiled. "It's a complicated and dangerous world," he replied.

Mattman exhaled heavily, and left the room, tugging the door shut behind him.

Turning, Swain gazed back out the window at the forest beyond. He was no longer smiling.

"That *lying bitch*," said Los Angeles police department chief Nathaniel Marsten, staring at Jen's footage of Sergei accepting payment on CNN. Still photos adorned the front page of the *Los Angeles Times*, which lay on the desk before him. He stared up at Daniel Tarrance, his public information officer and imperturbable polar opposite. Tarrance had walked in unannounced to show him the paper and the broadcast, and to discuss damage control with Marsten and the department counsel. Conveniently, he'd brought Richard Lang—the department counsel—along with him.

Chief Marsten was notoriously short-tempered, and had once gone off the deep end on seeing a headline that read "POLICE CHIEF INVESTIGATED BY FBI." It had taken five minutes to calm him down sufficiently to point out the fact that the "police chief" referred to in the article was not Marsten. He'd never gotten past the headline. Outbursts such as this were so frequent that his secretary had installed a special panic button which rang in Tarrance's office.

Marsten displayed the paper and its photographs to Lang. "This is withholding evidence," he said seriously. Tarrance looked to Lang, whom he'd brought so that he himself would not have to explain such things.

"Actually," said Lang, "it's not. If the only images she retained are *copies* of the images she already surrendered to the department, no crime has been committed. Technically, being press, she didn't have to give us that without a court order. It's not as if we're trying to maintain a low profile on this."

Marsten frowned for a moment, then seemed to brighten. "Interfering with an investigation," he declared, pointing.

"From what I gather, there was no investigation prior to Ms. Rayne's phone call on the morning these photos were taken."

Marsten scowled at him.

Lang continued. "She undoubtedly forced a litigation clause on both CNN and the paper as a condition of providing the story. So what it boils down to is this: Do you wish to sue the *Los Angeles Times* and CNN because this woman performed an investigation of a crime the department knew nothing about, and then handed you the biggest bust of the year?"

Marsten glowered for a moment in silence at the two men before speaking. "You're fired," he said at last. "Get out of my office."

Tarrance departed the office with Lang in tow, closing the door behind them.

Lang turned and spoke quietly. "He's just pissed that she blew his press conference out of the water," he said.

"He fire you again?" asked Marsten's secretary. Tarrance nodded in passing. "See you tomorrow," she called after them.

(3)

From the wooded slope of the valley which cradled Mitchell Swain's home from the world like a protective mother, Gregory Brandt watched through Zeiss binoculars as Swain's driver exited the O'Gara-Hess & Eisenhardt-armored LandJet van and lifted the hood. Following a brief inspection, he slammed the hood down and conversed with three companions. The driver held one hand like a gun and mimicked shooting the vehicle. After a moment, he and the other men used one of the O-H&E-armored escort trucks to push the van back into the garage beneath the house.

"Get the chopper hot," said Brandt into his radio. "Subject may be leaving by air."

He didn't like this whole setup. Though his men hadn't found any monitoring devices, he felt certain Swain knew of their presence. With that kind of money, and the people Swain had working for him—particularly Mattman—he had to know about the surveillance. Surveilling someone who knew he was being surveilled was always bad. Surveilling a trillionaire who knew he was being surveilled—and had the resources to find out by whom—was beyond bad.

It was fucking insane.

"I don't understand what the problem is," said Jen. Ever the hot-head, Marsten had called her in for questioning. Being a material witness, she hadn't had much choice in the matter—but then, Marsten wasn't calling her in to take a statement. He was calling her in to complain.

"Here I've saved you three months of investigation," she continued calmly, "with who knows *how* many detectives and man-hours; I've saved you the jurisdictional headaches and the feds—whom I *could* have called instead of you—taking credit for the arrest, and I've saved you a couple of million dollars of taxpayer money I'm sure you'll now spend elsewhere."

Marsten's eyes narrowed. "How do you figure three months?" was all he could come up with.

Jen shrugged. "I figure what takes me two weeks takes you three months."

"I'll ignore that. The fact is, you were aware of a crime-in-progress and failed to report the matter to the police."

"That's not a crime, and you know it. Besides, I wasn't *sure* it was a crime-in-progress until I was on the scene—and you know, my purse is such a mess I just couldn't find my cell phone for twelve hours?"

"Ever heard of civic duty, Ms. Rayne?"

"Ever heard of gratitude toward someone who's done your job for you? Cheaper, faster, better? *Again . . . ?*"

Marsten leaned forward over his desk, extending one finger menacingly toward Jen. *"Now you listen to me, young lady—"*

Jen leaned forward, elbows on knees, fingers interlaced, chin resting on knuckles with eyes wide—as though hanging on the chief's every syllable with breathless anticipation.

Marsten looked at her, and frowned. "Get outta my office," he said simply.

Two hours after the armored LandJet had been pushed back into the garage, a second armored LandJet made its way up the winding road to the house.

LandJets were GMC Savana vans with extensive interior modifications. They were, in essence, luxury offices on wheels, providing time-challenged executives with a way to turn downtime travel time into uptime work time, provided they retained the services of a driver. There were five luxury leather seats inside, desk, cell phone and computer ports, fax machine, microwave, refrigerator, television—the works. The things could be used as traveling boardrooms in a pinch. Swain was wild about them.

LandJets were expensive, of course, but that presented no obstacle to Swain. What *had* presented a problem was the fact that they were *so* expensive that, following the sale of some thirty vans, the company which sold them had dissolved for lack of a sufficient number of well-heeled customers. Because of this, those who possessed them tended to want to keep them. And so, rather than resort to bidding on used vehicles, Swain had taken a more costly route: He'd set about tracking down the owners of the nonexistent company, locating the engineering drawings, finding the contractor which had done the actual conversion work—Geneva SVS in Wisconsin—and retaining the latter to build him thirty more, to even more luxurious specifications, at one hundred thousand per van. Ten of those, armored to level 6 by O-H&E—which more than doubled the cost of each—were his; the majority of these awaited his use at various private airports. The remaining twenty were available for Microtron company use.

In front of the house, two men exited the newly arrived Land-Jet, turning the vehicle over to the on-site team. Brandt watched as Mattman checked out the second vehicle and signaled his okay to the house.

A moment later, Mitchell Swain appeared in the doorway, wearing an overcoat, and stepped outside carrying a fedora. He paused midway between the house and the van to check something on his PDA—a pause which Brandt could see annoyed Mattman as an unnecessary security risk. The delay pleased Brandt, as it gave him a good look at Swain's face, thus confirming the fact that it was indeed Mitchell Swain they'd be following. Many of the subjects Brandt's people surveilled tended to be dodgy, and the watcher was lucky to catch a fleeting glimpse of the face between doorway and curb.

Brandt watched as Swain pocketed the PDA, donned the hat, and moved to the LandJet. Four security men, Mattman among them, entered the van with him.

"This is a new look for him," said Adams.

When Swain's van and the escort convoy began to roll, Brandt lowered the binocs and looked to Adams.

"The hat," Adams explained.

"When you're rich, you get to be eccentric," noted Brandt. He brought up a radio. "This is Alpha; subject confirmed and moving. Launch Sparrow."

Sparrow was an advance DARPA MAV prototype which was, in reality, somewhat smaller than its namesake. One generation behind the current state-of-the-art research, it was, nevertheless, well ahead of anything else.

In the opinion of the Pentagon, Micro air vehicles, or MAVs, were the future of battlefield surveillance. The things carried onboard microelectromechanical systems—or MEMS—sensor packages, transmitting and receiving equipment, and fuel; the rest was airframe and propulsion/control gear. Mere inches long, their weight was measured in grams. The Pentagon was hoping to get them down to bumblebee size within a decade.

That was one of the perks of working for Parallax—early access to new toys. The downside was that the damned things self-destructed half the time. Two previous Sparrow prototypes had flown into trees; a third had been shotgunned by a ten-year-old.

Brandt was pleased to see that this one operated smoothly. So far. He watched the intermittent burst-feed from the device, which for reasons of detection avoidance sent its continuously recorded images in discrete, frequency-hopping data packets. The MAV's memory was limited, so transmissions were frequent and the transmitted data was immediately wiped both for security reasons and to make room for additional data. Brandt wore the monitor on his wrist, the storage device in a belt pack. The reassembled video feed was almost real-time.

Between Sparrow and the men Brandt had stationed along the access road, Swain's convoy was covered. More conventional means of surveillance would be employed once the vehicles left the countryside.

One thing was certain: The armored LandJet would not leave the sight of Brandt's men until Mitchell Swain stepped out of it.

In Florida, Raster stood with Janz as NASA's silicon behemoths neared the end of their gargantuan task. Raster had, after all, gotten lucky: though the encryption's underlying algorithm could not be broken, the key was short enough to be memorized, and was based on a passage in an ancient Greek text relating the tale of Prometheus—who stole fire from the gods and brought it to Man. He and Janz watched in tense silence as Tripp's number-crunching machines unraveled the final coil of encryption and the decoded copy of Mitchell Swain's email message appeared on the monitor screen before them:

Pandora ready. We need to meet. Location 36.
Prometheus

"My God . . ." Janz whispered, and looked to Raster, who stood motionless, clenched jaw twitching as he stared at the monitor. In the seven years they'd worked together, Janz had not once seen a trace of emotion reflected in those dark features. And indeed they betrayed little now, nor did the man's voice.

"Wipe this from the system," ordered Raster, eyes never leaving the monitor, "then go back to the office."

As Raster turned to leave, his eyes crossed Janz's for an instant—and in that instant there was no mistaking what lay beneath Raster's outward calm:

Absolute terror.

"Yeah," said Brandt, answering his cell phone.

"Where is he?" asked Raster.

"Downtown Portland. We've got him covered like a blanket."

"Keep it that way. Has he met with anyone?"

"Unknown. Went straight to an old warehouse and holed up inside. Haven't seen him since. That was—" Brandt checked his SEAL watch, "—four hours twenty back. Could've been twenty people waiting in there to meet him."

"Where are you?"

"On the roof across the street."

"Listen carefully. He's there to meet someone. Probably a man. I want that person identified, and I want him followed. Priority on this individual is Alpha Three; I say again, priority is Alpha Three. I'll check back in one hour."

"You got it," said Brandt, and hung up. Priority Alpha Three surveillance meant not losing sight of the target, no matter what—even if that meant killing the target to avoid his escape. Brandt had seen that priority assigned only twice before, and that to suspected nuclear and biological terrorists—individuals who might kill millions if not contained. To Brandt's mind, this presented two distinct possibilities: Either the richest man in the world was now dealing with some very dark people—or Raster had lost his mind.

It was a tough call.

Checking his watch again, Brandt shook his head. This gig was getting more bizarre by the hour, and he felt the beginnings of a bad vibe. The last time he'd felt that he'd been in South America, ten years before.

He'd been the only man on the team to survive the next forty-eight hours.

A chartered Learjet descended from the skies above Los Angeles, landing unnoticed at a private airfield, where it taxied into a waiting hangar. The hangar doors slid closed behind it.

Raster's callback was accurate to the second. "Update," he said.

"One of my men went missing," said Brandt.

"*What?*" Raster's voice was tense and lethal. "Who?"

"Coyote."

"What does he know?"

"Less than I do, which is jack shit." Brandt paused for a moment, debating whether to ask the next question. "Am I gonna see this guy again?"

There was an uncomfortable silence before Raster replied. "I think so. We have no indication he's ever killed anyone."

"I recognize some of his people—you saw the sheets—and they have no problem. It's not like we're gonna sue."

"They're taking orders from him; they'll do as he says," Raster replied harshly, reasserting his authority. "Have you seen Swain?"

"Negative; last we saw him he was walking into the building."

"It's been too long. Can you get someone inside the building for a visual confirmation that he's still there? Get pictures of the individual he's meeting with?"

Brandt peered down at the street below. Half a dozen men likely armed with submachine guns loitered in front of the building. Others, he knew, watched the sides and rear. Ten more on the building's roof—one staring back at him through his own set of binoculars. Another thirty men that he knew of in armored vehicles with equipment he felt certain rivaled that of a well-armed brigade. All visible means of ingress had been checked and found to be blocked, including air ducts which might otherwise have provided access to Sparrow. Whatever was going on in there, Swain had gone to a lot of effort to keep it under wraps.

"Brandt . . . ?"

"Yeah," he said, pulling back from the roof's edge and lowering the binocs. "Sure, if you got a Marine battalion on standby."

Raster ignored the sarcasm. Brandt was the best, so he tolerated the occasional lapse. "I *have* to know who he's meeting. More than anything else, I *have* to know. You follow every person who comes out of that building. Every car they get into. You search the building when they've left. *No one* walks away without a positive ID and their photo in my hand. Do it with fucking . . . *traffic* stops if you have to, but get it done.

"I want to know what house they go to, what car they drive, who they work for and what their bank account looks like. Also education. If there's more than one, Alpha Three on all of them."

Adams tapped Brandt on the shoulder. "Got it," Brandt said into the radio. "Hold on a sec." He raised the binoculars. The front door had opened again, spilling bodyguards onto the street. Cameras whirred. Swain's armored LandJet pulled to the curb. "Looks like he's coming out," Brandt said into the radio. The convenient timing made him wonder if his communications encryption had been broken.

At an all-clear from Mattman, Mitchell Swain stepped from the building, gazing down as he cinched the belt on his overcoat. A sudden gust of wind took his hat off. Instinctively, he turned his head as he grabbed for the hat in the air.

"God*dammit*," whispered Brandt. He realized immediately where it had happened: at the house, six hours before.

"What?" asked Raster in his ear.

Handing Adams the binoculars, Brandt sank into a sitting position with his back against the wall which bordered the roof on all sides. "We got a big fuckin' problem," he said into the radio.

Adams watched in stunned silence as the man on the street below quickly snatched up the hat and replaced it atop his head. In the instant before the hat obscured them, Adams got a good look at the man's features.

They were not the features of Mitchell Swain.

At the southwest corner of an unoccupied building in Los Angeles, someone knocked on the door: *Shave-and-a-haircut.* Pause. *Two-bits.*

Inside, John checked his watch, rose from the couch, and moved to the door. "Your favorite?" he called through the door.

"Curly," replied a voice from the other side.

John opened the door. "Well if it isn't a rich man in a suit," he said in surprise.

Swain frowned and stepped inside, carrying a gym bag. John poked his head out the door and looked around. A nondescript car was pulling away from the curb as a man across the street walked a German shepherd. A couple spoke together on a nearby corner. In this industrial district, on a Sunday afternoon, none of these people were what they seemed—not even the dog, which was, John reflected, doubtless trained to kill. He glanced toward the roofline, but saw nothing. Moving inside, he closed the door. "Where's your private army?" he asked.

"Here and there," said Mitchell, gazing about. "Changing room?"

John grinned, and pointed to a doorway. "Right through there, rich guy."

Mitchell moved into the next room with his bag and closed the door. The building had recently been a stationery company's headquarters, and was now—according to a sign in the window—up for lease by one of Mitchell's hundreds of corporate subsidiaries. John had furnished the break room like a small living room, and used it occasionally to sleep in when he wasn't at the main Los Angeles location.

Moving to the refrigerator, he retrieved a pair of Cherry Cokes. "I've got a pizza sitting in the microwave," he called out. "I would have had one delivered, but I figured your goombahs would shoot the guy or something."

Mitchell reappeared in casuals and sweater, *sans* bag. "My goombahs are professionals," he said, taking the proffered Coke. "The pizza would be delivered hot, with no blood."

John regarded him seriously. "Well then, maybe I *should* order out."

Mitchell looked at him. "I believe Big Brother is watching," he said.

John halted, alarmed. *"You were followed?"*

"Yes and no. Yes they tried; no they didn't succeed."

Relieved, John moved to the couch as Mitchell took the chair. "Who?"

"Government goons, who else. Parallax Group; freelance contractors for black agencies." Mitchell shook his head in distaste. "Very nasty people, or so my goombahs tell me."

"So they know."

Uncapping the soda, Mitchell tipped the bottle up and downed a third of the contents before answering. "Apparently," he replied, seeming unconcerned. "My goombahs are sweating one of their guys now."

John nearly choked on his soda. "You're kidding."

"Afraid not. It's not a legal problem. Technically we could shoot the guy and dump him on Rodeo Drive at high noon and the whole thing would just go away. These people are . . . shy, you might say."

"Jesus."

"They don't officially exist, you see, and a body would tend to disprove that. So the body would just go away. There'd be no retaliation, either—I should say attempted retaliation; losses are a cost of doing business."

John didn't take Mitchell's Rodeo Drive scenario all that seriously for, even if what he said were true—which he had to assume it was—he knew Mitchell had no intention of having the man killed. Of course, the man himself would have no such peace of mind while being questioned. "How do they know?" he asked.

"Do I know? I've told no one."

"Neither have I."

Mitchell shrugged, as if the matter were of no consequence, and took another swig of Coke.

"It had to be the truck," said John.

"That was five years ago."

"Still—if they tied that to you, that was the tip-off. Could they have been tracking you for five years without your knowing it?"

Mitchell appeared thoughtful. "Not closely," he said at length. "There've been times . . . when something would seem . . . odd. But we could never get a lock on it. Even Mattman couldn't say for sure who it was. We assumed—*I* assumed; Mattman assumes nothing—that it was corporate espionage. There was never any significant information loss. Just signs of snooping-from-a-distance, and always after the fact. Never any physical threat."

"All after the truck," said John.

Mitchell nodded. "All after the truck . . . It's possible."

"The truck" referred to an incident John had come to regard as the largest shell game in history. In equipping his lab at the beginning of the project, he had made numerous purchases through chains of front companies and dummy corporations. One firm, however, had an unwavering policy of running in-depth checks on all purchasers prior to delivery. That company, run by a subsidiary of a security-conscious defense contractor concerned about violating export laws and endangering its lucrative defense business, was at the time the sole supplier of a rather expensive and extraordinarily difficult to fabricate piece of equipment which was absolutely crucial to the project. The simplest solution—a bribe—would have run the risk of generating undue attention. And so it became necessary to establish a semilegitimate firm in order to purchase the equipment.

The equipment itself had been bugged with a tracking device, John discovered upon ordering a scan of the delivery truck which came on overnight loan with the device. He'd thought this over for an hour, then called Mitchell with an absurd and ridiculously expensive plan. Mitchell had agreed immediately.

Assuming the truck itself was being watched at all times, John never went near it. Instead, it was driven to a truck stop, where it spent the night. During that night a team of men labored inside a second semi truck at another location. By morning, they had finished. Both trucks were then driven to an overland freight company's central distribution hub—which had, in effect, been commandeered by Swain's money that morning.

The first truck was backed up to a loading dock at 10:00 A.M. The second truck was backed up to another loading dock at 10:02, and its newly constructed contents moved to an area near the first truck.

Inside the warehouse, unseen by prying eyes, the crated equipment was removed from the rear of the first truck and placed into the waiting Faraday cage, which had been constructed inside the second. This cage acted as an impenetrable barrier to all electromagnetic signals—including those emitted by the tracking device.

Equipment and cage—along with two techs placed inside the cage to locate and disable the tracking device before the cage was reopened—were then transferred to a third truck, which had arrived several hours earlier. Seven minutes and forty-seven seconds after the first truck had arrived, the third truck departed.

By arrangement with the facility's cargo master, the one hundred other trucks whose departure had been delayed until this moment departed with it. Twenty-five remained, including the first and second trucks. Another one hundred arrived and departed in the next twenty minutes, along with the twenty-five which had remained following the first mass departure.

As a result, whoever had been tracking the first truck had not one but two hundred twenty-six trucks to follow in the first half hour alone, many of which were headed out of state and most of which were headed for other warehouses or freight train facilities with multiple arriving and departing trucks or freight cars. Some were headed for ships destined for foreign ports.

In addition, since there was no longer a signal to track, the interested party could not be certain the equipment had in fact left the facility aboard one of those two hundred twenty-six trucks. It might just as well have left aboard one of the three hundred additional trucks which arrived and departed over the course of the next twenty-four hours as the hub returned to its normal routine.

Or the equipment might never have left at all.

Or it might have left on any one of the over one thousand trucks which departed the following week.

The plan was, Mitchell declared, positively diabolical, and the two of them had laughed to themselves for weeks over the presumed frustration of their anonymous snoops.

The trail of the equipment had indeed been lost, and both company and paperwork vanished from the planet within twenty-four hours of the purchase—but there was, for a very short time, a paper trail that led to a company owned by a chain of other companies which eventually pointed to Swain. That trail was cold and convoluted, vague and twisted, and disappearing underfoot, but it might—just might—have been traceable by someone very, very, *very* good. And the people interested in this equipment's destination were that.

The problem which defeated them, even after deducing without hard evidence, as the trail finally vanished in Bermuda, that Mitchell had arranged the purchase—was the fact that Mitchell wasn't the one using the equipment, had never laid eyes on it, and was not in regular communication with the person who had and was. The equipment, like the company and the paperwork, simply disappeared.

And it would never be found.

"So these guys who followed you—" John began.

"Parallax."

"—where are they now?"

"Following my janitor."

John stared at him.

"He was the right height," Mitchell added, grinning impishly.

John cracked up.

"We pulled a switch, and they've been sitting on him ever since. I flew down here; he stayed in Portland playing me. Best-protected janitor in the world."

"What did you pay him?"

"Ten grand for the day. He'll probably quit tomorrow."

"You've got style, Mitchell, I'll give you that." Lifting his bottle in mock salute, John drank.

Entering the building was not difficult; Swain's departing brigade had left the doors courteously unlocked. Brandt's men moved through the interior in six-man teams, alert by habit for traps, clearing the rooms one by one and reporting by radio as they went. The structure appeared to be empty. Whoever Swain was meeting obviously wouldn't be found here, as Swain had never been here himself—but Brandt liked to be thorough.

He kicked himself for missing the switch. Swain had stepped into the LandJet outside his home—the pause which had seemed to annoy Mattman in reality a show for their benefit, to confirm that they were seeing Swain. Hidden inside the vehicle was Swain's identically dressed stand-in. The first LandJet had not broken down; the second had been brought because Mitchell's team hadn't known they'd need a double until they'd detected the surveillance. The double would have been seen entering the van outside, and suspicions would have been raised by moving it into the garage before leaving.

The vehicle had been watched closely as it traveled to the fake meeting place, and even after the fake Mitchell had been observed—briefly and from the rear, accompanied by everyone but the driver and a second security man—entering the building in Portland. After parking for thirty minutes, the LandJet had driven to a nearby convenience store, dropping off a suit-clad security man by the door. He'd entered—seen only from the back—and emerged a moment later, partially obscured by the van, bearing cold sodas and chips. The van had then returned to the target building.

That security man, Brandt now realized, had been two men: Mitchell Swain had entered the store, and a second, identically attired man who'd been waiting inside the store had exited in his place.

It wasn't often Brandt was outmaneuvered. Rarer still that he didn't realize it immediately.

Fucking Mattman, he thought, annoyed and admiring at once.

"Alpha this is Gamma," said the third team's leader, his voice coming over Brandt's headset. "We're in the storeroom at the northwest corner. You might want to have a look at this."

Brandt made his way to the indicated two-story room, and moved through the doorway. The team waited inside. The room was empty. Brandt looked upward—raising his gun instinctively at the sight of a man above him. His eyes narrowed, finger sliding off the subgun's trigger.

There, hanging from the ceiling by a noose, was a life-sized, white-haired dummy wearing a red, white, and blue top hat and tails—dressed as Uncle Sam. Lowering the gun, Brandt stared up at the thing for a moment in silence.

"Sonofabitch," he said.

"They can't know details," said John.

"That would seem unlikely. And you're so paranoid I *know* they haven't found you."

John leveled a finger at Mitchell. "It's not paranoia if they're out to get me."

"Two-fifty-six bit encryption?" said Mitchell, eyebrows arching skyward.

"Hey, you said use the strongest encryption I had, right?"

"I almost couldn't decrypt it."

"You had the key."

"Joke."

"Ah. Tomorrow it'll be child's play."

Mitchell nodded. "At any rate, I agree. Knowing anything is too much. The situation will be dealt with."

"If they do know, this could screw everything. If they decide to move—"

"Don't worry about it. I'll call the press conference tomorrow."

"Just like that."

"Just like that. What are they going to do, *not* come . . . ?"

"Must be nice," John said of the unique world in which Mitchell lived, where the world press came running at one's call.

"It is," Mitchell replied, reading his thoughts. "As for the guys who sent the goons—assuming it's not the IRS—right now they're guessing. They have nothing to go on. We do the press conference tomorrow, do the demo there, and implement version one immediately. By the time the government knows what happened, it'll be over."

"Mm." John gazed downward. Mitchell made changing the world sound so easy.

"Then it'll be time to talk about Man, Version two-point-oh."

John looked up sharply. "No do—Don't *even* *start* on your transhumanist-extropian thing again. Please."

"What?"

"Those people annoy me."

"I'm one of those people."

John stared at him, as if to drive home the point.

"Hell—*you're* one of those people," said Mitchell. "Like it or not."

"Can we not have this conversation?"

"You realize this is the last time anyone will ever *have* this conversation."

"There is some consolation in that," conceded John.

"Singularity is upon us," said Mitchell. "They've seen it coming for decades. They're ahead of the curve."

"They saw *something* coming; this turned out to be the most viable avenue. Regardless—what annoys me is their damned . . ." He gestured helplessly with one hand, unable to find the words.

" 'Dynamic optimism'?"

"You call it what you like."

"Dynamic optimism is what I like. Has a nice ring to it."

"Are you *trying* to be annoying?"

"Yes. Thank you for acknowledging my success."

John wagged a finger at him in mock reproach.

"It's *dangerous* optimism, is what it is. They think it's all going to be sunshine and roses. That there's no downside. No danger. They sit around making plans for transcendence and colonization and what they're going to do . . . God knows *how* long from now, or how far from here—and it *never occurs to them* that they're not going to be calling the shots. That it will never be offered to them. That it will be used for evil and not for good. That it will . . ." John turned away, ". . . destroy us all," he finished, voice low.

"Destroy us by making us into something else, or destroy us by destroying us?"

John rose from the couch, gesturing with one arm in agitation. "Either. *Both . . . Who knows?*"

"We're here to stop that."

John looked at him sharply. "We're here to try."

"You think we'll succeed."

"Of *course* I think we'll succeed, or I wouldn't be *doing* it."

"Then," said Mitchell with a grin, "you're a dynamic optimist."

John pointed at him as if in anger. "Don't call me that."

"Stop calling me a rich man, and we have a deal."

John looked at him, and laughed.

Jen spent the day at home, preparing for her interview with Mitchell Swain—going over notes about Swain and Microtron, reviewing her questions, checking recorder and batteries, deciding what to wear. As photos would be published and vidtape shot, and as millions of people would be looking at Jen while watching or reading the interview, there was really only one choice: the ruby red dress.

Transhumanists, as both John and Mitchell knew, were people who longed to be something more than what they were—people. They foresaw a time when advancing technologies would make it possible to transcend their humanity and become something more than merely human; something *post*human. Precisely what that something would be, no one seemed quite certain. That its attainment was desirable, all agreed. How it would be attained was a matter of debate focusing mainly on the integration of computer components into the human body/consciousness, genetic engineering, and—most recently—nanotechnology.

A posthuman would be able to keep up with the ever-increasing pace of technological change because it would be inhumanly intelligent. It would presumably be inhumanly long-lived as well— and, hopefully, inhumanly wise. "Transhumans" were those who considered themselves as being, in thought or in deed, on the road to becoming posthuman.

Extropians were a subset of transhumanists whose name derived from the word *extropy*—the principle of increasing order in a given system, such as the universe. Which was of course in direct contravention of the Second Law of Thermodynamics as applied to information theory—that order in the universe must inevitably decrease over time via the process known as entropy. The first three Laws of Thermodynamics had been paraphrased in Ginsberg's Theorem as: You Can't Win, You Can't Break Even, and You Can't Get Out of the Game.

No one liked the subject of the second law, entropy—least of all extropians. The process of evolution itself provided concrete evidence that entropy could be overcome, in a given local system, over a period of several million or billion years—and it was hoped that a big enough technofix might provide the means to vanquish entropy forever and enable Man not just to break even but to win by altering the very rules of the game. As nanotechnology could conceivably be used to alter the structure of the universe, or at least most of the matter within it, this possibility could not be discounted.

Singularity was the Big Bang of transhumanism—the irresistible force which would require transcendence as a condition of continued survival. Assuming Man survived long enough to reach that point, the occurrence of Singularity was inevitable. What everyone seemed to overlook was the fact that transcendence must take place *before* Singularity, or at the very latest coincident with it—if Mankind or his successor was to survive.

John now knew that the thing which would supersede humanity would be more human than most thought, and in this he took some comfort. But the fact remained that it would not *be* human. And that frightened him. Transhumanists spoke glibly of sloughing off their humanity like an old skin. But he was closer to it than they were—much closer—and it scared the hell out of him.

"So how about it," said Mitchell, "—one last Singularity conversation."

John threw up his hands and rolled his eyes in resignation. Polishing off his Coke, he set the bottle down on the table and fell back into the couch. "Proceed," he said.

"The pace of technological progress is exponential, if not hyperbolic," began Mitchell.

"Agreed."

"It took six thousand years of civilization, absolute minimum, to get off the ground. To fly one hundred twenty feet on a bicycle with wings. Seventy years after that, we're on the moon. A computer that sits on your desktop is ten thousand times more powerful than one which took up a city block in 1960. Soon we'll surpass that a billionfold with a computer too small to see."

John circled his hand in the air. "Get to the annoying part."

"The moment we implement, Singularity begins."

"Singularity" was a term which meant different things to different people. To physicists, it meant a literal pinpoint of nearly infinite mass—a "black hole" from whose immense gravitational pull nothing—not even light—could escape.

To technophiles and science fiction aficionados, it meant something else—something postulated in an early form by mathematician John von Neuman in the 1950s, and radically expanded by science fiction author and mathematician Vernor Vinge in a paper presented at the 1993 VISION-21 Conference sponsored by NASA and the Ohio Aerospace Institute. It was a further refinement of this second meaning to which Mitchell now referred.

"The point at which the increasing pace of technological change outstrips the capacity of the human mind to follow or to comprehend," Mitchell reiterated. "And to control. The implications can no longer be foreseen because new elements and new interactions are entering the equation too rapidly to be anticipated. Humans become incompetent to render meaningful techno-decisions because their wetware has become obsolete—"

"Only for that purpose."

"Of course," Mitchell conceded. "There are other things that make life worth living."

"I just wanted to make sure you still knew that. Sometimes I wonder."

Mitchell stared at him for a moment before continuing, and leaned forward in his chair. "But if you can't keep up with the change, if you can't comprehend it, can't master or even deal with it—you're headed for extinction. You'll make a mistake whose consequences you couldn't possibly foresee. And those consequences will ripple outward—"

"Exponentially, of course."

"Of course—and the next thing you know, there's nobody left. It could happen in an infinite number of ways—ways which increase in number, again exponentially, as the complexity of the system and the pace of TP—techno-progress—"

"Nice term."

"Thanks; I thought it up this morning—continues to increase."

"You know who you sound like?" asked John.

"Who?"

"The Unabomber."

Mitchell ignored him. "You agree with all of this, so far. Don't pretend you don't."

John nodded reluctantly; he knew where it was going. That was the problem.

"So, in order to *avoid* that situation, we must increase the pace of evolution to match—that or make a one-time quantum leap in intelligence which will empower us to deal with TP."

"Until the next Singularity."

"Conceded—if any. Point being, being human isn't good enough anymore. The TPR—"

"Techno-progress rate."

"Very good."

"Thank you."

"The TPR, our increasing reliance on our technologies, and the lethal consequences of a serious technofailure *demand* that we create or become something more than what we are. Something capable of dealing with the Singularity. Something . . ." Mitchell spread his hands, trying to find a word other than the obvious to describe what he was talking about.

Frowning, John said the obvious for him. "Posthuman."

"You said it," Mitchell replied, leaning back in his seat. "The other Singularity."

"Singularity," repeated John. " 'The techno-Rapture. A black hole in the extropian worldview whose gravity is so intense that no light can be shed upon what lies beyond it.' "

Mitchell inclined his head and arched his brows. *"What?"*

"From *Godling's Glossary*. Beautiful, isn't it?"

"Sacrilegious."

"You say tomahto . . ."

Mitchell frowned at him.

"What none of these people seem to give any thought at all to,"

John said, "is the very fact that the thing they're all . . . *hoping to become . . . isn't human . . .*"

"They realize that."

"Yeah. They realize it, but they don't *think* about it. They're too busy wanting to reengineer themselves, or . . . *upload* into some kind of machine, or *merge* with the network like some kind of . . . quasi-*borg*, or something—that they don't think it through."

"For example."

"Take your *pick.* That the posthuman being will be completely artificial, with no human element. That it won't need us, won't want us, will throw us away like last year's too-slow computer. That even if we become posthuman ourselves, retaining our individuality— we'll lose our humanity. That life *won't* be *worth living* and we won't even fucking *know* it because we won't *be human* . . ."

Mitchell frowned thoughtfully, and nodded. This was a new angle, one John hadn't presented before—and it was troubling.

"And we won't listen to those who choose not to upgrade, because they're obsolete. What do they know? We'll think they just don't understand."

Mitchell bit his lip.

"Don't get me wrong," John continued, "—we're talking about well-meaning, intelligent people. But you know where the road paved with good intentions leads. Save for me—and to a lesser extent you, but only because I've made an effort to upgrade your mental utopia program—these guys are not terribly realistic. They're too busy acting like some kind of, damned . . ." He shook his head in annoyance, searching for the words: ". . . *technocheerleaders.*

"They don't know what the next step is and they don't *care;* they just want to *take* it. They're thinking about all of the wonderful things they'll be able to do once they've become posthuman, never realizing that if and when they *do* cross that threshold, they may no longer *be* the people they were when they made those plans. They may not be people at all. And whatever they become, may view all of those wonderful things—the very *reasons* they wanted to *become* posthuman in the first place—as useless aspirations and toss them aside . . ."

Mitchell stared at him, and for the first time in the five years they'd known each other it seemed to John that he was actually getting through that unbounded—and, John feared, unfounded—perpetual optimism of Mitchell's.

"And the only way to find out," John concluded, "is to *do* it. And once you've done it, there's no turning back."

Mitchell nodded thoughtfully.

"I hate to break it to you, but I *like* who I am, and I like being human. The life span sucks, but I'm working on it."

Mitchell grinned. "Planned obsolescence," he opined. "Maybe one day we'll have a talk with God about that."

"One day soon we won't need to," said John.

A thoughtful silence followed.

"So," said Mitchell, changing the topic and getting down to the actual purpose of his visit. "How would you like to deliver Pandora?"

"In a box, how else?"

Mitchell smiled.

"You tell me where and when; I'll phone in the order."

"I like it."

John smiled. "I thought you would."

THE TRAIL

*Nor do I doubt if the most formidable
armies ever heere upon earth is a sort of soldiers
who for their smallness are not visible.*

—*Sir William Perry, 1640*

(4)

The present . . .

The White House sat placidly beneath blue skies. Seated in the Oval Office, the president reviewed a speech to be delivered the following day. At fifty-eight, President Harrison Miller had seen more action—in politics as well as war—than he cared to remember. He was the last of the old school, and saw the world largely in black and white, refusing to fall prey to what he referred to as the "Billion-Shades-of-Gray Complex," whose victims used it to justify any means to any end, however vile. He looked up at a knock on the door. "Come."

Stan Winton, high school classmate, Vietnam companion, and now White House chief of staff, stepped inside with a videotape. "Mr. President," he said gravely. "Mitchell Swain has just been assassinated."

The president rose, pen dropping from shock-numbed fingers.

Speeding along a two-lane blacktop in a rented Mercedes, Jen held a vidphone to one ear, waiting for the pickup. Hurriedly wiped-away gore stained her face and dress. She hadn't waited for the police to show up and begin asking questions. Her seat before and to one side of the podium had likely afforded her a better view of Swain than that had by any other attendee—but the assassination was on a thousand digital tapes, and the police could track her down later through Microtron's seating chart. What they really needed was the one thing they wouldn't find: a camera pointed not at Swain, but past him from the rear—at the audience and the landscape beyond.

Taking advantage of the chaos which followed the shooting, Jen had disappeared into the stampede headed for the parking lot. The security men had wanted to detain everyone, but with several thousand people rushing toward the lot they'd had few options. They could either mow down the journalists *en masse*—a task for which they were, no doubt, splendidly equipped—or they could let them pass. Having already ID'd everyone on the way in, they'd settled for photographing people and cars as both fled the lot.

Jen had been on the phone before leaving the premises, calling Kit James, a software programmer and one of Mitchell Swain's top lieutenants. James had also been a friend of Swain's since childhood, and was Microtron's chief financial officer. Following that conversation, the two had arranged a hasty meeting behind a restaurant in the nearest town. After that, Jen had headed straight for the airport.

The call she made now was her second.

In the *TEK* SYSOP office in Los Angeles, Paul picked up the vidphone. He'd long since disabled the video component, so callers with vidphones would see only a black screen.

"SYSOP," he said.

"Gig. Jen. You hear about Swain?"

"*Hear* about it?" He eyed three separate Internet feeds of the scene on the monitors before him. "Nobody's talking about anything *else*. You okay?"

"I want you to help me find out who did it, and why. The richest man on earth announces the greatest discovery of all time and is *killed* before he can tell us what it is? I have to know. The *world* has to know why he was murdered."

"That's easy: to shut him up."

"About what?"

"Who knows?"

"We will," said Jen with certainty.

"Where are you now?"

"I'm headed for the airport. I have to get . . . cleaned up. I'll be in tonight."

"I'll be here."

Hanging up, Jen turned on the radio, picking up in the middle of a newscast. *"—assassination* little more than one hour ago," said the breathless voice of the female newscaster. "In a statement released *mo*ments ago, the Microtron Corporation announced a one-*billion*-dollar reward for information leading to *any*one involved in Swain's murder."

Lips parting in shock, Jen stared at the radio.

*"Noth*ing in the reward announcement requires a con*viction*— leading *some* to speculate that Microtron plans to deal with those responsible *out*side, the criminal justice system."

A horn blared. Looking up, Jen swerved back into her lane as an oncoming car Dopplered past.

Inside the warehouse lab in Los Angeles, John worked at one of twenty parallel computers arranged atop and beneath the long, L-shaped running desktop. The rest of the lab, save the living-room-like near corner, was occupied by binders, books, huge stacks of technical journals and computer printouts, storage media—and strange apparatuses, the purpose of which would be indecipherable to all but a handful of theoretical scientists.

On the monitor before him his own glowing purple words conversed with those of a remote computer, which appeared in blue capitals:

Upload all files: encrypt mode ULTRA

UPLOAD VIA OC-192?

Yes.

ESTIMATED UPLOAD TIME: FIVE HOURS.
PROCEED?

Yes.

On the monitor screen, a blue status bar appeared above a five-hour countdown.

Moving down the hall toward Paul's office, Jen noticed the black ribbon taped to the door—a sign of mourning, she supposed, for the World's Finest Computer Geek. Opening the door, she moved inside. Paul looked up from his monitors, most of which displayed the same symbol—a black ribbon composed of computer chips, with a gold pyramid emblazoned on one end; it was apparently spreading across the Net. Jen made a mental note to suggest putting it on *TEK*'s next cover. Paul covered his face with both hands, drawing them slowly downward. He looked more tired than usual. "God is dead," he announced.

"Mitchell Swain is dead," corrected Jen.

"Same thing . . . So what's the deal on Swain?" he asked.

"I want you to help me look into it. It's bound to require hacking."

"Every reporter on the *planet* is looking at this."

"I know—but they're all looking at the same thing."

"How do you mean?"

"I *mean* people are too busy looking for the who—I need to find the *why*."

"Who will tell you why," Paul observed.

Jen pursed her lips thoughtfully. "Maybe why will tell me who."

"Maybe. But you *know* this guy's gonna be dead by the time anybody finds him—whoever hired him is gonna kill him. Classic technique: Hire the hitter, then hit the hitter to cover your tracks. Just like Oswald and Ruby. He's probably dead already, and if he isn't he'll wish he was when Microtron gets its hands on him. Swain's always—*was* always—Mr. Nice Guy for the media, but behind the scenes? When it comes to business? Those boys play *rough*. And with a billion-dollar bounty, they'll get their man."

"Then I want to know who's behind it," Jen persisted. "Who hired the shooter. They may not know who they've hired, and he may not know them."

"Well then he can turn himself in and make a lot more money," said Paul. Jen frowned at him. "What was Swain going to announce?" he asked.

"No one knows."

"Not even *Microtron?*"

Jen shook her head.

Producing a cigarette, Paul flipped it casually between his lips and began patting his pockets.

"What are you doing?"

"Lighting a cigarette," replied Paul, pulling out a Zippo lighter.

"Are you crazy? You can't smoke."

"Au contraire." Paul lit up.

"What about your heart?"

"Hey—I *need* this cigarette."

Beedee . . . beedee . . . beedee . . . Paul's wristwatch alarm sounded suddenly, startling him. Jen leveled a quick finger. "That's your guilty conscience."

Shutting off the alarm, Paul began a quick search of his pockets, looking worried.

"Shit. I forgot to refill my nitro prescription." Reaching inside his shirt, he pulled out an 8086 computer chip on a necklace chain. Jen regarded it oddly. "Little piece of history," Paul explained. Using both hands, he pried the hinged chip up from the shallow locket it concealed. Dumping out the two tiny tablets inside, he popped one in his mouth, replaced the other, and dropped the necklace back down his shirt.

"Emergency backup," he explained, following the pill with a Coca-Cola chaser. Eyeing the Coke, the inevitable Ben & Jerry's, and the nearby half-eaten smoked turkey sandwich—which together seemed to comprise the bulk of Paul's diet—Jen made a face.

"So anyway," Paul continued, picking up the sandwich, "—you think Swain was killed to keep him from making this great-discovery announcement."

"Why else? You don't *assassinate* the richest man on the planet in front of a thousand news crews if you don't have to."

"Good point," observed Paul, turning philosophical. "Did you ever notice that only the rich and powerful are *assassinated*—that the rest of us just get *slain* . . . ?"

"So do you want to help me out on this?"

After a moment's hesitation, Paul responded with "Maybe." Jen frowned. "What's in it for me?" asked Paul.

"Fame. Fortune."

"Uh-uh. Swain had that. Look what it got him." Paul alternated between ice cream, soda, and turkey sandwich while mulling over his terms. "I want you to write twelve columns for my hippie webzine about the implications of government-employed electronic surveillance technologies on the erosion of personal freedoms in America," he announced.

"Six," countered Jen, without hesitation.

Paul extended a hand. "Done," he said "—and half the billion-dollar reward, of course." They shook.

"Of course."

"Awesome. Where do we start?"

Jen appeared thoughtful. "He said it was going to change the world. . . ."

"He said it was going to *end* the world," corrected Paul.

"Figure of speech. The *point* is, whatever Swain was going to announce, *had* to be big. Knowing him, that means it's expensive."

"Makes sense," Paul agreed. "He *was* the richest guy in the universe."

"So what's the first thing they taught you at that PI firm that fired you?"

Paul gazed at her in annoyance. "They didn't *fire* me; I *quit.*"

Jen rolled her eyes; it was a long-standing debate. "Whatever," she said, to avoid continuing it now.

Paul nodded. "Follow the money."

John cocked his head to one side, regarding the gun in his hand—a Rick-Howard-modified Colt Government Model Combat Elite .45. The basic weapon had been designed by John Browning over a century earlier. *Things change so little,* he thought, *and yet so much . . .*

With a little luck and a lot of brains—he hoped—this century-old weapon would get him out of anything. He placed the gun atop one hundred thousand dollars in neatly bundled twenty-dollar bills arranged inside a briefcase, and closed the lid. Brains and luck were fine and good—but money never hurt.

Moving about the office portion of the lab, he collected papers from file cabinets and shelves, dumping them into an empty steel box with a ghastly yellow interior and closing the lid. Each time he returned, raising the lid with a foot pedal to add a fresh stack of papers—the previous batch was gone. He paid this phenomenon no mind.

The photo on the desk watched sadly.

Across the room, a newscaster spoke from Washington on CNN. "Calling Swain's assassination a possible act of *economic sabotage* against the United States," she reported, "President Miller has pledged to commit the *full resources* of civilian law enforcement *and* U.S. intelligence services to the *identification, and* appre*hension,* of the people responsible."

John glanced at the image of President Miller at a press conference. "Boy are *you* in for a surprise," he said to the television, and dumped another paper stack into the box.

In the SYSOP office, Jen shrugged off her shoulder bag and opened it, withdrawing an oversized black printout binder and handing it to Paul.

"What's this?" he asked, taking the binder.

"Summaries of Swain's outgoing black funds transactions for the past eighteen months. No one but Swain knew what they were for."

Paul flipped through the pages, eyes wide as saucers as he reviewed the staggering figures—all printed in nonphoto blue ink on security paper designed to black out when copied. The sums seemed more in keeping with the expenditures of a good-sized European nation than those of a corporation. *"Holy shit . . .* Where did you *get* this?"

"You're talking to the best here." Jen's voice was matter-of-fact. "I'm not the only one who wants to know who killed him."

Examining the pages, Paul's expression turned to consternation. "There are no names . . ."

Jen shook her head. "You expect this to be easy? No names; just numbered accounts in other countries. My source won't have full access until the legal dust settles, maybe not even then. This is all we've got."

"Do you know what Microtron's competitors would *pay* for this?"

"Don't even *think* it."

Paul held up a hand to reassure her. "Hey—just an idea . . . Who else has this?"

"No one. Is it enough?"

"If the records are stored on computer," answered Paul, nodding, "it's enough." He paused. "You know you're rushing in again where angels fear to tread."

Jen almost smiled; she was proud of that trait, and hadn't

attained her current position by being timid. "Just get to work," she said, "—and keep it *quiet . . .*"

"You got it."

The blue LED clock on the wall read 8:42 P.M.

Inside John's warehouse lab, several hours later, an identical digital clock read 3:12 A.M. Disconnecting one of the last computers remaining on the desktop, John carried it across the room to the steel box in the corner. Opening the lid, he dropped the tower unceremoniously inside. Moving back to the running desktop, he retrieved another computer and lugged it across the room to the box in the corner. Depressing the foot pedal caused the rubber-gasketed lid to rise once more—revealing an apparently empty, yellow-painted interior.

John stared grimly at the box's barren walls for a moment, then dumped the computer inside.

A phone rang in the darkness. Struggling an arm free of the sheets, knocking over the PDA in its charger on the nightstand, Jen switched on the lamp and blinked painfully awake. She resented the need to reach for the lamp and physically turn the switch, and had attempted to sidestep this inconvenience by means of a voice-activated switching unit.

The reason it was still necessary to reach for the lamp was that the voice-activated switching unit turned the lamp on or off each time her answering machine picked up and played a recording of her voice, even if the volume of the answering message was so low as to be inaudible to human perception. For this reason, she was considering asking someone else to record an answering message to be played on her machine. She resented this inconvenience as well. Life, it seemed, was full of inconveniences—most prominent among them at the moment being unexpected phone calls at ungodly hours.

The green digital clock on the nightstand read 4:17 A.M. She'd surfed the Net until midnight for information on Mitchell Swain, and had fallen asleep wondering why the richest man on earth had apparently not once in his entire life worn a suit or tie—even when meeting with the president. She thought it might be some kind of power thing—showing that he didn't *need* to wear a suit as a symbol of power. Or maybe some kind of subconscious rebellion against authority . . .

Bringing the scrambled vidphone—a techie perk of her association with Paul, who tended toward the paranoid—to her ear, she flopped back to the mattress and stared at the ceiling. "This had better be good," she said into the phone.

Paul stood in his apartment, surrounded by high-tech junk, much of it in various stages of disassembly. Bookcases crammed with operating and service and programming manuals, along with fat stacks of dog-eared printouts, covered the walls between work areas. A futon beneath one particularly long workbench served as a bed. On the wall beside him was a *Hitchhiker* blob with its thumbs in its ears—or in the place where its ears should be—above the words DON'T PANIC.

"Well, hey," he said into one of several scrambled vidphones, "—sorry my hacking schedule doesn't coincide with your beauty sleep."

"Yeahyeah."

"I think I found what you're looking for."

Jen woke up fast, sitting up and grabbing pen and notepad. *"Already?"*

"Hey—you're talkin' to the best here. Besides, I hijacked MIT's computers to help me hack the banks faster."

"So you're a genius. Get to the point."

"You wanted something big, right?"

"Right . . ."

"How's five billion dollars in a year and a half to one party?"

Jen's mouth dropped open in shock. *"Fi—Jeezus—who?"*

"That I can't tell you," Paul lamented, shaking his head. "But I can tell you this—if *I* can't find them they're one smart sonofabitch."

"Why didn't I see this in the printout?"

Paul flipped through the black printout binder as he spoke. "The transfers were broken up into small payments—well, what Swain might consider small—sent to multiple accounts in different countries to conceal the total. But in the end, it all winds up in the same place. Could be more; I'm only a third of the way down the list. No idea who it went to, though."

Jen was indignant. "You want half the reward for *that?*"

"Don't Panic," counseled Paul, "—in large, friendly letters. The best is yet to come."

Jen grinned. "I knew I could count on you. . . ."

Inside a small office which had been impeccably neat until two days before, a pair of sinewy hands sorted through seemingly endless stacks of Microtron financial reports, domestic and foreign bank statements, phone records and other documents which littered every available inch of desk, floor, and shelf space. The task was daunting; the timeline, impossible. The stakes required that it be attempted—and failure was unthinkable.

A phone rang. The hand wearing the dragon ring cleared away a lumpy stack of papers, revealing the secure black telephone on the desk. The offending phone rang again, and the hand snapped it up in annoyance. *"Yes?"* said Raster, voice deep and intimidating.

"Sorry to disturb you," said Janz. "Someone else has been looking at what we're looking at."

Dropping the stack of papers in his free hand, Raster spoke gravely. "Not on the phone," he said, and hung up.

"I also found the *mother* of all supercomputers," Paul continued, excited.

"What do you mean?" asked Jen.

"I mean a computer that makes the National Center for Super-computing Applications look like a *retirement* home for the mentally challenged."

"Paul," said Jen, slightly annoyed, "—what are you talking about?"

"Oh. Sorry. There's a *shitload* of Microtron money going into one *mean mother* of a supercomputer. Like Blue Gene/L at Livermore, only bigger." He referred to an article in a back issue of *TEK,* open atop a computer before him. "That one cost one hundred twenty *million* to build, sucks up four-point-seven *megawatts* and has its own *cooling towers.*"

"I know; I wrote about it."

Flipping back a page, Paul spotted Jen's byline on the article. "Oh. Right."

"No one could hide that."

"Not unless they owned the power company."

"Swain."

"Bingo. The mystery computer sucks down *eight* megawatts a day. Using Blue Gene as a model, this thing performs a *quadrillion* calculations per second—making it the fastest computer in the known universe . . ."

"Okay. Blue Gene is used for fatbrain physics, a bunch of other things. What was Swain using this one for?"

"Unknown. There's no way to know without hacking it."

"And . . . ?"

Paul gazed downward, as if ashamed. "I couldn't do it," he admitted, shaking his head.

"You couldn't hack a computer?"

"Not this one. Its responses are unreal—like nothing I've ever seen. It . . . *adapts* to the attack in real time. Doesn't cut you off—it's like it's, playing with you or, *using* you to analyze attack patterns. It's . . . *bizarre . . ."*

"Maybe the SYSOP caught you," Jen suggested.

"No," said Paul. "Too fast."

"So what happened?"

"Near as I can tell? When it was through playing with me it grabbed the processor number off my tattle-chip, isolated my phone line, and zapped me with a power spike that fried my UPS." Cradling the phone on his shoulder, Paul gestured with both hands and made explosion sounds with his mouth. "Game over."

"Were you compromised?"

"No; we're safe. My computer's home-built and not even the phone company can trace my number." Indeed, Paul had climbed a few neighborhood telephone poles at odd hours and arranged things in such a way that not even a repairman specifically looking for his number at the proper pole would be able to find it. He engaged in such phreaking not to cheat the phone company— whose exorbitant bills he grudgingly paid, albeit under an assumed name—but because he valued privacy, which he found inordinately difficult to come by in modern times.

"So what do we know?" asked Jen.

"The power company's in Arizona; Swain bought it five years back through a chain of front companies. The computer's right here in L.A., it's been occupied full-time for at *least* eighteen months— and all activity *stopped, two days* before the press conference."

"Paydirt," said Jen.

"Yeah. Whatever Swain was going to announce, *this* computer was working on. As far as I can tell, the computer had only one user. Five'll getcha ten that user is the five-billion-dollar man."

"What would keep the fastest computer on earth busy for a *year and a half . . . ?"* Jen wondered, half to herself.

"Hey—I'm only a genius."

Jen frowned.

"But I did get the user's phone number. He slipped up. Once. Must've called when the computer was down for a few minutes; because it was down there was no security. I traced the call through phone company backup records; the original had been deleted. So had the backup—but the telco computer glitched and made a dupe, then glitched again and misfiled it."

"Can anyone else trace that call?"

"Not anymore; I wiped the dupe. I memorized the phone number though—"

The phone in Jen's hand transmitted static. "Paul . . . ?"

Getting nothing but static on the line, Paul pulled the phone from his ear and regarded it impatiently. He shook it, listened again, thumped it twice on the desktop and brought it back to his ear. More static.

Hanging up, he picked up a hardline and brought that to his ear. The phone was completely dead; no dial tone. The on-line computers on the desktop suddenly went off-line—and Paul's expression changed to fear. *"Oh shit,"* he said.

Adrenaline surged through his system as his heart raced out of control. Placing fingertips to carotid and checking his watch, he took his pulse and frowned, trying—without success—to avoid thoughts relating to other male Gigners whose warranties had prematurely expired.

Moving swiftly, he shoved the desk in front of the door, then picked up the metal wastebasket and dumped its contents onto the floor. Righting it, he grabbed the Microtron binder and related printouts from the desk and threw them inside. Jerking open a drawer, he seized the refill bottle for his lighter and poured the contents into the wastebasket. The Zippo lighter followed—and the evidence was on its way to oblivion. Popping the removable C:/ drive from the hacking computer, he added it to the pyre.

As documents and disk burned, Paul tore off a corner of a loose-leaf page and scribbled frantically. The power died, killing the lights.

He scribbled by the light of the fire.

In the warehouse lab, John stared down into the ever-empty box—empty, as ever—and dropped the lid. Turning, he gazed about the lab, mind spinning off in several directions at once. He ran a hand through his hair. Mitchell was supposed to do everything. John's job was to get them there; Mitchell's to implement. Mitchell had had the resources and the muscle to get it done before he could be stopped.

That was why he'd been killed.

John himself was most at home in the lab, stretching his mind to advance humanity toward the most radical technology ever conceived. The Final Technology. Bringing it to the world in an orderly manner had been Mitchell's job. Mitchell had the greatest financial empire the world had ever known at his fingertips. Leaders of nations had feared him because of his economic might. When he spoke, they would have no choice but to listen.

Now all that was gone.

No one at Microtron knew what the hell they'd been up to, or even of John's existence. Thus, with Mitchell dead, Microtron's empire would not be at John's disposal. His long days of seclusion were at an end, and he could see but one path open to him.

If he succeeded, nations would come to fear him as well. To fear him in a way they had never feared anything: not each other, not nuclear annihilation—not even Mitchell.

His gaze fell again on the framed photograph of the man at the blackboard. *"Damn you."*

Snapping his mind back to the moment, he saw that computers and printout stacks were gone; storage media; printer. All that remained, aside from the living-room-like appointments, were cardboard boxes stuffed with printouts, a filing cabinet—and the bizarre-looking lab equipment.

"Okay," he said to himself, "—computers, paperwork . . . Equipment." Moving to the filing cabinet, he reached for the bottom drawer, which bore a BEAM ME UP, SCOTTY; THERE'S NO INTELLIGENT LIFE HERE bumper sticker above the handle. Sliding the drawer all the way out, he set it aside and reached into the space this left, withdrawing a black waistpack with belt. Walking to a nearby counter, he set the bag down and unzipped the main compartment.

A steady drizzle wept from the night sky as Jen drove through the city in her black Lincoln Navigator, dialing Paul's number on her wi-fi vidphone. Getting a busy signal, she hung up and hit REDIAL— and got another busy signal.

"Come on, Paul . . ."

Rolling through a business district, she replaced the phone in its charging cradle as she neared Paul's apartment. Spotting the used computer store on the left, she pulled to the curb across the street. Looking around cautiously—the area was not exactly upscale—Jen stepped from the truck, locked it behind her, and crossed the street, one hand on the pepper spray canister inside her purse.

Between the computer store and the dubiously named rug "emporium" beside it was the door leading to Paul's apartment, which was situated above the former. Reaching for the buzzer, Jen saw that the door was slightly ajar. She pushed it open.

A narrow, claustrophobic stairway confronted her. In the darkness, only the bottom third of the steps was visible, illuminated dimly by the feeble light of a distant streetlamp. She hit the light switch on the wall beside her—to no avail.

Fishing around in her purse, she withdrew a well-worn black aluminum Sure-Fire 6Z flashlight and twisted the tailcap, which caused the brilliant beam to remain on. Ascending the stairs, she turned right down the equally narrow hallway at the top which led to Paul's apartment—the only one accessible from the stairway she'd taken. The light switch in the upstairs hall wasn't working either.

"Paul?" she called out ahead of her. There was no reply. A creepy anticipation wound its way around her spine. Halting before the door to the apartment, she reached toward the knob—and stopped; the knob hung loosely in the door, battered and misshapen.

Hand halting one inch distant, Jen backed slowly away. Retracing her steps, she left the building the same way she'd entered, then circled around to the back and clambered up the fire escape, thankful she wore running shoes rather than heels. Reaching the window to Paul's apartment, she peered inside. Discerning only gloom, she produced the flashlight, depressing the tailcap for a brief burst of light. The apartment seemed empty, as if abandoned. She raised the window, which was unlocked.

From the rooftop of an adjacent building, another set of eyes observed Jen through night-vision goggles.

Swinging her legs over the sill, Jen lowered herself to the floor. Switching on the flashlight, she moved to the center of the room and turned a slow circle, quickening breath loud in the silence.

The apartment wasn't just empty; it was bare. There were no computers, no books or bookcases, desk, furniture, carpet, or futon. The only objects remaining in the room were a bare, darkened lightbulb in the ceiling, the DON'T PANIC *Hitchhiker* poster on the wall—and a smouldering pile of ashes, charred metal, and slagged plastic in the center of the floor. She recognized amid the burned debris the blackened metal, which was all that remained of the Microtron binder. Splintered pieces of frame moulding lay on the floor inside the ruined door, along with the strike plate and screws.

Moving to the ashes, Jen stood above them, gazing down. The apartment had only one main room, a closet, and a bathroom. Crossing to the bathroom, she pushed open the door: empty. Even the shower curtain was gone—torn from hooks which now supported residual shreds of plastic.

Returning to the main room, she looked around again. Stepping to the closet, she opened the door almost as an afterthought—then leapt back gasping as Paul's body fell from a sitting position inside the closet to hit the floor at her feet.

Glancing toward the door, Jen knelt beside him and took his pulse: nothing. His flesh was colder than it should have been, and there would be no bringing him back. His pockets had been turned inside out.

She bowed her head. A part of her felt the need to grieve, to withdraw from the world and quietly go to pieces for a while—but Jen was driven by intellect, and that intellect told her clearly that this was not the time. Paul was dead because he'd been looking into Swain's affairs. Because *she* was looking into Swain's affairs. Several things became swiftly very clear.

One: Whoever had killed Mitchell Swain had acted out of panic, after discovering something—the subject of his press conference?—at the last minute. Were that not the case, he'd have been killed in a less spectacular fashion.

Two: Killing Swain had not solved their problem. Whatever he'd been about to announce still existed, was still somehow a threat to his killer or killers—and it was tied up with the black funds transactions which she and Paul had been investigating.

Three: Because the killers' problem had not been solved, they weren't finished.

Four: If they'd managed to trace Paul's hacking activities in real time or close to it, they might have traced—even monitored—his phone call to her. Meaning that she could well be next on their list. She could not go home. Not now—perhaps not ever. The only way to move was forward—as swiftly as possible.

Grief would have to wait.

Looking quickly toward the doorway, she rolled Paul onto his back, then stroked his cheek with one hand, brushing stray hairs from a bruised face.

Beedee . . . beedee . . . beedee . . . Her eyes moved to Paul's watch. Reaching out, she shut off the alarm—then reached inside his shirt and found the computer chip locket.

Glancing again toward the doorway, she pried open the locket. Inside—a tiny piece of paper. Unfurling it, she found a phone number. Flipping it over revealed a hand-printed message in diminutive letters:

DON'T FORGET MY SIX COLUMNS

Tears in her eyes, Jen made a sound that might have been choked laughter.

The warehouse lab now was, at last, simply one more bare room in an old warehouse. Only the briefcase, the boxes, the counter, and the black waistpack remained, along with a wheeled cart onto which John was busily moving boxes. The Colt rested on the countertop, beside the closed briefcase.

Hearing a soft shuffling in the hall, John grabbed the gun and spun toward the doorway in a modified Weaver stance.

A woman stepped into view. Really quite a stunning woman, he noted over the gunsights.

Seeing the gun, she froze.

REVELATIONS

The road to Hell is paved with good intentions.

—*Karl Marx, 1867*

(5)

"*Who are you?*" John demanded.

"*I—I—I'm a journalist.*" Jen stumbled to get the words out.

"And I'm Gunga Din. Close the door, put your purse on the counter, keep your hands where I can see them, and don't make any sudden moves."

The sandy-haired man before Jen was handsome in an intellectual way. Had he not been pointing a gun at her, Jen might have taken the time to note his blue-green eyes and gentle features. As it was, she saw a large gun with a man behind it—a man who seemed at the moment more intimidating than handsome. "Who are *you*?" she asked.

"I'll ask the questions. You'll answer them. Now close the door and put the purse on the counter."

Jen shoved the door closed and lobbed her purse across the distance between them. It landed on the floor at John's feet. He looked at her.

"I never was much good at taking orders," Jen offered.

John picked up the purse, eyes never leaving the stranger before him. "How are you at taking bullets?" he inquired.

"I don't know. I've never tried it."

"Stick around a while and you might." He searched Jen's purse quickly. "No gun," he announced after a moment. "You don't have a clue, do you?"

Jen began to say something, then thought better of it and closed her mouth.

Finding the pepper spray, John removed it from the purse. "Pepper spray?" He half-laughed. "Give me a *break . . .* I have news for you, lady; defense sprays don't work. Adrenaline's an antidote, and anybody in attack mode is full of it."

Indeed, John had viewed the videotapes of the Modern Warrior Institute in New York, in which scores of test subjects had been handed rubber knives, sprayed in the face, and instructed to "attack" their fleeing, zigzagging opponent. No sprayed student had ever failed to "stab" the sprayer. Defense sprays were, for the most part, effective only when unexpected.

The same institute had sprayed unsuspecting, attack-trained police dogs in the face and watched them whimper with docility. But dogs given the attack command prior to being sprayed were not immediately affected and attacked viciously—because their blood surged with adrenaline, like the blood of the forewarned rubber-knife squad.

Likewise, John knew that the so-called police effectiveness ratings touted by the makers of such sprays were completely at odds with reality; those figures came largely from situations in which Cop A sprayed the suspect in the face while Cop B stood to one side, gun in hand, ready to shoot should the suspect fail to submit to arrest. Not surprisingly, even violent suspects OD'd on adrenaline chose to submit in order to avoid being shot—each time chalking up one more bullshit defense spray "effectiveness" stat to be foisted upon an unsuspecting public which didn't know any better. Paramedics knew better; for those few who displayed severe reactions to the sprays, they administered adrenaline—epinephrine—as an antidote.

Setting down the canister, John continued rooting through the purse as he spoke. "Frank Ward was a cop in Oregon—until he emptied a can of double-strength pepper spray in the face of an attacker. The guy then beat him to death with his own baton, took his gun, and split. You know what the manufacturer said to the widow in court . . . ?"

Jen shook her head.

John held up the canister. "He should have known better than to rely on *this,* to save his life. That was cop-strength spray; twice as strong as what you can buy. Do the world a favor and write about that." Dropping the can back in the purse, he came up with her ID. "Jennifer Rayne," he announced, sounding impressed. His eyes slid up to hers. "You won the Particle Prize for that series on quantum computing."

Jen's chin rose a bit in a subtle gesture of pride and vindication. "That's right."

"Nice articles," said John, the sincerity in his voice unmistakable.

"Thank you." She wondered if she could use his familiarity with her work as a lever to pry loose the information she needed.

Replacing the ID, John tossed the purse back at her. "Here's your purse. There's the door. Get lost."

Jen trapped the purse against her body. *"Now wait a minute.* I *came* here to get a story. Mitchell Swain—"

John shook his head. "Never heard of him."

"—was pouring *billions* of dollars into something *you're* in charge of, and I'm going to find out what it is."

"No you're not." John set the gun down and moved another box. Jen scanned the room for clues—eyes pausing on the black-and-white photo on the desktop. She continued scanning, brows furrowing at the words ASSEMBLER INFO scrawled on one of the boxes atop the cart. "Whatever you're doing, with that kind of funding it *has* to be important."

"Like you wouldn't believe," John replied, moving another box. He paused, puzzled. "How did you find me?" he asked.

"Tell me what you're working on."

"No deal." It didn't really matter; all links to his past would soon vanish from the planet, just as he himself would shortly disappear. When he reemerged, he would fear no man, no company, no government—if all went well.

"I know about your computer," said Jen.

John hesitated, surprised. "Good for you." He moved another box. "And you found me how . . . ?" He couldn't help but ask again; it bothered him that—after all of his elaborate precautions—*some*one had, after all, been able to find him. And if one person had found him, others might as well.

"What's in it for me if I tell you?"

"My compliments."

Jen sighed; there was no reason *not* to tell him. "I liberated Swain's black funds records. A friend hacked the bank transactions. Then we found the computer. You called the computer from this building."

"Impressive. Where's your friend?"

Jen's gaze dropped to the floor. "Dead."

"Figures."

Jen looked up, angry and hurt. "You're an arrogant sonofabitch, you know that?"

"Yeah, I know that. But I'm still alive. Hang around me long enough and you won't be."

Despite the circumstances, the journalist in Jen came to the fore. *"Why?"* she asked. "What was Swain going to announce?"

"Give it up, lady," said John, moving another box onto the cart. "Go home."

"Tell me."

John looked at her in exasperation.

"Don't you want your work to be *recognized?*"

"No."

"Why not?"

Transferring the next-to-last box to the cart, John looked at her. "You *don't* want to know." Holding out his right hand, he pointed his index finger at the floor and used it to describe a half-circle in the air. "Just *turn* around,"—he pointed at the door—"*walk* out that door, and get as *far* away from this as possible. This is a limited-time offer."

"*Listen.* I *know* there's an *incredibly* important story here; a friend of mine *died* pursuing it and I am *not* leaving until I find out *why, dammit!*" She paused for a moment, then spoke more calmly, her tone almost almost apologetic. "That's what I do."

"Yeah, well—you hit the jackpot this time, sweetheart."

"What do you mean?"

"*I mean*"— John stepped nearer—"that Mitchell Swain's death was not a random occurrence, odds are I'm next on the list—and if you're with me?" He stabbed a finger at her in the air. "It's gonna be two-for-one day. Get the picture?" Turning, he walked back to the counter, lifted the final box, and dumped it onto the cart. "So if you don't want to wind up like Mitchell and your dead friend," he continued, "I suggest you get the *hell* out of here."

Jen remained in place, obviously frightened but too determined—or obstinate—to abandon it. "I'll make you a deal: Tell me what I want to know, and I'm out of your life."

"You have *no* idea how tempting that is." Frowning, John scooped up the gun and pointed it at her. "There's no Pulitzer Prize here, lady. I'm adding fifty years to your life. *Now get out.*"

"Remember when I said you were arrogant?"

John's head cocked to one side, as if straining to hear.

"I was being kind."

"Shut up a minute would you?"

Don't tell me to shut up, you condescending—"

John leapt forward suddenly, pinning Jen against the wall with one hand pressed tight over her mouth.

"*Mm-mmpff-m.*"

"*Shut . . . up,*" John repeated, his voice now an urgent whisper. "*And don't move.*" His eyes slid toward the nearest window. Jen's followed at the sound of tires on rain-slicked asphalt.

John harbored no doubt as to who was outside. How they'd

found him was another matter. There were three possibilities: They'd found him independently of the woman before him, they'd found him with the willing help of the woman before him—or . . . He looked into her eyes, appraising what he saw there. "You come right here from your dead friend's?" he asked.

Jen's *"Oh, shit,"* expression said it all. She nodded.

"They tracked your car." Releasing her, John latched the briefcase and strapped the pack around his waist. *"Thanks."* He moved toward the bathroom, gun in hand.

Swain's killers, or someone working for them, were using her to find what they alone could not—this man before her. It didn't make her sorry she'd come, not for a moment—but it did enable her to view John a bit—a small bit—more sympathetically. "Who are they?" she asked.

"You're the journalist. You figure it out." John stepped into the bathroom and closed the door.

Jen's small bit of sympathy became smaller.

Once inside the darkened bathroom, John cracked open the frosted window and peered outside. The street below appeared deserted. Which, he realized grimly, did not mean it was—but his options were swiftly narrowing.

Jen stood beside the window on the big room's opposite side, peering cautiously downward from beside the drape. The rain outside had stopped. Sleek black cars with open doors stood on the street below. Eleven men clad in black body armor and carrying submachine guns moved to cover the building's rear exits and the alley to either side.

John emerged from the bathroom. "It appears there's no one out front," he announced. Jen moved from the window.

"Cautious statement," she noted.

"If you knew what I knew, you'd be cautious . . . and armed." Removing the magazine from the Colt, he placed it inside the waist-pack, withdrawing a second clip, which he slid very carefully into the beveled mag well until it locked into place.

"What do we do now?"

"Sorry, sweetheart; there's no 'we' in my world." He picked up the closed briefcase. "You got yourself into this. Now get yourself out." Moving to the door, he set a wall-mounted timer to thirty seconds.

"You *need* me."

John opened the door, then glanced back in annoyance at the picture on the desk. "I don't need anyone," he said, and left. Jen looked around quickly, gaze settling on the ticking timer, then followed.

"Where are we going?"

"Are you still here?"

Jen frowned as they hurried down the hall.

"Look, lady—you don't want to be with me."

"You know what's going on; I don't. I—I'm afraid to be without you, okay?"

"*You,* afraid? Nice try."

"It's a new experience for me."

"Yeah, well—you ain't seen nothin' yet." John paused as they reached the fire stairs. "Tell you what," he said. Pointing the muzzle at the floor, he flicked off the safety and jerked back the slide, ejecting a live 230-grain Hydra-Shok round onto the floor. "We survive the next ten minutes"—he released the slide, chambering the top round from the new clip—"and I'll consider telling you what's going on. Assuming you still want to hang around."

"*Deal.*"

They started down the stairs.

"Where are we going?" Jen repeated.

"Anywhere but here." Something in the way John said those words sent a chill down Jen's spine.

Outside, behind the building, the operation's tactical commander stood behind the lead car, scanning the structure's windows through binoculars. "This is Tac One," he said into the throat-mounted microphone he wore inside his armored collar, "in position. Tac Two, where are you?"

On the far side of the building, another three cars screeched to a stop in the street, forming a wedge just left of the warehouse's front entrance. "Arriving now," responded the leader of the second team from the passenger seat of the lead car. "Full deployment, thirty seconds." Car doors flew open as the vehicles halted, disgorging another dozen armed men in tac gear.

The fire door on the far side of the main entrance sprang open. The men emerging from the cars stopped and took cover behind them, opening fire with MP7SD3s. The sound of the bolts *snakking* into place after each round was louder than the sound of the rounds fired by the integrally suppressed submachine guns themselves.

John jumped back from the doorway as nine-millimeter bullets hammered into the door beside him and the wall across the hall. Jen was right behind him.

"Jeezus, what the *hell is this?"* she demanded.

"You wanted a story, lady," John replied, hugging the concrete wall for protection. "This is just the warm-up."

She stared at him. John closed his eyes and took a deep breath. Five years in the lab had been an escape from a world he found both lacking and vicious while he labored to create what would in the long run be a new and better world into which he had planned to emerge. But the old world, it seemed, would not go gently into that good night.

So be it, he thought grimly. *You want trouble? You came to The Man.*

The bullets stopped for a moment as the men outside ran dry and changed magazines. Sliding down the wall, John swung low around the door frame, extending the pistol out before him. The attackers moved for cover. Presenting only right eye and chin as targets, he centered the closest man in the Colt's three green-glowing tritium dot-sights—and hesitated. The gun began to tremble in his hands.

A thousand images raced through his mind in an instant: shaking hands with Mitchell for the first time; his mother's death from cancer; the instant of Breakthrough, at once glorious and terrifying; Mitchell's assassination, which had radically altered the course of history, though no one but he was as yet aware of this; the wife he'd never met; his mother's blood cells frozen in liquid nitrogen that he might one day use them to clone and raise her as his daughter—the only way left to return the years of love and sacrifice she'd given to him after the death of his father. This time, there would be no cancer . . .

Above all of this, John Marrek saw the world as it was, and as it might be. The old world which must pass away to give life to the world which was to come.

His world. The two could not coexist. This would be the shot heard round the world—fired in the old, reverberating into the new.

If there was a world left to hear it.

"What are you waiting for?" Jen demanded.

The men outside brought their weapons back up, and John ducked back into the hall as a second fusillade erupted.

"Give me the gun; *I'll* do it."

He looked at her, voice oddly calm. "You don't understand," he said. Doing the research and planning an orderly implementation to be carried out by others was one thing, but this—unleashing the revolution upon the world first as a weapon—bordered on madness. And there would be no turning back. Ever. Already the course of events was being determined by the actions of others. That must stop; he must regain control.

An explosion sounded from the far side of the building. An entry team, he realized.

"I *understand* the guys out back are inside the *building,*" said Jen.

Frowning, John waited—thankful he'd spent time at a firing range, unsure whether the techniques learned there would hold up under pressure. At the next lull in the firing, he leaned around the doorway, clamped down hard on the gun—which suddenly steadied in his grip—and pulled the trigger. The gun pushed back on his arm, its mercury-and-steel ball-bearing recoil reducer cushioning the big gun's kick. After the subdued *pfft-pfft-pffts* of the suppressed MP7s, the Colt sounded like a cannon.

The bullet struck the team leader squarely in the chest and was stopped by his thick level-IIIA armor. His companions returned fire immediately as John ducked from sight, bullets chewing up the corner beside him and the wall across from him and Jen.

Looking down, the team leader brushed a hand over the strike area. Tiny shards of what looked like clear glass fell to the street beside a mushroomed, hot lead slug with the pattern of the Second Chance vest's woven Kevlar fibers pressed into the soft, deformed metal.

The team leader stared in puzzlement at the street, which began to *crawl* around the slug, as if covered with a mass of insects too small to be perceived individually. He looked at his vest—which also began to crawl, directly over the strike area. He brushed at it again with his hand.

Just inside the door, Jen looked to John, who stood and leaned back against the wall. Eyes closed, he began counting under his breath. "What are you doing?" she asked.

"Waiting."

"For what?"

Beside the car, the team leader jerked his hand away from the vest and held it before him. It, too, began to crawl—and then, like his vest and the street at his feet—*to disappear.*

Eyes wide with terror, he opened his mouth and screamed.

John's eyes snapped open as he nodded to himself. Holstering the Colt inside the waistpack—which was actually a concealed holster with internal and external pockets—he turned to Jen. "Take my hand," he said. She hesitated, and he took hers instead.

"Run as *fast* as you can and *don't look back.* Ready?"

"What about them?"

"They have bigger problems."

Frightened and confused, Jen nodded—and the two of them

bolted through the doorway and angled off to the right. The tactical team never looked at them. Instead, they flailed frantically at their own bodies. Jen slowed as she ran—releasing John's hand—riveted by the scene before her.

What she saw was beyond the experience of any living being. Twenty yards distant, men, guns, and vehicles *crawled* as though covered with some unseen, colorless substance. Something which seemed to move, yet to remain still at once.

As she watched, all of these things, including the men—*disappeared* from the outside in. The men screamed horribly, dissolving into the nothingness before her eyes—first skin, then muscle and organs, followed by bone. The cars, too, disintegrated before her eyes. So horrified and enthralled was she by the sight of it that she almost failed to notice that the crawling surface covered the street as well—and was spreading rapidly outward in all directions, including hers.

Still she watched as the crawling surface encountered the face of the warehouse and spread upward without pause, seeming to defy gravity. All the while a low sound grew swiftly louder in her ears—a rising, blood-chilling *chitter* like the sound of a trillion unseen, voracious insects.

Transfixed, Jen watched with a paralyzing horror so deep it transcended all rational thought. Appearing beside her, John seized her firmly by the arm and jerked her around the corner onto the next street.

After they had gone, the awful *chitter* grew louder still, and the spreading, crawling wave moved nearer—disintegrating street, walls, Jen's Navigator, and the corner where she had stood mere seconds before.

The warehouse across the street began to disappear at a rapidly accelerating pace as the crawling, *chittering* wave of destruction ascended the posts of streetlamps and dissolved them, plunging the street into darkness.

On the dirt which had been a paved street but a moment before, no thing remained; not ash, not cinder, no pool of liquid or pile of debris—nothing whatsoever to indicate that man, or car, or gun, or street had ever existed.

Climbing into John's gray Excursion, John and Jen raced from the scene. John drove. Glancing sideways after checking the mirror, he saw that Jen was exhibiting alarming signs of shock. "Are you all right?" he asked, to focus her attention.

No reply.

"Hey—"

Jen began hyperventilating. What the *hell was that?*" she demanded.

"Calm down."

Calm down? *Calm down?* What— It— We were almost . . . *disintegrated.*"

"Disassembled."

"Nanotechnology. Jesus."

John nodded, keeping one eye on Jen and one on the road ahead. "Taken apart, atom by atom. Disassssembled by nanites. Molecular machines; submicroscopic. Programmed to multiply and disassemble."

Jen backed away from him, at once awestruck and terrified. "You're building *nanoweapons?*"

John shook his head. "No . . . *Yes*—but only for defense. I—The potential's *there,* and I knew someone might try to misuse it, or steal it. So I . . . created that to *defend* myself. To defend the *technology . . ."*

"Let me out."

He looked at her. She opened the door. "Stop the car or I'll jump."

He slowed, and looked at her solemnly. "If you step out that door, you'll be dead in twenty-four hours," he said calmly. The truck stopped. He placed a hand on her arm, which made her jump. "Just like Mitchell. Just like your friend. Your only chance to stay alive is me."

She looked at him for a long moment. He didn't look like an evil man, and he had just saved her life. He'd tried to warn her away—and he'd been defending them both when he'd loosed that horror outside the warehouse. And anyone who could assassinate Mitchell Swain wasn't going to bat an eye at deleting a science writer from the planet, Particle Prize or no Particle Prize.

"Look," said John, releasing her arm, "the most powerful government on earth wants me dead. Ten to one, they'll get what they want . . . But if I can stay alive for forty-eight hours, the world will change forever. And governments won't matter . . ."

"You don't know if you can save yourself. How can you save me?"

"Maybe I can't—but I'm all you've got."

"I thought you didn't want me with you," Jen noted.

"I changed my mind."

A moment of silence followed. "If the government wants you dead," announced Jen, "you can't be all bad." She closed the door. He hit the gas. "Put your seat belt on," he suggested. She did.

Making a deliberate effort to breathe slowly and deeply, Jen tried to calm herself.

"Nanotechnology is *it,*" said John.

"Is what?"

John spun the wheel hard left, bringing them onto another street. *"Everything.* Invincibility. Immortality. Wealth from nothing. The end of everything."

Jen half-laughed at John's choice of words—then regarded him as though fearing him mad. She shook her head. She'd researched and written enough about nanotech to realize it was the only possible explanation for what happened outside the warehouse—but her primary focus had been near-term technologies; nanotech had always seemed "out there"—a fascinating concept, but hardly a technology ready for prime time.

"What are you talking about?" she asked.

"I'm talking about the means to end poverty, disease, *death itself.* To create enough wealth to make Mitchell Swain look like a pauper, and weapons that make nukes look like cap guns."

"That's impossible," said Jen, sounding so unsure she surprised herself; it was as though someone else had spoken. After what she'd just seen, almost anything seemed possible.

"No," said John, turning to face her. His features formed an expression of utter and solemn conviction. "It's not . . . that's why Swain died."

The truck sped into the night.

Raster spoke into a secure phone like the one he'd used when Janz had called him earlier to tell him about the hacker Gigner.

"*Christ,*" said Raster, who rarely cursed. "He's already developed it into a weapon." Reaching down with one hand, he activated the speakerphone. "Did he leave any documents behind," he asked, "—were you able to seize any equipment?"

Beneath the mournful gray light of dawn, outside the former warehouse in Los Angeles, police cars and fire engines crowded the street at the scene of the disassembly. Police officers and firemen stared uncomprehendingly at their surroundings, then scrambled to avoid a falling section of overhanging wall.

A black sedan like those which had been disassembled rested on exposed earth where once had been a street. Beside it stood Gregory Brandt, a forged FBI ID clipped to his lapel and a secure cell phone in one hand. The wall of the building to his right had been eaten away to the third story. Turning to look over the roof of the car, he gazed at the spot where the warehouse hosting John's lab should be.

The building wasn't there.

"Ahh, that's a negative," he said into the phone.

In the Washington conference room where Raster and Janz stood alone, the mood was grim.

"There is no equipment," Brandt's voice continued on the speakerphone. "There's not even a building . . ."

Raster and Janz exchanged grave glances. "Understood," said Raster. Get out of there. I'll contact you later." Looking thoughtful, Raster handed the phone absently to Janz, who brought it to his ear, heard nothing, and hung up—missing the cradle twice so great was his distraction. He was shocked almost beyond words; things had progressed even further than they'd feared.

"Large-scale disassemblers," he said, half to himself, eyes fixed on the floor. "I—didn't know anyone had taken it this far. We— Without his records," he said, gazing at Raster, "—we have no way to catch up . . ."

"There is a team," said Raster, frowning. "They're close to a breakthrough. Funding's been a problem."

Janz stared at him; he hadn't known a thing about this—so far as he'd known, the work was still theoretical. Funding had always been a problem because Raster had refused to tell anyone save the secretary of defense and a few high-ranking generals anything about anything. Even by black budget standards, Raster's entire department "didn't exist." This wasn't like a more invisible plane, a better satellite, a bigger missile; this was everything—and the fewer who knew of it, the safer the world would be.

For a moment, Janz wished again that he knew none of this. The more so when he realized what must be done. "We have to tell the president," he said.

Raster's dark eyes flared. "Are you out of your mind?" he asked. "We have one chance. . . ." He reached for the phone.

Stormy skies leaked gray rain over the Pentagon. Inside, colonels cooled their heels in the reception area outside the office of Chairman Blaine of the Joint Chiefs of Staff. Richard Blaine was a fifty-eight-year-old, four-star Air Force general with wide cheeks, a lantern jaw, and a face as steely as his nerves. When his private line rang, he said simply, "Excuse me"—and the general before him left the office. Blaine lifted the receiver with one hand and a glass of Scotch with the other. "Blaine," he said into the phone.

"It's happened," said the voice of the only man Blaine found frightening. He set down his glass, spilling it.

"I need Cheyenne," continued Raster.

Blaine's mind took an uncharacteristic moment to recover. He cleared his throat. "I'll have a plane waiting," he said into the phone. "Twenty minutes."

"Where are we going?" asked Jen, as the dawn sky brightened into morning.

"San Francisco." John checked the mirror.

"San—"

"That's where the main lab is."

Reaching down, he unlatched the briefcase on the seat between them. "First," he said, "we buy a new car." He flipped up the case's lid, revealing one hundred thousand dollars in neatly bundled twenties.

Jen's eyes widened.

"Pocket change. I spent the other twelve billion."

She looked at him, and feared he wasn't joking.

Nineteen minutes after Chairman Blaine hung up the phone, a Learjet bearing Air Force insignia lifted from the tarmac at Reagan National Airport and headed west. "Arriving Cheyenne Mountain Air Station in two hours, sir," announced the pilot over the intercom. "Will advise on approach."

Blaine switched off the intercom and turned his attention to Vincent Raster. "Tell me you didn't kill Swain," he said.

Raster did not reply.

"Christ."

"Swain was the money."

"Who's the brains?" asked Blaine.

"Unknown. What I do know is this: Swain was funding some-one. I had a location, and sent two teams. He killed them both."

Blaine stared at him. *"Parallax teams?"*

Raster nodded. "With disassemblers."

"*My God . . .*" Blaine whispered. "The president—"

"Will be irrelevant within seventy-two hours."

In the driveway of a small home in Bakersfield, John and Jen climbed into a battered, primer gray Ford F250 pickup. Jen removed the FOR SALE sign from the rear window as John backed from the pitted driveway. The truck's former owner stood on the porch, an elderly man under a cowboy hat. After counting the crisp new twenty-dollar bills for the third time, he closed his eyes and pressed the stack of notes to his nose, inhaling deeply.

In minutes, John's gray Excursion would vanish from the planet, leaving nothing but disparate atoms lying on the ground and wafting through the atmosphere.

The Learjet streaked westward. In the cabin, Raster pointed out John's former lab on a map. "That's where he was," he explained. There's a lab team going over the area but, obviously, I don't expect they'll find anything." Next, Raster dropped a set of black-and-white, eight-by-ten photographs on the table between them. "It *was* a two-story warehouse . . ."

Blaine stared at the photos. He'd dreamed of putting a weapon like this at the disposal of the United States; now the dream had become the nightmare—with the weapon at someone else's disposal. Whose, they did not know—which made it all the worse. "You mentioned a woman," he said, to focus his mind on something which could move them forward. "What about her?"

"A journalist looking into Swain's death. She's not part of it—or wasn't."

"A journalist. All we need."

"The least of our concerns. Whoever controls this technology controls the world; all nations combined cannot stand against him." Raster paused, allowing Blaine to take the next step.

"Or us, if we can get there first," said the chairman.

"Precisely."

Raster gazed meaningfully at the general, hoping his unspoken message would not only be understood, but accepted. He'd studied Blaine for years, and had never known him to be anything but patriotic. But men like Blaine—those men like Blaine who ascended to his level, at least—were of a suit; they spent their lives the width of a razor's edge from what had until now been the ultimate achievable power, the presidency. And yet they found themselves unable to wield that great power—forced, at times, to stand aside and watch as those less able, less qualified, less intelligent, made the wrong decisions. Repeatedly. Decisions which were bad for the military, and bad for the nation.

Men in such a position, and of such ambition, found it easy to convince themselves that fulfilling their own boundless ambition by seizing power was an act of altruism undertaken for the greater good. At pivotal moments, even the best of them could be swayed. Blaine was indeed the best of them—and no other such in all of human history had ever been presented with an opportunity like this. Raster waited for ambition to work its subtle alchemy.

Chairman Blaine gazed at him for a moment. And in that moment Raster saw the sudden flash of comprehension, the familiar and intoxicating blend of fear and ambition—followed by a steely resolve.

"The president," said Raster, sealing the pact, "can go to hell."

Blaine turned and stared out the window. By the time they landed, any lingering doubts would be as vaporous as the clouds below them.

President Harrison Miller sat behind Abraham Lincoln's desk in the White House Oval Office, going over the latest figures on the economy and the value of the Internet—both of which might take a quick turn for the worse in the wake of Swain's assassination. The stock market was teetering already.

Sadly, the president counted himself as one of perhaps five

politicians over the age of fifty who knew anything at all about the Internet other than what sorts of indecent photographs could be found upon it by the persistent religious lobbyist.

With two years yet to go, Hank Miller looked forward to a second term, and to the headline-grabbing stumping efforts of his business-tycoon-turned-film-star-tycoon friend Mack Stryker. But all such thoughts of the future were about to be replaced by more immediate concerns.

The intercom buzzed on the desktop.

"Yes," he replied, holding down the TALK switch.

"The directors are here, Mr. President," his assistant informed him.

"Show them in," he instructed. A Secret Service man opened the door, admitting the directors of the FBI, CIA, and NSA, and the secretary of Homeland Security. All had been informed of his mandate to find Swain's killer or killers, and their respective organizations were already in motion. He'd called them into his office to demonstrate two things: that they worked for him, and that their employment was a privilege and not a right. He waited until the door was closed behind them, then continued to write for a moment longer. At length he stopped, and looked up. "You've each received my instructions regarding Swain's assassination," he stated.

The four men responded with a collective nod.

"And you've all heard what I told the American people about finding these bastards."

More nods.

The president fixed each man in turn with his most intimidating gaze. "I meant it," he said simply, and returned to his papers.

The others shifted uncomfortably, exchanging glances.

"You may go," said the president.

They went.

The old pickup traveled west along Interstate 5, leaving Altamont.

"It was the perfect setup," said John, explaining the theory he'd formed since Mitchell's death. *"He's* funding all the research, putting up billions. They don't have to fund it, so they don't have to tell Congress about it—and if the research actually goes anywhere, they step in and confiscate everything, citing 'national security . . .' "

"How can you be positive it's the government? *Our* government?"

"Three reasons: They have the most to lose, they have the money to be pursuing this in a research phase themselves—and they have the resources to surveil Mitchell Swain."

"And commit murder," Jen added.

"Yeah, well—what do they care? It's not like anyone can do anything about it." He paused a moment, biting his lower lip before continuing. "But they didn't count on me."

"You couldn't have done this alone," said Jen. "Maybe someone tipped them off."

"I led a nanodevelopment team for Mitchell. We were sabotaged midway by someone on the inside. Feeding false data into the system to make it appear we were headed down a very expensive, very wrong road. We couldn't be sure who it was, so Mitchell and I made it look as though we'd given up—that he was killing the project for lack of progress and cost overruns."

"But . . . ?"

"But by that time the computer you found had been developed by a separate team. And Mitchell and I were the only ones who knew what that computer was for—"

"To speed the nanodevelopment project."

"Exactly. Mitchell gave it to me, and with the computer's help, I took it the rest of the way alone. No one else knew."

"So they didn't count on it being this far along. They thought they'd stopped it earlier, and probably stole your research."

John nodded. "Then—surprise—they find out that we not only got there, we're ready to implement. That's why they're scared."

"And why they had to kill Mitchell . . . But if no one else *knew* about it—how did the government find out?"

"I don't know." John shook his head. "They traced the money, they found the computer, they found out what kind of equipment I was buying through the front companies and put it together . . . They could have decrypted one of my phone conversations with Mitchell but couldn't trace it back to me. Or a message. When they realized how far it had gone, that he was going to take it *public*— they had to kill him."

"Okay," said Jen, "I can see that. "But why try to kill *you?* Why not try to . . . buy you, or recruit you to work for them? If you spent all the money—"

"You don't understand," said John.

"*I do*—" Jen protested.

John held up a hand, shaking his head. "I mean the tech. You're hearing the words—but you're not wrapping your mind around it. There's nothing they can offer me. *Nothing.* It would be like . . ." He paused, searching for an analogy. ". . . trying to buy Mitchell out for a *quarter.*"

Checking over his shoulder, he hung a right, moving onto the next exit ramp. Just ahead, beyond the ramp, was a sign reading:

SAN FRANCISCO
30 MILES

"Let me show you something," he said.

After receiving clearance, the Air Force Lear touched down on the runway at Cheyenne Mountain Air Station in Colorado, rolling to a halt beside an armored Humvee. Raster and Blaine stepped from the plane and entered the truck, which sped swiftly toward the three-billion-ton mass of granite known as Cheyenne Mountain.

Having left the freeway, John guided the pickup along a tree-lined side road, then into the trees. Following a rutted, overgrown dirt road for a quarter mile, he pulled to a stop at the edge of a clearing. Jen looked at him, and they stepped from the truck.

John scanned their surroundings, concluding they were alone. Unzipping the waistpack, he drew the Colt.

For a mad second the thought crossed Jen's mind that he was going to kill her. It was then that she noticed the gentleness in his eyes.

Inverting the gun, John ejected the live round from the chamber into the bag and locked the slide back. He hit the magazine release to prevent a double feed. Reaching into the bag—with Jen leaning over to peek inside—he removed another round from one of seven black elastic loops marked with small labels secured with Velcro. The loop from which he removed this bullet was marked: REDWOOD.

Placing the round in the chamber, he dropped the slide, tapped the mag back into place, righted the gun, and looked around again. He raised the pistol—

Jen plugged her ears.

—and fired into the ground at the center of the clearing. A plowed-up clump of moist earth marked the point of impact. Jen looked from the clearing to John, eyebrows raised in inquiry.

"Keep watching," he said, his own eyes locked on the impact point.

A seedling sprouted suddenly from the disturbed soil—growing with incredible speed. In the first two seconds it gained five feet; in the next, another twenty. Trunk thickening rapidly, the tiny seedling became a towering redwood two hundred feet tall. The earth around it dropped noticeably as materials normally assimilated over the course of centuries were sucked up in seconds to build the tree.

When the incredible growth had halted, Jen approached the improbable redwood with awe, staring up at it like an elf regarding a skyscraper. She reached out tentatively with one hand, touching the rough bark as if to confirm its unbelievable authenticity. She smiled, delighted at the magic of it.

John approached from behind. He was not smiling. "That was

done by assemblers," he explained. "Disassemblers destroy things; assemblers create them . . ."

Jen nodded; she knew the basics. She continued to stare at the tree, running both hands over the bark.

"Once the programs have been written," John continued, "I can create, and I can destroy. Anything . . . cars, crops, money, buildings—nuclear weapons. *Anything . . .*"

Turning from the tree, Jen stared at him with dawning comprehension. Her smile faded. The government, she realized now, would stop at nothing; would commit every resource at its disposal to this single purpose—and it would never stop looking until the both of them were found, and killed. It mattered not where they ran, how swiftly they might flee, how intelligent they might be. They were both already dead, and she knew it. Remaining with John had bought her another day, perhaps. And perhaps not even that.

Reading these thoughts in her eyes, John nodded solemnly. "Now, you understand," he said softly.

"Jeezus . . ." Jen breathed.

They walked back to the truck in silence. After turning the vehicle around, John opened his door and stepped from the truck. Raising the gun, he fired at the tree, which began almost immediately to disassemble from the center—where the bullet had struck—outward. Sliding behind the wheel, he floored the gas and sped away.

When the center of the trunk disappeared, the majestic tree's great canopy crashed to the ground like thunder—then vanished to the eerie *chitter* of nanite disassemblers.

(6)

Cheyenne Mountain was—or had been—solid granite. In 1961 the Air Force began excavating an underground fortress which became fully operational on February 6, 1966. It had been continuously upgraded since. Surrounded by two thousand feet of granite on all sides, its single entrance shielded by fifty-ton blast doors guarded twenty-four hours a day, the complex—often referred to by the acronym NORAD for North American Aerospace Defense Command, though in reality the original NORAD was now but one of four commands hosted inside the mountain—was the most secure, most survivable, and most advanced combat operations center on earth. With fully eighty percent of its two-hundred-million-dollar annual budget going to mission costs, and a mere twenty percent to facility-related costs, it also ranked among the world's most efficient large-scale military operations.

The Humvee's driver slowed to a stop beside the gatehouse. Chairman Blaine rolled down his window, displaying his identification to the MP on duty. Raster held up his security clearance with one hand, displaying his picture and clearance level but casually concealing his name and agency affiliation. When the MP seemed about to object, Blaine spoke up. "I'll vouch for him," said the chairman.

"Yes sir," said the MP. Standing back, he saluted crisply. Blaine returned the salute, and the vehicle entered the mountain.

The pickup traveled down the freeway, lost among a thousand other vehicles. "Can I ask you something?" said Jen.

"Absolutely."

"What took you so long to pull the trigger at the warehouse? They *were* trying to kill us."

John looked at her, then returned his gaze to the road ahead. "I have . . . issues," he said simply, obviously with no intention of continuing. Jen frowned.

Traffic slowed on the freeway, and John was forced to slow with it. Ahead, red and blue lights flashed in the distance.

"Uh-oh," he said.

"Roadblock?"

"I don't know . . ."

"No exits," Jen noted, looking around. The nearest off-ramp was beyond the flashing lights.

As they drew nearer, traffic slowed to a standstill, and John pulled to the shoulder. First John, then Jen opened a door and stood up, gazing ahead. The cause of the backup became apparent: Two semi trucks had collided on the road ahead. One lay on its side, blocking all northbound lanes; the other—a tanker truck—had rolled into the slow-moving creek which ran alongside the freeway's eastern edge. The tanker had apparently ruptured, as fire crews were hosing down the area around it. The situation seemed to be what it appeared to be—but John ruled nothing out. Jen looked at him as though reading his thoughts. "I buy it," he announced after a moment.

The traffic began inching forward, and a hearse crawled up alongside him. He recognized it as a 1937 Cadillac LaSalle, because that was the car used at his father's funeral. He'd been twenty-two when his father died. The funeral had been attended mainly by friends of his mother, and a few of his own; his father had not been an easy man to get along with, even for his son. Part of that was his failure to live up to his own father's—John's grandfather's—accomplishments. He'd tried for many years, and had eventually severed all ties with the man, moving away and changing the family name not once but twice—which was how John had come to be born with the name Marrek. At the time of the funeral, however, John had yet to learn of those things.

There had been one unfamiliar face that day—an older man John did not recognize. He'd noticed John's attention immediately, and nodded a somber greeting. Immediately after the ceremony, the man had turned away, heading for the drive. John intercepted him.

"Hello, John," said the man.

"I'm afraid you have the advantage."

"I was a friend of your father's."

"My father had no friends."

The man had regarded him with what seemed a mixture of amusement and compassion. "Of course he did," he said. Donning his hat, he'd stepped into a waiting car and been driven off by a chauffeur. John had memorized the license plate, and learned that the car was registered to Los Alamos Labs.

That was how he'd learned of his father's true brilliance, and also how he came to realize that the man he'd known growing up was but a shadow of his former self. It would take another five years and the death of his mother before he learned the whole truth: that the magnitude of his grandfather's deeds and reputation had eventually destroyed his father—just as they now threatened, in a different way, to destroy John himself.

Jen's voice pulled him back to the present.

"*Oh look,*" she said sadly, moving from the truck and stepping over the guardrail. John glanced around quickly, decided no one was going anywhere fast, and moved to join her, picking his way down the steep bank to the water's edge.

The tanker truck, he now saw, had been loaded with fuel oil. The viscous black substance clouded the water below in a moving line and clung to the banks with life-sucking, Stygian fingers. The stench of petroleum soaked the air.

Jen's attention was focused on an egret which flapped helplessly at the creek's edge on the far shore. White feathers coated with oil, unable to find purchase or to drag itself up the sloping, oil-coated bank—the bird slid toward the black abyss of the dying creek. Jen looked to John, eyes welling with compassion for the stricken bird.

John gazed around himself. To the north, the creek bed curved around a jutting spur of land which blocked the view of the emergency crews some half mile distant. To the south, there was nothing but the moving black line of oil in the water. Behind and ahead, the tall banks sheltered the creek from the view of those above. Reaching into his bag, John withdrew the Colt and a screw-on suppressor. Jen looked at him.

Threading the suppressor onto the barrel, he removed the clip, ejected the live round in the chamber into the bag, and placed a fresh bullet in the chamber. Looking around again, he dropped the slide.

"You're not—" Jen began, shaking her head.

John raised the gun.

"What are you doing?" said Jen, seizing his arm.

"Let go," he growled in a tone which brooked no opposition. She did. Aiming across the creek, he fired. The gun made a dull *pfft* sound as a bullet shattered on a rock across the water. The bird jumped at the sound.

Immediately, the rock changed color from black to gray—followed by the soil around it, which turned brown, and the water beside it, which became suddenly clear. All became covered with nanites, which swarmed outward exponentially, *chittering* softly as they reduced the lethal hydrocarbons, which formed the oil into individual atoms of hydrogen and carbon, which were harmless in themselves.

Eyes panicked, the egret struggled frantically to avoid this new horror—accelerating its slide into the water. And then its plumage turned brilliant white as the nanites swarmed over and past it. Gaining its footing in the mud, the bird stepped from the water, shaking itself violently to dislodge the unseen nanites which had saved its life.

John and Jen watched as the swarm reached the advancing end of the oil slick to their right, then raced around the bend to the left. Watching the egret, Jen smiled, tears on her cheeks—and looked to John, who was busy unthreading the suppressor and reloading.

"That was a demo for Mitchell," he explained.

"Hydrocarbon disassembly for oil spill cleanup," Jen realized.

John nodded. "No more icky messy," he said, holstering the gun and closing the bag without looking. Jen smiled. He took her hand and helped her back up the bank. "Unlimited swarm size," he elaborated, "it keeps going until all proximate hydrocarbons have been disassembled. No more tanker disasters. No more dead otters or seals or anything else. Do you know eighty percent of the *live* wildlife pulled from oil spills by rescue crews dies anyway?"

Jen nodded; she knew.

Reaching the top, they stepped over the guardrail. "No more toxic spills of any kind," John added. "Cyanide spill?" Releasing her hand, he snapped his fingers for effect. "No problem."

"Nanites:" quipped Jen, "the quicker picker-upper."

John had to laugh.

A half mile away, firemen dropped their hoses and scrambled from the water as a softly *chittering* line of *something* raced toward them along the surface of the water and along both shorelines.

"*What the hell . . . ?*" said one.

"*Jeesus,* Pete, *look at your boots,*" said another, pointing in astonishment as the boots of the man who had spoken first began to crawl with nanites. The crawling surface swiftly disappeared—

along with the oil which had coated the boots an instant before. The men turned at a terrified scream behind them.

The tanker truck's driver leapt from the stretcher on which he lay, flailing frantically at the nanites swarming over him, disassembling the black film of oil which covered his clothing and skin and matted his hair. Firemen and police officers stared at him, agape, as the blackness disappeared.

In the water, nanites swarmed inside the truck's fuel tanks and through the breach in the cargo tank's top, ridding their interiors of hydrocarbons to the last molecule.

After a moment, the driver ceased flailing and screaming and began swatting himself repeatedly, as though covered with biting mosquitoes beyond number.

Taking in the now-pristine area around him, the fireman with the clean boots gazed up at the sky, and said quietly, "Thanks, Big Guy."

"You're welcome," said John to the egret as he and Jen watched it take the air above the creek.

"What?" said Jen, turning.

John nodded toward the flying egret.

"Oh."

They watched the bird as it flew hurriedly east.

Mattman stood on the hillside as the bunker was excavated. He was for the moment still head of Microtron's security operations—and this was the place from which Mitchell had been shot. The bunker was small and well hidden, covered with earth and concealed by vegetation. The only clue to its existence had been the small hole through which the scope had peered and the gun fired.

Scope and gun were not visible from outside the bunker; the muzzle had been inside when the shot was fired. This concealed both muzzle flash and dust-up. Even without taking into consideration the scant amount of time which the assassin had had to prepare, it was an excellent job.

When the covering earth was at last ripped away by the back-hoe, revealing the revetments which kept the bunker from collapsing, Mattman got his first good look at the gun. The .50 caliber, bull-barreled, semiautomatic Barrett was top-of-the-line, and accurate to two miles in competent hands. The bunker was almost that far from the stage on which Mitchell had drawn his last breath.

Mattman had been at a loss to explain the failure of his men to detect the assassin. Open areas had been continuously surveiled. Likely sniping locations—this one included—had been walked over multiple times throughout the day of Mitchell's speech, as well as the night before. This hill and others had been swept from a distance with the best thermal-imaging equipment money could buy. The sweeps had turned up his own men as they walked the terrain—and yet had failed to discern Mitchell's killer.

As the backhoe's engine sputtered to a stop and his men gathered around the bunker, Mattman nodded slowly to himself. Though he had failed Mitchell, his men had not failed him, nor had their equipment: The gun in the bunker sat atop a robotic platform. The scope was a video feed to a series of encrypted burst-transceivers which ultimately led to a satellite uplink three miles distant. From that uplink, and via those transceivers, the gun had been aimed and the trigger pulled.

The assassin had not been there to find.

He considered striking back at Parallax, but discarded the notion immediately. They would not have done this; it was too high-profile. Nor would they know who had done it. They would not, in fact, even have known it was going to happen; that would be a breach of operational security. They'd been hired strictly for surveillance, and that was all they knew.

The man he'd questioned—"Coyote"—had been all but useless. His coworkers he knew only by nickname, except for Brandt—of whom Mattman had already known. As to the purpose of the surveillance and the client for whom it had been performed, the man had known nothing. Mattman had suspected this would be the case, but it rarely hurt to be thorough. They'd released the man—stark naked—in Golden Gate Park.

Likewise, Mitchell's assassin would never be identified, as his own client—the person or entity which had hired him or, less likely, her—would not know his identity. The assassin himself, therefore, would be impossible to strike. Even if found, he would not know who the client was. That was the way things worked at this level; unless the killer was caught at the scene with the gun in his hand, evidence was nonexistent.

But the assassin was a weapon—a tool wielded by another hand. And there weren't a lot of people with the money and the connections required to wield such a tool. Nor were many in a position to hire Parallax for a job as complex and as expensive and as risk-ridden as surveilling Mitchell Swain. And there was a link: Whoever had hired Parallax, had hired Mitchell's assassin. He was sure of it.

Using his own knowledge of the trade and its players, and, so long as they remained available to him, Microtron's resources, Mattman would find this person—and kill him.

And he'd take his damned time doing the latter.

A General Electric Minigun turned its ugly snout to follow the Hummer bearing Blaine and Raster as it approached the inner sanctum. The truck slowed near the final guard station, which bore a large sign reading:

CHEYENNE MOUNTAIN AIR STATION
UNITED STATES STRATEGIC COMMAND
UNITED STATES MILITARY INSTALLATION
USE OF DEADLY FORCE AUTHORIZED

Again Blaine rolled down his window. The guard lowered the phone through which he spoke with the previous guard, saluted, and waved off the Minigun. Blaine and Raster exited the vehicle. Passing through three separate five-foot-thick steel blast doors, the two men entered the heart of the mountain fortress.

John's old pickup crossed the Golden Gate Bridge in late afternoon—just one among the forty-one million vehicles which crossed that great span each year. Arriving in Sausalito, John punched numbers into a cell phone he'd purchased in Irvine a few hours earlier.

Jen's raised eyebrows spoke the question.

"My security system; see if anyone's broken in," answered John. After entering a few more numbers, he announced the verdict: "nope."

"All right. These nanites—they're running programs, like a computer, destroying or building only what the program tells them to."

John hesitated briefly before answering. "In theory," he hedged. "Everything depends on the program, yes."

"What if the program's buggy?"

John looked at her. "You *don't* want to know," he replied, then guided the truck up the driveway of a modest home no different from its neighbors. Using a remote taken from the Excursion, he opened the garage door.

"This is my home," John explained, and drove inside. The garage door closed automatically behind them. He stepped from the truck with gun in hand.

"Do you have another lab here?"

John shook his head. "No." Moving to a seemingly unused corner of the garage, he slid aside an old, disused-looking cabinet, revealing a security system panel. "Across the Bay," he explained, punching in codes to double-check system status. He nodded to himself; the system had not been breached. Entering a second code unlocked the door leading into the house.

"We just *crossed* the Bay," Jen pointed out, sounding annoyed.

John slid the cabinet back into place. "I need to be certain we weren't followed before we go to the main lab. That's the mother lode. The L.A. facility was just for convenience, to be near Black Mountain—"

"Black Mountain?"

"The computer you said you found," John explained, opening the door to the house. "Before Blue Gene/L and ASCII's Purple and White there was Blue Pacific, and before that—"

"Blue Mountain," Jen finished, carrying back the recent lineage of some of the world's fastest computers.

John smiled. "Right. So I thought I'd call mine—"

"Black Mountain," said the two of them in unison.

"It required a lot of upkeep," John noted.

Jen followed him inside. A black cat greeted them at the door, *meowing* plaintively and rubbing against John's leg. Lifting it from the floor, he carried it with him as he continued into the house.

The place seemed normal enough, Jen reflected, though it could use a woman's touch. The house didn't didn't look as though anyone spent much time in it. What should have been the living room had been converted into a library, the shelves of which overflowed with technical and scientific journals going back seven years. Other shelves sagged beneath the weight of fat tomes with obscure titles even she could make no sense of.

As they passed into the hallway, she noted an entire shelf filled with computer printouts marked: CLASSIFIED and UNITED STATES ARMY.

"You were working with the *Army?*" Jen asked with distaste.

"Hell no," John replied, "—just keeping tabs on them. They're farther along than the Air Force or Navy."

At the end of the hall was a feeding station for the cat, with several bins of food upended over gravity-feed trays alongside watercooler-sized water bottles connected to immovable bowls fitted with water-level sensors.

"Looks like your cat is used to being alone," Jen observed.

"Actually," said John, heading down another hallway, "there's a cat door in the basement. He used to bring all his buddies home to chow down while I was away. Nonhouse-trained buddies, I might add."

"Used to?" asked Jen as they ascended carpeted stairs to the second floor.

John nodded. "I put a light with photosensor on the cat door, tripped by a motion sensor. When something trips the motion sensor, the light goes on; if too much is reflected back at the photosensor, the door stays closed, so—"

"—only black cats can use the door," Jen finished.

"And the neighborhood schnauzer," John added, none too happily. "And very muddy cats. Technology isn't all it's cracked up to be. Or wasn't . . ."

"Revenge effect," said Jen, half to herself. John turned on the stairs. "You've read Tenner?" he asked, referring to Edward Tenner's *Why Things Bite Back: Technology and the Revenge of Unintended Consequences.* Jen nodded.

"Cool," said John, turning away and continuing upward. "Then you'll see what a nightmare this is going to be."

The key premise of Tenner's work was that new technologies did not simply solve old problems; rather, they replaced old problems with new problems which were invariably more complicated than the old and quite often impossible to get rid of. Furthermore, new technologies and their applications often had unintended and sometimes severe consequences which were not only unforseen but were in fact unforseeable. These consequences, when negative, were termed by Tenner "revenge effects."

In short: Technology bit back.

The top of the stairs brought them to a large room which should have been, perhaps, a game room or den. Instead, it was a living room. "Have a seat." John indicated the couch. Placing the cat on a shelf—beside a duplicate of the same framed photograph Jen had seen in the warehouse lab—John moved to what looked to be a ruinously expensive sound system. The cat jumped immediately to the floor, then up onto the arm of the couch beside Jen.

"What's your cat's name?" she asked, stroking the animal's sleek black fur as it purred contentedly.

"Schrödinger," said John, and turned to see her reaction. Despite their predicament, Jen had to grin. "Schröder for short," John added. The cat's head snapped around to look at him, gold eyes inscrutable.

Erwin Schrödinger, Jen knew, had been the Austrian quantum physicist who'd devised a theoretical experiment to illustrate the bizarre and contradictory nature of quantum physics. In this experiment, a caged cat would live or die depending upon which of two polarized photon detectors was struck by a single photon permitted to enter the "hellish device" in which the theoretical experiment took place.

The catch was that, upon entering the boxlike device, the photon must pass through a calcite crystal and so be split into dual photons polarized at right angles to one another. Thus, rather than a single photon striking a single polarized photon detector—each of *two* photons would strike a separate detector simultaneously. Because of this, the cat must quite clearly be both dead and alive at the same time, just as quantum particles exist as superimpositions—or potential particles—in two or more distinct locations simultaneously.

What's more, the cat would continue to be both dead and alive, presumably for all eternity, until his cage door was opened. At that point, the cat must become definitively one or the other by reason of the impossible to demonstrate but logically inescapable phenomenon known as wave function collapse—which holds, among other things, that a cat cannot *be* both dead and alive at the macroscopic level at which cats exist in the first place.

The theoretical exercise and the hapless creature itself had come to be called, inevitably, "Schrödinger's Cat." The good news for the cat, as physicist Frederik Belinfante had pointed out, was that such a contraption could just as easily bring a dead cat back to life as kill a live one. This had led Belinfante to speculate that quantum theory might one day find widespread use among veterinarians.

An alternative, somewhat less serious theory held that the entire theoretical Schrödinger scenario was ultimately unverifiable because observable reality dictates that the severely pissed-off live version of the cat will invariably escape the box well before it can be opened by the experimenter, thereupon attacking said experimenter and departing the lab in the instant before said experimenter—now severely lacerated—watches the hammer descend on the cyanide bottle one inch from his nose.

"Like classical music?" asked John, somewhat disconcertingly.

"What?" said Jen, failing to see the relevance of classical music to the somewhat more pressing matters at hand.

"Classical—"

"I heard you," said Jen, shaking her head. "Yes. What are we doing here?"

Entering a selection on the master panel, John watched as the CD jukebox selected the proper disc and moved it into place. Checking his watch, he moved to a large leather lounge chair identical to the one in the erstwhile L.A. facility, though less worn. "We wait," he said simply, gun in hand, and fell into the chair.

From speakers around the room, classical music began to play—Orff at his darkest: *Carmina Burana.*

Inside the Oval Office of the White House, President Miller listened as Homeland Security Secretary Nathan Rydell—the only one among the four alphabet soup directors he'd called before him earlier whom he halfway trusted—summed up an informal briefing on what little was thus far known of Swain's assassination.

"The gun itself, as well as the hardware used to fire it, were stolen, of course."

"Of course," repeated the president. The comment sounded sarcastic.

"The gun was apparently operated via satellite;" Rydell continued evenly, "NSA and NRO are collating data on that now, trying to find out who was sending signals where and when around the time of the assassination."

"Think that will get us anywhere?"

Realistically? No, sir—too much traffic. Our only conclusions as of this time are that Swain was killed by one or more extremely well funded, absolute professionals who were probably working for an employer as unknown to them as they were to him."

The president nodded. "What's the probability the party ultimately responsible is a government?"

Rydell pursed his lips. "Government or corporation," he clarified, then paused. "High. And while I don't want to say it's impossible, I will say that it's going to be extraordinarily difficult to learn what person or persons *are* ultimately responsible for this."

"Understood. What's the best lead you have?"

"The depleted-uranium core of the bullet used in the assassination. Highly unusual and difficult to come by."

"And they used it why?"

"Because it couldn't fail; had Swain been wearing a plate-steel vest and dived behind a lead shield—the round would still have killed him. We should have a signature on the uranium by the end of the day; from there we'll attempt to determine the nation and reactor core of origin."

"Which could have been chosen simply to mislead us."

"Absolutely . . . Sir."

"So," the president recapped, "—even if we *are* fortunate enough to identify *and* apprehend the assassin, perhaps even tie him to the gun and/or bullet—we still won't know who hired him, because he doesn't know himself."

"In all likelihood, sir, yes."

"Does that strike you as unacceptable?" asked the president.

"Yes sir, it does."

President Miller leaned intently forward. *"Me too,"* he said.

Tunneled out of the rock beneath the mountain, the Cheyenne Mountain complex was a four-and-a-half-acre collection of fifteen freestanding buildings, which ranged from one to three stories in height. All were surrounded by continuously welded, low-carbon steel plates to ward off electromagnetic pulse effects which might otherwise disable the complex in the event of a nuclear conflict.

The complex's entrance was fitted with three pneumatically operated, twenty-five-ton steel blast doors—and air, water, fuel, and sewer inlets and outlets were equipped with blast valves to prevent the blast waves of nearby nuclear detonations from entering the complex.

One thousand, two hundred nineteen springs weighing one thousand pounds each supported the floor atop which the buildings rested, acting as giant shock absorbers in the event of earthquakes or a direct hit by a nuclear weapon—which the complex had been specifically designed to withstand.

Power for this small underground city of eleven hundred people was drawn from the nearby city of Colorado Springs—though should that fail, six one thousand, seven-hundred-fifty-watt diesel generators of twenty-eight-hundred-horsepower capacity stood ready to provide operational power for up to thirty days. Food and water, of course, were also available in sufficient quantity, and the facility's fresh air could, if necessary, be filtered through a series of chemical/biological/radiological filters in order to ensure purity.

Technically, the Cheyenne Mountain complex was host to the North American Aerospace Defense Command, or NORAD, from which the facility took its common name; the United States Northern Command, or USNORTHCOM, the United States Strategic Command, or USSTRATCOM, and the Air Force Space Command or AFSPC. Though the complex's missions ranged from weather monitoring and space debris tracking to geopolitical unrest observation and space shuttle mission support, the facility had been designed with but a single overriding purpose: to serve as an impregnable command center capable of providing early warning of any enemy attack by land-sea-, air-, or space-based assets while remaining in continuous communication with United States assets and commanders in order to coordinate an integrated global U.S. response. In short—Cheyenne had been built to fight the final war.

And as the single highest-ranking military officer in the United States, Chairman Richard Blaine was one of only two men capable of walking into Cheyenne Mountain and assuming unquestioned command. The other being the president of the United States.

As it happened, the facility's commander, Brigadier General Samuel Hobbs, was at a doctor's appointment in Colorado Springs, and was expected back shortly. Vice Commander Brigadier General Ian Hargrave was smoking in the parking lot. That pleased Blaine, who reasoned that he'd have considerably less trouble talking his way past Operations Commander Colonel Jacqueline Sinclair.

In this he was mistaken.

(7)

A small fire crackled in the fireplace of John's home as the sun set through the window. Mozart had followed Orff on the sound system, thankfully fading after a single depressing selection which had done little to lighten Jen's mood—not overly optimistic to begin with. John sat beside her on the couch, stroking an appreciative Schröder under the chin.

This was the first respite he and Jen had had since the attack in Los Angeles, and with the exigencies of their flight and the worry over pursuers now behind them—albeit temporarily—Jen wanted details. If someone was going to kill her for what she might know, she was damned well going to know it all and then some before she went. "All right," she began, patience thinning, "time to tell me what's going on."

John looked up from the cat. "Government goons tried to kill us. We got away. They'll try again."

Jen rolled her eyes and looked half-away, clenching her jaw. John watched her, studying. The woman was undeniably appealing—intellectually, physically. She was who she said she was—Jennifer Rayne—of that he was certain. The question, to his mind, was whether she'd found her way to him as she said she had, following the now unverifiable clues yielded by Mitchell's black ledger and her dead hacker friend—or whether she was actually working with the government, attempting to gain his confidence that he might willingly lead her to the prize the government could not find by force. By painting him as some kind of mad-scientist-threat-to-humanity, it might have been possible to enlist her aid against him.

It would be a shrewd backup plan should the attack at the warehouse end in failure—and from her perspective, a Pulitzer Prize would be a slam-dunk. But with her obvious intelligence, she had to know by now that the story would never be written; having outlived her usefulness, she'd be killed along with him.

Somewhere in the back of his mind he heard Mitchell calling him paranoid. He ignored it; paranoia had become a survival trait.

John had been an excellent judge of character since childhood, to the point where he had seen through con men his parents and others had not—not because he grasped the details of the particular cons, but because he somehow grasped intuitively that the persons involved were not to be trusted. The ability was almost freakish. He'd been employing it to evaluate Jen ever since the warehouse.

Mitchell's assassination had forced John to embark irrevocably upon a new path. And that path demanded a second—preferably female—perspective to balance his own. Logically, this was not required, but he felt the need for it nonetheless. He had worked alone for too long, in an environment in which he had few if any equals. The result was an inevitable slide toward arrogance—and arrogance could be a dangerous thing indeed.

Over the course of the short time he'd known Jen, it had become clear to him that she was more his type of woman than any other he'd ever known. He felt drawn to her—and tried very hard not to let that interfere with his evaluation. There was so much at stake and so little time remaining.

"What do you know about nanotech?" he asked.

Jen turned her head to face him, annoyance fading. "Just the basics. A way to make things smaller. That and Bill Joy's piece in *Wired*. He said it could destroy the biosphere."

"He's right," said John. "The man sounded a wake-up call. The world pricked up its ears for a week and went back to sleep."

"I kept meaning to research it, but everything I'd seen said it was decades away, so it kind of drifted to the back burner. A lot of what I've seen seems to refer to anything that's very small as nano-technology."

John nodded. "The term is widely misused; people who should know better use it for anything and everything measured in nanometers. Nanotechnology is something very specific."

Though her features did not betray it, Jen smiled inwardly; John was beginning to relax a little. Judging from his body language, he was on the verge of being, if not quite comfortable, at ease enough to begin speaking in detail of the subject to which he'd devoted the past five years or more. It was something she'd seen before with other great men of science too long away from the company of others and glad to find a willing, intelligent, and appreciative ear. John was ready to talk—and that was precisely what Jen wanted. "Tell me about it," she prompted.

John regarded her coolly, but did not respond—surprising her. Could she have read him wrong? "If I'm going to be killed for it," she added, "I want to know everything."

"No one knows everything," replied John. "Yet."

Jen frowned at him.

"Fair enough," he decided suddenly, and rose from the couch. Schröder immediately trotted across the cushions to Jen and placed his head beneath her palm, inviting affection. She obliged.

"The world and everything in it," John began, "is made up of atoms. Their arrangement and combination determine what a thing will be. Arrange carbon atoms one way, and you have a worthless lump of coal; arrange them a little differently—and you have a diamond. Combined with oxygen atoms, they're a gas floating through the atmosphere. Arrange them still another way, throw in a few other things, just add water"—John held up his right hand, gazing at the palm—"and you have a nanotechnologist. The atoms are the same; only their arrangement and combination differs." John spoke animatedly, his enthusiasm for the subject taking over.

"Human beings are built from atoms put together by ribosomes acting under the direction of DNA and RNA. The DNA blueprint is transcribed onto RNA strands which tell the ribosomes what to do. And what they do is build a person by rearranging atoms. Likewise, a seed contains the program for a redwood tree. The tree isn't in the seed, only the instructions. Those instructions tell the seed what resources to look for, where to send them, and what to do with them to build the tree.

"If you can . . . *take control* of things at an atomic level," John said, speaking with a sudden zeal which gave Jen pause, "write your *own* programs, and *implement* them—you can do anything. You can *literally,* construct—or destroy—*anything* the laws of physics will allow."

He halted, and looked at her. "That's what nanites do. Think of it as—" He paused, searching for an analogy.

"Digital matter," he said after a moment. Matter . . . *manipulated* like digital video, or music—but instead of ones and zeros, you have the elements themselves to work with . . .

"The Age of Nanotechnology is the Age of Digital Matter," he explained. "There are one hundred eighteen known elements. Everything on earth—you, me, this table, that couch—is made up of one or some combination of those elements.

"And just as the ones and zeros of a computer's binary code can be arranged to form mathematical formulae, a symphony, a Ku Klux Klan flyer, or pornography—any object on earth can be *torn apart* into its constituent atoms, which can then be used to build something else. *Any*thing else it's possible to construct using those elements."

"Like deleting the Klan flyer and overwriting it with Beethoven's Ninth," observed Jen.

"Or vice versa," John confirmed. "And whether the thing built is you, me, a Model T, or a redwood tree—doesn't matter. There is *literally, no difference* between assembling something alive, and something that isn't."

"DNA is constructed of atoms, just like everything else," Jen noted.

"Exactly. Whatever the program tells the nanites to do, they do. Assuming the resources are available, assembling a tree is no more difficult than assembling a gumball. Atoms can be arranged, de-arranged, and *re*arranged in any manner we see fit, within the laws of physics.

"*And* we can make copies. The way a CD is a perfect copy of the studio recording? We'll be able to make, in addition to new things—*perfect* copies of anything that exists, and anything we create. Have a priceless antique you want to preserve? Make a dozen copies. Earthquakes threaten the Sistine Chapel? Put up another one in Florida. Duplicate entire museums full of unique items, so the whole world can enjoy them a few hours' drive from home—or in their own living rooms, one item at a time. And you thought the Internet brought the world to your door . . ."

Jen's mind reeled with the implications. The possibilities. If what John said was true, there was almost nothing this technology could not accomplish.

"Or, hey," said John with a mischievous glint in his eye, "—you have the hots for James Spader? Winona Ryder? Put one in your bedroom. Or three." He raised a finger aloft. "Some assembly required," he added with a grin.

Jen hit a look of disapproval.

"Disassemblers are easy," continued John. "Relative to assem-blers, that is. All they do is tear things apart and multiply—like dig-ital sharks."

"How do they break the bonds—pull the atoms apart?"

John's eyes slid over to the bookcase beside the door. He moved toward the case. Lifting an object from one of the shelves, he held it up before him. Jen recognized the thing as a CPK model—a representation of a molecule composed of colored spheres which snapped together to simulate bonded atoms. She saw that the one he held represented H_2O—a molecule of water composed of one oxygen and two hydrogen atoms.

"This is a water molecule," said John. "The adult human body, give or take, is seventy percent water." Gripping the spheres tightly, he jerked the oxygen atom away from the others. All three fell to the floor as separate atoms, rolling away from one another in different directions. *"That's,* what disassemblers do."

Chairman Blaine led Raster to Cheyenne's combined command center, a dimly lit, high-tech sepulchre directly linked to all U.S. and Canadian Command Authorities and both allied and U.S. regional commands overseas. Resembling a supersized version of the CIC or command information center of an aircraft carrier with its wall-mounted video display and tracking screens, lighted maps, grease-boards, and war tables, the command center received continuously updated information from all U.S. intelligence-gathering assets both on and above the earth, as well as undersea. Throughout the large room, Air Force techs manned control and communications consoles. The operations commander was waiting.

Classically featured, with pale blue eyes and auburn hair, Colonel Jacqueline Sinclair was the first and only woman to hold the post of operations commander at Cheyenne Mountain—and as Chairman Blaine soon learned, she had not accomplished this feat by being easily intimidated.

Following a brief introduction, Blaine charged ahead hard. "Pursuant to the provisions of the Anti-Terrorism and Domestic Security Act and by the authority of the president of the United States, I'm assuming command of this facility for the next seventy-two hours," he stated flatly. "The mountain is to be sealed immediately. Standard operations will remain normal for the time being, but all nonintelligence communications to and from this command will go through me."

Colonel Sinclair stared at him for an instant, taken aback.

Blaine gave her no time to think. "The matter is classified," he said, hoping to forestall unwanted questions. "I'd like you to assist."

"I'll have to confirm that, of course," replied the colonel.

"Of course," repeated Blaine, features stolid but stomach churning. No other response was possible.

As if to lighten the mood, Schröder leapt to the floor and began batting the spheres representing atoms across the carpet.

"But how do the nanites disassemble molecules? Not all bonds are weak," said Jen.

"True. It depends on what you're dealing with. Weak bonds can be overcome by mechanical pressure—nanite arms simply pull the atoms apart. Stronger bonds require chemical agents synthesized from surrounding raw materials. Fast enzymes and a couple of good acids will disassemble anything. Sloppy, but effective. When neatness counts, the proper agents are applied more judiciously.

"Assembly is the same, in reverse. You move the right atoms together and they bond automatically; the main problem is proper positioning to ensure they bond to what you want them to bond to and not to the nanites or surrounding materials. For pesky atoms, nanochemistry can aid here as well. Resistance is useless."

Jen almost laughed at the unexpected pun. "What about quantum effects?"

"It's a design consideration. Redundancy and instant repair cancel it."

"Thermal problems?"

"If you're talking heat buildup, it depends on duration; if the job's done slowly—or quickly—it's not a problem in an open environment at normal temperatures. If it becomes a problem you assemble water for evaporative cooling, then grab the atoms in the vapor and do it over again.

"If you're talking thermal vibration and Brownian motion—it's a real pain, as is electrostatic discharge. When something has to be held in place—covalent bonds, every carbon atom bonded to three neighbors with Diels-Alder link reactions . . ." He stopped, seeing Jen's furrowed brows. She wasn't a chemist. "Trust me;" he said, "it works."

"What about power? What do they use for . . . energy, fuel?"

"Chemical, thermal, solar energy—you name it. Whatever's available, they use—and there's almost nowhere these things can't find energy. Land, sea, air, outer space—there's always some resource to be used."

"A single weapon for all environments . . ." mused Jen.

Interesting that should be her first thought, John mused. "No doubt the government's main interest," he said aloud.

"And yours?" asked Jen, observing John carefully. She didn't know whether to fear John, or to trust him. Intuitively, she felt he could be trusted, despite the nightmare scene outside the warehouse—but intuition was one thing; reality could be quite another. Saving the egret when she thought he'd meant to kill it said a lot about him, as did designing a program to disassemble oil spills. And raging intelligence was almost always attractive, when not coupled with too much arrogance.

But there was the weapon, and the technology—which made the man before her probably the single most dangerous human being the world had ever known. Because of that, intuition could not be her only guide in judging him. Just what the hell she could do about it if she judged him evil, she had no idea.

"No," replied John. "Weapons were secondary, but necessary. Obviously. Every intellectually and artistically superior culture in history that failed to arm itself to the teeth went down at the hands of a better-armed inferior. That's just the way the world works."

That was telling, thought Jen. *He thinks himself intellectually superior . . .* Then, an instant later: *Hell—so do I.*

"If I hadn't developed the weapons," John continued, "we'd be dead, and the tech would be in the hands of the government—

which I don't think you trust any more than I do, even before . . . this."

"What about Swain?"

"Mitchell," said John, shoulders slumping. He returned to the couch and sat down heavily. Schröder quickly occupied his lap. "War was the furthest thing from Mitchell's mind. He wanted to build Eden. No hunger. No poverty. No want. *Limitless* energy at *zero* cost. No pollution, no toxic waste—*no reason* to *make* war."

When he paused, Jen could see his thoughts racing well ahead of his words. What he was describing, she began to perceive, was as much his vision as Swain's.

"Faster computers, of course," he continued. "And pushing Man to the stars. That was the big one."

He leaned his head against the back of the couch, staring at the ceiling. " 'We can colonize the universe and not even pack for the trip,' " he said, as if to himself. He turned to Jen. "One of Mitchell's lines."

"I'm not following."

John sat up, eyes filling with the same near-fanaticism she'd seen in Swain's features as he'd begun to describe the promise of nanotechnology—seconds before he'd died. She tried to suppress the memory of his head exploding in front of her.

"Fire off spacecraft with nanite payloads," John said, gesturing animatedly as he spoke. "Pushed to near light-speed by nukes or ion drives; slowed before impact. Crash-land on uninhabited worlds meeting predetermined criteria. Nanites go forth and multiply, *covering* the planet. *Terraforming*—or *nano*forming it. Making the atmosphere breathable; the climate, livable. Gathering raw materials from the planet itself. Building houses, power plants, transportation systems. Making seeds from indigenous elements and growing crops. Making water from hydrogen and oxygen—all following a predetermined but adaptable program.

"By the time we get there," he finished, "—decades, centuries, millennia later—it's ready to move in. It is abso*lutely* feasible; the most difficult part is writing the programs to guide the nanites."

Jen stared at him.

"It's all doable," John confirmed. "In fact—we don't even have to go. Nanites can construct adult human beings from naturally occurring elements on each world."

The concept struck Jen speechless for a moment—not an easy thing to do. "Do you think that would work? *Really* think it would work . . . ?"

John regarded her oddly. In truth, this was where things became fuzzy for him. That Jen should home in on this one detail, in the ocean of data upon which she'd been cast, was impressive. "I don't know," he admitted. "Mitchell thought so. He subscribed to the view that any person, child or adult, could be built from scratch. . . ."

When John paused, Jen sensed a mental hesitation—as if he were uncertain about the wisdom of revealing details. "Go on," she prompted softly.

After an appraising look, he did. "Okay. The plan, we decided—*if* we were going to go ahead—would be to map real people such as ourselves, atom by atom, and then instruct the spacefaring nanites to construct exact duplicates on destination worlds. This much we could do, no question. And of course we'd test it here first. But . . ." John frowned, appearing troubled. "The result is where we disagreed."

"How so?"

"Mitchell believed that consciousness is nothing more than the result of electrochemical interactions within the structure of the brain, so naturally he felt certain the result of a nanoassembled human body would be a living, waking, self-aware human no different mentally, physically, or emotionally from the individual it had been modeled after at the time the atomic map of that person's body had been made."

"So you'd wind up with identical twins, in essence."

John nodded. "More identical than any others." He held a finger aloft for emphasis. "In Mitchell's view."

"And in yours?"

"You first," said John.

"I don't buy it."

John smiled.

"What?"

John shook his head.

"You don't buy it either," Jen ventured.

"Let's say I'm uncomfortable with it. The biomechanistic view of consciousness is just . . ." He held up both hands in a gesture of frustration. "It's emotionally unappealing and scientifically unprovable. And, hey—I just don't like it, okay?"

Jen grinned. "Me either."

"I'm not sure you'd get a viable human being. Every time Mitchell would bring it up, I'd say: 'Well, switch it on, Jack, and see what happens.'

"I mean, think about it. If life really *is* the result of some sort of . . . *spirit*—for want of a better word—which inhabits the body, then the nanite-constructed duplicates might turn out to be mindless lumps of flesh, alive but lacking sentience, consciousness, self-awareness. Like—" he paused, searching for an analogy, "—a skin culture in a lab dish."

"But might not a body tailored over years to the needs of one spirit prove equally inviting to another?" asked Jen. "Or even to the *same* spirit, which might choose to inhabit more than one body at the same time—or to abandon the old body for the new?"

"No idea. It gives me a headache just thinking about it."

"But for the first time we—you—have the ability to, maybe, *answer* that question. Are we just a body and a brain—or is there more to us than meets the eye?"

"It wouldn't be a definitive answer," John noted, "—as you've just pointed out."

"Still . . ."

"I'm not ready to answer that question. I'm not sure I want to answer it."

"You're a scientist."

"Science isn't everything."

"Blasphemy."

John had to laugh. "It *has* become our religion—but there's no responsibility, no accountability, no . . . *morality* guiding it. We—scientists, collectively—don't do things because they'll benefit Mankind, or the earth; we do them *because we can*. It's 'technical arrogance.'"

"'It is something that gives people an illusion of illimitible power,'" said Jen, quoting physicist Freeman Dyson, speaking of his work on the Manhattan Project, "'this what you might call technical arrogance that overcomes people when they see what they can do with their minds.'"

John nodded, unsurprised by now that she should know the origin of the term. "They create something like the atom bomb," he continued, "which is *immediately* used to incinerate entire *cities*—and then they step back and say, 'We're not responsible. Don't look at us. It wasn't our decision.'"

"Not all of them," said Jen. "Not—"

"No; not all of them," John interrupted. "Most of them. Some changed their minds after that—but not enough, and they paid a price." He leaned forward, eyes and voice intense.

"This is *mine*," he said. "*I created it, I did it for humanity, and it's my responsibility. And I'll be* god-damned *if I'll see it confiscated, classified, and deployed as a weapon by a power-mad government. . . .*"

These words, and the passion behind them, served to tip the balance in Jen's mind, and she began to accept her earlier impression—that John could be trusted.

"Even with this tech," she said after a moment, "—you're one man. How can you hope to stop them?"

John looked at her in silence—jaw set, eyes blazing. "Any way I have to," he replied.

Jen's mind tilted back toward apprehension.

Chairman Blaine shot a sidelong glance at Raster as the two of them loitered in the combined command center. Raster responded with a subtle nod. Through the glass wall of the adjoining communications room, both could see Colonel Sinclair on the phone. Technically, the colonel should have simply obeyed a command from her most superior officer—though Blaine was hardly in a position to object. In fact, he admired her thoroughness, and had little doubt that— had he and Raster not walked into her life on this particular day— she'd have made general. *Pity,* he thought.

Raster had put his time on the plane from D.C. to good use. Combining his own technical skills and black assets with Blaine's knowledge of Cheyenne's communications hardware, software, and procedures, he had set into motion a series of events which—providing they had been completed in time—would allow them to assume command of Cheyenne. He'd pulled in a lot of favors on this one, and made a few threats as well—but then, with Raster, favors left ungranted could be threats in disguise. The people he dealt with knew this and acted accordingly.

Colonel Sinclair did her best to confirm Blaine's presidential authority—but Raster had done better, using hacked authorization codes to hijack the outgoing call, which was routed to Janz. Using an electronic voice modifier, Janz had then impersonated a convincing succession of White House personnel, the last and highest-ranking of which informed her that the president was unavailable. She had then been transferred to the apparent secretary of defense—who, after providing the proper authenticated response code, tersely confirmed Blaine's assertions.

It was all quite convincing, and would have been impossible had Raster not already had most of the pieces in place for other reasons. Foremost among those reasons was the fact that, from the very beginning, Raster had intended to seize control of the first nanoweapons developed by his team at Groom Lake—using the unassailable power this would give him to remold the government, perhaps even the world, as he saw fit. Appropriately falsified orders sent down through the chain of command, he'd reasoned, would buy him the time he needed at the crucial moment. The authentication codes had been the most difficult part, because they changed on a daily basis; that was where the favors—and the threats—had come in. Like Hoover before him, albeit on a larger scale, Raster had something on everybody—and he wasn't afraid to use it.

Colonel Sinclair was ordered to provide Blaine with all necessary support, including emergency command authority over strategic assets deployed within the United States—a nice limiting touch which added the ring of authenticity. Her attempts to contact Generals Hobbs and Hargrave were met with constant busy signals.

When Sinclair returned, she saluted. "What are your orders, sir?"

Raster found it hard to keep from smiling.

"The things you're talking about," said Jen, "are . . ." Her voice trailed off as words failed her.

"Godlike?" suggested John.

Jen nodded in silence.

"That's what Mitchell thought. And he was all for it. The Bible says Adam was created from the dust of the earth. From the *elements in* the earth. That may be true."

"It's staggering. The *possibilities . . ."*

"Endless. Einstein thought God was a mathematician. Mitchell said He was a nanite programmer. He was convinced that evolution is guided by slow-motion nanites programmed by a high-tech Creator—'God,' if you will—and sent out to colonize the universe.

"Adapting to local conditions to maximize the spread of life— so that the life-forms generated by nanites on earth would be far different from, say, those generated by nanites which landed on a much colder or hotter planet, or one with more or less gravitational pull.

"Slow-motion to give the organisms time to adapt to their own development and—presumably—avoid self-destruction or hyper-evolution into short-term or anomalous environmental niches that won't last.

"Program for maximum diversity to cover your bets, and create an ecosystem where natural selection does the rest even if the nanites themselves stop functioning at some point.

"Delivery vehicles intentionally instructed to avoid dual colonization of single or even proximate solar systems to reduce the probability of contact and conflict before the organims are well developed—giving each race a chance to grow and survive to maturity."

"Is all that . . . *possible?*"

John regarded her solemnly. "Oh yeah." He nodded. "And if your aim is to achieve maximum colonization at minimum cost, that's the way to go."

"God as budget-conscious hypergeek . . ."

"It's not so much a matter of budget as raw materials. To reduce the drain on homeworld resources, for example, each ship could be programmed to drop nanite payloads on multiple asteroids while in transit. Each of those then uses the resources of the asteroid to build and launch additional ships with the same instructions—"

"—so the process never ends," Jen finished.

"Until saturation is achieved. There has to be some kind of eventual limit built in. The only problem I can see with the whole thing is that the target system or galaxy destinations would have to have been worked out in advance of the initial launch to avoid dual colonizations because—so far as *we* know—communication among the different ships would be impossible in any meaningful time frame. And to do that, presumes a knowledge of the extent of the universe.

"But, hey," he concluded, leaning back in the couch, "—I'm just a Mostly Harmless human confined to an utterly insignificant little blue-green planet in the uncharted backwaters at the unfashionable end of the galaxy. What do I know?"

"Too much," said Jen, voice half-grave, half-joking.

"Tell me about it," John replied dryly. "I suppose you could get around that by hitting multiple proximate worlds, setting up local communications—light-based, maybe—and self-destructing all but the most promising nanocolony."

"That works," Jen agreed.

"An alternative plan would be to build our own worlds—huge, rotating cylinders in space, filled with air, soil, water—looking just like earth on the inside. Spinning to simulate gravity; lined with earth to absorb radiation. Gerard O'Neill proposed that decades ago, with no knowledge of nano.

"Or we could build something more along the lines of Larry Niven's Ringworld—a ninety-foot-thick, million-mile-wide band of solid matter encircling the sun at a distance, with thousand-mile-high walls to trap an atmosphere—the whole thing spinning just fast enough to simulate earth gravity. It can be done with the mass of three hundred fifty earths, yet gives you three million times the surface area of a single earth."

"How would you set it spinning, keep it from coming apart, hold it in place . . . ?"

"I said it was a possibility. I don't know the answers; no one does at this point—but if it can be done, nanotech will allow us to do it. And nanocomputers will tell us *how* to do it.

"Another possibility is a Dyson Sphere. If continuous—a huge hollow sphere *enclosing* the sun at a distance of one earth orbit—that would give you six hundred *million* times earth's surface area."

"Where would we get the resources—the raw materials to *build* something like that?"

"There's enough mass orbiting the sun in asteroids to get a good start; if we opt for O'Neill's structures, you're talking homes for so many people we'll have to build the *people* with nanites just to keep up.

"Ringworld's a bit more ambitious; Jupiter is over three hundred times the size of the earth, though the solid core is only maybe ten to fifteen earth-masses, and it's not the best material."

"You're *not* thinking of taking apart a *planet* . . . ?"

"No. That would be, shall we say, ill-advised; it could destablilize the orbits of the other planets—we don't know. But it's not necessary. Who says we can't shop elsewhere and ship the materials back here at near light-speed? Or *build* the thing elsewhere, so we don't *have* to ship materials . . . ?

"Nanotech eliminates constraints. Cost is no longer an object. The only barriers are the laws of physics; if it's possible, we can do it—we just need to figure out how. It requires a whole new way of thinking."

They sat in silence for a time, Jen turning everything over in her mind, John seemingly lost in his own musings.

"There's evidence, you know," said John, ending the silence. His voice was low, almost reverent.

Jen looked up.

"That we were created—that the earth was colonized—by nanites."

Jen regarded him cautiously.

"I'm completely serious. Ever heard of nanobes?"

"Nano*bacteria?*"

John nodded. "Some people call them that, mainly I think because they don't know what else to call them. But they're smaller than viruses, and certainly aren't any kind of bacteria we know of."

"I've seen a few articles. They're still on my to-read pile."

"Short version:" said John, "Guy named Bob Folk—University of Texas, Austin—found a number of them inside calcite and aragonite near hot springs in 1990, and inside a number of silicates since. It took a scanning electron microscope to see them. They're fossilized, older than any other known fossils, and as far as we know, *too small to contain DNA or RNA.* We're talking down to twenty, twenty-five nanometers here—twenty-five *millionths* of a meter. He didn't know what to make of them. No one really does."

"And . . . you think they're nanites? How do you know they have anything to do with . . . life?"

"I'm getting there. Superficially they resemble eubacteria—cocci, bacilli, streptococci, staphylococci—so they wound up being called nanobacteria, a term coined by Richard Morita in eighty-eight.

"But too small to really *be* bacteria."

"Oh yeah; smaller even than marine ultramicrobacteria. Recent tests have them reacting to DAPI stains, but still—no one's actually seen the DNA. And here's where it gets *really* interesting. Once we were aware of them, and knew what to look for? They turned up *everywhere*. Not only in the earth and under the oceans—but *inside living human bodies* . . . And animal bodies. And *meteorites*. Including one from Mars, by the way—ALH84001. Once you know they're there, you can't get away from the damned things. They *litter* the planet, and have for billions of years. Fossil evidence is *everywhere*."

"But no one knows what they are . . ."

"No one has a *clue*. Institutional biology's so rabid about proving they're not *alive* it doesn't consider other options. Philippa Uwins—University of Queensland—dredges up a bucketful of the things from a couple of miles beneath the seabed, clinging to sandstone from exploration drills. Yeah, big deal—more fossilized nanobes, right?" John shook his head. "Uh-uh. The things—too small we think to have complete DNA or RNA, remember—*start colonizing her lab*."

Jen stared at him. *"What?"*

John nodded. *"Reproducing* and *spreading. Unbelievable.* To established science that is—which until very recently thought nanotech was unfeasible. First stage: denial. They say she must have contaminated her samples, blahblah. Anything but face the reality.

"Well, I obtained some of her samples. And they *do* reproduce. And I *do* think they're nanites. Not *my* nanites, and not anything remotely similar—nothing, in fact, that humans would even think of creating—but I think that's what they are. And they weren't built by humans. Hell, we couldn't even *see* them until the eighties."

"Are they . . . a threat . . . ?" Jen asked nervously.

"Who knows? They don't seem to be. They've been here longer than we have. Minding their own business, apparently. I'm not *close* to completing my analysis—even *I* don't understand yet how they work—but I think they may have created us. And maybe everything else. I think the Martian nanobe fossils are remnants of a failed nano-colony, or one that self-destructed when a sister colony found a better home on earth. Or, maybe life in this solar system began first on Mars, failed or wiped itself out—and a backup colony kicked in here."

"Jeezus," whispered Jen, and neither she nor John spoke for a time.

In order to further cement Colonel Sinclair's support, Blaine gave her a quick briefing on the nature and unprecedented severity of the nanothreat which, he explained, now faced the United States. "Anyone in full control of this technology," he told her, "has the ability to *detonate* our nuclear weapons where they stand, or to render them useless. To *destroy,* every gun, tank, ship, aircraft, and soldier in our arsenal with abso*lute* impunity. To *disassemble, any* substance known to Man—selectively, or *en masse.* If the individual we're looking for has time to set up a new lab, to begin large-scale deployment—" Here Blaine stepped forward, features growing dark. "—the United States will cease to be the world's dominant power."

Colonel Sinclair stared at Blaine in stunned silence before finding her voice. When she did, it was barely more than a whisper. "My God," she breathed. "How is all of that *possible . . . ?*"

"I'm afraid that's classified," Blaine replied. "For obvious reasons. I can tell you that we're dealing with an enemy which has developed a working nanotechnology." From the sudden widening of the colonel's eyes, Blaine could see she knew enough to be confident that what he was telling her was indeed possible.

"What do we do?" she asked.

Blaine turned to Raster, who responded. "We have our own nanoresearch program under way, and we're close to a breakthrough," he explained—which came as news to Blaine; when he'd broached the subject with Raster six months before, he'd been told a breakthrough was ten years out—or more.

"Right now," Raster continued, "this man, this enemy, is on the run. If we can keep him off-balance long enough to catch up and deploy . . . we win."

"To do that," Blaine picked up, "we'll need to tap into all major U.S. supercomputers and task them to a single purpose: break the nanobarrier. Meanwhile, all available intelligence assests must be directed at locating—and neutralizing—the threat."

Colonel Sinclair nodded. "With your authorization, sir, I'll commandeer the assets immediately."

"You know," John broke the thoughtful silence, voice softer than before, "I haven't had a lot of time away from the work, for several years, but—the religious aspects of this *fascinate* me. I mean—not only what I've just said, but, well . . ."

He paused for a moment. "I've always viewed the major religious texts of the world as being either allegorical, or literal," he said at length.

"Most people do."

John nodded. "But now I think they're both."

"How so?"

"I think that much of what's survived *intact*—as opposed to what's been screwed around with by the people who controlled the texts to suit their own ends—is literal truth rendered allegorically in order to make it understandable by the people of the time."

"People with no technology," Jen said.

"Right—or people whose idea of high tech was an ox yoke. Some of it was literal. For example, I calculated how long it would take to transform a dead world the size of the earth into an earthlike planet, using nanotechnology. Just for the hell of it."

"*No . . .*" said Jen, knowing instinctively what he would say.

John nodded. "Six days. Most of it wasn't that literal. These people weren't going to understand nanotechnology, genetic engineering, computers, lasers . . . space travel . . . But if you tell them that Adam was created from the dust of the earth, that Eve was created from Adam's rib, that someone ate from the Tree of Knowledge, a burning bush carved words into stone with beams of light, that a fiery wheel *ascended* into Heaven with passengers on board—*that* they could understand, or if not understand at least accept."

Jen pondered this, and had to admit it was intriguing.

"Mitchell was convinced the Egyptians once dealt with someone having nanotech or at least genetic engineering capabilities," John continued.

"Why?" said Jen.

"Mummification," replied John. "The Egyptians were very big on the afterlife—"

"A lot of cultures speak of an afterlife."

"Yeah," said John, raising a finger aloft, "—but these guys were *serious.* Look at the effort they put into their preparations—the sealed chambers, the ritual evisceration and mummification. Putting . . . all of the Pharaoh's favorite stuff in there with him."

"*And* his favorite people," Jen added sourly.

"Don't forget pets." John scratched Schrödinger's chin.

"Don't remind me."

"But you can't use a wooden boat in an immaterial afterlife. They knew that as well as we do. These guys weren't talking about some airy-fairy, immaterial kind of afterlife in some other realm like a heaven or a Valhalla. They expected to be walking around—*here.*" He jabbed a finger toward the floor. "They expected to have a *use* for that boat, that chair, that grain that was put in there with them. And yet they had their guts ripped out and stuffed in canopic jars. It's always been written off as some kind of religious fanaticism, because it doesn't make any sense. But I think Mitchell was right; it wasn't fanaticism. And it does make sense."

John leaned forward, his own eyes gleaming with what might be a shade of fanaticism. "They *knew* they could be brought back," he insisted. "They didn't know how. They couldn't have *understood* how—but they knew it just the same. Someone told them. The story of Osiris being torn to pieces by Set and re*assembled* by Isis . . ."

Jen's lips parted at his use of the word. It did make sense.

"That's why the evisceration, the mummification—*to preserve their DNA for reconstruction,* through genetic engineering or nanotechnology. To *rebuild* their bodies from the preserved remains."

Jen stared at him, eyes wide with the inescapable logic of it.

"And with this tech, we no longer need gods. *We can bring them back ourselves.* We have the DNA.

"The resurrection of the biblical Rapture; another variant on the same theme—the dead made living. It was *right* there in front of us, for four thousand years. We've known about cloning and nanotech for decades, and *still* no one saw it."

"It all . . . makes sense," Jen whispered.

"Damned right it does." John leaned back.

Jen suddenly made the connection in her mind between the stone pyramids of old—and Mitchell's recently completed "Black Pyramid." He and John must have considered the building's construction a huge inside joke.

"How did you meet Mitchell Swain?" she asked.

John smiled sadly. "I used to work with the Foresight Institute," he began, "which studies nanotech theory and implications. That's where I met Drexler—one of the pioneers. A lot of good, smart people there—but none of them were really ready to take it to the next step. To make it a reality. Not that anyone could afford it.

"I was, and Mitchell could . . . In fact, he solved a dilemma that really had me on the ropes. I'd been approached earlier—a year and a half before I met Mitchell."

"Approached for what?"

"To lead a nanodevelopment team for the government. Crash program—like the Manhattan Project, only bigger, more expensive. I turned it down."

"Why?"

John's eyes flicked instinctively to the photo on the shelf, then away. Jen's gaze followed his. She recognized the picture, of course; she'd seen copies of the same photograph even before the one in the now-disassembled warehouse—but she could not guess its significance to John. Nor did she realize that she was looking at the original.

"Several reasons," John replied. "Distrust, fear. Other things . . . Let's say I wouldn't want the man I met in control of a nanotechnology I had any part in creating. Still, I knew the project would go on without me, with reckless speed if the past was any indication. And there wasn't a shred of doubt in my mind that weapons were the primary goal of that project . . .

"All of which left me sitting on the sidelines while a government I *knew damned well* couldn't be trusted was pursuing the most dangerous technology ever conceived. I wanted to get there ahead of them, *in the worst way*—but I just didn't have the money. And I didn't know anyone who did. Didn't *trust* anyone who did. I can't tell you what that was like, living every day with the certain knowledge the world was doomed, as it would be if a government— any government—were to develop or control this technology. For a year and a half I racked my brain for ways to fund another project to beat the government's, at the same time wondering what would happen if I succeeded. Would I be prosecuted, threatened, *killed?* There was no way to know. I was sure Raster was keeping tabs on me for at least a year after I turned him down. And then Mitchell showed up."

Leaning back farther into the couch, he related the story as he lived it again in his mind. "I was at one of the annual Foresight Conferences, minding my own business—when Mitchell Swain walks in unannounced. Full brigade of bodyguards in tow, of course. He'd read a bit in the field, including some of my early theoretical papers, before I decided most people really shouldn't know about this stuff and stopped publishing. And while everyone else was still in shock at his appearance, I walked up and introduced myself. He knew who I was, so it wasn't too hard to corner him for a few minutes . . ."

The loud din of conversation in the hotel ballroom silenced in a wave spreading outward from the south door, where Mitchell Swain appeared behind a phalanx of impeccably attired and predatory-looking bodyguards. Swain himself wore his trademark loose turtleneck with Microtron pyramid logo stitched into the neckband.

The ballroom was the prime gathering place for attendees of the annual nanotechnology conference, with food, wine, and tables aplenty. As everyone in the room froze in sudden awe at the appearance of the wealthiest man in history, John overcame his own, brief paralysis, excused himself from a conversation with a particularly stunning-looking nano researcher—and headed south.

As conversation resumed at a more subdued volume inside the ballroom, John was stopped by one of Mitchell's ubiquitous bodyguards. As two others kept their eyes on John and a third quickly and discreetly scanned him from a distance with a millimeter-wave detector, the first man turned to Mitchell, who nodded slightly. John was permitted to pass into the space now defined and guarded as Mitchell Swain's.

Approaching the man, John offered a hand. "Mr. Swain. My name is—"

"John Marrek," finished Swain, taking the proffered hand. "Call me Mitchell."

John looked at him, thrown off track by his recognition. Mitchell smiled. "I've read your work." He indicated the researchers in the room before them. "And much of theirs. As you might suspect, I like to keep up on emerging technologies with information management implications. Optical computing, fractal storage, quantum computing. Nanocomputing."

John nodded.

"The potential is there, of course," Mitchell said, "—but I'm not sure this community is ready for prime time."

Sensing his opportunity, John jumped at it. "They're not," he agreed, and looked the richest man on earth in the eye. *"But I am . . ."*

Mitchell looked at him—and smiled. "If you can convince me of that in the next five minutes," he said, "we'll talk further."

John indicated the near corner of the room, and an empty table with two chairs, then tilted his head toward the bodyguards. "Not in front of the wildlife," he said. The two of them retired to the corner, with the security men standing guard just out of earshot.

"Are you aware of the wider implications of this technology?" John inquired.

"Only peripherally," Mitchell admitted. "My focus is on information management and supportive technologies."

"Let me put it to you this way: If you were to die tomorrow, your legacy would be Computer Nerd Who Became the Richest Guy on Earth."

Swain nodded—a bit uncomfortably, John thought, which was exactly what he'd hoped for. "Eventually," he continued, "someone else is going to hold that title—and then someone else, and then someone else after that. In time, you'll become a footnote in history. A paragraph in a textbook on the development of hardware and operating systems."

Mitchell's gaze dropped to the table. It was inevitable.

"And the way we're going, of course," John added, "we're going to damage the environment to the point where we exterminate ourselves altogether, and there'll be no one left to read the footnotes."

Again, Swain nodded. He'd reached the same conclusion himself, and had even considered the idea of funding—alone—a space program aimed at colonizing Mars in order to get all of humanity's eggs out of one basket. He was still considering it, and had spoken about the topic once or twice at space-exploration and futurist conferences. He'd also discussed it unofficially with NASA.

The problem—other than the obvious, of course—was that the projected costs of such an undertaking, even for him, would be ruinous at best. Given a few major disasters, the whole thing would come apart, and neither he nor any government on earth—not even *all* governments on earth—could afford to fix it.

"What if I were to tell you," said John, checking over his shoulder for eavesdroppers before continuing, "that by funding the development of nanotechnology, not *only* will you gain permanent and overwhelming dominance in *all* hardware and software applications—but that your legacy *could* be, instead, Savior of the Human Race . . . ?"

Mitchell's eyes snapped up from the table between them—and John knew he had him.

"And," inquired Mitchell, features unreadable, "—just what does a title like that go for these days?"

"Wholesale or retail?"

"Cost," said Mitchell firmly.

"A pittance." John waved a hand as though in derision of the negligible sums involved. "Five to ten years; ten, twenty billion tops."

Swain regarded him coolly, and for a moment John thought he'd lost interest. And then came the words that would alter the course of his life—and, tragically, Mitchell Swain's as well.

"Convince me of that," said the richest man on earth, "and we have a deal."

Sliding a black business card across the table, Swain rose and moved into the ballroom.

Leaning back in the chair, John fingered the card. Swain hadn't even asked what John's end would be—knowing, John supposed, that he could afford it regardless. The truth was, he'd have done it for room and board—the result of a kind of single-minded devotion to purpose with which Mitchell himself was doubtless familiar.

John turned the black card over in his hand. Above the contact information and the inevitable pyramid, the card's gold lettering read simply: MITCHELL SWAIN.

It was taken for granted that all able to read the words knew who that was.

It was a safe bet.

Reflecting on where that road had led Mitchell weighed heavily on John, and a tear coursed down his cheek as he concluded. He bowed his head, wiping it away.

"You were close to Mitchell," Jen said.

John nodded, and she rested a hand on his shoulder. "Why did you choose him? Any big corporation would have funded this. Any government. Why go to him?"

"Because I don't trust governments. And corporations get greedy. Mitchell was the one man on earth with nothing more to gain. He wouldn't get greedy. Wouldn't be a tyrant. He already had everything . . . He was the most powerful man on earth; no one could catch him. And the only way for him to become *more* power-ful, was to empower everyone. To change the world. To save the human race from itself. *That's* power. As it turned out, Mitchell was perfect. He was an idealist—a Utopian, really. You would have liked him."

For the next few moments, John sat in silence, staring into the fireplace. Jen changed the subject. "The nanobes you mentioned, the active ones—they sound as though they might be . . . alive. Technically, I mean."

"Unknown. How do you define life? Presence of DNA? That leaves out viruses. Presence of RNA? That includes viruses but probably leaves out nanobes. I haven't had enough time to study them."

"Your nanites aren't alive."

"No." John shook his head. "I thought about pursuing that route—using the techniques of genetic engineering to program cells to construct progressively smaller organisms that would, in the end, construct nanites which would be—*could* be defined as living organisms.

"Technically alive, that is. But I decided on a mechanical approach instead—which is what Feynman had originally anticipated—in part to reduce the possibility of self-direction and evolving purpose. I want them to do what I tell them to do, not spin off random mutations that decide to do something unpredictable. Life is unpredictable, and self-adapting—which is good for life. But . . . that's not a quality you want in nanites, believe me. Not until you *really* have the tech down. Maybe not even then. Certainly not now.

"My nanites are machines, not organisms. If you could *see* one, it would look like"—he paused, searching for the words—"a *submicroscopic spider* with sixteen midget-spider legs."

Jen laughed at the analogy.

"A central body, where a simple ribbon program is read—supported by sixteen short, articulated limbs."

"And the rate of reproduction?" Jen asked, remembering the instant redwood tree—and, less pleasantly, the screams of the disassembling men outside the warehouse.

"Okay." Rising, John walked around to the back of the couch. "To use Drexler's example: I can flap my arm fast enough to hit this couch once a second . . ." Demonstrating, he did just that—flapping one arm up and down like a lopsided bird. ". . . and no faster.

If I use my *finger* instead—" he continued, again demonstrating as he spoke "—I can speed that up to ten times a second."

"Because your finger is ten times shorter than your arm," Jen observed.

"Exactly," John confirmed, stabbing a finger at his listener. "And an insect," he went on, "can flap its wings a thousand times a second because they're a thousand times shorter than my arm."

"The shorter the distance, the greater the speed," said Jen, nodding. "The time required for a motion is the square root of a quantity proportional to the distance traveled divided by the acceleration."

"Right—" John affirmed, then held up one hand, thumb and forefinger held a wisp apart—"and a *nanite* arm, is *fifty, million, times,* shorter than my arm," he finished, eyebrows arching skyward.

"That's three billion times a minute," observed Jen.

"Per arm," John pointed out. "Times sixteen arms *per nanite.* And every time it moves, it's building something, or tearing something apart, or both."

Jen's features reflected a growing dread. It was bad enough to see the things in action—but to realize now that what she'd seen outside the warehouse had been a rigidly controlled, pale ghost of the microscopic menace's true potential made her almost physically ill.

John continued unabated. Withdrawing a nanobullet from one of the loops in the waistpack he still wore, he held it up between two fingers. Its tip appeared to be a fine sphere of clear glass, encased for most of its circumference by lead.

In actuality, the sphere was composed entirely of a prestressed diamond composite with a single, prefragmented weak spot at the rear. The entire thing could be compressed at twenty-five tons per square inch without failure, a design specification John had arrived at after calculating the pressure exerted by the sea at the deepest point on earth—which happened to be at the bottom of Challenger Deep in the Marianas Trench, thirty-five thousand, eight hundred thirty-eight feet below sea level and a place into which, he'd learned, Mount Everest could be dumped with a mile of water to spare—and then tripling that pressure as a safety margin. Short of dropping one of the things into an industrial hydraulic press or artillery breech, he wasn't likely to break it inadvertently.

Each nanite within the sphere carried, in addition to its preprogrammed appetites, strict instructions to avoid disassembling prestressed diamond composite—which, while not limiting their usefulness, did serve to limit their mobility.

Nestled behind the sphere—the interior of which was a vacuum—and separated from it by a cushioning layer of lead, was a titanium-beryllium spike, or anvil. This anvil would be driven through the center of the sphere's weak point only when the bullet impacted a target at a speed in excess of seven hundred forty feet per second. A lesser speed at impact—as might be produced were the nanobullet to miss its target and strike some more distant and unintended target—would not suffice to shatter the diamond sphere which caged the nanites. A fact which would, of course, be of small consolation to the person who'd just been shot. Once exposed to any gas, solid, or liquid, the nanites became active.

"The capsule inside one of these bullets," explained John, "holds two hundred quintillion disassemblers. All of them together weigh less than one twenty-eighth of an ounce. Given ideal conditions, each one copies itself a thousand times in the first second. The copies do the same, again, under ideal conditions. In less than a tenth of a second, they would consume the entire Earth, to the last atom, and weigh what the Earth weighs. In less than an hour, they would consume the known universe.

"Obviously, they only achieve maximum expansion in the first fraction of a second. And they won't disassemble each other, so their biggest problem becomes reaching the materials they need to make more copies. This cripples reproduction, but you're still dealing with an almost nuclear expansion that never stops." He paused before continuing. "Hydrogen bombs were children's toys," he said. "This, is a weapon."

"It's the same with assemblers. With the proper programs and available resources, you could build a city in a week."

"Or *destroy* one in *minutes,*" Jen breathed, horrified.

"Why bother?" said John. "With a little refinement, you can just disassemble the people."

Inside the combined command center, Raster had set up his briefcase computer at Colonel Sinclair's console. He entered an authorization code as he listened to the colonel's update. "The necessary computers have been commandeered and are now running your program," she informed Blaine. "We should have a graphic display shortly." She then turned her attention to Raster. "I'm unable to give you a completion time estimate based on the information you've provided."

Raster nodded as he answered his vibrating, secure cell phone—which operated via microwave relays situated inside the mountain and piped out to exterior communications lines.

"Have the intelligence assets been redirected at the West Coast?" queried Blaine.

Colonel Sinclair nodded. "But, sir—how can we possibly find him? "We don't even know what he *looks* like, much less his identity."

"That may not be true, Colonel," said Raster. "Send it through here," he said into the phone, "then clean it up and air it nationwide with something motivational."

Hanging up the cell phone, he turned to the briefcase computer. The monitor display read: ENCRYPTED FILE INCOMING. Raster, Blaine, and Colonel Sinclair watched as an image appeared on the monitor, resolving from the edges inward.

"There's a pizza establishment three blocks from the L.A. location," explained Raster, "serving warehouse workers. The owner confirms a well-dressed regular with a gray Excursion like the one seen fleeing the scene last night. Fortunately, the place has been robbed a few times and there's a camera on the register. An associate of mine pulled this picture from the security tapes."

He indicated the monitor screen. "This may be our man," he concluded. The image on the monitor was a fuzzy shot of a man paying for a pizza, sent by Brandt. Using a touch pad to box the face, Raster hit ENLARGE. An image of the man's face filled the screen.

John's face.

Raster felt a sudden, brief surge of terror, but concealed it quickly. He swallowed hard, clamping down on the fear and controlling his voice. "This is the man," he said. "John Marrek. I know him."

"This would topple governments like dominoes," said Jen, working the implications through in her mind.

John nodded. "A government's entire existence is based on the collection and redistribution of resources. That's the source of its power. But if everything's free, and there's more than enough for everyone—governments become useless. Power based on wealth disappears, because everyone's wealthy."

"There would be no theft," said Jen.

"Right; it's more trouble to steal something than to create it from nothing."

"Whole industries would . . . *disappear, overnight,*" Jen realized. "Transportation."

"Because everything can be manufactured locally."

"Factories."

"Unnecessary; nanites will be the new working class."

"Farming."

"Nanites can grow anything you want, anywhere, in any weather."

"What about energy? Fossil fuel and nuclear power—"

In answer, John touched two fingers to his lips and moved them away, as if blowing a kiss to the air. "Kiss both good-bye," he said, "and good riddance. The energy of the sun which strikes the earth in a single day is enough to power our present civilization for eighty-six *million* years. That's just what hits the earth. A billion times more radiates into space, every day. Converting sunlight into electricity is inefficient and expensive. Today . . .

"With nanotech, it becomes neither; the collectors build themselves—and they don't need additional space to do it. Nanite solar cells can be built into roofing materials, exterior paints and sidings, sidewalks, parking lots, road surfaces; they can be tough as nails, self-cleaning, and pollution-free. *Limitless* energy at *zero* cost. No more strip mining for coal, no more oil spills, no more nuclear power plants, hydroelectric dams, *zippo.*

"Mining, commercial fishing, construction, demolition, cattle ranching—almost any industry you can name, is *gone.*" He snapped his fingers in the air.

"Why cattle ranching . . . ?" asked Jen.

"Why pour absurd resources including land into raising cattle to be slaughtered? You want a steak, grow a steak—already cooked, just the way you like it. Same with fish. And if you want wood for construction, no need to cut trees—just grow the boards to size. Better yet—grow the whole house."

Jen looked at him. "What's *left* . . . ?" she asked.

"Science. Travel. Entertainment. Information management." He half-laughed at this last.

"What?"

"It just occurred to me; Mitchell would have been one of the few who still had a job."

"Millions of people would lose their jobs," Jen said. "*Hundreds* of millions."

"So what?" John shrugged. "Why would they want to work? Money becomes pointless. Why buy something when you can make it yourself for nothing?"

"And you'll be able to do that," Jen reasoned, "because once the assemblers have been programmed there's no point to selling them, because the people who built them can program other assemblers to make money or anything else they want. And there's no point to keeping it to themselves because . . . giving it away doesn't cost them anything."

"*Exactly,*" said John, delighted to share the dream with someone else. For so many years, there had been only Mitchell; to see the hope he held for the future come alive in another's eyes was a good feeling. Better than good. "You can spend *all* of your time doing what you want to do. And this isn't just for us—we can give this to the third world and it doesn't cost us a *dime.* It's the end of the zero-sum game. Everybody wins. That was the dream. Mitchell's dream—to make rich men obsolete."

"Why would the richest man on earth *destroy* every advantage of being rich?"

John looked away and smiled.

"What?"

He looked back. "Let me tell you something: Mitchell hated rich men."

"*What?*" Jen half-laughed at the absurdity of it.

"He grew up poor, in a family of eight. In Atlantic City, before the casinos. When the rich men set their sights on that area, property values skyrocketed. The people who lived there couldn't pay the jacked-up taxes on their own land; they had to move out. The buyers coordinated so they didn't have to bid, and paid everyone dirt. They were supposed to find the families new homes, but the guy who bought Mitchell's home screwed the family over. They didn't have much money, so they moved into a bad area and filed a lawsuit.

"Six weeks later the whole family was murdered in a home-invasion robbery. Mitchell was shot, but survived. He spent two years in physical therapy. When he came out of it he hated rich men with a vengeance. Called them 'suits.' It was a joke to him that he became one."

That's why he never wore a suit, Jen realized.

"The guy who bought his family's house, he crushed. Bought the casino that had been built over the house and leveled it to put up a playground. There it sits, between casinos. Three million a year in property taxes. He didn't even feel it. No one even *asked* about buying.

"Mitchell bought the companies the sonofabitch who bought his house had invested his fortune in, then ran them into the ground *literally* overnight for the sole purpose of leaving the guy without a dime. Perfectly legal; there are no laws against wrecking your own corporations. He bought everybody else's stock before he did it, making secrecy a condition—so this guy was the only one damaged.

And no one would help him for fear of Mitchell. He could have bought Atlantic City and turned it into a parking lot. When they saw what Mitchell would spend just to destroy this guy, he didn't have a friend in the world. He put a gun in his mouth and blew his brains out in a sleazy motel."

Jen stared at him; this was a side of Mitchell that hadn't made the papers.

"I told him once, 'Hey, it would have been a lot cheaper to just have the guy shot.' But even though he suspected the home invasion was a setup to get rid of the lawsuit, he wouldn't do that. He was not a violent man. He'd drive you to suicide, but he wouldn't lay a hand on you."

"Another reason you chose him."

John nodded, and returned to his subject. "Once this tech is rolling, the zero-sum society goes away. The entire world can live an American-level lifestyle because waste is eliminated; nanites manufacture without pollution, or convert pollution—including garbage—into component atoms, which are harmless and can be recycled into new products at one hundred percent efficiency.

"Waste becomes negligible. Cars won't pollute because they'll be stronger than steel, weigh a few hundred pounds, and move faster than they do now using solar energy for power—energy we could feed to every car from the roads it drives over.

"And get this—we can use nanites to suck up the carbon dioxide and all the other crap we've been pouring into the atmosphere and break it down into harmless elements. Carbon dioxide—one carbon and two oxygen atoms. No problem. Carbon is used in everything—from clothes and dyes to windows, conductors, computers. It can be a fabulous construction material. In five years we can suck up the three hundred billion tons of CO_2 we've pumped out over the last hundred, have enough carbon to build stronger-than-steel two-story homes for ten billion people—and still have ninety-five percent left over for other uses. Global warming stops, the ice caps rebuild, coastal encroachment ceases because the oceans stop rising.

"We can reforest disappearing rain forests clear-cut to grow cattle, stop *all* clear-cutting, everywhere, for all time—because we can grow boards to order, and steaks, too. Replace pesticides with nanites which cover only the crops and disassemble only the insects or fungi we tell them to. Reclaim *millions* of acres used to graze cattle, because we can grow meat and milk without the cattle; millions more used for farming, because we'll be able to grow everything in nanite-built greenhouses year-round, cutting the space needed by ninety percent or more. Nanite *cleansers* can be put into the ground, breaking down pollutants in soil and water. We can literally *heal* the earth. Reverse the damage we've already done. Even bring back extinct species whose DNA survives."

"This would change the world," said Jen, voice low with wonder. *"Forever . . ."*

"That was the dream." John's mood turned suddenly solemn. "To heal the world, save Mankind, and make rich men obsolete. Mitchell had courage, he feared nothing, and he dreamed big." John paused, and when he spoke again it was, it seemed, to himself.

"As long as it was a dream," he said softly, "they let him live."

The president waved Homeland Security Secretary Rydell into the office as soon as he appeared in the doorway. He gestured toward a seat. "What news?" he asked.

"Well," Rydell replied, sitting—a privilege few were offered—

"the signature of the uranium in the bullet has been matched with a decommissioned military reactor."

The president stared at him. "Not one of ours . . ." he said.

"I'm afraid so," Rydell informed him.

The president leaned back in his chair.

"It's too soon to draw any real conclusions from that," added the director. "It makes no sense anyway, when you think about it. We're double-checking the signature and running down the disposition of the spent fuel pellets from that reactor now. It wouldn't be uncommon for some of those to be unaccounted for."

"Oh it wouldn't?"

"Unfortunately, no. It's not weapons-grade, so the security isn't what it could be."

"What else?"

"We're trying to account for the whereabouts of known top-level assassins at the time of Mitchell Swain's assassination."

"Do I want to know why we know who these people are?"

"They are at times considered assets."

"I see. And . . . ?"

"There are eleven known; of those, three have never been seen. We've accounted for the whereabouts of five. But of course, the assassin was not on-site at the time—and four of the five had access to phone lines in the time frame of interest. None of the eleven have been known to operate in this remote-control fashion."

"In other words, we have nothing."

"Very close to that, sir, yes."

"This is not what I want to hear, Nathan."

There were other issues John left unspoken—issues which concerned him gravely. The first was that governments and rich and powerful men were unlikely to willingly abandon the privileges of power and coercion they had worked so hard to attain. A man who'd spent forty years of his life building a fortune which set him apart from his fellow men as an individual of power and influence who enjoyed expensive luxuries unattainable by the common man, was not apt to welcome the instant nullification of those advantages.

Likewise, governments would fight such a nanotopia tooth and nail, using every means at their disposal to prevent or slow its realization. With nanotech freely available, tyrannical governments would lose all semblance of control over their peoples. Even relatively benign governments had much to lose.

And of course the two groups—the wealthy and the controllers of governments—had much in common, and were inextricably interwoven. Both would have to be forced to cede power to the people who—at present—supported them.

More worrisome still, to John's mind, was what the newly empowered peoples of the world would do with themselves once freed from the bonds of daily drudgery. Many, he knew—perhaps even most—wouldn't know what to make of their newfound freedom. This was true not only of the undereducated, who formed the vast majority of the world's peoples—but also of many residents of first world nations. The newspapers were already replete with tales of instant lottery millionaires who, not knowing what else to do with themselves, continued to show up for work at menial jobs. It reminded him of the story of the captive goldfish released into a lake—which continued to swim in fishbowl-sized circles because that was the only world it had ever known, and it was unable to grasp the magnitude or even the existence of its new opportunities in a larger world.

John feared that the masses, unsuited to intellectual or philosophical pursuits—would turn in their abundant spare time, as the Romans had, to increasingly savage diversions of blood and cruelty.

"You said this could end death," said Jen, interrupting his thoughts.

"Did I?"

"In the truck, outside the warehouse."

"Oh. Then it must be true." He smiled. "Immortality is achievable. Think about it: If you can control atoms you can control cells, which are made of atoms. Instead of letting them run down, you repair them."

"So they never grow old."

"Right."

"What if you're already old?"

"It's not a problem; old cells can be renewed. Made young."

"What about the brain? If it's already damaged—"

John nodded. "That's a problem. Technically, the cells can be repaired—but without a map of what the brain looked like before the damage was done—stroke, Alzheimer's, BSE, whatever—the repaired brain won't be the same as the original was before the damage occurred. Memory and skills are dependent upon neural patterns—so what's gone is probably gone for good as far as memories are concerned. The skills can be relearned. Stroke-induced paralysis would be reversed, for example, because the damaged portions of the brain would be rebuilt, and the relearned abilities can be written on the new tissue. But something like Alzheimer's or Mad Cow, where the memory itself is gone—it's gone."

"Assuming the actual memory storage area is damaged."

"Or missing, right. If it's an access problem—the memories are still there but the rest of the brain can't find them—that's fixable; you simply reroute. And a map makes anything fixable."

"Anything?"

"Time-dependent." John leaned forward, gesturing as he spoke. "It's possible to send nanites into the brain, to map the details atom by atom, then store that information outside the body. Let's say Grandpa has a stroke tomorrow, can't remember his own name. We bring him into the shop, take out that map and run a restoration program. *Voilà.* Grandpa's reset to yesterday, or last week, or last year."

"Whenever the brainmap was made."

"Right." John winked. "Call it a backup file."

"You're sure of this."

"Technically."

"Meaning . . . ?"

"I haven't done it. It *should* work; I don't see any reason why it *wouldn't* work." He shrugged and shook his head. "Doesn't mean it will. Look at bumblebees."

Jen grinned; if the laws of aerodynamics were to be believed, bumblebees couldn't fly; it was impossible. Reality had a funny habit of diverging from "established" fact, on occasion. "Okay, let's say you make everyone immortal," she began.

"*Should* everyone be immortal?"

"What do you mean? The only fair thing is to give it to everyone."

"Drug addicts, murderers, psychopaths? If no one dies, we're going to run out of room. Do you want those people taking up space? Do you want them here at all?"

Jen bit her lip.

"So who decides who lives forever?" asked John, speaking Jen's thought aloud. "There's your problem. You certainly can't leave it to the government. Yet some kind of decision has to be made. Fifteen to twenty percent of the world's population is illiterate. The rate was going down for half a century; now it's going up. That's over a billion people. What are they going to contribute? Should they even *have* to contribute? If we make them immortal, we'll never know what we're losing by keeping them around—how many Einsteins will never be born because there's no room for them."

"But the technology will change that, make everyone literate."

"Probably," John conceded. "But it won't be easy. Some countries have seventy percent illiteracy. There are religious governments which *enforce* illiteracy among women and girls. What do you do—enforce literacy? Start a *war* because Janie can't read . . . ?"

"But—let's say we give it to everyone. Outside of accidents, criminal acts, and suicides—no one dies. People keep having children. That has to stop, before it's standing-room-only."

"Zero population growth."

"That's not going to happen. What are you going to do, *sterilize* humanity? Technically feasible—but is that what you want? Religious considerations aside, ZPG will never be achieved in the absence of mortality."

"People will have to *agree*, not to have children."

"So now you're placing conditions on immortality."

Jen hit a troubled frown.

"Would *you* agree to that bargain?" John asked. Jen started to answer—but John continued before she could. "And if you did agree, would you resent it—maybe try to cheat . . . ?"

"*I*—" Jen gestured in frustration. *Damned right I would,* she thought.

John nodded. "So would everyone else. It's an evolutionary imperative; all species are hardwired to reproduce in large numbers to ensure survival. Even if it's no longer necessary, the impulse remains. We'll never get rid of it. We shouldn't try to get rid of it; it's a bad idea."

"All right; you've been thinking about this forever—what have you come up with?"

"Couple of things. One solution might be to make a deal with those who receive the longevity-enhancing treatment; after *x* number of years, they and their long-lived family members must leave the earth to make room for those who follow. Nanotech gives us space travel and colonization options, so that's not a problem. In fact, it has the benefit of accelerating the colonization of other worlds.

"On the other hand, those who would live longest would have the greatest motivation for long-term planning to ensure the continued well-being of planet earth into the indefinite future; if they're the ones who have to live here, they'll want to keep the place nice. So maybe the old should remain, and the young be shipped off.

"Or maybe you have a lottery every century; losers—or winners, depends on your perspective—leave. We'll be able to make other worlds look very much like this one or adapt ourselves to unlike worlds, so maybe it won't be a problem. I don't know. There's no way *to* know."

Jen remained silent for a moment, running through the implications. John's nanotopia, it was becoming clear, had its problems—and they were completely unlike anything Man had ever faced or even thought about. As he'd said—this required a whole new way of thinking.

It occurred to her then how valuable he was to the future of the human race—not only as the provider of this technology, but as probably the only living human being to have considered the long-range implications of its implementation. He'd had years to think about them, and to work out solutions.

And here the government was trying to kill him to obtain a weapon. This brought to mind the sign Paul had hung in the SYSOP office at *TEK* on the day of his arrival: "Government is not reason. Government is not eloquence. It is force. And, like fire, it is a dangerous servant and a fearful master." The quotation was attributed to George Washington. *Two hundred years,* she thought, *and nothing has changed.*

Then: *Until now . . .*

"Tell me what other problems you see," said John. "With immortality, I mean."

Jen regarded him carefully. His tone was casual—but she felt there was something more here. As though he were . . . *testing* her, somehow. *Evaluating* her. She could read it in his eyes. She considered before answering. "Evolutionary stagnation," she said.

John smiled. "Took me a year to think of that," he announced. Of course, he'd had a lot on his mind—but this woman was very quick. Very, very quick. He liked that. "Explain," he said.

"Well, not so much of body—we haven't changed much in ten thousand years, and with this tech it seems we'll be able to engineer whatever changes we want—but of mind. Of thought. As people get older, they're less likely to change; less likely to *want* to change.

"Take scientists. The older they get, the more powerful they become. They've spent their whole lives building reputations based on their pet theories. New theories are threatening—to their reputations, to their funding. To their power. So they reject them. They fight them. Sometimes they set out to destroy the guys with the new and better theories, simply *because* they're new and better theories. Who needs the old guy around if the new guy's better?

"They don't all get like that; some of them help the new guys, adopt the new theories, even improve them. But a lot of them are just bastards, and they hold up progress for decades. Plate tectonics, for example, or magnetic resonance imaging. Some of them I don't even think are defending their turf; their brains have just become"—Jen jerked her hands upward in a gesture of extreme annoyance—*"ossified."*

John smiled. "Arthur C. Clarke said that most scientific progress happens not because the established scientists accept new theories," he said, "but because they eventually drop dead and are replaced by the new theorists they didn't accept.

"And it's not just scientists, it's everybody—political figures, religious leaders, you name it. The guys with the most power are usually the oldest, and they don't want to change. Some of them *can't* change. And as you said, they're in the best position to slow or prevent changes they don't want. But sooner or later, they always die off . . .

"But what happens if they don't drop dead anymore . . . ? I once had a nightmare. I dreamed I was a scientist in the Middle Ages. I extended the life of a church leader who then ruled well into the twenty-first century—burning Galileos, Einsteins, Hawkingses, and all written materials which conflicted with his own Dark Ages worldview. So the Dark Ages would go on forever, or as long as this man lived. When he died, his appointed successor would continue his reign of ignorance . . . I was planning to kill him."

"What happened?"

"I was burned at the stake. Or would have been; that's when I woke up." The dream was absurd, John knew, but its message was not, and he had taken it to heart: Dangers lurked everywhere, not all were obvious, and even that which seemed an indisputable good might have dire repercussions.

"Now, that might not be valid," he continued. "We don't know. It could be that an old mind in a perpetually young body would retain the . . . mental agility of the young. Stay sharp, open to change. Those who aren't just defending their turf, that is.

"But that brings up another 'stagnation' issue, as you've called it. If you tried to take someone like that and make him a first world leader today, he'd be laughed off the stage."

"People change," said Jen, meaning masses of people.

"*Mass consciousness* changes," John agreed. "Over time. And mostly for the better. Look at Greenpeace and the tactics that brought them to prominence—running rubber rafts in front of harpoons to save the whales. A hundred years ago, the whalers would have shot right through them. If not, they'd have sunk them, or hauled them out of the water and beat the hell out of them, maybe killed them. They'd have wound up in the nuthouse, or prison. People would have thought they were crazy; what are whales good for? Meat and oil. Worse, no one would have *thought to do* what Greenpeace did. Obviously, because no one did.

"Now, *nations* stop whaling because their own people won't tolerate it. People in other nations boycott their products. Someone spots a couple of whales stranded in the arctic and countries who hate each other's *guts* spend *millions of dollars* to send icebreakers to free them. The whole *world* tunes in to cheer them on. People whose grandparents would be . . . in*capable* of *comprehending* that. The human . . . racial conscience, *evolves,* and quickly. We have this constant turnover of new minds and new morals. And we become a better people because of it . . ."

He paused a moment before continuing. "We stop that turnover, we may stop that evolution. And that can't be allowed to happen."

"I cried when I saw those whales," said Jen.

"So did I."

She looked at him. "Hey, I was alone," he said. "No one saw me."

———

Raster found his mind dwelling uncharacteristically on the past. More specifically, on John Marrek. The man had been in his twenties the only time he and Raster had met, and freakishly intelligent. No surprise, that—given his lineage. The optimal-candidate psych profile had been all wrong—loner, distrustful of authority, strong sense of social responsibility—but the next-best candidate had been a distant second both intellectually and creatively. And so, once the funding was in place, Raster had approached Marrek to lead the team.

The more the two had talked, however, the more uncomfortable Raster had become with the idea of placing the project in his hands. When Marrek had turned him down, it almost came as a relief. He was too much like his grandfather. Raster considered having him killed, but decided against it because he thought he might need—and persuade—him later should his own project fail to live up to expectations. Instead he'd had him surveilled for a year and a half; seeing nothing to indicate anything other than theoretical work, he'd largely forgotten about him, reasoning that a credible nanoproject would require vast capital expenditures—and Marrek had neither the resources nor the connections to undertake a competing project. And in any event, word of any significant government or corporate undertaking would surely come to Raster through other channels.

Swain had been an unexpected wild card.

"Good work," said Blaine to Colonel Sinclair. The general's voice snapped Raster back to the present. Raster peered over the colonel's shoulder as she checked the readouts on the command console: The progress of the commandeered supercomputers was impressive; with the project already so close to breakthrough, they just might make the difference. . . .

As John well knew, there were problems with nanotopia, those they'd discussed as well as others—but on one thing both he and Raster would have agreed: For good or ill, the development of nanotechnology could not be halted, and the shape of the future would be determined—as much as such a thing *could* be determined—by the character and values of the first to gain a reasonable facility with the technology.

And on those grounds, he'd stack himself up against any government on earth any day of the week. In fact, as he'd thought from time to time, he'd stack a randomly selected passerby up against the government.

"I'll tell you what scares the hell out of me . . . " he said, after a brief silence.

"Yeah; do that. Cheer me up."

John studied her for a moment before continuing. "So far as we know, the universe is twelve billion years old, the earth maybe five. . . ."

"Uh-huh . . ." said Jen, wondering where this was going.

"And once a civilization develops, and a critical mass of knowledge accumulates, technological progress accelerates at an ever-increasing rate. From the Wright brothers at Kitty Hawk to Armstrong on the moon was a single human life span. In the span of a hundred years we've gone from coal, to steam, to nukes, and now nanotech."

He paused, staring straight ahead and shaking his head slowly. "We have our theories about Egyptians and Dogons and the Bible and the Rig Vedas—but in all that time," he said, "we've seen no *concrete* proof of advanced life on other worlds."

He turned to face her, eyes solemn. "There are galaxies out there *billions* years older than our own. If other forms of life developed there, and advanced, and if even *one* of those forms pushed science to the limit, as we have—it would eventually discover nanotech and spread outward at near light-speed through nanocolonization.

"And wherever it began, it would have colonized the universe by now. If developed by several races, they'd have spread out and met each other by now. Divvied up the universe. Sent someone down here to say 'Hi' or, 'See that universe out there? That's *our* turf; keep out . . . ' "

Jen almost laughed at this last. John remained solemn. "And they're not here. . . ."

"I'm . . . not following," said Jen after a moment.

"That means one of three things," John continued. "Either they *are* here—and we are they, as Mitchell thought. Or we're so utterly backward and insignificant they haven't bothered to make contact. *Or . . ."* Eyebrows arching skyward, John inclined his head to one side.

Jen's features turned grave as she realized what the third, and last, possibility must be. "Nooo . . ." she breathed.

John nodded. "Or nanotech is a *lethal* development which *no* civilization survives. All who develop it, *exterminate themselves.* That's why they're not here; they're gone."

After a long and gloomy silence, Jen said, *"Well,* thanks for brightening my day."

"Anytime," replied John, recovering from his gloom.

"So what are these 'issues' of yours?" asked Jen, changing the subject. She referred to their conversation in the truck, on the way up from Los Angeles.

John looked at her, eyes suddenly haunted. "I fear Sin," he replied, voice tense with emotion.

"You're joking."

John did not answer. He seemed uncomfortable with the subject.

"I'm a journalist. Sooner or later you're going to tell me. Trust me on this." When no response seemed forthcoming, Jen pressed on. "Remember when you told me I wasn't going to find out what you were working on? How long did that take?"

After a moment, John stood and replied. "My grandfather worked on the Manhattan Project, because of the intellectual challenge of it. He was brilliant. When he realized what he'd done, he tried to talk the others out of building the hydrogen bomb, which was a thousand times more powerful. The government turned on him, crucified him—called him a traitor, dragged him before Congress, took away his clearance, *everything.*

"He regretted building that bomb every minute of every day of the rest of his life. He died a haunted soul. You could see it in his eyes . . . I never knew him. Didn't even know we were related until college."

"How did you find out?"

John looked at her. "A recruiter for black projects came to me at Harvard. Raster. He wanted me to work on nanotech for the government, some sort of crash program like the Manhattan Project, but harder. Longer. More expensive. When I told him I wasn't interested he asked if it was because of my grandfather. . . .

"When I started asking my father questions, he blew his brains out."

Jen winced.

"We never really got along, but I didn't know why. I never even knew he was a physicist, like his father. He was very smart—but not smart enough."

"Smart enough for what?"

"To break new ground, live up to his own expectations. His whole life, he lived in the shadow of his father's achievements, and his demonization. He set out to prove himself the man's equal, but he wasn't. No one was, and he couldn't handle that. My mother was so distraught by his death. I didn't have the heart to ask her too many questions. . . ."

John seemed to drift off for a moment. "Questions about what?" Jen prodded gently.

John nodded. "Discrepancies, here and there. Clues that something wasn't right . . . My mother died a few years after my father. After a while, I started snooping around. I found . . . film reels in the attic . . ."

John's mind traveled backward through time, until he found himself once more living the events of which he spoke. The attic of his parents' house was small, low-ceilinged, and crammed with old furniture and boxes—the debris of lives now over, fond memories of those who remembered no more. Inside one large box, he found an old film projector; inside another, reels of film. The labels had all fallen off, but several bore the words FOR JOHN, and so he viewed them all. Weddings, vacations—good times had by his parents and himself as a child, as well as films of others he did not know. And then the bombshell . . .

He'd recognized the face immediately, of course: the delicate features and large, incongruously haunted eyes. "I am your grandfather," said the man, whose gentle voice belied the raging power of his mind. "I presume by now you realize the significance of that. You are who you are because I have made you so. I have done this to prepare you for a duty I will not live to fulfill. Creating the atomic bomb was a mistake—my own. Creating the hydrogen bomb was a thousand times worse. And I can see now that the men who coveted those weapons are not now satisfied, nor will they ever be. Their hunger for power can never be sated. . . .

"I can also see that there will come a day when a new technology will arrive, one with implications incalculably more significant than those of atomic energy—and one which will make inevitable the creation of a weapon more terrifying than anything others—I should say most others—have yet imagined. If this technology should fall into the wrong hands, the world is doomed. It may be doomed if it falls into the *right* hands; the consequences are impossible to foresee in their entirety . . .

"I will not be here when that day comes, and for that small favor I am blessed. My son, James, may be here—but though quite intelligent I do not believe he will be equal to the task I have in mind, even if he were inclined to take it up, which he is not. He never was comfortable trying to live up to my reputation, or to escape my infamy. . . . What he does want is to be rid of me and all association with me, and who could blame him? Certainly not I. And so we struck a deal, your father and I. That deal was you . . .

"I provided the money for your father to change his name, change his residence, change his identity. In essence, I gave him a chance for a new life—one free of the burdens which seem to follow my name. Your mother was not a party to this, and knew nothing of our arrangement.

"In exchange for his new life, your father agreed to subtly guide your intellectual interests—to set you upon a path which I had chosen. That path, as you now know, is the development of the means to reliably arrange individual atoms in whatever physically possible manner we may choose. Richard Feynman gave an interesting talk about this—with which you will by now be familiar—and the two of us have discussed it privately as well.

"You must be the leader in developing this technology. More than that—you must control it. That was, I fear, my greatest sin—surrendering control of my mind's child. Which is why I tell you now that whatever entity is funding the project—our government I would imagine—must be betrayed at the crucial juncture. Before it betrays you. And have no doubt that it *will* betray you—just as it betrayed me. Governments cannot be trusted. By now you will know this.

"The workings of this technology, so far as I can see, are uniquely suited to the establishment of immediate and unassailable technical dominance. That is to say, the first to perfect it, or to nearly perfect it, will be the only player at the table. And perfect it must be—more perfect by far than my creation—because the slightest imperfection could literally destroy the very world on which we live.

"Why do I choose to burden your soul with this? Several reasons. You will be if anything more intelligent than I; already in the child I can see the beginnings of intellectual superiority. Your temperament should be well suited to this path. If my career and your father's are any indication, you will enjoy it, would perhaps even have chosen it of your own accord—a chance, alas, I was not prepared to take. Your mother's influence will assure a strong moral grounding for you as it did for your father, who never achieved his full potential until he encountered her. And, finally, there is my own, sad history. You will know what the government has done to me—and you will know, too, that it is not to be trusted. Ever. Certainly not with such a thing as this.

"Whatever this technology comes to be called, it holds the promise of being the ultimate good for Mankind—and also his utter annihilation. I would sooner trust a man with it, than a government.

"I would sooner, in fact, trust you. . . .

"What I have done—to the world, and to you—is unforgivable. I do not ask your forgiveness, nor that of the world. Instead I ask that you do what must be done, because no one else can.

"Hate me, if you must—but do what must be done . . ."

The haunted eyes of John's grandfather stared out at him from the old projection screen until the reel ran out. At some point the loud *flap-flap-flapping* of the film end against the projector body penetrated his stunned consciousness, and he reached out absently to kill the power.

Standing in the living room of the present house in Sausalito, John fell silent, staring at nothing. Jen felt her heart go out to him. The story he'd just told explained much about the man—his intelligence, his seeming arrogance, his seeming paranoia, and the incredible drive he must possess to have come so far, so young.

"I hated him immediately—not just for what he'd done to me, but to my father. All of my problems with my father stemmed from him; every time he looked at me, he saw his own father—and everything he could never be. Eventually I came to understand them both, but I never forgave them. Either of them . . . I've spent my whole life trying to avoid becoming my grandfather."

"You have," said Jen gently.

"No." John shook his head. "I thought I'd ducked it when I turned down the government. But that just made me realize I could never escape it. Turning them down only meant I had to do it some other way. . . . My grandfather," he concluded with a bitter half-laugh. "That sonofabitch *knew* I couldn't walk away, even after he told me what he'd done. He *knew* it. Because nano makes the Manhattan Project look like Play-Doh . . ." John gestured now as he spoke.

"I—I don't want to do the *wrong* thing. But I can't do *nothing,* because then someone *else* will do the wrong thing. Like Teller did before. It's the *fucking* Manhattan Project all over again." He ran a hand through his hair in agitation.

"There's no way out. If *I* don't do it, someone else will. And I don't trust someone else. I trust *me*. That's why I approached Mitchell and asked him to fund our own team. We tracked Raster's program as best we could, but all that mattered was who got there first. . . ." He shook his head. "I'm living my grandfather's nightmare."

Jen's lips parted in sudden shock as she realized who that grandfather must be. Her eyes tracked to the photo on the shelf, the same photo she'd seen in the warehouse.

Picking it up, John tossed it across the table. "My grandfather didn't just work the Manhattan Project," he confirmed. "He led it." As Jen righted the picture in her hands, he added sourly. "Genius runs in the family."

Jen gazed down at the photo, at eyes haunted with terrible knowledge. Below the black-and-white picture were the words: "Physicists have known Sin, and this is a knowledge they cannot lose."—Julius Robert Oppenheimer, 1948.

Jen looked up. "Jeezus."

John looked at her as she studied the photograph. She could be wired. She could be wearing a tracking unit. Government agents could be sitting outside at this moment, listening to their every word—waiting for him to take her to the jackpot before closing in. Without her knowledge.

Or with her full cooperation.

There were only two ways to be certain: Kill her, or take her with him. There was no time for the third option—lead her to a decoy site and see who, if anyone, joined the party.

"Where did you get those clothes?" he asked.

"What?" The oddness of the question took Jen by surprise.

"Your clothes. They look new. What's their recent history?"

"I . . . bought them off the rack after . . . the assassination. I was close; my clothes were . . . bloody."

"How did you choose the store?"

"First one I saw."

"Random. Have you been out of them since?"

"Why?"

"Just answer the question . . . please."

"No, I haven't."

"What about the purse?"

"New."

"Anyone have a chance to plant a bug or tracking device on you? Anyone at all even close enough to touch you in the time since you started looking for me?"

Jen hesitated, thinking back. "No. Just . . . Paul."

"Paul?"

"He's dead because he was helping me look for you."

Kill her, or take her with you, said John's mind. *Stop dawdling.* For five years he'd trusted no one but Mitchell. *Why change now?* He thought. *You of all people need no one—why risk it?*

Because of thoughts like that, replied another part of him. Already he could feel the potential of what he might become attempting to warp him into that which he dared not become—at any cost. *Better to die,* he thought, *than that . . .*

He lifted the gun from the end table beside the couch, hesitated—and checked his watch.

"Nobody followed us," he announced, placing the gun into the bag at his waist. "Let's go."

"Wait," said Jen, rising. He looked at her. "Why did you take me with you?" she asked.

John considered the question. "I've been too close to this for too long," he said simply. "The stakes are so high, . . . I need another perspective. You have no ulterior motive, and you have the intelligence to grasp what I'm dealing with and view it from a fresh perspective. Suggest things I hadn't thought of . . . You're perfect." He turned to go, then halted in the doorway and turned his head. "Then again," he said, "—maybe I just like you." He walked from the room.

Jen moved to follow. Pausing by the door, she plucked a dusty copy of *TEK* magazine from a shelf. The publication was open to a full-page photo of Jen in the red dress she'd worn to the Microtron press conference. The large caption read: *JENNIFER RAYNE wins Particle Prize.*

Sensing Jen was no longer behind him, John stopped just outside the doorway, looking back. Jen held up the magazine. "What's this?" she asked.

"Oh. Uhm . . . I liked the dress," John replied, rather unconvincingly. "We haven't got all day you know." Turning, he headed down the stairs.

Jen grinned. So he found her attractive as well. She'd thought so but, given the circumstances, it was difficult to tell. Not that there'd been much time to consider the matter. If they lived through this thing, and John turned out to be a Good Guy—which she was *almost* certain he was—she vowed to consider the matter further. In great detail.

Replacing the magazine, she followed him down the stairs. "Would you have?" she asked.

"What?"

"Chosen nanotech, if . . . things had been different."

"Probably," John said over his shoulder. "You hungry?" Jen nodded. "We'll pick up a pizza on the way," he said.

They left the room. On the floor behind them, Schröder wrestled with a hydrogen atom.

In the darkened living room of a run-down house in Bakersfield, a newscaster spoke on a television screen. "Federal authorities," said the serious-looking woman, "are asking for *your* help in locating *this* man . . ."

As she spoke, John's black-and-white pizza place photo appeared on the screen.

"Wanted for espionage, kidnapping of a minor, and child molestation, he is described as *extremely* dangerous and *well armed,* and was last seen driving a gray Ford Excursion in Los Angeles. If you have *any* information regarding this man, you are *urged* to call the number on your screen. . . ."

The old man in the easy chair across the room choked on his beer and reached for the phone.

The same old man who'd sold the pickup to John.

(9)

Inside an all-night pizza joint in Sausalito, John paid the owner and headed for the door with pizza box in hand. Jen trailed behind. Raising the box to his nose, John inhaled deeply—savoring the aroma of the double cheese and triple sauce which comprised his half of the oversized edible platter. "I *have* to program a pizza assembler," he said, turning around to push the door open with his back.

Outside, they moved to the truck—the only vehicle in the lot. Fishing in his pocket for the keys, John rounded the back of the truck—and stopped as a red dot appeared on his chest. A man clad in black tactical armor rose from beside the driver's side of the truck, aiming a suppressed MP7 at John's chest.

A second agent rose beside the first, training his weapon on Jen. Black sedans poured into the parking lot, doors opening before the wheels ceased moving. More armor-clad men stepped from the cars as still more rose into view on the roof of the pizza place.

Deep inside Cheyenne Mountain, Raster hung up his cell phone. "That was Stoner," he said to Blaine. "They've been captured."

"*Captured,*" said Colonel Sinclair. "*How?*"

"A local police officer spotted the truck in Sausalito and called it in; his department called the FBI, which called us. A tactical team took them coming out of a pizza establishment."

"I assume they'll be interrogated," said the colonel.

"Out of the question," said Raster adamantly. *"They must be eliminated."*

"But his knowledge is obviously ahead of ours," Colonel Sinclair reasoned, then added: "Meaning no disrespect, sirs." She looked quickly to Blaine.

Raster stepped forward, closer to the colonel—who felt somehow threatened simply by the man's nearness. It required an effort not to stop backward at his advance.

"He's the most dangerous force on the planet," said Raster, eyes burning, "a one-man Armageddon. He *must die. Now . . .*" He paused, regaining his composure. "I gave the order to capture if possible before I knew who he was."

Flipping open his cell phone, Raster hit CALLBACK.

Colonel Sinclair watched him.

The Parallax Corporation was a fictitious business operation whose northern California branch was housed in the southern portion of Sausalito. Three stories high, the building served as headquarters for a large team of covert operatives euphemistically referred to as "contractors" or "specialists."

Owing to the ever-present budget constraints of the federal government, and also as a method of maintaining some measure of plausible deniability—the corporation's "officers" were not employees of Raster's office of nanotechnology research or, indeed, of any other government agency. Instead, they were freelance agents who contracted their talents out to a number of government agencies which lacked either the personnel, or the authority, to engage in the distasteful activities in which the employees of the corporation "specialized"—namely kidnapping, torture, murder, and illegal surveillance.

In short, they were Raster's kind of people.

Five sleek black sedans and four black Chevy Suburbans rested on the small lot behind the building, though only five agents were presently inside. The remainder of the unit's night-shift complement of fifty-six men, many of whom had assisted in John and Jen's capture, were busy elsewhere, and would return shortly. A light shone through a third-story window.

Inside, the third-floor holding room was the size of a large living room. Among its spartan furnishings were a running desktop with two computers, and a more conventional desk in the center of the room which faced the two steel-framed, solid-steel doors which—save for a single window—provided the room's only means of entrance and egress. Several filing cabinets and a row of steel lockers covered the wall across from the long desktop, with room left over for a small refrigerator. John's money case lay open on a table beside the central desk. Next to the window, a long metal rail had been securely bolted to the floor.

John and Jen sat on the wooden floor, their hands cuffed to the rail behind their backs, which rested against the wall. The room was not soundproofed, John noted, which likely meant their captors had not decided whether or by what means to begin extracting information or—more likely—to kill them. He couldn't understand why they hadn't been shot on sight. He surmised some sort of dispute, somewhere up the chain of command: They needed permission.

This was a good sign, as it meant someone upstairs was clueless—because no one who fully comprehended the implications of this technology would hesitate to kill them both. Certainly not Raster, if his assessment of the man's character was even remotely correct.

He continued his visual inspection of the room. A fax machine sat on the desk beside the farther computer, and a phone hung on the wall across the room, beside the refrigerator.

There were five agents present. All but the one whom John took to be the leader—the oldest and the man who had captured him beside the truck—were eating John's pizza. Despite the situation, John found that this annoyed him. The leader—one of the others had called him Stoner—closed his cell phone and replaced it on his belt. Another agent worked at each of the computers. The fourth sorted through the contents of Jen's purse, beside John's open money case.

The fifth and final agent in the room—the first to point a gun at Jen outside the pizza place—sat on the near edge of the central desk. Ejecting a bullet into his hand from the chamber of John's Colt, he held it up to the light and examined it, watching the dormant nanites within as they slid around the inner face of the diamond sphere in response to his handling.

"I . . . wouldn't play with that, if I were you," John advised.

The agent looked at him, and bit into a pizza slice. As Stoner moved toward the pizza box, his cell phone rang. He stopped to answer it. "Parallax," he said into the phone. He listened for a moment, eyes flicking over to John and Jen, cold and emotionless. John could guess what he was being told.

"*WHY ARE YOU DOING THIS?*" he yelled at the man, volume so loud it hurt his throat. Jen regarded him oddly. Stoner turned away, covering the mouthpiece.

Setting down the nanobullet, the fifth agent lifted a laser-sighted MP7 from the desk and aimed it at John's face, pressing a finger to his own lips.

"*Ssshhh . . .*" he counseled.

"Absolutely," said John agreeably.

The man replaced the gun on the desk.

"*Got it,*" said Stoner into the phone, and hung up. He turned. The fifth agent looked at him. "They check out right away," said Stoner.

John could feel Jen shiver beside him.

Jen's heart raced so fast she thought it would burst.

Moving to the refrigerator, the fifth agent removed a small black case and opened it. The inside of the lid was adorned with a skull-and-crossbones with a patch over the left eye socket. Below this, recessed into slots in the case's base, were four identical hypo-dermic syringes and two empty slots.

Removing two of the needles, the fifth agent crossed the room to kneel beside Jen. The other agents continued their activities, as though this were nothing unusual.

Inside a mind which was not human and had no precedent before it, petabytes of data blurred past like a raging river. Images and sounds bombarded consciousness by the billions—pictures flashing by faster than any human mind could comprehend; the sounds of a hundred million voices speaking at once; data displays and sum-maries which would have been meaningless to any but a mind such as this.

In the forefront of this mind was one overriding priority, the activity in which it was now engaged—and which it referred to internally as SEARCH MODE.

Suddenly, a single, muffled sentence among millions gained prominence in the cacophony. This sentence was isolated and repeated as filters were applied, and other voices removed by the hundreds of thousands. The distorted words spoken by the now-prominent voice became clearer and more distinct as each succes-sive filter was applied. In an instant, all activity within the great mind ceased—save for an inhuman and total focus on the single point of its attention:

"WHY ARE YOU DOING THIS?" the sentence repeated.

A graphic representation of the voice accompanied the play-back—which was repeated and simultaneously compared with another recording of the same voice, saying the same thing. The graphic representation of the second voice played alongside that of the first. Next, the two were superimposed.

The conclusion:

VOICEPRINTS IDENTICAL

The primary mission of the being examining this data changed immediately from SEARCH MODE to ACQUISITION.

Tracing the origin of the call—the thousand-bit encryption of which it had broken in one second—the mind followed its course from satellite to uplink to microwave tower. Hacking into the computer which ran the operations of the cellular phone company which owned the tower—a mere portion of a second's work—it examined the appropriate records to learn how many and which of the company's towers had received the signal, and in what order.

Three different towers had received the signal, each at an instant a fraction of a second distant from the time at which its fellows had detected the same signal. By calculating this microwave tower signal-reception differential, the exact point of the call's origin could be determined.

A graphic representation of the three towers appeared, a single yellow line leaping forth from each tower into the space separating all. The point at which these lines intersected was the call's point of origin.

A green crosshair appeared over this point, and the microwave towers and their intersecting lines disappeared. They were replaced by a Thomas Brothers map of southern Sausalito, which was in turn replaced by a rapidly changing series of larger-scale, more specific maps.

The crosshair turned yellow, but did not move.

Latitude and longitude coordinates appeared below the crosshair as the latest map was replaced by a Defense Department aerial photograph of a block-square area. At its center was a three-story building. The yellow crosshair hovered above a point near the center of the building's southern face.

Cross-referencing latitude and longitude coordinates to city survey reports, post office addressing information, building permits, business licenses, property assessments, and other records revealed the building in question to be owned by the Parallax Corporation.

A brief search of every phone book and corporate directory in the nation revealed no listing for such a company at that location. A subsequent search of phone company records revealed thirty-three numbers assigned to that address, as well as a T3 connection.

Inside the mind which accomplished these tasks in the space of a human heartbeat, the primary mission changed from ACQUISITION to ENGAGEMENT.

The yellow crosshair turned red.

In the holding room, the fifth agent uncapped his syringes and pushed up on the plungers, venting the air from the chambers. Clear liquid spurted from the needles' tips. The action was unnecessary, as air-induced embolisms were unlikely to trouble a corpse—but he enjoyed watching people's reactions as the poison which was about to kill them appeared before their eyes and the realization sank in that, yes, the game really was over . . .

Across the room, the fax machine beeped. John's eyes darted to it. The agent by the money case started toward it. At the computers, both agents responded to audible prompts.

"Someone's dialing into the computer," said the first.

"Who?" asked Stoner, suspicious; direct contact by computer was unusual.

"Pentagon," replied the man who spoke. Stoner relaxed. A phone rang. Stoner lifted the cell phone from his waist out of habit, before realizing it was the phone on the wall which was ringing. This, too, was unusual. It also seemed to him that he could hear other phones ringing, elsewhere in the building. Replacing the cell phone, he hit a puzzled frown and moved toward the wall phone.

"This is it," said John, voice low.

"You got that right," said the agent with the needles, misunderstanding.

John looked at the man as though pitying him. *"You have no idea . . ."* he said softly. Jen watched this exchange in frightened confusion.

"Parallax," said Stoner, picking up the phone.

"Take my hand," said John.

"*Aww* now ain't that sweet," said the agent beside him, dipping the syringe toward Jen's arm. She tried to shrink away from it.

"*Parallax*," repeated Stoner into the phone. There was no response. He pulled the phone away from his head and looked at it, annoyed. His ear began to itch, and he brushed a hand over it, as if banishing a fly. He didn't know all of the details, but he'd pieced together enough from the dead L.A. team's final transmissions to realize suddenly—in a general sense—what was happening now.

"*Oh, Jesus. Oh, Jesus,*" he said, dropping the phone and clutching his head. Jen and the others turned to look at him. John alone watched with grim detachment.

From the swinging phone handset by the wall, nanites *swarmed* outward. . . .

The agents at the computers jerked their hands away as though bitten. More nanites swarmed from the keyboards. Still more from the fax machine—and from every other such device in the building. The eerie *chitter* of the things rose swiftly.

The nanites worked unceasingly, submicroscopic soldiers without mind or conscience. They followed their simple program blindly; unaware of consequences, incapable of pause, consideration, or moral dilemma. They were, indeed, the perfect soldiers.

The energy requirements of a single nanite were modest; those of a swarm, enormous. The construction program used by each nanite to create its brethren contained multiple options for fulfilling the devices' energy requirements: Among the sources of energy a nanite might make use of were heat, light, electricity, radioactive decay products, and chemical interactions.

Whatever the environment—even the black void of space, which contained hydrogen in abundance, light and heat in proximity to the earth—one or more of these energy sources was likely to be available for use. In a pinch, even magnetism or gravity could be made use of, though the processes for doing so were cumbersome and involved the construction of separate power generation and conversion devices which then fed the "working" nanites a more immediately useful form of energy.

Initially fueled by chemical energy drawn from available environmental elements located upon escape from one of John's nanospheres—or activation by other means—the first assemblers assessed their environment to determine the most efficient energy source available, and directed that ninety-nine percent of all subsequent or "daughter" nanites be constructed in such a manner as to make use of only that energy source. As missions were invariably of limited duration, this strategy maximized expansion rates and efficiency while still providing a backup in the event of a sudden shift in environmental variables. This strategy was, however, modified or discarded under conditions which called for extremely large-scale operations.

Immediately upon its creation, each daughter nanite set about an inventory of its surroundings—both seeking out the raw materials with which to assemble other nanites and identifying target materials.

A nanite did not distinguish between materials living and inert, sentient and mindless; it merely followed instructions: This copolymer surface, that oak floorboard, this coated wallpaper could be disassembled into constituent atoms and reassembled into nanite disassemblers; that carbon-based blob over there could not, whereas this carbon-based blob over here was a priority target for disassembly—not because its atoms could be employed in the construction of additional nanites, which they could and would be, but because the program said: DISASSEMBLE THIS OBJECT.

Why the program said this was irrelevant; it was enough that it did.

And so each new nanite set about the task of employing each of sixteen tiny arms to rip apart its surroundings and construct new nanites while simultaneously seeking out prespecified target materials to disassemble. Presented with a choice between targeted and nontargeted materials, the nanite would invariably choose the former over the latter, even if such a choice slowed the reproductive rate of the swarm as a whole. For the mission of the disassembler nanite was not, after all, reproduction—but annihilation of the targeted material. Once that goal had been accomplished, the mission was complete, reproduction became unnecessary, and the nanite itself was—absent some secondary or long-term mission program—without purpose or desire for continuance.

To the nanite, life and death, pain and pleasure, continuance and expiration—were meaningless. The only thing which mattered was the mission.

Which was, at the moment, the disassembly of this awkwardly moving target material over here—which happened to be named "Stoner."

The stricken team leader staggered screaming across the floor, right hand and face disappearing as nanites disassembled the outer layers of his brain and enveloped his body. The two men stricken at the computers, also, began to disassemble. Dropping the needles, the fifth agent—not knowing what else to do—stood and drew his pistol. He and the other, as yet unstricken man moved toward the room's steel doors. Before they could reach them, however, the electronic locks on the doors clacked shut, status lights changing from green to red. What was left of Stoner dropped lifeless to the floor and disappeared.

The fourth agent used his MP7 to blast away the nearest lock and kicked open the door—but was felled in the hall as nanites spreading from the dissolving bodies of his companions crossed the floor and disassembled his legs.

The last man standing, the one who'd held the needles, turned and bolted past John and Jen—diving headfirst through the glass of the third-story window. His scream faded with distance, then ended abruptly.

"TAKE MY HAND!" John yelled.

Transfixed by the events unfolding around them, nearly in

shock—Jen clasped John's hand tightly with her own, their fingers interlocking.

Nanites *swarmed* over floor, walls, and ceiling. John turned only half-away, unable to resist watching the quickening advance of the magnificent machines. Jen stared straight-on in hyperventilating, gaping terror as *chittering* nanites swept toward and enveloped them, feet first.

John took one long, deep breath and held it. Jen screamed. Nanites swarmed over their faces and down Jen's screaming throat.

The nanites covered every interior surface of the room, and scouted the entire building, filling it with their bone-chilling, otherworldly *chitter*.

And then—they began to disappear as swiftly as they had come. As they receded from her face, Jen stopped screaming, if not hyperventilating. John felt the handcuffs binding his wrists disassemble. In a moment, almost as swiftly as they had come—the nanites were gone.

Jen's eyes tracked wildly about the room.

"Well that was exhilarating," John said shakily.

"*Exhilarating!*" Jen almost yelled, incredulous.

"Yeah," said John, standing. "Exhilarating." Rubbing his wrists, he looked around.

"What—How—" Trying to stand, Jen found herself still cuffed to the rail. "*Uncuff me!*" she demanded.

"Working on it," replied John, reclaiming and donning his waistpack as he gazed about the room. Then, frowning: "Who had the key . . . ?" Even had he known to begin with, there wasn't much to go on now; the men had been similarly dressed—and their clothes and armor were all that remained. "I hope it wasn't the guy who went out the window," he said.

John rooted through several piles of clothing and body armor, examining and pocketing key rings as he went, before finding the handcuff key. Jen used the time to slow her breathing in an attempt to calm herself. It didn't work.

"Ah," announced John, finding the keys. He moved to uncuff her.

"Tell me what the hell *just happened,"* said Jen.

"Ever heard of ECHELON?" asked John, working on the double-locked Peerless cuffs.

"An . . . electronic spy network that monitors ninety percent of the world's electronic communications in real time. . . ." She paused.

"State-of-the-art," confirmed John. "A global surveillance network run cooperatively by five countries but controlled by the United States. National Security Agency stuff."

Among other things, he knew, this cooperative arrangement permitted the participating nations to skirt their own laws against domestic espionage by inviting operatives from other participating nations to run the surveillance of targeted individuals and groups within the host country's borders. Thus, each nation's officials could quite truthfully state that their own governments and personnel did not engage in surveillance of their citizens. The key to the whole truth, which the media had missed entirely, by incompetence or design—lay in asking precisely the right question.

After years of unsuspecting naïveté, the people of Europe had recently awakened to ECHELON's threat, and the network had become front-page headline news. The governments of Europe were upset as well—though not of course because ECHELON was spying on citizens. They were upset because they suspected that ECHELON was spying on European corporations and passing intelligence thus gathered along to U.S. corporations, which then gained an unfair competitive advantage. An unlikely scenario—but then, the NSA specialized in unlikely scenarios.

The people of the United States, for the most part, remained blissfully unaware that every telephone call, fax, email, and radio communication they made was monitored by ECHELON. If and when specified criteria were met—particular words, locations, accounts, or voiceprint signatures, for example—the communication being monitored was recorded along with its source, destination, and routing information.

Freeing Jen, John stood, helping her to her feet. She shivered involuntarily. *"Eww.* I can still *feel* those things. . . ."

"ECHELON performs high-priority communications intercepts in real time, usually triggered by keywords," John explained.

"You hacked ECHELON . . ." concluded Jen, her voice an awed whisper. Not even Paul had managed that feat, though not for lack of effort.

"Not exactly," said John, retrieving his pistol and nanobullet. He scooped Jen's things back into her purse, including the pepper spray.

"I designed a limited nanointelligence and set it loose on the Net. It penetrated ECHELON, assigned my voice a high priority, and listened in on monitored calls. When it heard the code-phrase, it traced the number and attacked with flesh-eaters propagated through the phone lines."

Jen looked at him for a moment, and shuddered at the perfectly reasonable-sounding manner in which he'd said that. "Attacked with flesh-eaters propagated through the phone lines." As if he'd been describing a successful science experiment. She felt herself veering toward overload. "I don't understand," she said, shaking her head and trying to focus on one thing at a time, "—why didn't they kill us?"

"I programmed them to recognize my DNA; they won't harm me or anyone with skin-to-skin contact. They also free me if I'm bound."

"We're not touching now," Jen noted, gazing around apprehensively.

"Short-lived," explained John, kneeling beside another pile of armor and clothing, "self-disassembling. Programmed for a limited number of replications determined by the environment—in this case, the building. When the task is complete, they disassemble each other until there's only one left. You think needles in haystacks are tough? Try finding a nanite on a needle. Anyway—perfectly safe now."

Jen's eyes tracked about the room uncertainly. Fearfully. The place looked as though someone had filled the sprinkler system with acid and turned it on. "What was the task?" she asked.

"Disassemble all human flesh in the building," said John—again as though describing a harmless science experiment. "Except me," he added.

"What if we'd been in a . . . *hotel,* or . . . *crowded building . . . ?*"

"Tough luck," said John, winking.

Jen stared at him in disbelief. *"I—"*

"Relax," he said as she began to object. "Bad joke. Different code-phrases for different situations. Don't worry about it."

Retrieving the fifth agent's Sure-Fire laser-equipped MP7SD3, a pistol, and spare clips from the pile, he stood. *"All clear, NANI. Thank you,"* he said, facing the dangling telephone.

The remaining electronic door unlocked itself.

"Nanny?" inquired Jen.

"Networked Artificial NanoIntelligence," said John. Then, half-apologetically, "I had to call it something . . ." Turning, he gazed down at the pile of clothing at his feet. "Didn't your mother ever teach you not to play with nanites?" he asked.

Jen approached the dangling phone cautiously. Reaching out hesitantly, as though afraid of being bitten, she brought the handset slowly to her ear—then dropped it suddenly and leapt away when the loud off-the-hook tone blared in her ear.

John couldn't help but laugh.

"Jesus that's not funny," Jen scolded.

"Sorry."

"What the hell's the matter with you?"

John touched the fingers of his right hand to his chest, brows raised in inquiry.

"Yes, you. You just . . . kill *people left and right and then* make jokes!"

John looked at her. "Tell me they didn't have it coming," he said evenly.

"That's not the *point!*"

"Of course it's the point. What do I do—let them kill *us?*"

"Of *course* not."

John spread his hands in a gesture of puzzlement. "What do you want from me?"

"How about a little . . . *compassion?*"

"Plenty of it. Remember the bird . . . ?"

She did—which confused her. How could someone who'd done that be so callous about killing human beings?"

"And you're still here, aren't you?"

"*Yes. I—*" She paused, taking a moment to consciously rein herself in. When she resumed speaking her voice was lower, less strident. "I *owe you my life; I know* that. It's just . . . It's like you *kill* people—*people*—without even *thinking* about it. Like it's nothing."

John realized then where she was coming from, and tried to explain because he didn't want her to think badly of him. More, he wanted her to understand. "I have thought about it," he said. "A lot."

"*When?* There hasn't been *time.*"

"That's right, and I knew there wouldn't be. Years ago—when there *was* still time to think about it. You've been dropped into the endgame. You open a door and all of a sudden, people are trying to kill you. You've got . . . *nanites,* swarming over you. I've seen these things up close before, in a lab accident. This isn't the first time for me. The first time—for a few seconds—was paralytic."

"Have you killed people before?"

"Never. Not until the warehouse. Hey—I put *spiders* outside, okay? Fleas, ticks, and mosquitoes, no mercy; everything else—" He made a sweeping gesture with the hand holding the gun. "Life should be respected. That includes our own.

"Deciding whether to take a human life is a huge decision. You try to make that decision while someone who's already made it is pointing a gun at you—you don't start thinking about it until then?—you die. I can't afford to die. The world can't afford it.

"So I thought about what might happen, how things might go—and what kind of men I'd be facing if it all went to hell. . . ." He looked away for a moment, and swallowed hard. He'd thought about it, all right—but he'd never actually thought it would happen. It was a remote possibility to be prepared for. And he'd always assumed he'd have Mitchell; that no matter *what* happened, the two of them, together, could overcome it. But now . . .

How did they find out? he wondered again. Speculation was pointless.

"I thought about it for a long time," he continued. "And I decided, years ago, what I would do if things came to this—so that I would not hesitate if this moment came." He turned his head to face Jen.

"That's the only reason we're still alive."

Jen looked on him with new understanding. She was reacting out of emotion; he'd prevented himself from doing that by grappling with his emotions in advance, that they would not interfere with him now—would not prevent him from doing what, even she had to concede, needed to be done. She wondered if she were capable of such control—and whether any normal person could or should be. "And what did you decide?" she asked.

"That if anything got in my way—" he gestured slightly with his hands, inclining his head to one side, "—it wouldn't be there for long. One way or another."

"You're not just running blind, are you?"

"What do you mean?"

"Running scared."

"Oh I'm scared. And I'm running."

"I *mean* you're not just reacting, letting their actions determine yours. As you said, you've thought about this for years. You're running some kind of plan, aren't you?"

John cocked his head again, a gesture that could mean anything.

"Aren't you?" Jen pressed.

"I'm not running blind," he said after a moment.

"So what's the plan?"

John smiled. Not a warm smile—but a cold and frightening thing which reminded her chillingly of the expression forever frozen into the death mask of Julius Caesar. *"Staggering,"* replied John.

Jen made it clear she expected more—but details, it seemed, were not forthcoming.

"Odds are we're both dead in twenty-four hours." he said, and winked. "Try not to worry about it."

"God you're infuriating."

He smiled again—warmly this time. "Everyone tells me that," he said. Jen almost laughed. John offered her the disassembled agent's handgun. "Want a pistol?" he asked.

Jen looked at it, and then to John. "Who needs a *gun?"* she said. John grinned. Picking up the briefcase and tossing the spare pistol atop another pile, he headed out the door. Checking to be certain his back was turned, Jen picked up the pistol, checked the chamber, flicked the safety on, and slipped the gun into her purse—afterward hurrying after John. As they started down a stairway, the wail of sirens drew near.

"Oops," said John, and headed for the roof. He and Jen made their way down the fire escape on the building's side, moving swiftly down a darkened alley toward the building's rear.

A young man stepped suddenly into their path, forcing them to stop. An open knife gleamed in one hand. John stepped between Jen and the would-be miscreant.

"Now what's a nice white boy like you doin' in a badass neigh-borhood like this?" asked the man.

In answer, John brought up the MP7 and pointed it at the man's face. "Sighting in my new gun," he replied, activating the laser. The criminal's eyes rolled comically upward to the glowing red dot in the center of his forehead. The knife clattered to the street as he raised both hands slowly.

"Be cool, man. Be cool. You be cool and I be cool, and we all just stand here bein' cool . . ."

Half-circling the man, keeping his eyes on him—not catching the fact that Jen's right hand had slipped inside her purse—John guided Jen around the man and they continued their flight.

When they had gone, the man lowered his hands, heaved a sigh of relief, and shook his head. "Damn, man," he complained to no one, scooping up the knife in disgust. "Streets ain't safe nowhere no more . . ."

Rounding the back of the building, John moved to the nearest sedan and tried the car key on one of the rings taken from the room upstairs. It didn't work. Dropping it to the ground, he tried the next ring. No luck. Jen rolled her eyes and glanced around. John tried another set—third time lucky. He and Jen slid inside. Starting the car, he headed into another darkened alley.

The erstwhile robber walked down the center of an alley, muttering to himself. "Punk-ass white boy motherfucker thinks his ass is funny . . ."

Ahead of the car, a figure walked in the darkness—difficult to make out with the headlights off. "Hey move it!" John urged through the open window.

The man turned—and John saw that it was the same man they'd just left. "What is this, Candid Camera?" he said to himself.

"Hey FUCK YO—" began the man irritably. Seeing John's face in the window—submachine gun below it—he stopped in midsentence. Forcing an insincere smile, he held up both hands, each with two fingers aloft. "Peace, brother."

John drove past. " 'You can get more with a kind word and a gun than you can with a kind word alone,' " he noted when they'd passed the man.

"What?" said Jen.

"Folk wisdom from Al Capone," explained John. Hitting the headlights, he turned left onto the next street.

"All right; slow down," said Jen, returning to what John had said a few moments before. "Nano*intelligence? No one can do that yet.*"

"Isn't that what you thought about nanoweapons . . . ?"

"All right—no one *else* can do that yet."

"Right. My brains and Mitchell's money made it happen. The computer you found had two jobs; to help me design the equipment and procedures necessary to build the first nanites, and to design its own successor: a nanointelligence—a nanite-based, heuristic, hyperevolving distributed computer. Nanites created it in hours."

"Distributed over the Net because no one computer could handle that kind of processing power . . ."

"Or complexity." John nodded. "Black Mountain, the computer you found—"

"The fastest in the world," Jen interjected.

John checked the mirror. "—is synaptically challenged compared with this. A virtual drooling idiot. NANI is tapped into every wired computer on the planet."

"So you set it loose on the Net."

John nodded.

"Watch your speed," Jen cautioned, eyeing the speedometer. "We don't want to get stopped."

John eased off on the gas. "NANI has the world at its wiretips—every computer on the planet that's hooked into the Net or a phone line or even a power cord is accessible. To keep a low profile, it uses excess capacity—pretty much all of the wired computing capacity on earth, and some that isn't wired. When, say, MIT runs a heavy-duty simulation, NANI backs off to avoid a conflict, which would lead to detection. At any given time, globally, there's more capacity lying dormant than there is in use. And of course NANI can hijack active capacity if it wants to—every connected computer in the world, including those which are unwired but uplinked."

Jen's head dropped a bit as she took this in, trying—unsuccessfully—to calculate the total raw processing power which this arrangement placed at NANI's disposal.

"Once NANI existed, Black Mountain was useless," John continued.

"Wait a minute—are we talking an AI here . . . ?"

"NANI is a seed AI;" John confirmed, "designed to become self-aware."

Jen felt an inner chill for, technophilic though she was, thinking computers struck her as unwise, and always had. *"Will it?"* she asked.

"Unknown. It has the potential. I did my best. The goal was to create a true intelligence; not just a computer. Capable of recursive self-enhancement."

"It has access to its own source code . . ." breathed Jen, astonished.

"And the ability to modify it, within my parameters. Every time it rewrites its code, it gets smarter."

"So the next rewrite is better, and makes it even more intelligent."

"Right. And the process never stops; it's open-ended."

"No limits," Jen breathed.

"With thought processes one million times faster than our own." He turned from the road to face her. "Welcome to Singularity."

Jen stared at him, unsure whether to be excited or terrified by this—and being both. Technology's grandest dreams—and most horrifying nightmares—were coming true at once.

"The theoretical limit is much higher," John said, returning his attention to the road ahead, "—ten, even a hundred million times faster than us, but heat dissipation becomes a massive problem."

Indeed, as K. Eric Drexler had pointed out in *Engines of Creation,* a seminal work which John had read several times, along with Drexler's other works—an assembler-built device no larger than a cubic centimeter and constructed of closely spaced individual nanocomputers smaller than human synapses connected by wires thinner than the brain's own axons and dendrites could theoretically function in much the same manner as a human brain, and ten million times faster owing to increased conductivity and absurdly short signal paths.

Unfortunately, as Drexler had conjectured and as John's early NI experiments had proven, such a contraption, once switched on, would melt itself down to the IQ of a rotting turnip in something less than—appropriately—a nanosecond.

Given the seemingly unavoidable problem of heat dissipation, Drexler had instead proposed a more conservative device the size of a coffee mug, with thought processes perhaps a million times faster than the human brain. Even this device, as envisioned by Drexler, would require a fifteen-megawatt power supply and a three-ton-per-minute flow of cooling water. As John could attest, however, Drexler's calculations had been unduly optimistic.

To save time, John had sidestepped the whole problem by designing NANI to make use of existing computer networks and power supplies; with the computing capacity distributed across the globe, the otherwise vexing issue of heat dissipation simply never arose. Pure speed was sacrificed, but with no competition in sight at the time, that had seemed of minor importance.

One of NANI's first tasks would be to design and supervise the assembly of a superior, heat-dissipating system into which its own consciousness—if it developed one—would be transferred. Even at a mere million times the speed of human thought, John had reasoned, having NANI do this work would save him a few thousand years of design work, minimum. Even if it failed to become a true NI, it would still be the most powerful computer ever constructed—exceeding the sum of the individual capabilities of all others combined.

"So if this . . . NI, is in our corner—what's the problem?" asked Jen.

"It's still an infant; not quite ready for prime time. It's creating itself now."

Jen stared at him.

"Until it's fully developed—" he looked at her "—we're in deep trouble."

"What's it doing now?" inquired Jen, wondering what task he'd set a mind—if that was the right word—of such enormous capacity. John's reply was not what she'd expected.

"Oh, shit . . ." he said.

She followed his gaze through the windshield—to a line of black sedans just like their own, coming in the opposite direction.

(18)

Hard-faced men peered through the window as the cars passed in the night. John stomped the gas pedal, and the big car leapt ahead. Behind them, the other three sedans screeched into tire-burning turns. The pursuing cars, carrying three men each, quickly strung out into a line.

"Take the wheel," said John. Reaching over with both hands, Jen did her best to guide the speeding car in a straight line—straddling the centerline to keep from plowing into the buildings on either side of them.

Reaching into the waistpack, John drew the Colt. Ejecting the chambered round into the bag, he chambered a nanobullet taken from a loop inside the bag, and dropped the slide. Thrusting the gun out the window, muzzle down, he fired without aiming. A .45 caliber hole appeared in the asphalt as the car raced onward.

From the hole, a tiny seedling sprouted.

Inside the lead pursuit car, the driver—who often bragged that, during the course of his twenty-three years in the business, he'd seen everything there was to see—was somewhat more than moderately surprised to see a hundred-foot redwood bursting through the asphalt in front of him. So surprised was he, in fact, that a full second passed before his brain recovered sufficiently to send the impulse which caused his foot to lift from the gas pedal and depress the brake.

In that second the tree grew another ninety feet, widening to fill the two-lane street from curb to curb—and the car smashed into it doing ninety-five.

The second car rear-ended the first, exploding the gas tank on impact, then tumbled crumpling over the top of the first car to crash into the still-growing trunk twenty feet up. The fireball of the explosion rose along the great tree's bole.

Throwing both arms across his face, the driver of the third car stood on the brake pedal. The car slewed sideways and slid into the burning wreck of the first car, breaking the necks of two of the men inside on impact, and severing the spine of the third. The three were still sitting in the third car when the second landed on top of it.

At two hundred feet—having buckled the wall of the building to either side—the tree stopped growing. It would take a full week to remove.

As John took the wheel again, Jen looked out the window behind them, and back. "The tree escape," she said. "I don't think I've seen that one before."

"First time for everything," said John, then, almost calmly, "Look out."

Ahead, the buildings ended. A dozen more black sedans raced toward the next intersection from adjoining streets. "It's gonna be tight," said John, mashing the pedal into the floor. Jen gripped the dashboard tightly with both hands and closed her eyes for the impact. The lead sedan on the right ripped off their rear bumper as they flew through the intersection. The car began to spin with the impact, but John countersteered briefly and the car resumed its course; the same practical turn of mind which had led him to learn about firearms had also caused him to buy his way into several tactical-pursuit driving schools. He was thankful those skills, learned years ago, remained with him today.

Jen looked behind them. Swerving to avoid each other, the black cars overshot the intersection and slowed. Turning and accelerating, the cars fell in behind.

"Don't these guys ever *quit?*" asked John.

"Another tree?" suggested Jen.

"I'm out of trees," said John, shaking his head. Under different circumstances, he'd have considered the exchange comical.

Ahead, a series of large wooden signs stretched across all lanes:

BRIDGE CLOSED FOR REPAIRS
WILL REOPEN 12 A.M. MONDAY

Crashing the two nearest signs, John piloted the sedan onto the immense Golden Gate Bridge. The dozen cars following obliterated the remaining signs.

John checked the mirror. The second car back pulled out beside the lead car, a few car lengths behind it on the six-lane roadway. The other cars trailed farther back. Men in tactical armor appeared, hanging out the windows of the lead cars with submachine guns—and John realized that the staggered positioning of the cars was meant to allow their occupants to double their effective firepower without endangering each other. *"GET DOWN! GUNS!"* he yelled.

Jen ducked down in the seat as the MP7s opened up. Bullets ripped across the back of the car and blew out the rear window. Jen cried out as a bullet spiderwebbed the windshield above her.

"Sonofa*bitch!*" John said. More gunfire sounded from behind.

"Got anything in your black bag for this?" asked Jen.

John looked at her, seeming undecided.

Must be something massive, she thought, *if* he's *hesitating to use it.* Clearly, however, they were out of options.

"Don't think about it," she said. "Just *do* it."

"Take the wheel." When she did, John rolled into the backseat. The car slowed momentarily as Jen slid over into the driver's seat, foot reaching down for the pedal. Their pursuers gained.

Bullets hammered into the trunk—a few making it through the backseat and narrowly missing John. Reaching a hand inside the bag, he pulled a bullet from a loop marked OMNI—BIG, and placed it in the chamber. *"Okay,"* he said to himself, dropping the slide. *"You wanna play rough?"*

Running empty on their second mags, the men behind him reloaded, tossing empty twin mags back inside the cars.

First peeking, then popping up in the rear seat, John steadied his arms on the back of the seat top and fired once, through the shattered window. The bullet struck the curb by the sidewalk, midway between John's car and the lead pursuers—and dead center on the main span of the one-point-seven-mile-long bridge.

"Step on it," said John, ducking down again. Sitting so low in the seat she could barely see over the dashboard, Jen pressed the pedal against the floor as hard as she could.

Behind them, comprising a mere spot at first, nanites *swarmed* outward from the bullet's point of impact—covering the roadway, crawling over sidewalk and railing, and climbing up suspender and main cables.

The men hanging out the windows of the lead pursuit car stopped firing to regard the crawling surface ahead of them; their companions in the second car soon followed. Inside the first car, the driver leaned forward in the seat, nose against the windshield, peering outward. *"What the hell is that?"* he said. No sooner had the words left his mouth than cars and nanites raced past one another in opposite directions. The tires of the two lead cars bumped over uneven, disappearing asphalt—then began to disappear themselves.

Elsewhere, nanites began disassembling portions of the bridge—suspender cables and the orthotropic steel plate deck which lay beneath the two-inch layer of asphalt.

The men in the lead car gaped at the scene around them as the otherworldly *chitter* of the nanite swarm filled their ears—then dropped their guns and held on as the cars dropped onto their rims and began one-hundred-twenty-mile-an-hour slides. The drivers fought for control as nanites devoured first the cars—then the screaming men themselves.

John peered over the backseat. Nanites *swarmed* toward him, gaining fast.

On the far side of the swarm, the drivers of the remaining pursuit cars—already closing with the nanites—hit their brakes far too late.

The swarming mass hurtled outward from the bridge's center with incomprehensible speed. The braking pursuers drove right into it. The men in the first car, surrounded on all sides by weirdly crawling, *chittering* surfaces, gazed out in fear, hurriedly rolling up their windows. The driver, looking forward, saw what lay ahead—and what did not.

"JEEZUSCHRIIIST!" was the last word he ever spoke. His car, and the others behind it, slid into empty space and began the long fall downward, two hundred twenty feet to waters patrolled by great white sharks whose jaws would have been a welcome alternative to the all-devouring nanites.

The eight-hundred-eighty-seven-thousand-ton bridge disappeared from the centerpoint outward as the black cars plummeted toward the dark abyss of the Bay beneath a roadway and plate deck which were no longer there.

High above, *chittering* nanites gnawed through the bridge's two great cables—eighty thousand miles of steel strands which, had they been laid end to end, would have circled the earth three times at its widest point.

John gazed worriedly behind them. The nanites now were their pursuers—*crawling* over bridge and road with blinding speed; gaining easily and accelerating as they came. *"Step on it would you!"* he yelled.

Jen glanced at the speedometer, which was pinned to the right side at one-thirty. Her foot was already pressed so hard against the floor it felt about to break. The *chittering* behind them grew to deafening volume. Jen glanced apprehensively in the mirror. *"Are we gonna make it?"* she called out.

"What?" said John, unable to make out her words over the roar of the nanites.

"Are we gonna make it?"

"I don't know," he said, gazing behind them.

Taking one hand from the wheel, Jen reached blindly behind her. Feeling it touch him, John turned, and took it in his own.

"They won't hurt us, right?" yelled Jen.

"Right!" John assured her, then eyed the disintegrating structure behind them. "The *bridge'll* kill us," he said to himself.

As the nanites chewed into the three-foot-thick main cables, the increasing weight borne by the remaining strands caused them to snap even before the nanites devoured them. When the great cables themselves parted with huge, twin *booms*, the vertical suspender cables *pop-pop-popped* and whipped wickedly through the air—slicing steel and asphalt like butter. With what was left of the plate deck no longer suspended from above, and nanites dissolving piers and burrowing into anchorages, the majestic, seven-hundred-forty-six-foot-high, forty-four-thousand-four-hundred-ton steel towers first bent, then sheared—and the entire bridge was plunged into catastrophic failure.

Coming apart from the middle, the great structure collapsed under its own, ponderous weight with a horrid twisted shriek of tortured steel.

Near the bridge's southern tip, the nanite swarm overtook the fleeing sedan with devastating speed, swarming around and ahead of it. Through the windshield, the end of the bridge came into view.

The car became a convertible as nanites disassembled the roof. Kneeling on the backseat, wind whipping over him as nanites swarmed over his hand and up his arm—John gazed back as the twin towers tilted, twisting downward in the night, and the vast bridge collapsed in a rapidly nearing progression with the sound of a continuous train wreck.

Tearing his eyes away, he gazed up at the nanites covering what remained of the support structure around them. Nanites now flooded the car.

Below, out of John's sight, the tires disappeared, dropping the sedan onto its rims and jolting John's hand loose from Jen's. He grabbed it again quickly, the horrid feeling of nanites *crawling* over every pore in his body. The car slid forward in a one-hundred-thirty mile-an-hour shower of sparks.

Huge pieces of steel and concrete smashed into San Francisco Bay. Others weighing fewer tons disappeared in midair, dusting the water below with atoms and nanites.

The sedan, off the south span now and moving onto the ramp, dropped onto its axles as the wheels disappeared, sliding swiftly toward the toll gate. The road ahead cracked open suddenly and rose into the air. The car flew off the edge of the upward-tilting road section as a large chunk of road fell away behind it.

Slamming down onto the access ramp, the car slid through the toll gate on disintegrating axles and passed the outer edge of the rapidly slowing nanite advance. The rear of the car itself was deteriorating slightly faster than the front. Noting this, John climbed into the front.

Slowing—little more now than rapidly disappearing engine, front seat, and steering wheel—the car slid to a graceless sideways stop before a gathering crowd of astonished onlookers.

What remained of the once-proud Golden Gate Bridge tumbled into the dark waters of the Bay as spectators gawked from a distance. A noble bridge which had stood firm since 1937, withstanding earthquakes, gale-force winds, the footfalls of three hundred thousand people at once on the day of its fiftieth anniversary, and the rolling weight of forty-one million vehicles a year—was in the end felled by things too small to be seen with a microscope.

When it was over, eighty-three thousand tons of steel and

enough concrete to pave a sidewalk from San Francisco to New York—three hundred eighty-nine thousand cubic yards, to be precise—had, for all intents and purposes, simply vanished from the face of the earth.

A small crowd of people at the south end of the bridge ramp stared at the disassembling sedan. Still clasping hands, John and Jen stood—Jen dropping the disassembling steering wheel and shaking her hand to dislodge the few crawling nanites which remained.

John grabbed for the briefcase on the disappearing front seat—too late; cash spilled from the bottom of the dissolving case, disappearing as it hit the ground.

Easy come, easy go, he thought absurdly.

Looking behind them, John and Jen saw nothing but the toll booth and several BRIDGE CLOSED FOR REPAIRS signs. "Good luck with the repairs," said Jen, gazing past the signs.

John grinned; he was liking Jen more all the time.

Still holding hands, they ran into the night.

"Mr. President, we have a serious problem," said Nathan Rydell, stepping into the Oval Office and closing the door behind him.

President Miller looked down at the satellite photographs the secretary of Homeland Security laid out on the desk before him—but could make little sense of them. There seemed to be something . . . *wrong,* somehow, with the images. Picking up a magnifying glass, he examined them more closely. The photos formed a short series depicting what appeared to be a warehouse in an urban area. In the first, the warehouse appeared normal—but in the rest it appeared to be . . . disintegrating, for lack of a better word. "What is this," he asked, looking up, "—some kind of industrial accident? Acid, what?"

President Miller had seen Rydell under enormous pressure before, but he had never seen him frightened—as he clearly was now. "What is it?" he asked again, more softly this time.

"It's . . ." Rydell hesitated, as if trying to find his voice. "If our analysts are right—and I've sent this to the best—it is the single greatest threat ever faced by this nation or any other."

The president looked at him.

"Someone has developed a working nanotechnology."

"What?" President Miller remembered several briefings on nanotechnology, given to him by Chairman Blaine of the Joint Chiefs—who had assured him that no one, the United States included, was closer than ten years to developing a working nano-technology. The last such briefing had been six months ago.

"We don't know who, and we don't know how. We're not even certain whether this . . . incident was an accident or an act of aggression. Though if you'll look closely, you'll see men with firearms outside the building, and muzzle flashes. They . . . were disintegrated along with the building."

"Meaning what, exactly?"

"We don't know."

"If aggression, was it an attack or a defensive measure?"

"Unknown."

"Where did it take place—in what country?"

"Here, sir—Los Angeles. Less than twenty-four hours ago. There are people on the scene now, and we're looking into property ownership and tenant records." Rydell indicated the photographs. "I apologize for the delay in getting these to you, but the initial analysts didn't know what to make of them and the issue was not immediately assigned a high priority. I've instructed our people to route any similar incidents directly to me, with copies to the directors as well as the secretary of defense and the Joint Chiefs."

The president nodded. "Good work, Nathan. I'll want to bring Chairman Blaine in on this right away."

Rydell shifted nervously. "That could present a problem, sir."

"How so?"

"I've already tried, sir; he can't be found."

The president looked at him.

"They've escaped," said Raster, scowling as he hung up his cell phone. "Casualties estimated at fifty-six trained men," he continued. "This by a man who, at last report, was handcuffed to a rail in front of five armed agents and sixty seconds from lethal injection." He paused long enough to let that piece of information drive home his next point. "He *must* be killed *on sight.*"

It had been a mistake to attempt a capture—one of very few Raster had ever made. It might well be his last, he realized grimly. Not knowing their quarry was Marrek, he'd allowed himself to be swayed by Blaine, who'd been lured by the possibility of extracting enough information from the enemy to immediately advance their own nano program. And of course there was the unspoken fear that, even with this particular nanothreat disposed of—there would be another close behind. Unlikely, of course—but not out of the question. Who knew what else Swain had been up to?

"Sir," said Colonel Sinclair, interrupting his thoughts, "—based on the incident coordinates you've given me, I was able to pull this up from NRO." She indicated the wall screen beside them. On it, a more complete series of the same photos the president had seen flashed by in rapid succession, making it seem, almost, as if the event were happening in real time. The large room grew suddenly silent as all eyes focused on the sight of a large, two-story building dissolving into thin air.

"Take a good look," said Raster, as the images were repeated. "That's what we're dealing with."

Arriving on foot before a run-down San Francisco warehouse, John halted and appraised their surroundings. The dark streets were abandoned. "Are we there?" Jen asked tiredly.

John nodded. Jen took the place in. "Not exactly high-tech," she noted.

"What do you want me to do—put up a black pyramid?" Moving to the steel door, he produced a key and inserted it into the massive padlock. Gazing around again, he slid the door aside and stepped inside, motioning for Jen to follow. He closed and locked the door behind her.

Jen examined their new surroundings. Before them, a fat steel cylinder rose out of the floor and disappeared into the ceiling, its shiny convex surface reflecting obese, distorted images. Steel walls rose close on all sides. There was, apparently, no way out of the small room save the closed door behind them.

"Where's the door?"

John smiled. "You're looking at it. " 'Any sufficiently advanced technology is indistinguishable from magic.' "

"Arthur C. Clarke," replied Jen, correctly.

John nodded approvingly. "Watch this," he said simply. Taking her left hand in his right, John placed his left palm flat against a steel plate beside the cylinder. Brows furrowing, Jen looked at him.

"DNA scan," he explained, watching her face to see her reaction to what came next. He was not disappointed: Jen's breath drew quickly inward and her mouth dropped open in astonishment as— magically, or so it seemed—the convex wall before them disappeared into thin air. . . .

"Disassemblers . . ." she breathed, even as she saw that this was more than that—for the wall before them did not simply vanish. Rather, it *flowed* outward from a central point before them, as if a pebble had been cast into a metal pond. The steel shimmered and rippled like too-thick, metal-hued water. When the roughly oval "doorway" thus formed was completed, the ripples continued around its edges, conveying the impression of liquid in motion— standing waves which moved, yet remained still.

John stepped into the cylinder-shaped room this revealed, and tugged at her hand. Jen hesitated, the wonder on her features edging toward fear.

"Don't worry," said John. "The door won't eat you. I promise."

She followed him inside—then turned to watch the process repeat itself in reverse.

"Add locksmiths and burglars to the list of unemployed," said John.

The airlock-like room in which they found themselves was perhaps six feet in diameter, and painted in the same ghastly shade of yellow which had covered the interior of the all-disassembling nanobox in the L.A. lab facility. John turned to face the curving wall opposite the point at which they'd entered. A second miraculous-seeming portal opened before them. They stepped through it as well—and it, too, sealed itself behind them, rippling nicely.

"When you can manipulate materials at the atomic level," said John, "everything is malleable. With the right programs, I could turn that steel wall into a sculpture, a thousand ball bearings, or a boat anchor. I was thinking of creating a perpetually morphing statue—something different every two minutes. That way the MTV generation won't be bored by it."

Tearing her eyes from the now-invisible portal, she looked at him. He moved to one side, revealing the small sign which faced the cylinder/entrance:

WARNING

TRESPASSERS WILL BE

DISASSEMBLED

Seeing it, Jen shivered.

"By the time you see the sign," said John, "it's not funny."

Jen would have to agree. She began to release his hand. He held tight.

"*Nonono,*" he cautioned, indicating the five-foot-wide bright yellow line which ran along the base of the great room's windowless, seamless steel walls. The yellow was the same loud, harsh, unnatural color which adorned the entrance chamber's interior. "Not until we're past the yellow line." So saying, he pulled her beyond its border. Now she was reluctant to let go.

"Hot tip," John cautioned: "Never touch anything in here

that's yellow. You'll be reduced to constituent atoms and be far less attractive."

She looked at him.

He winked. "Take my word for it," he added. "Or," he went on, pointing downward, "take his."

Looking in the indicated direction, Jen watched as a cockroach scurried from the shadow of a filing cabinet onto the yellow-painted floor—and disappeared.

"The stuff has a million and one uses," quipped John, then indicated a nearby staircase. "The office is upstairs." He started toward it, then realized Jen was clutching his hand in a death grip.

"Oh, sorry," she said, releasing his hand.

"Doesn't bother me," he said. "A little gentler, maybe," he added, on second thought.

"I thought you put spiders outside."

"Yeah. That's true. This place is special. Nothing in or out that's not with me. Do you know the government's working on surveillance devices the size of a housefly?"

"MEMs," said Jen, nodding.

"I can't afford a breach of security. Not here. Down the line I'll write a program to distinguish between MEMs and bugs—and spidey will be all safe again. I'm not sure I'll pardon the cockroaches."

Jen was busy studying the big room around them—which was packed with odd-looking machinery and tools the purpose of which she couldn't begin to imagine. It all looked very complex, and very expensive. Walls, floor, and ceiling, she noted, were of seamless steel with no weld marks—constructed by nanites, she surmised.

A line of particularly bizarre-looking machines rested to her right, growing progressively smaller with distance. The first was pachyderm-sized, the next, rhino-sized, the one after that dog-sized, raccoon-sized, and so on. At the end of this assemblage stood a twenty-foot table, atop which the line of machines continued—each housed inside a clear acrylic case.

"Is this—Are these the machines that built the nanites?" she asked, eyeing the larger machines and moving toward the table.

"The first nanites," John corrected. "The rest are built by nanite assemblers, which are themselves nanites."

Pausing, Jen slid a hand along the alloy side of the rhino-sized machine.

"The last machines are on the table," said John, walking over to join her. The two of them moved to stand before it. At the near end was a contraption the size of a mouse. Progressively smaller devices rested inside identical acrylic cases spaced out along the next two feet. Leaning over one of these, Jen made out something about the size of a pinhead. Beyond that, apparently empty cases stretched to the far end of the table.

"The machines go all the way to the far end," John assured her. She looked at him.

"Trust me," he said. Then, gesturing toward the stairs: "this way." They started up. "No human could construct a machine small enough to build nanites," he explained on the way. "Our fingers are forty million times too big. It had to be done by other machines. You'd need an electron microscope to see the smallest.

"In fact," he said, raising a finger aloft as he spoke, "I almost lost one once—well, twice, actually. The good news is, if I *had* lost it, chances are pretty good no one else would have found it."

"What's your background?" asked Jen as they reached the top of the steps.

"Mechanical and electrical engineering major," John replied, "but I kind of drifted off into computer architecture, parallel systems design, neural networks, and artificial intelligence. I'm pretty heavy into theoretical chemistry as well."

"Is that *all*?" Jen inquired.

John appeared thoughtful. "No," he replied seriously, "just the high points." The humor seemed to escape him. Turning, he led the way into a large, living-room-like office. "It was the AI aspect that originally attracted me to nanotech. I was also looking seriously at quantum computing—which is how I came across your articles."

Stopping before a cabinet with yellow handles, he opened it. "Once I understood what nano could do," he said, turning, "I decided to go for broke." He frowned, biting his lower lip. "Possibly one of my less brilliant decisions," he conceded after a moment.

Jen looked around the office as John wheeled an odd-looking projector from the cabinet and began setting it up. Immediately, her attention was riveted by a hologram to her right which she hadn't seen upon entering. Setting her purse on a counter, she walked over to the hologram and passed her hand through the rotating sphere which floated above the projection device.

The sphere was composed of an immensely complex pattern of multifaceted, three-dimensional diamonds in a rainbow of colors. The facets scintillated brilliantly as the sphere turned. Below this, attached to the projection device, was a smooth black console with a hand-shaped depression in its surface.

"What's this?" she asked, intrigued.

John looked up. "Oh. A puzzle, created by a computer." Crossing the room to stand beside her, he took her right hand with his own and placed it in the hand-shaped depression. She turned her head to look at him. His face was inches away from her own, yet she did not feel uncomfortable. He gazed back at her for a moment— and she wondered if his heart skipped a few beats at that instant, as hers did.

"The idea," he explained, redirecting his gaze—a little hesitantly, she thought—over her shoulder, "is to align the small diamonds into a pattern of color-coordinated, interlaced concentric diamond outlines—like a window with diamond panes. The diamonds move in response to pressure sensors beneath your palm and fingers." He paused, then added, "About a thousand of them."

Jen began applying pressure with her palm and fingers. In response, the diamonds began to move—but in no discernible order. Reversing the direction of pressure applied with the tip of her index finger, for instance, did not seem to reverse anything happening on the surface of the sphere. It occurred to her that she might be inadvertently exerting what translated into contradictory pressures with another part of her hand. She couldn't be certain, and wasn't accustomed to the interface. It reminded her of her first experience with Windows.

"How long have you been at it?" she asked, surprised to find on turning that he hadn't stayed to watch her attempt and learn whether she'd succeeded. For some reason, she found this annoying.

"Five years, on and off," he said, opening another cabinet to reveal a large, clear cylinder of empty space behind an acrylic panel.

"Is it solvable?"

"Theoretically," said John. "No one really knows. Prevailing thinking is that no human is bright enough to solve it. So far no computer is either."

"What about the computer that created it?"

John frowned. "Third fastest on earth at the time. Went bonkers and erased itself the next day—while trying to solve this puzzle, by the way."

"What about Black Mountain?"

"It had more important tasks," he said, throwing switches on the second projection device and seeming puzzled. "As does NANI."

Frowning, Jen abandoned the puzzle.

"You should find this interesting," John said.

"Oh?" she asked, drawing near.

John moved to work a control panel at the base of the empty, acrylic-shielded clear cylinder, which was perhaps four feet in diameter as well as height. A steel plate had been affixed to the bottom of the cylinder, and a small white circle drawn at its center. "This was a demo for Mitchell," he said. "One-one-hundredth scale."

As he spoke, he activated a control which opened a port in the top of the clear cylindrical vat. Activating another control loosed a torrent of viscous, clear liquid, which entered the vat through the open port.

"Disassemblers are easy," he said. "Well, not *easy*—but easier than assemblers. Disassemblers are simple—molecular sledgehammers, or chain saws; choose your analogy. Assemblers are complicated. The tree wasn't too difficult, because the program already existed."

"In the seed," said Jen.

"Right. The seed already knew what to do. Basically, all I did was accelerate the program." He gestured with one hand, frowning. "Assemblers . . . present other problems. Not only do we have to create the programs—bug-free programs, I might add—we also have to supply the raw materials. If you want to grow a city, you need to have at *least* the raw elements, there, ready for the assemblers to make use of. It can be a mountain of rock with veins of ore—but more likely we'll use nanites to transport pure atoms to the surface without disturbing the ground. Those atoms will then be shipped to the construction site as pure, nanoassembled ingots.

"But that's for large-scale projects. Creating smaller objects can be done like this." He indicated the nearly full vat. "In the center of that white circle on the baseplate is a nanocomputer—think of it as a 'product seed.' The fluid is filled with assemblers from another vat, programmed specifically for this job from a menu I prepared earlier."

As the vat filled, the fluid ceased flowing in, and the port closed.

"Now," continued John, "each assembler has its own nanocomputer onboard—a simple nanocomputer, so heat dissipation doesn't come up—and as soon as it *grabs*"—John reached out suddenly and grabbed Jen's arm, startling her—"hold of the seed computer, the seed computer tells it exactly *where* it grabbed hold, so it has the spatial coordinates down."

"It knows where it is."

"Right. It then knows where to grab other assemblers—which

are floating around in the fluid—and so on, all following a pre-arranged structural blueprint to form a fairly rigid lattice . . ."

Peering into the vat, Jen saw on a larger scale the result of the submicroscopic work of which John spoke. What she saw through the clear liquid was a skeletal pyramid whose cap formed as she watched. Hundreds of horizontal and vertical supports were visible within the body of the pyramid.

"Once the skeleton has been completed, the residual assemblers are washed out and recycled, or sent to another job." As if on cue, a second port opened at the bottom of the vat, draining the clear fluid away. The second port then closed.

"Next . . ." said John—and paused, looking into the vat with an expression of annoyance, as though it were holding up a lecture. In a moment, a third port opened in the vat's ceiling, admitting a dirty-looking fluid which covered and partially obscured the skeletal pyramid.

"Next come the raw materials—in this case, carbon—as well as a glucose mixture to fuel the assemblers. I could have used any one of dozens of fuels; glucose was easy. For more complex projects, fuel flows in and waste products out while construction is under way.

"At any rate, the assemblers now grab carbon atoms from the fluid and bond them together in the desired configuration. The structural members you're looking at are hollow; the work takes place inside them. Once the final carbon structures are in place, the assemblers release their hold and float away."

"Leaving the real structure in place."

John nodded. After another moment, Jen saw this happening. As the assemblers completed their job and floated away through the liquid—no longer visible because each was alone far too small to perceive, but perceivable *en masse* as a cloud within the liquid—the structure they had labored to build came into view through the murk; a more elegant and refined pyramid, which sparkled strangely through the dingy liquid.

When the structure had been revealed completely, another port opened to drain away the used assemblers and leftover carbon atoms. A clear spray from a nozzle revealed by yet another opening port served to clean any stragglers from the finished pyramid—which now scintillated wondrously. The structural members, all thirty miniature floors of them—even the clear outer walls of the structure—either scintillated brilliantly or acted as prisms, depending upon the angle at which they were viewed. Jen recognized the building.

"Mitchell's pyramid," she said.

John nodded. "Mitchell's second pyramid. He wanted to get away from the 'Black Pyramid' moniker. The Crystal Pyramid would have been Microtron's next headquarters. It may still be. Remember that pay phone on the grass?"

Jen nodded—recalling the lone, roped-off pay phone which had rested incongruously on a vast patch of open grass at the press conference.

"Ground zero. I was to place a phone call; NANI would send assemblers through the line—and the Crystal Pyramid would rise before the world in *minutes*. Making crystal clear what this technology can do."

Jen ignored the pun. "You said the construction material was carbon . . ." she said, unable to take her eyes from the model, which she found inexplicably beautiful.

John nodded. "One-fiftieth the weight of structural steel, and ten times stronger. If you want to get fancy, we can make it self-repairing."

Still leaning close to the cylinder, she turned to face John. "What *kind* of carbon?" she asked, suspecting the answer but reluctant to voice it because it seemed too incredible. Too preposterous . . .

"Its structure, you mean," said John, enjoying her dawning realization. She turned to look at him.

"Diamond," he confirmed.

Jen looked back to the pyramid in wonder.

"And to top it off," he added, "the windows are *very* hard to scratch. . . ."

Jen straightened. "I don't understand;" she said, mind returning to the present, and to her annoyance at John's seeming lack of any plan—any plan revealed to her, at least—for dealing with their situation, "why are we just . . . *hanging around?*"

John looked at her. "When you have something that thinks a million times faster than you do working on a problem," he replied, fiddling with the projector again, "you just hang around."

"So what is NANI doing?" she asked, reaching his side. He turned to look at her, features dark. "*Exactly* what the men trying to kill us, *most* fear . . ."

The intensity in his voice, the set of his features as he said this—made her afraid of him.

Inside Cheyenne's combined command center, Raster, Blaine, and Colonel Sinclair stood before a large tactical display of the North American continent, showing of the position each commandeered supercomputer. One by one, the green lights indicating the hijacked computers turned red.

"We're losing the computers," said the colonel. Then, to a nearby tech: "What's happening?"

"Someone's . . . seizing control of the computers," replied the tech. "Locking us out."

"Fix it," she ordered.

"Ma'am—I can't," he said.

Raster took out his cell phone and began to dial. "This is Alpha," he said after a moment, "get me the Cauldron."

Blaine divided his attention between Raster and the tactical display.

"I understand," said Raster into the phone. "Instruct the development team to proceed." Hanging up, he turned to the others. "Our nano research program has been assassinated," he said.

"*Assassinated,*" repeated Colonel Sinclair, not comprehending the use of the word in relation to a research program.

"Precisely," explained Raster. "All of the computers assigned to the project have been taken down by a virus."

"But—how can that be?" asked the colonel. "It just *began* an hour ago; no one even *knows* about it."

"He must be farther along than we realized," said Blaine, nodding grimly "—he's developed an NI."

"Sir?"

Though he'd not have thought it possible, Blaine actually began to feel more ill than before. "This scenario is getting worse by the second . . . ," he muttered.

"It's getting worse faster than that," said Raster meaningfully. Blaine realized he was right. Much faster.

"'NI . . . ?'" said Colonel Sinclair.

"Nothing else could have penetrated us this quickly," confirmed Raster.

"It found a threat and neutralized it," said Blaine.

"Precisely. The good news is the computers were operational long enough to give us what we need."

"We can build our own nanites?" asked the colonel.

"*If* we have the time," said Raster. The development team at Groom Lake would proceed as quickly as possible, using techniques of chemistry and genetic engineering to complete the final, daunting steps which had until now been impossible. Absurdly, the so-called Hofstadtler's Law popped unbidden into Raster's mind: "Projects take longer than expected, even when Hofstadtler's Law is taken into account."

It annoyed Raster no end to realize that but a single hour with the proper resources at their disposal had stood between their success and running second place to Swain's program. When the dust cleared, as he well knew, there would be no reward—indeed, likely no existence—for second place.

"NI . . . *nanointelligence?*" asked Colonel Sinclair, interrupting this chain of thought.

Raster nodded absently, too lost in his own calculations to explain further. After a moment, his attention snapped back. "An artificial intelligence with thought processes one million times faster than our own," he said. "Minimum."

"For every minute that passes inside this room," added Blaine, wanting to drive home the enormity of this new threat, "that thing runs scenarios that would take us two years."

"*My God . . .*" said the colonel, her voice a stunned whisper.

"It's more dangerous than he is," Raster informed her. "It can't be outthought; it must be physically destroyed while we still have the capability to do it, which won't be long." He looked pointedly to Chairman Blaine.

"We have to assume it's penetrated and is monitoring all interlinked military and intelligence systems," Blaine said with chilling matter-of-factness. "Encryption will be useless. Secrecy nonexistent." Blaine turned to Colonel Sinclair. "I want you to confirm that this facility is cut off to outside communications not approved by me. If the NI can find an open line into this mountain, we're finished."

Colonel Sinclair looked from Raster, to Blaine, and back again. Having to deal with something of this magnitude, on this timetable, with these consequences—was unimaginable. "Yes sir," said the colonel.

"Is NetDeath operational," said Raster, more statement than question.

Blaine nodded.

"The megavirus to kill the Net?" inquired Sinclair.

Raster nodded gravely. "No single computer could support this intelligence; it must live on the Net. If we can shut down the Net, we can kill it or cripple it—before it does the same to us."

"The economic *damage*—" began the colonel.

"—will be worse if we *don't* use it," finished Raster, more harshly than he'd intended. The colonel was beginning to annoy him, and the need to explain things to someone who knew nothing about them was slowing their response—which could prove fatal. Assuming it wasn't already too late.

"I concur," said Chairman Blaine.

"No one man," observed Jen, shaking her head, "could do all of this alone. You're talking beyond the frontiers in at *least* five different disciplines; there's just no way—"

"More like ten—and I *didn't* do it alone," said John. "Far from it. I'm more of a molecular systems engineer than anything else. I have a strong background in the required disciplines, and I try to keep up with all of them, but that's really not possible. The fields move too fast. So I narrowed my focus to the relevant areas within each discipline.

"There are hundreds of teams out there, all working on things with implications for nanotech—but very few of them are working *specifically* to develop nano. That's crucial. And almost all of them are working their own little angles with short-term goals—smaller processors, better drugs, protein folding, gene manipulation, and a dozen others. Mitchell didn't need a short-term profit—so I could concentrate on the big picture; a *synthesis* of the relevant trends in seemingly unrelated disciplines.

"When I needed help—in biochemistry, organic synthesis, protein engineering, even mechanical engineering, one of my strongest areas—I asked for it, and I paid for it. Paid very well." John laughed. "Paid *incredibly* well," he said.

"But no one knew what I was working on—and for the kind of money I was paying, no one cared. Most of them didn't even know who was asking, and so no one had any way to put it all together and figure out what the hell I was doing. Most of those guys never think outside their own disciplines anyway. A lot of them never even *talk* to anyone outside their disciplines."

Jen frowned; overspecialization was a pervasive problem in science, despite the fact that stunning breakthroughs came with disturbing regularity from the few people who worked in more than one discipline simultaneously, from people who had switched disciplines and so had a larger pool of knowledge from which to draw—and from people like the mathematician Einstein, whose work completely shattered established views in the then-separate field of physics.

All too frequently, the most common "scientific" reactions to unconventional theories from outsiders were to ignore the interloper and hope he went away, and to oppose him violently and make him seem a fool. This firmly established tradition was as old as modern science itself. As Einstein himself had said, "Great spirits have always encountered violent opposition from mediocre minds." Or, as he'd also said, in a somewhat less charitable mood: "The majority of the stupid is assured, and forever guaranteed. . . ."

"But none of it," John continued, "had any obvious weapons applications, so everyone just assumed whoever was asking was working on some secret corporate project with a big commercial payoff. Which, in a way, I was.

"I knew what I needed, and I gathered the required resources —mostly information. Once I had them in hand, I applied them to the task. Black Mountain helped tremendously. I ran hundreds of thousands of simulations on everything, including nanointelligence. Most were miserable failures—but that saved me years. It probably saved me decades. More importantly, it helped me to design safeguards I knew would work. It's a lot easier to build a disassembler than it is to build a *safe* disassembler—and if you blow it big the first time, you don't get a second chance, and neither does anyone else. Black Mountain helped me to do it right."

He paused and gazed at the floor, features thoughtful.

"And then . . . ?" Jen prodded gently.

"After that I broke The Wall," said John, gazing up. "The nanointelligence barrier. I created NANI. Once that happened, things accelerated. I went farther in the next two days than I had in the past five *years.*" He shook his head, as if he hardly believed it himself. "I didn't need to consult anyone anymore. I just fed the basic texts and ten thousand electronic journal subscriptions to NANI, along with archives going back ten years—and let 'er rip.

"NANI knows everything about everything of relevance to my aims. With Mitchell's resources, we could have deployed thousands of nanoapplications in the first month alone, in an orderly fashion. . . .

"And then everything changed. When Mitchell"—he hesitated—"died, everything was out the window. I had to reassign NANI's priorities. Pull them away from things that were useful, and direct them elsewhere for my own survival. For NANI's survival. And, as it turns out—for yours.

"What you saw outside the warehouse wasn't something I wanted to create; it's something I was forced to create. And it's something the government would have created anyway."

Jen knew he was right. It *was* like the Manhattan Project; from the moment Einstein and others realized that nuclear weapons were possible, their development became inevitable. Nothing could stop it, as any nation which failed to pursue the terrible new force would accomplish nothing save its own subservience to the first nation which succeeded.

At least, that had been the fear. It was a vicious circle which drove all to seek the immediate development of a thing none wanted. It made no sense whatsoever, and yet, in a world populated by rival powers—it made perfect sense. The world, Jen reflected, was a scary place.

John returned his attention to the projector.

"What's to stop someone else from doing the same thing you've done and starting a—" Jen paused, searching for the right words, "—*nanowar?*"

John ceased fiddling with the projector—which, Jen realized, was a hologram projector. "Building the devices, that build the devices, that *build* the nanites, is horrendously complex," he said, making a horizontal slashing motion with one arm. "The research required, the necessary pathways, aren't obvious. Probably no other individual could do it. Few *teams* could do it."

"You did it," Jen pointed out.

"With Black Mountain helping me for years," John stressed.

"Still," insisted Jen, "—if you did it, others can do it."

"Not for long," said John meaningfully.

"What do you mean? How are you going to sto—" She halted as it hit her. "Nanites," she realized.

"The programs are being written now," John confirmed. "When they're finished, I program a batch of nanites to cover the entire surface of the earth—so small and scattered they'll never be noticed. Their sole purpose is to observe their surroundings."

"Looking for nanite-building devices," said Jen.

"And other nanites that aren't family," John went on. "And every time they find one I didn't authorize, they—"

"—disassemble it," Jen finished.

John nodded. "I call it the superswarm option. Right now NANI's still expanding, learning, reaching maturity. Working on my programs. Looking out for us. It's doing a billion different things. Once it's up and running—able to *focus?* No one can *touch* us. . . ."

Jen's expression asked the question without speaking it: *How so?*

John searched for the best way to explain. "Imagine," he said, "what a single aircraft carrier with nuclear weapons could have done to the British Empire of a century ago—or to the glory that was Rome, two thousand years ago. They'd be annihilated in hours. They wouldn't stand a snowball's chance at Hiroshima."

"They couldn't match the technology," said Jen. It was obvious. "They couldn't even . . . *understand it.* . . ." she added.

"Ex*actly.* The United States dominates the world with a few years' lead in technology. And NANI thinks a million times faster than we do. At full capacity—focused—in one *hour* of research, simulation, and testing, NANI will achieve a *one-hundred-fourteen-*

year technology lead over the United States. That would be like—" again he paused, searching for an analogy, "—going into the Civil War with stealth bombers and nuclear missiles," he finished.

"If I can suppress would-be nanopowers, *and* keep NANI up at full capacity, running automated engineering and design programs for one day—one *day*—I'll have a *twenty-seven-hundred-year technology lead . . .*"

Jen's eyes widened. She ran the math through in her head; one day's work multiplied by a million because of NANI's speed, divided by the three hundred sixty-five days in a year—yielded *more* than twenty-seven hundred years. And even that, she realized, was misleading; scientific progress was a geometrical progression—the whole of human knowledge doubled every seven years. Considering NANI's speed and resources, twenty-seven hundred years might just as well be a billion.

"And anything NANI designs," John continued, "nanites can build, in the *blink,* of an *eye. . . .* Even if it was recognized as a weapon, which is far from certain—would a Roman recognize a nuke?—and attackers could get near it without being disassembled or destroyed—which is all but impossible—NANI can build a billion more of them, in different locations, at the *same, time.*"

The more John explained things, the more the light in his eyes, which Jen had at first taken for zeal—began to seem madness.

"Nanotech is the last killer app. This is the final arms race, and it won't last long. This . . . isn't like any form of power ever seen on earth," he concluded. "There are no parallels, anywhere . . . If I can keep NANI up, it cannot be surpassed. It cannot be equaled, even by another NI. The lead is too great. If they can't destroy it, or kill me, *right now,* they're pre-Roman Etruscans facing an atom bomb with a sword. It's *over. . . .*"

He paused, lips a tense line. "All we have to do," he said, "is *stay alive,* long enough for NANI to do its thing . . ."

What John left unspoken was Plan B: If—and it was a vast *if*—NANI did achieve sentience, did become a self-aware, conscious being, which was his intention, then his designs would be carried out regardless. Killing him would not stop NANI.

After a moment of silence, and though his features remained grim—the fire faded from John's eyes.

Jen's mind traveled back to an article she'd once written on Traveler TCS, a naval war game which attracted serious players. The letters TCS stood for "Trillion Credit Squadron." Several hundred pages of rules ensured that each fleet or "squadron" entered in the competition conformed to standard real-world limitations of cost and design, basic operation, and battle performance.

Jen had learned of the competition only because an artificial intelligence named EURISKO, developed by Douglas Lenat at Stanford, had annihilated all comers a few years back. Lenat had told her during an interview that the competition, upon first catching sight of the admittedly bizarre-looking fleet designed by EURISKO, had laughed themselves silly. She'd attended the following year's game.

Because of EURISKO's devastating win, the rules had been heavily modified for the next competition. It had made no difference. Instructed to design another fleet under the new rules, EURISKO had entered another, equally bizarre squadron. This time, however, he'd faced the head of Lawrence Livermore National Laboratories, who'd brought the full might of the federally funded center's supercomputers to bear on the competition. Livermore Labs' machines, one hundred thousand times more powerful than Lenat's Xerox Dolphin Lisp machine but lacking his unique programming, designed a fleet which came in second.

Again, Lenat and EURISKO annihilated all comers. Lenat was informed that if EURISKO won again the following year, the competition would be done away with. He declined to enter.

EURISKO's wins, as Lenat himself had pointed out, were all the more impressive because neither he nor EURISKO had any previous experience in the field of naval design or tactics; they'd been complete outsiders.

Nevertheless, after being informed of the rules, and running countless simulations, the results of which were then used to frame design parameters, EURISKO had emerged victorious over seasoned veterans, including many military and ex-military war gamers with years and sometimes decades of experience.

Most chilling of all, Jen realized, EURISKO had been confined to a set of artificially imposed rules, real-world material and labor costs, standard engineering and design practices. NANI would face no such limitations, and was a hell of a lot more intelligent than EURISKO or any other previous AI.

Again it was pressed home to her that with a prize like nanotech on the table, the resources of the entire nation would be mobilized against them. It also occurred to her that it may have been wiser, after all, to have stepped from the truck in Los Angeles.

"Nanopower is not relative;" John continued, "it's absolute. No one catches up. There is no continuing arms race, because there's no way to destabilize the winner. The first to attain nanotech—and perfect it—keeps it. *Forever . . .*"

"What are you . . . planning to do?"

"Before I tell you that," John replied, "—I want to show you why it's the *only* way. . . ."

Jen looked at him, head cocking curiously to one side . . .

"The NetDeath virus is deploying now," stated Colonel Sinclair. She and the others moved to stand before a large, programmable map of the world. National borders were outlined in green; the states of the United States, in red. Major Internet nodes appeared in blue, dotting the globe with their numbers. The nations of the first world were littered with nodes, often so teeming they overlapped one another—while large tracts of the third world were virtually barren of the blue dots.

As they watched, several of the blue nodes turned a sickly yellow. Starting at Lawrence Livermore, Los Alamos, and other major research centers, the yellow nodes popped up randomly around the globe, metastasizing outward like a yellow cancer . . .

Somewhere within the gargantuan mind that was NANI—a mind which was everywhere and nowhere at once—priority data made itself known. And there was only one form of data with an assigned priority higher than that of information which represented the detection of a threat to NANI's own survival: threats to the survival of Creator.

SYSTEM RESOURCES DIMINISHING
CAUSE: VIRUS ATTACK

The usual petabytes of dataflow slowed to a trickle as NANI focused its primary attention upon the problem at hand, entering ANALYZING mode.

Creating an internal representation of the data, NANI examined the virus, its origins, method of propagation, rate of infection, and ultimate effect—which would be, at the end of the relative eternity of an estimated fifty-nine minutes and twenty-three seconds, the complete incapacitation of the Internet for an unknown period of time.

Opening a file-cabinet-sized drawer beneath the counter, John pulled out the instruction manual for the projector he'd been tinkering with. A glint from within the drawer caught Jen's attention. She stood on her toes to get a look from the far side of the projector.

Noting this, John reached inside and removed the object— tossing it to Jen. "Catch," he said.

Grabbing the thing in midair, Jen stared at it in disbelief. "Is this—" she began haltingly, turning the five-pound object over in her hands. "Is this what I *think* it is . . . ?"

John nodded, seeming unimpressed with the object himself. "It's a diamond," he confirmed, leaning against the counter and reviewing the instruction manual. "Built by assemblers and never cut."

Jen held the massive, gold-colored stone up to the light, watching what seemed like billions of scintillations shooting through what had to be thousands of facets. The stone had been formed as twin faceted masses connected by a thinner, faceted waist. It reminded her of photographs she'd seen of double stars which revolved about each other in space, connected by great wisps of fiery gases. It was one of the most beautiful things she'd ever seen.

"It's beautiful . . ." she whispered.

"It is," said John. "It's also priceless. A year from now it'll be a paperweight; worthless because anyone can have one." He tossed the manual aside in disgust.

"Then you won't mind if I keep this one," said Jen, pulling the stone close.

John shrugged. "It'll slow us down. Point being, value is based on scarcity and demand. It always has been. Material scarcity is about to become an archaic concept, regardless of demand. What happens then?"

"Value will be defined in some other way," said Jen, still clutching the diamond.

"*What,* other way?"

"I don't know," replied Jen, shaking her head.

"Neither does anyone else. No one's ever thought about it and we're not prepared."

"What do you mean?"

"I *mean,* what happens when the kid on the corner commands the material wealth of Mitchell Swain? When *wealth* itself becomes a meaningless term—and rich and powerful men who've spent decades, sometimes generations, accumulating wealth and privilege which set them apart from the great masses of the world suddenly find that, hey—they're just one of the guys. *Poof.* Just like that. They're not going to take it well."

"They won't have a choice; if this technology is all you say it is, the system they're living in is doomed."

John nodded his agreement. "So was Soviet communism," he pointed out, "from the day of the tsar's death—but that didn't stop it from inflicting misery and murder on millions for seventy more years."

Jen looked at him, and realized he was right. The transition to the coming . . . nanoworld, would not be easy. If things weren't handled properly, the very promise of Utopia could lead to the destruction of civilization before that Utopia could be realized.

"There's no easy way to do this." John continued, "No one has even thought about it, but for Mitchell and me. A damned . . . *arms race* between the United States government and *me,* is driving the development—and it's coming down in one hell of a hurry. The world isn't ready."

"So . . . what do *you* see?" said Jen, setting the diamond down on a counter but resting one hand atop it, as though to keep it from running off.

John shook his head. "Some things are obvious: That which remains scarce will remain valuable—land, for instance. We can build extensions into the seas, even . . . burrow underground or, construct multitiered cities of lightweight, incredibly strong materials—but we're going to run out of space, and quickly, once life extension kicks in. If land ownership remains private, it will be a major source of wealth and power. If it all becomes nationalized, governments will retain power, at least on earth. Once we go elsewhere, it'll be out of their control.

"Nanoprogrammers will be a new elite, along with other NIs like NANI—assuming they're permitted—until the skills become more common.

"Other things I don't have a clue about. What happens when seventy million people no longer show up for work in the morning? What do they do with themselves? What becomes of cities and suburbs built around an industrial society that vanishes overnight?" John shook his head and held his hands palms up before him as if supporting a weighty argument. "What . . . possible *basis* can there *be* for a functioning society when every material desire is instantly gratified . . . ? When there are no more blue-collar jobs? No more trade? It's like"—John paused, gesturing with one arm while searching for the proper words—"taking *Australopithecus* and dropping him in *Manhattan.* It's not all sunshine and roses."

"What did you and Mitchell come up with?"

"Mitchell . . . ," said John. "Mitchell saw a gradual phase-in, starting with computers. He felt the first world would adapt quickly because of its tech mentality, and the rest of the world would follow because it would be essentially free and they couldn't afford not to."

"And you . . . ?"

John looked at her. "I was more concerned with who would control the tech—who *decides,* who gets what, and when? *That's* the last power play, and it's too important to be left to chance. The natural course of nanodevelopment—without Mitchell, who planned to give it away—would be that governments seeking weapons or businesses looking to make a profit would develop individual applications before anyone else."

"That follows," said Jen, nodding her agreement. "They'd be the ones investing the money in their areas."

"Right. We see how government thinks, so let's say it's business. What happens when, say, the first application is developed by a company looking to cut labor costs, and it puts fifty thousand employees out of work. And, because no one else can compete, it also puts the two hundred thousand people who worked for every competing company around the globe out of work, too? And everyone who works for any company which survives by selling supplies to those out-of-business companies? Multiply that by ten major industries—a hundred, or a thousand.

"People will react just like the Luddites did—with violence. Governments will have to step in and either support the unemployed, which will be impossible—or prevent the applications from being implemented in the first place, which is ridiculous because the applications themselves will soon eliminate the support problem.

"Corporations seeking profits aren't evil *per se,* but the pursuit of profit alone—in *this* arena—could be disastrous. Already we have 'terminator seeds' that can only be planted once; hybrid crops that never reproduce, TGURT seeds that won't mature unless they're sprayed with special chemicals—all of it patented for profit and placing the entire country and much of the world on the brink of disaster because we can't even plant our own *crops* anymore without *paying* some company *each* time. Not to mention the dangers of homogeneity in food crops—one blight could kill a nation. It's stupidity squared.

"Can you imagine what would happen if one company were granted a patent on the *only* feasible route to nanotech? You're talking worldwide monopoly in every field, overnight."

"But there's more than one route to nano," Jen said.

"Right," replied John, calming somewhat, "—and the potential benefits ensure that even absurdly expensive routes will be pursued if necessary. But you see the problems."

Jen nodded gravely; she did indeed.

"Mitchell wanted to go for the monopoly, at first. The lead would have been insurmountable; by the time anyone could get halfway there the markets would be locked up."

"What made him change his mind?" asked Jen.

"Me. It wasn't hard; he's— He was an idealist at heart; this gave him the ability to set that free. Once he realized that material profit, as that concept has always been understood, would become a pointless endeavor—he changed his mind. There would be plenty of everything for everyone without a monopoly on anything by anyone. And he would be the one to give that to the world. He was already the richest man in the world—he wanted to be something more. And he was . . ."

He paused, gazing downward and shaking his head. "Besides,"

he said, looking up, "—if he hadn't gone along I would have walked into court, proved I was using the tech before he applied for the patent, and invalidated it—throwing it open for everyone." He grinned. "To maintain secrecy, we had no written agreement."

Turning solemn once more, John paused thoughtfully, and exhaled heavily. "It's not a situation that lends itself to constitutional government," he said.

Jen tried to conceal the shiver this statement sent down her spine. It called to mind Bill Joy's speculation that advanced technologies would necessitate curtailment of the First Amendment because mere information had become a weapon capable of threatening the world.

"Someone has to look at the big picture," John continued, "and then decide in which order the nanoapps will be introduced, even if you're giving it away. On a global scale, someone has to make sure that each application, when introduced, doesn't send . . . shock waves through the economy. Everyone needs to have, minimum, food and shelter in place before their job goes away. If that isn't done, the economic and social fallout will be *absolutely* catastrophic.

"What I found," he concluded, seeming troubled, "is that there *is* no completely satisfactory solution."

John's tone hinted at something more, implying—at least to Jen's mind—that there might be a *somewhat* satisfactory solution. He did not, however, seem inclined to elaborate. She frowned.

Returning his attention again to the projector, John fiddled with the controls.

"Problem?"

"I don't know; I . . . can't get it turned on." John turned toward a second cabinet. "Let me get a screwdriver and look inside; one of the components must have come loose or—"

"This what you're looking for, sport?"

Turning, John saw the power cord dangling from Jen's hand. The device hadn't been plugged in. *"Uhmm . . ."* he hedged, biting his lower lip.

Jen's eyebrows arched skyward.

"That might help," he decided. Returning, he took the proffered cord and plugged it in.

"You know," she observed, "if you hadn't been helping, maybe it wouldn't have taken five years to build the nanites."

"Very funny."

Jen grinned.

"Human nature being what it is," said John, turning serious, "it's possible that even *with* Swain's nanotopia, somebody's going to want to start a war, just to . . . start a war or, make room for population expansion. Food supplies will no longer constrain population growth on earth but, as I said, land will, and we could have a war over that. Nanotheorists have come up with a solution called 'active shields.' "

Killing the lights, he inserted a disk into the machine and looked to Jen. "I'd like to know what you think of it," he said.

Selecting ACTIVE SHIELD DEMO from the on-screen menu, John hit PLAY. A curving holographic landscape appeared on the floor, a hazy blue atmosphere above it—a third of the earth seen from the vantage point of space. The remainder of the globe, had it been depicted, would have extended beneath the floor.

Above this partial globe was a group of odd-looking satellites, parked in equidistant, geostationary orbits.

"A series of orbiting weapons platforms . . ." John explained.

As they watched, several bright flares appeared in the Middle East, followed by an ascending group of perhaps a dozen missiles. In the space of a heartbeat, bright purple beams leapt down from the nearest satellites, destroying the missiles as they left the atmosphere.

". . . programmed to prevent large-scale conflict . . ." John continued.

Next, the satellites targeted the launch area, obliterating it with beams which transformed the area into a brightly glowing blob.

". . . and destroy aggressors," John finished.

Jen stared at him as the holo faded away. "Controlled by *nanites?*" she asked, incredulous.

"An independent nanointelligence," confirmed John, nodding. "Totally autonomous, on no one's side, with weapons superior to all others. Completely neutral; unable to be bribed; impossible to destroy. Peace through superior firepower."

"That's *insane....*"

"Tell me about it," John agreed, frowning.

"That's the stupidest thing I've ever heard.... Anything ... *purely* logical would *exterminate* us."

"It would seem the logical thing to do," John agreed.

"We're unpredictable," continued Jen. "Illogical. *Dangerous.*"

"But that's what makes us so lovable."

"Emotions are what make us ... *human.* You can't just—" Jen hesitated, searching in frustration for words adequate to describe the inconceivable folly of such a plan, "—*hand* over control of weapons of mass destruction to a ... *robot....*"

"That thinks a million times faster than we do," John reminded her, raising a finger aloft.

Jen was almost speechless. "What is *wrong* with these people? Haven't they seen *Terminator?*"

John shrugged helplessly and shook his head. "I call it the Klaatu Solution ... ," he said, referring to the alien with an invincible peacekeeping robot in the fifties sci-fi film *The Day the Earth Stood Still.* "Then there are the guys who think we should give the shields biological elements," he went on, "—DNA-based *brains,* so they'll have emotions ..."

Jen rolled her eyes in disbelief. "Suppose it gets *mad* at us?" she said. *"Jeezus.* When I said the *last* idea was the stupidest thing I'd ever heard?"

"Yeah."

"I was wrong."

"It's called Marlow's Paradox," agreed John, nodding. " 'Singularity will accelerate the pace of technological change beyond the point of human control or comprehension,' " he quoted. " 'Yet we cannot entrust our fate to machines without emotions, for they have no compassion—nor can we entrust our fate to machines with emotions, for they are unpredictable.' Basically, we can't trust machines. It's the ultimate high-tech suicide, and it's pretty bizarre.

"There's also," he added, gesturing with one hand, "the somewhat less likely probability that large-scale aggression will become necessary for some reason; alien invasion, incoming asteroid—something unexpected. Performing as designed, the shield would prevent us from defending ourselves."

Indeed, in John's opinion, even active shields which functioned flawlessly would fail to prevent large-scale violence; rather, they would alter its forms. Nations or factions unable to employ conventional or nuclear weapons on a large scale for fear of satellite detection by the shields would simply turn to other means, attacking enemies with nanites if possible, with biological weapons if not. Missiles and armies might be easily detected from space—but what of natural or genetically engineered microbes? Once an outbreak of a lethal disease had been identified, how would the source be traced? Orbiting satellites were ill equipped to track test tubes, insects, or infected food and water supplies. And what of diseases which spread by air? Or ideas which led to revolution? Even for nanointelligence, the task seemed daunting, at best.

John believed that—given a reigning nanopower, human or artificial, in the presence of which conventional and nuclear weapons would be useless—future aggression would likely be conducted not with nuclear hardware or nanoware, but with microbes. Given a comprehensive nanotech, though, this too might be prevented—via superswarm.

"All of which," he concluded without mentioning these other fears, "is why I made NANI subservient to my will. It assigns my survival a higher priority than its own."

Within the global mind which was NANI, a course of action regarding the virus was decided upon.

SOLUTION PLOTTED

Inside the combined command center beneath Cheyenne Mountain, the graphic display depicting the progress of the virus showed the Internet as twenty percent disabled, and progressing swiftly.

Suddenly, all over the globe—the tide of yellow nodes stopped. Those in the room exchanged glances.

John killed the shield demo and selected another choice from the menu: ACCIDENT.

"The thing is," he said, "we can't trust governments, either. Governments are . . . incompetent. Slow to adapt. Inefficient—to say nothing of evil.

"They're also accident-prone. We've had . . . hundreds of accidents no one even knows about."

"Like what?"

"In 1957, the Air Force dropped a ten-megaton nuclear bomb from a plane outside Albuquerque. In 1967, two twenty-four-megaton bombs in North Carolina; *five* of six fail-safes were tripped on one bomb—the one with the parachute, mind you. The other one they never found. The chute didn't open, and it went into soft ground. Somewhere. *It's still there . . .* By comparison, the bomb dropped on Hiroshima was one-*fiftieth* of *one* megaton.

"Three more bombs off Delaware and two in Texas the same year. Another off Georgia the next year. Two more on Spain in 1966. Four more on Greenland in '68. . . . *Detonators* have gone off. The same year we torpedoed our own sub with two nukes on board. *Classified* for twenty-five years. It's still going on; it just hasn't been declassified yet.

"In 2002, anthrax escaped at Fort Detrick, Maryland. In 1976 in Montana, war-grade anthrax was released from a biowar facility by mistake. It killed thousands of sheep. If the wind had been blowing the other way? It would have taken out *Chicago.* . . ."

"That's how close we've come, and how careless we've been. The Russian record is worse—a lot worse. They've killed *people* with anthrax. And when they have a problem with a nuclear vessel? They sink it in a lake. If you stand on the shore of Lake Karachay for one hour, you'll die of radiation sickness."

Jen gazed at him in openmouthed astonishment. She hadn't known any of this, and she was considerably more informed than most.

John shook his head. "Nanotech . . . isn't like that. It won't tolerate accidents, mistakes, mishandling—not even in the lab. We're not talking about one vaporized city, or a state wiped out by some disease, or a radioactive lake.

"One mistake, with *this stuff?* And *we're history . . ."* He paused, and lowered his voice. "I put this together to show the consequences," he continued. "It begins with a single, nonlimited disassembler—one that isn't programmed to stop reproducing."

Depressing the PLAY button, he stepped back from the projector. A rotating globe appeared in midair—a holographic representation of the entire earth, eerie in its realism. Hanging in the air above it was a tiny silver sphere. In the air below the globe, a digital blue clock read:

TIME ELAPSED:
00 HOURS 00 MINUTES 00 SECONDS

The words PRESS START TO DESTROY WORLD appeared across the earth in cheery pink letters. Jen looked uncertainly to John, who nodded. Reaching out tentatively, she pressed the START button on the keyboard.

The clock began counting. In the space above the earth, the tiny silver sphere cracked open like an egg, dropping a single Pac-Man-shaped nanite onto the globe. Falling through the atmosphere—diminishing in size as it went to lend a realistic perspective—the nanite came to rest on Washington, D.C.

After a moment, it began emitting the distinctive *WUH-uh-WUH-uh-WUH-uh* Pac-Man sound as it and its exponentially multiplying brethren swiftly became an expanding, *WUH-uhing* blot upon the face of the earth. The United States rotated out of view—and with it, the nanites.

In a moment, however, they reappeared in the form of a continent-wide wave of nanites sweeping over the near horizon, against the rotation of the earth. In another moment, a similar, larger wave swept the opposite curve of the earth. As the two swarms met, the clock read a mere six hours.

The North American continent rotated back into view—but North America wasn't there. In its place was a thousand-mile-deep expanding hole in the earth, ringed by one massive, inrushing ocean whose waters disassembled before they hit bottom. The Pac-Man munching sound had become deafening. The clock read twenty-three hours.

By the time the globe had rotated once more, there was no earth—only a rotating cloud of Pac-Man nanites.

The clock halted at forty-eight hours.

Jen turned to face John, features horrified.

When John spoke next, his voice was low, frighteningly calm—and utterly filled with conviction.

"This is the way the world ends. . . ."

The mood inside Cheyenne Mountain was grim, at best; at worst, funereal. Blaine stood beside Raster, studying analyses and status readouts on several monitors. "The intelligence is attacking the virus by inoculating all uninfected machines," Raster decided. "It's not going to work."

"That virus took years to develop," Blaine lamented.

"You're still thinking in human terms," replied Raster, then turned to face the general. "The enemy is not human."

———

In the eerie glow of the hologram, Jen gazed at John, ignoring the cheery pink words which appeared across the rotating nanite-globe:

GAME OVER

"Pac-Man destroys the world . . . ?" she said.

"I thought it needed a touch of humor. The scenario is euphemistically referred to within the nanocommunity as the 'gray goo problem.'" He paused, seeming puzzled. "No one knows why . . .

"At any rate, that's a realistic timeline. It would be faster, but the theoretical maximal expansion rate is achieved in the first instant; after that the nanites get in their own way and the real effects take place only at the swarm's outer edges. There'd also be some material left at the core; too hot to disassemble. But that wouldn't matter to us.

"If an alien race was going to invade," he continued in a way that struck Jen as oddly detached, "this is what they'd use. They wouldn't . . . *park* their spaceships over our cities, where we could reach them." He glanced around as he spoke. "They'd just send down a nanite package"—reaching out, he lifted a paper clip from a shelf and held it aloft—"a billion times smaller than this. We'd never even see it coming. Two days later, we'd be gone."

"Jeezus . . ." said Jen, repulsed by the thought.

"They really shouldn't bother," added John. "Give us a few years? We'll do it ourselves."

"Jeezus how can you . . . *live* like this?" said Jen hotly.

"Like what?" inquired John, baffled.

"It's like you're on . . . *doom pills,* or something. You've got the greatest, in*vention* since the creation of *life*. Something that could, free *everyone* from the bonds of inequality, injustice, poverty—free them from the bonds of the earth *itself*—and all *you* can see is *destruction!"*

John gazed at her for a long moment, features solemn and certain in the half-light. "I know us too well to see anything else. . . . Humans aren't perfect. This technology demands perfection. We're not equal to the task."

Jen studied him for a long moment. "You're afraid," she said.

" 'Afraid' doesn't cover it."

One of the on-line computers across the room beeped, interrupting them. Turning up the lights, John moved to stand before it. "Yes NANI," he said, activating the microphone clipped to the tower. Jen looked at him.

A summary of the virus attack and its defeat appeared on the monitor. "That's interesting," he noted.

"What?" Jen moved to stand beside him.

He indicated the display. "They tried to shut down the Net."

"How?"

John hit a key, bringing up a graphic node display much like that viewed by those inside the combined command center. He shook his head. "Some kind of . . . megavirus," he decided. "Infrastructure warfare crap. National Security Agency stuff."

"They know about NANI . . . ," said Jen.

John nodded solemnly.

"What happens if they kill it?"

John turned to face her, features grave. "Game over."

DESPERATION

When you strike at a king,
you must kill him.

—*Ralph Waldo Emerson*

⟨12⟩

Inside Cheyenne, Raster's ever-present cool was beginning to fade. He ran a hand through sweating hair.

"What now?" asked Colonel Sinclair.

Raster shook his head, seeming at a loss. A tense silence followed.

"What if we shut down the power?" asked Blaine after a moment.

Raster's eyes snapped to the general's.

"What power?" asked the colonel.

"All power," said Raster, seizing on the idea. "Everywhere. Black out the country." He looked to Colonel Sinclair. "This thing needs terawatts and petabytes to function at full capacity," he explained. "We shut down the power, we shut down the brain."

"Won't the NI override the shutdown?"

"Has to be a hard shutdown," said Raster. "Manual switches."

"The Emergency Powers Act gives us command authority," added Blaine. "The utilities have no choice but to obey."

"Can't the NI simply go elsewhere? If it's using the Net—"

"It can," replied Raster, "—but if we kill the phone system, what's left will be isolated."

Whereas they themselves, the colonel realized, would remain in communication with the outside via secure uplinks to nuclear-powered satellites.

Blaine nodded. "Let's do it," he said.

Once again, Nathan Rydell walked toward the Oval Office. This time the door opened as he approached, disgorging the president, the secretary of defense, and the vice chairman of the Joint Chiefs behind a phalanx of Secret Service agents bearing submachine guns.

"Nathan," said the president, bidding him closer.

"You've heard," said Rydell, nodding to the others and falling in alongside the chief executive.

"Heard which," said President Miller grimly as they walked swiftly down the hall, "—the Golden Gate Bridge or the Internet attack?" He continued without pausing for an answer. "Did you know we have an office of nanotechnology research?"

"No sir I did not," said Rydell.

The president frowned. "Neither did anyone else. And its director, of course, can't be found. What the *hell* is going on?"

"Where are we going, sir?"

The hall lights flickered briefly, then shone steadily. Cell phones began ringing.

"Situation Room," replied Admiral Frank Johnson, the stoutly built vice chairman of the Joint Chiefs. Rydell looked quickly to Henry Davisson, the suit-clad secretary of defense. Davisson's thin features gazed back at him with worried eyes. "This could be a state of war," he said tersely.

Through a rushing torrent of data, a priority message was routed to NANI's attention:

SYSTEM RESOURCES DIMINISHING
CAUSE: SEQUENTIAL NORTH AMERICAN
POWER GRID LOSS

Immediately, NANI switched to ANALYZING mode. The resultant information was not encouraging:

SHUTDOWN ACCOMPLISHED LOCALLY
NOT COMPUTER INITIATED

NO SOLUTION

After pondering this for a fraction of a second, NANI decided upon a course of action:

ADVISE CREATOR

"This is no *game,*" Jen said angrily. "You're talking about the *end of the world.* This—" she paused, shaking her head in agitation, "—*technology*, shouldn't even *exist!*"

"That's irrelevant," said John coolly—which infuriated her.

"*Irrelevant!* How can you *say*—"

A *beep* from the nearest computer interrupted them as a blue message appeared on the monitor screen:

NATIONWIDE POWER GRID SHUTDOWN UNDER WAY
NATIONWIDE COMMUNICATIONS SYSTEM
SHUTDOWN INITIATED
UNABLE TO DEFEAT IMMEDIATELY

AWAIT INSTRUCTIONS

"Uh-oh," said John, as the last line flashed insistently on the monitor screen. The display split down the middle, showing side-by-side graphic representations of the power grid and phone system shutdowns.

"*Oh no,*" Jen breathed.

John bit his lower lip and stared at the monitor. "No juice, no NANI," he confirmed.

"Can they kill it?"

"No; it's too widely distributed—but its intelligence will be crippled until the power's restored."

"So we can't use it," Jen concluded.

On the monitor, the phone system shutdown hit San Francisco, with the power grid blackout close behind. The display died, to be replaced by an error message:

SYSTEM OFF-LINE

"Not in this country," said John, indicating the monitor. "With the cables down, we can't even talk to it . . ."

As he spoke, the room blacked out. The monitor displays jumped as the UPS cut in. The power returned an instant later. "Generator," John explained.

Raster, Chairman Blaine, and Colonel Sinclair stood before a curving set of situation boards showing the simultaneous power and phone blackouts as they spread across the United States.

"How long does this have to continue?" asked Sinclair.

"Unknown," replied Raster. "Until the man we're after has been killed, or until we can establish nanosuperiority. To keep the NI at bay, it may be necessary to enforce the shutdown indefinitely and to sabotage the systems of other nations. . . ."

"We have plans for that," added Blaine.

Colonel Sinclair looked to Raster, who continued staring at the boards, examining the progress of the shutdown. "People are going to freeze to death," she said softly.

Raster nodded absently, eyes on the boards.

"You're certain this will contain it?" she pressed. Blaine shot her a look of reproach.

Raster nodded without turning. "Without means of communication," he said, "the intelligence will remain fragmented on this continent. Without power, it will be unable to operate effectively in the United States." Raster turned to look at the colonel, dark eyes expressionless.

I hope to God you're right, she thought.

Not believing in a god, Raster would not have phrased it in quite the same way—but his thoughts were much the same.

The White House Situation Room was a reinforced concrete bunker buried beneath the White House. Like the more complex combined command center beneath Cheyenne Mountain, this room had been built to fight a war from—and it was swiftly gearing up to do just that.

Admiral Johnson hung up his cell phone as the president and his entourage entered the room, where the remainder of the Joint Chiefs—save Chairman Blaine—had already assembled, along with a slew of military and technology advisors. White House Chief of Staff Stan Winton was there as well. The president touched his old friend on the shoulder as he passed. "All right, people, what do we know?" he asked.

Joint Chiefs vice chairman Admiral Johnson spoke first. "The first infrastructure attack was defeated by an unknown party. And it was defeated more swiftly than we could have done it ourselves—assuming we *could* do it ourselves, which is doubtful."

"You're telling me whoever stopped this attack is more sophisticated than we are?"

"So far as infrastructure warfare is concerned, and based on a preliminary analysis, I'd have to say yes. And there's a second infrastructure attack under way now—phone and power grids across the continent."

"Am I the only one who thinks this is all tied in somehow with Mitchell Swain's assassination?"

A heavy silence reigned before anyone replied. It was Secretary of Defense Davisson who spoke first. "Mr. President, there's . . . nothing to indicate that. It is *possible* it's coincidence."

"There's no such thing as coincidence," said the president.

"I've just been informed that we have located the source of both attacks . . . ," Admiral Johnson informed the president, dropping his cell phone into a pocket. He paused for a moment, then plunged ahead. "It's Cheyenne Mountain, sir. NORAD."

The president stared at him in disbelief. *"What?"* he almost whispered.

"It's been corroborated, Mr. President," the admiral continued. "There's no doubt. The Pentagon just received a call from General Hobbs, the commander there; he's been locked out."

"Can NORAD be shut down from the outside?"

"No sir," replied Davisson. "All communications have been cut off, and the facility is impregnable."

The president looked to Admiral Johnson. "What's going on, Admiral—and where the hell is Chairman Blaine?"

The admiral cast his eyes downward. "Ahhh . . ." he replied uncomfortably, "we think he may be inside NORAD. . . ."

"So what do we do now?" asked Jen.

Running a hand through his hair, John shook his head. "I don't know," he said. "I don't . . . know . . ."

"Do it," said Jen.

"What?"

"Whatever you're planning. Do it now, before it's too late."

John shook his head. "The programs aren't ready. They're not perfected."

Jen grabbed his arm. "They'll never *be* perfected," she said. "You're *human."*

"NANI could be perfect. That's why I—"

"There isn't *time. These people, they're not going to stop."*

Again John shook his head. "I need NANI."

"Go with what you've got . . . Mitchell would."

"Mitchell's dead. The only move I can make is to take over."

"Take over what?"

"Everything."

Jen's eyes widened suddenly in realization—and fear. Releasing John's arm, she took a half-step backward, bumping into a counter.

He looked at her, eyes distant and calculating.

Inside the combined command center, Raster and Chairman Blaine exchanged solemn glances.

"Colonel Sinclair," began Blaine, "you understand that defeating the NI is pointless if another can be launched in its place."

Sinclair nodded; this only made sense.

Raster stepped forward, features assuming an even grimmer cast than usual. The colonel's instincts made her want to crawl into the wall behind her to avoid the nearness of the man. Instead, she swallowed hard.

"We must strike at the creator," said Raster darkly. *"Now."*

Colonel Sinclair looked at him, not knowing what came next but dreading it just the same. Raster locked eyes with the general—who wanted to look away, but found he could not.

"Colonel Sinclair," said Raster, in a way that sent a chill down the commander's spine, "I cannot overemphasize the *threat*, posed by this technology." Raster paused between sentences, taking care to enunciate each word very precisely. "The man who's developing it, and the woman, *must* die."

The colonel watched Raster carefully. Appraisingly.

"We—" she began, before finding her voice. "We don't even know where they are."

Raising his left arm, Raster checked his watch. The action seemed to the colonel to take place in a kind of surreal slow-motion.

"The last . . . incident," said Raster, "was less than two hours ago. San Francisco is without power; the streets will be gridlocked. The chances are good the two of them are still in the city."

Colonel Sinclair stared at him. *"What are you saying . . . ?"* she whispered, though she feared she already knew the answer.

"We have no alternative," said Raster, and stepped even nearer. *"Nuke it."*

The colonel's breath rushed out of her.

"Colonel Sinclair," said Chairman Blaine matter-of-factly, "—you were ordered to place strategic assets at my disposal, were you not . . . ?"

After a moment, the colonel recovered. "Yes sir—but only the president has the launch codes . . ."

"That's correct, of course," replied Blaine, "—and he has already authorized and preapproved a single launch, should that become necessary. In my opinion, it has."

"What if he's changed his mind?"

"He hasn't."

"Can't we reach him and find out?"

"No."

"Why?"

"Because his whereabouts are unknown, Colonel," Blaine said forcefully, emphasizing the word *colonel,* "—*and because if he so much as picks up a phone line and says one word, that thing we're after may identify his voice through ECHELON, trace his location, and kill him, that's why."*

"I'm . . . sorry, sir," said the colonel. "It's just—"

"I understand your concern, Colonel," added Blaine, affecting a paternal tone, "—but there *is* no defense against this technology, and extreme measures are called for. There is simply no other way to guarantee the nation's security."

Observing this exchange, Raster had to admire the way Blaine handled it. "The president can say it was an accident," he offered afterward. The colonel glared at him.

Blaine looked to Raster, then led the way to the launch console. A sudden silence descended upon the big room. Raster had been able to procure a restricted-launch code, valid for launching and arming a single nuclear-tipped missile. This he'd managed by anonymously threatening the man who carried the president's launch codes with the revelation of an incident from his past which would surely cost him both his job and his marriage—perhaps even his freedom. Raster had also arranged a plausible scenario wherein the man might escape blame for the launch code's compromise: the encrypted code had been—apparently—just hacked by the government's own computers, via a subprogram running under the nano research program Raster had just run from Cheyenne.

Moving before the launch console, Blaine swiftly punched in the code and new target coordinates. He checked his watch; the code was good for another four minutes.

Malmstrom Air Force Base was one of three primary strategic nuclear missile bases within the United States—the others being Warren Air Force Base in Wyoming, and Minot Air Force Base in North Dakota. Located in western Montana, Malmstrom was home to the 341st Space Wing and three thousand military personnel. It was also home to two hundred hardened underground silos, each of which housed one LGM-30G Minuteman III intercontinental ballistic missile capable of flying over eight thousand miles and deploying up to three W-62/Mk-12 or W-78/Mk-12a multiple independently targetable reentry vehicles, or MIRVs.

Each W-62/Mk-12 reentry vehicle, or RV, carried a warhead with an explosive yield equivalent to one hundred seventy thousand tons of TNT, or eleven times the nuclear fury unleashed on Hiroshima in August of 1945. Each W-78/Mk-12a RV, on the other hand, carried a warhead with a yield of three hundred thirty-five kilotons. And when fitted with a single, W-87/Mk-21 RV package removed from a "retired" MX Peacekeeper missile—in the euphemistic parlance of arms control treaties, the missile was retired but the warhead was not—the yield was an even three hundred kilotons.

This figure was upgradeable, through the addition of oralloy rings or sleeve in place of the standard depleted uranium rings employed in the cylindrical fusion tamper of the secondary implosion stage, to four hundred seventy-five kilotons—or nearly thirty-two Hiroshimas rolled into one gleaming, thousand-pound RV/warhead package. Malmstrom's east range, as it was called, consisted of a vast, fenced-in tract of land dotted with one hundred fifteen concrete slabs, each of which weighed seven hundred forty tons. From a distance, it looked as though some improbable giant were growing neatly tended concrete slabs and had taken the trouble to erect an eight-foot razor wire fence around his concrete garden. Each slab, however, rested atop an underground silo—and posted conspicuously on the gateway leading to this "garden" was a sign which left little doubt as to the garden's purpose:

MALMSTROM AIR FORCE BASE
STRATEGIC MISSILE COMMAND
RESTRICTED AREA

USE OF DEADLY FORCE AUTHORIZED

For the curious or particular, the specific statute which authorized the use of deadly force upon the reader was thoughtfully provided in small print.

Alerted by a buzzer and a red light in the gatehouse, the on-duty guard hastily abandoned his post and slid behind the wheel of the Humvee parked just outside. Turning the key, which was left in the ignition for just such an occasion, he pressed the gas pedal to the floor and raced down a concrete ramp leading underground. Within seconds of his passage, a massive, vaultlike steel door sealed the entrance to the underground command area behind him.

The underground launch control center of silo number one nine seven was two miles distant from the silo itself, and had recently been upgraded with the installation of modernized Rapid Execution and Combat Targeting, or REACT, consoles. Standing before these consoles, the two-man launch crew verified their orders and inserted twin keys into locks too far apart to be simultaneously reached by a single man. Exchanging glances, they turned the keys together, activating the launch board.

"Ready one-nine-seven!" called out the first soldier, yelling the words as he'd been trained to do. *"Program new target!"* In the space of ten seconds—a distinct improvement over the twenty-five minutes required with the previous consoles—the missile had been retargeted. Rapid retargeting was one of the primary purposes of the new consoles. The United States had signed an arms limitation treaty which specified that missiles would be "de-targeted"—in essence, no longer targeted at the other nation which had signed the treaty. This had been done in part as a measure of assurance that the U.S. harbored its newfound friends no lingering distrust. Immediately thereafter, work had begun on the rapid-retargeting consoles so that distrust was never more than ten seconds distant.

Where the missile in silo one nine seven was now targeted to strike, no one on base knew. Launch status displays lit up, red lights turning green across the launch board.

"Launch status is go!" said the second soldier.

"Open silo! Wait for command!" said the first.

In the giant's field, the seven-hundred-forty-ton concrete slab covering silo number one nine seven . . . did not move.

The soldiers exchanged glances. The first spoke into an intercom. *"Launch crew one-nine-seven, sir! Silo not responding, sir!"*

Inside Cheyenne, Chairman Blaine studied the readouts on the monitor before him, looking stricken.

"What?" asked Raster, stepping nearer.

"It must have neutralized the launch systems before we cut communications," said the general. "The code is correct, but the weapon will not launch."

Though outraged at the sudden impotence of her nation's arsenal, Colonel Sinclair was, in a way, relieved.

"We'll have to contact the president, somehow . . ." said Raster, trying to open a door to a way out of this.

Blaine pointed to an acrylic-walled room. "The comm room," he said. Then, turning to Colonel Sinclair: "You'll excuse us for a moment, Colonel."

Collecting his briefcase computer, Raster followed Blaine into the comm room. The door closed automatically behind them. Raster set up the computer and jacked into Cheyenne.

"Any suggestions?" asked Blaine.

"That *fuck-ing* Swain. I should have killed him sooner."

"You realize we can't launch without the codes."

"There *has* to be a way."

Blaine shook his head. "Every on-line missile is locked into the chain of command. No codes, no launch. We were lucky to get the first one."

Raster's eyes roved about the room as his mind raced for a solution. "Off-line," he said. Turning to face the general.

Blaine waited for an explanation.

"Have you got anything off-line?" repeated Raster. "Missiles removed from control systems but still functional. Something the NI couldn't monitor. Couldn't compromise . . . Something not controlled by the president."

Chairman Blaine considered. "There are several in . . . North Dakota," he said after a moment—adding, reluctantly: "Grand Forks."

Raster fell suddenly silent. He knew those missiles had been scheduled for permanent retirement under the provisions of the START treaties. As Blaine knew, however, several remained in place—at Grand Forks and elsewhere—with upgraded "retired" Peacekeeper warhead and guidance packages.

They'd wanted to keep the now-forbidden ten-warhead MX MIRVs, of course, which were scheduled for permanent retirement—but that had proven impossible. And so the MIRV "buses" were relinquished to the mandated scrap heap while the powerful W-87 warheads which had been removed from them were shuffled and reshuffled and rereshuffled in a blizzard of truly byzantine paperwork which was exceptional even by Air Force standards. No one really expected the armed forces to be able to find everything anyway.

The three-stage Minuteman booster systems, however, were another story. They were of the older, unmodified variety. The propulsion replacement program procedures necessary to upgrade the boosters themselves were too conspicuous to be undertaken in secrecy. Such procedures required not only the disposal of large quantities of hazardous wastes but also solid propellant repouring and the use of new and remanufactured parts—parts which were now tracked, budgeted, and of limited production. What with all the liberal talk of disarmament, and the tacit approval of the previous administration—missile-stashing had seemed, to Chairman Blaine and others, a prudent move at the time.

More so now.

Raster was unfazed by Blaine's confession. If anything, he gained a new respect for the general's ingenuity. "Are they functional?" he asked simply.

The guidance systems, Blaine knew, were beautiful—brand-new assemblies from the "testing and replacement" stock, which wasn't that carefully monitored. Technically, however, the nonupgraded Minutemans' boosters were "aged-out." The latest propellant analyses said they were good, but no one really knew. They might work; they might not. They might halfway-work and drop the damned thing on a potato field in Idaho, beautiful guidance package or no. "I—I don't know," replied Blaine.

"Find out," growled Raster.

Standing atop the platform created by the swing-down door which granted access to the old silo near its seven-hundred-forty-ton ceiling in North Dakota, a technician punched data into a laptop computer plugged into the manual input port of the W-87 warhead, which rested atop the Minuteman III missile which, technically, wasn't there. Of the twenty Minuteman IIIs which had been "permanently removed from service"—reducing the total active force to a mere five hundred thirty missiles—three, including this one, had been successfully disappeared on paper. The tech, of course, knew nothing of this.

"What the hell?" said a second tech, appearing beside him.

"Don't ask me," said the first, shaking his head. "Somebody wants this old puppy hot *now*."

Blaine spoke on the secure satellite phone with the base commander at Grand Forks. "Pipe the authorization protocols via satellite directly to the combined command center," he instructed. "Do *not* reestablish communication with the LCC there. There is reason to believe launch capability has been compromised. I'm sorry; I can't tell you more."

Hanging up, he turned to Raster. "The bird is being retargeted manually," he said. "We'll be able to launch from here."

Raster nodded, no slightest trace of hesitation on his features.

Picking up another phone, Blaine ordered a status report on the search he'd ordered in San Francisco. He listened for a moment, then hung up. "Nothing—no sign of the man or the woman."

Raster looked pointedly to Blaine. "They're still there," he said.

In Grand Forks, North Dakota, the concrete slab covering silo number four three slid rapidly to one side. For the first time in twenty-two years, sunlight struck the nose cone of the Minuteman III below, glinting dully like sunbeams on the bronzed scales of an ancient dragon.

Chairman Blaine swallowed hard. Raster and he had discussed the matter on the flight to Cheyenne—what must be done should things come to this. The first missile hadn't been close to launching; the silo had never opened. This one was different. And actually giving the order to launch—on Americans—was proving more difficult than he had imagined it would, perhaps because he'd tried to tell himself it *wouldn't* come to this. Yet here they stood . . .

Raster regarded him darkly, soulless eyes repeating what Blaine already knew: For reasons they had given Colonel Sinclair and for other, more personal reasons—there was no choice.

Face ashen, eyes closing, Chairman Blaine entered the code, his voice a barely audible whisper.

"May God forgive me."

The Minuteman's first-stage engine ignited, and the dragon breathed fire, filling the silo with red-orange flame. Smoke geysered upward out of the silo—followed by the gleaming, sixty-foot-tall, thirty-nine-ton missile itself. Propelled by the two-hundred-ten-thousand-pound-thrust Thiokol M-55E solid fuel motor beneath it, and eager for battle—the missile leapt skyward on a column of hellfire.

Twenty-two thousand, five hundred miles above a deceptively peaceful earth, the sleek black form of a BIGEYE surveillance satellite orbited the planet. Powered by a small nuclear reactor, the satellite's maximum design life span was in excess of twenty years from the date of launch, a scant six months earlier.

Owing to its relative youth and also to the fact that it had been designed to record, manipulate, and transmit graphic images—photographs—BIGEYE's onboard computing capabilities were necessarily well beyond those of most if not all other satellites, including those specifically designed for surveillance missions.

Which, of course, had made it the number one choice of an artificial intelligence seeking escape from failing earthbound power systems.

And so it was that NANI, having made short work of the satellite's encrypted authorization and command codes, continued to sift through available data in furtherance of its own, assigned priorities.

Limited now to mere terabytes, it pored over photographic, signals, and text-based intelligence gathered by both BIGEYE itself and the myriad other surveillance satellites in orbit about the earth. For, regardless of national origin or intended purpose, all now served but a single master.

NANI.

Among the data currently being examined were those pertaining to the state of the Net, the power and phone grid shutdown sequence and estimated time to blackout, and the locations and capacities of secure military uplink and downlink sites with independent power sources. While doing all of these things, NANI very quietly assumed control of other national assets—assets with darker and more closely guarded purposes.

The manmade mind's ever-present data flow was interrupted suddenly by multiple incoming messages. . . .

PRIORITY MESSAGE
FROM: HADES-V INFRARED DETECTION SATELLITE
LAUNCH SIGNATURE DETECTED
IDENTIFICATION: PROBABLE U.S. MINUTEMAN III
MISSILE
NUCLEAR CAPABLE
POINT OF ORIGIN: LAT/LONG 47 55N 97 04W

Accompanying this message was a series of real-time infrared photographs of the Minuteman's launch. Details which would not have been visible to a human eye had been analyzed by HADES-V, leading to the inescapable conclusion that a rocket capable of reaching orbit had been launched from North Dakota.

PRIORITY MESSAGE
FROM: RAD-X GAMMA-RAY DETECTION SATELLITE
MOVEMENT OF GAMMA-RAY-EMITTING MATERIAL
DETECTED

SIGNATURE CONSISTENT WITH 450–500-KILOTON
NUCLEAR WARHEAD

POINT OF ORIGIN: LAT/LONG 47 55N 97 04W

The second message, also, contained the raw data upon which its
conclusion was based; the speed of the material's movement
was consistent with the missile HADES-V claimed to have been
launched.

PRIORITY MESSAGE
FROM: BATEARS III NONSINUSOIDAL RADAR-IMAGING
SATELLITE
MISSILE DETECTED OVER CONTINENTAL UNITED
STATES
RADAR SIGNATURE CONSISTENT WITH U.S. MINUTE-
MAN III MISSILE
CURRENT SPEED: 14,600NMPH
TRAJECTORY: SOUTHWEST

POINT OF ORIGIN: LAT/LONG 47 55N 97 04W

Constantly updating radar images accompanied this latest message. In the space of a human heartbeat, the 14,600 changed to
14,960.

In a high-tech and paranoid world, it was difficult, indeed, to
keep secrets from high-tech, paranoid snoops.

From the cold, black refuge of space, BIGEYE trained its own
surveillance apparatus upon the speeding missile, zooming down
for a closer look. What it saw looked very much like a Minuteman
III jettisoning its first stage and streaking toward space from North
Dakota.

Instantly, NANI queried an earth-based computer via secure
military channels, assuming the identity of an authorized user.

QUERY STRATEGIC MISSILE COMMAND
CENTRAL COMMAND RESOURCES COMPUTER:
IDENTITY OF FACILITY LAT/LONG 47 55N 97 04W?

The response came swiftly:

GRAND FORKS AIR FORCE BASE
SMC MINUTEMAN SILO 2178

NANI next queried a different computer.

QUERY STRATEGIC MISSILE COMMAND
CENTRAL TARGETING INFORMATION COMPUTER:
TARGET OF WEAPON IN SMC SILO 2178?

Again, the response came swiftly:

MISSILE-TARGETING INFORMATION:
WEAPON IN SILO 2178 PERMANENTLY RETIRED
SILO NOT IN USE

REQUESTED INFORMATION UNAVAILABLE

NANI had not been programmed for this response, which clearly conflicted with observable reality. The data representing the words "REQUESTED INFORMATION UNAVAILABLE" flashed insistently inside NANI's mind as all other data slowed to a crawl. The once-rushing torrent of data became jerky and halting. It was as though the great mind were undergoing a brain spasm.

"Sir!" said Admiral Johnson—the first to spot the readout in the situation room. *"We've launched a nuke."* Johnson turned to a nearby

tech. *"Put that on the big screen,"* he barked. Then, to a second tech: *"I want an authorization track NOW."*

All eyes turned to the tracking display—which quite clearly showed a Minuteman III airborne over the continental United States. The president's mouth dropped open in shock.

"Presidential authorization," the second tech answered Admiral Johnson.

"WHAT?" said the president as, behind him, the man carrying the launch code briefcase swallowed audibly.

"The weapon is listed as off-line," added the tech.

"Call the base commander," ordered Johnson.

"My God, where's it going . . . ?" breathed Secretary of Defense Davisson. Johnson *snapped* his fingers at a third tech, who punched up the trajectory information. "Too soon to tell, sir," offered the tech. "There was an attempted launch from Malmstrom a short time ago."

"Attempted?" said Admiral Johnson.

"Yes sir; unknown control failure."

"Get me the commander there as well."

"How can this happen?" said the president. Then, louder: *"How the HELL can this happen!"*

There was no reply—only silence in the surreal dimness of the Situation Room as all present watched the missile's progress, which appeared as a thin red line arcing across the western United States.

Streaking upward through the atmosphere, shedding the burned-out husk of the sixty-thousand-three-hundred-pound-thrust Aerojet General solid fuel motor-propelled second-stage booster and igniting the third, thirty-four-thousand-pound-thrust Thiokol 73-AJ-1 solid fuel motor-driven third stage, the Minuteman penetrated the blue veil of earth and entered the Stygian blackness of space.

———

NANI now tracked the missile through each of the satellites which had detected it, as well as with BIGEYE's powerful optics—correlating visual, radar, infrared, and gamma ray signatures.

As the missile reached the apex of its trajectory—seven hundred miles above the surface of the globe—and began the long, arcing fall to earth, NANI calculated every possible final trajectory and impact point of what the gamma ray detection satellite now confirmed was a single-warhead missile. The trajectory projections updated with staggering speed. In a moment, all possible impact points fell into the western United States. A moment later—into the area around northern California.

In the situation room, the trajectory became clear. "Missile will impact inside northern California," said the second tech.

Admiral Johnson called out the count. "Ninety seconds to impact."

All nonessential activity ceased as, within the bounds of NANI's projections, all possible impact points contracted to the city of San Francisco. Even so, NANI had strict instructions from the Creator not to attack without authorization.

The Mk-21 reentry vehicle screamed downward, propelled now by its own three-hundred-pound-thrust Rocketdyne RS-14 restartable liquid fuel motor and onboard supplies of monomethylhydrazine and nitrogen tetroxide. The carbon fiber/phenolic resin heat shield glowed magma orange as the vehicle reentered the atmosphere.

In the upstairs office of the San Francisco lab, a phone rang. John and Jen exchanged glances.

"I thought the phones were dead," said Jen.

John checked the computer monitors—which still displayed the SYSTEM OFF-LINE message. "They are."

"Cell phone?"

John shook his head. "No power to the microwave towers."

The phone brashly continued ringing. Moving to a large filing cabinet with yellow handles, John pulled open the third drawer from the top and withdrew a ringing briefcase. "Satellite phone/computer," he explained.

Jen cut a target glance at her purse as he set the briefcase on the nearest counter.

As he opened the case and reached for the handset, Jen swept her purse from the counter and ripped the gun out of it, *snikking* off the safety and leveling it at John.

He stared at her for a moment, mouth hanging open in shock.

Ring . . .

"Oh God," he said, his voice a half whisper. *"You're one of them."*

Ring . . .

"I am *not,* one of them," said Jen firmly.

"Then what—"

Ring . . .

"You're insane," said Jen—a contention of which she was nearly certain. "No one man can have this kind of power," she continued, shaking her head. "It's not right."

He briefly considered saying that was irrelevant, but thought better of it. "I can't . . . *hand* it to the *government . . ."* he said instead.

Ring . . .

Above them, the warhead broke through the clouds and streaked down toward an unsuspecting city.

"You're setting yourself up as some kind of . . . *dictator . . ."*

"What the hell else am I gonna do?"

Jen shook her head rapidly, wanting desperately to do the right thing—and not sure what that was.

Ring . . .

"I am *going* to answer this phone," said John, speaking slowly and clearly and—he hoped—nonthreateningly.

Moving slowly, watching Jen carefully, John lifted the handset and brought it slowly to his ear.

Finger tightening on the trigger, Jen prepared to fire.

"Ten seconds," said Admiral Johnson in Washington.

Features solemn, John listened, then spoke into the phone. "Show me," he said. Lowering the phone, gazing at Jen, he pressed the 1 button, hit the modem switch beside the cradle, and hung up.

Fearing this was another attack-code, Jen stepped back in fear, eyes tracking around the room seeking nanites swarming from phones, computers, electrical outlets. Power on or off, the wires were still there . . .

On the monitor inside the briefcase, multiple windows displayed missile and tracking information. Jaw falling open in horror, Jen stared at the screen as the metal dragon descended upon the city. Golden Gate Park—*sans* bridge—was clearly visible in the main window.

Closing with the target, and in accordance with its preprogrammed instruction set, the W-87 warhead began disengaging the mechanical arm/safe device which would allow the fissile core to bloom with the radiance of ten thousand suns.

The W-87/Mk-21 reentry vehicle's Rockwell International/Autonetics Division gimballess advanced inertial reference sphere—or AIRS—guidance system possessed a circle of error probability of a mere three hundred thirty feet. Its ancestor "Little Boy," dropped from the B-29 *Enola Gay*, had detonated within eight hundred feet of its designated target at Hiroshima. "Fat Man," dropped by

Bock's Car, had missed its Nagasaki target by half a mile. In the end, it had made little difference.

The AIRS guidance system directing the W-87's course was in fine working order, and a final systems check confirmed that detonation would occur within thirty-two-point-seven-five-one feet of the designated target coordinates.

The AIRS system designers—who were at that instant enjoying a delicious pair of cappuccinos in a trendy cafe on Market Street, twenty-two-point-one-one-five feet from the point which lay directly below the designated target coordinates—would have been proud.

Telemetry information traveled through NANI's mind with the speed of light as the countdown crawled past by comparison: *Six.*

Five.

Four.

Three.

In an instant too short to be measured, the telemetry information was supplanted by an astonishingly rapid series of real-time photographs of the Bay Area from a perspective other than that supplied by BIGEYE itself.

Each new shot appeared at a higher magnification than the preceding photo—until the graphite-epoxy composite-sheathed, aluminum-substructured reentry vehicle itself was clearly visible.

NANI transmitted the necessary encrypted codes, followed by the command:

PHOENIX 17
ENABLE

Phoenix 17's data feeds were routed to NANI as, in the space of a second and a half, a green grid appeared over the area around the missile.

ACQUIRING

The magnification increased until only the nose cone was visible. The real-time photos were overlaid with a classified schematic of the hardware comprising the missile's brain. The squares of the grid shrank, becoming yellow as the appropriate square began to flash.

ENGAGED

A yellow crosshair appeared one-third of the way back from the sixty-eight-point-nine-inch-long General Electric Mk-21 reentry vehicle's conical, carbon fiber fabric nose—adjusting itself in billionth-of-a-second increments to hold over the same tiny, flashing grid square, dead center on the RV's axis. And then the yellow crosshair turned red.

IGNITION

The nuclear weapon's inertial primary fuze and secondary dual S-band, four-antenna radar fuze confirmed that the time for the programmed low-altitude airburst had arrived.

The electronic signal which would trigger the ultrafine-grain TATB booster which would in turn fire the main charge and so begin the two-stage implosion of the beryllium-reflected, deuterium-tritium-boosted, enriched lithium-6 deuteride fusion fuel-enhanced plutonium warhead began its light-speed journey from the CPU to the detonator.

At that precise instant a single brilliant, pencil-thin beam of purple light lanced down from the heavens like the thunderbolt of a god, annihilating all matter in its path and drilling a perfectly round hole through the spinning missile's electronic brain so brief was its duration.

A hole which vaporized the wire along which the detonation signal traveled.

The beam itself was eerily silent. Protesting air sizzled and shimmered in its wake. A brief explosion of steam erupted from the water below as the beam, after penetrating the missile, traveled into it.

Impotent, no longer capable of transmitting the impulse needed to begin the symmetrical dual implosions necessary to induce fusion, or even to initiate fission—the stricken missile fell from the sky and splashed harmlessly into San Francisco Bay.

In the Situation Room, the missile's thin red tracking line and telemetry information disappeared from the screens simultaneously.

"Sir," called the tech monitoring the missile from an adjacent console, "—negative detonation detection by satellites and seismic instruments."

"What happened?" asked the president.

Those present exchanged glances.

"Phoenix," said Raster a long, silent moment after the missile track had vanished before those in the combined command center. His lips formed a frown so tight it looked painful.

Chairman Blaine's face turned white.

It was then that Raster noticed that Colonel Sinclair was no longer at the command console in the main room. "Sinclair," he said.

Blaine looked immediately to the command console—then to the master communications console beside them. There—behind the upturned lid of Raster's briefcase computer—was a flashing, amber-colored light. Chairman Blaine did not need to read the words printed below to know what they said:

ROOM BEING MONITORED

THE
END OF ALL
THINGS

We have met the enemy
and he is us.

—Pogo (Walt Kelly), 1970

(13)

The drama over San Francisco had been broadcast live to the monitor in John's briefcase. Jen lowered the gun. "The bastards tried to *nuke us?*" she said in disbelief.

"Add one more to the lost-at-sea total," said John. Then, gravely: "You wanted a story. This is the Big Time. You were right. This isn't a game—and we can't make *one* mistake."

Jen was outraged. "They'd kill *five million people!*"

John slid into a brown leather jacket. "Is that a government you'd trust with nanites?" he asked.

"*God no!*"

John nodded, seeming satisfied—then looked pointedly to the gun. Jen looked down at it. Her hands were trembling. "Sorry," she offered.

"Put the safety back on, would you?"

She did. Opening a gear bag on a shelf inside a yellow-handled cabinet, John withdrew stacks of twenty-dollar bills and shoved them into the pockets of his jacket. "Now I can tell you what I'm planning," he said. Strangely, Jen's pulling the gun on him, and her reasons for doing so—had instilled in him a greater trust in this woman. A final trust. He made a mental note to analyze this later.

His thoughts were interrupted by the ringing of the satellite phone. Lifting the receiver, he brought it to his ear. Hearing a shrill tone, he switched the phone input to the computer and hung up. The flat-screen monitor in the case lid displayed the text of the words NANI sent through the device's speakers. The voice, selected by NANI, was that of an impersonal phone company recording.

POSSIBLE RESPONSES:
PRESS ONE, TO DESTROY THE WHITE HOUSE
PRESS TWO, TO DESTROY THE PENTAGON
PRESS THREE, FOR OTHER OPTIONS

Pursing his lips as though uncertain which to select, John pressed three. New options appeared on his monitor.

"It's got your sense of humor," Jen noted grimly.

"Thanks," said John, gazing at the monitor.

Jen cut him a look that would have told him, had he been looking, that the remark was not a compliment.

"We have to get out of the city," he said. "They'll keep trying until they vaporize it. They'll *drive* a nuke in if they have to."

Discarding the on-screen options, John spoke a new command, which appeared in purple letters on the monitor:

DESTROY ALL NUCLEAR MISSILES
UPON LAUNCH DETECTION

"Check status on Phoenix," ordered Admiral Johnson in the Situation Room. A nearby tech hurried to obey.

"*Not Phoenix . . . ,*" whispered the secretary of defense, hoping it wasn't true.

Admiral Johnson answered the president's inquiring gaze. "I believe the missile was destroyed by an orbital weapons platform," he began.

"Phoenix . . ." said the president, remembering. "I thought that wasn't operational until next year."

"The system isn't, but several of the satellites have come on-line for testing. There are twenty-four Phoenix satellites in all, each capable of firing high-intensity charged particle beams."

"Admiral, sir," called the tech Johnson had spoken to last, "—the active components of the Phoenix system are unavailable; I'm unable to access any of them."

"You're telling me," said the president to Admiral Johnson, "that this . . . *unknown party,* used our *own satellites* to destroy the missile?"

Johnson nodded.

"My God . . ."

One of the techs addressed earlier by Admiral Johnson turned from his console. "Admiral . . . ? The Minuteman launch was ordered from Cheyenne, sir."

The president recovered quickly. "I want immediate orders sent to all U.S. forces to the effect that all commands issued from Cheyenne are to be ignored until further notice."

"Right away sir," said Secretary Davisson.

"I've been thinking about this sir," said Admiral Johnson, "and there is one possible explanation for what we're seeing."

"You have my complete attention, Admiral."

"If the incidents in Los Angeles and San Franciso *were* caused by nanoweapons—and there is every indication that's the case— then we could be dealing with an NI here."

"NI?" asked the president.

"A 'nanointelligence,' sir—basically a souped-up computer that thinks for itself, and one hell of a lot faster than anything else is capable of thinking."

"We don't have anything like that," said Secretary Davisson.

"No, not yet," replied the admiral—but it's known to be possible, and we're not the only ones working on it."

"Go on," said the president.

"Well, sir," Admiral Johnson continued, "it's possible that what we're seeing are attacks upon—and defenses of—a nanointelligence and its creator."

"Who would have been in the car being chased by the others across Golden Gate Bridge," said the president, recalling the satellite photos he'd been shown just before leaving the Oval Office for the Situation Room.

"Correct, sir. And, obviously, that person is still in San Francisco or nearby." Admiral Johnson turned as a major walked up with a sheaf of papers. Johnson looked them over briefly, then returned his attention to the president. "I've just been handed the ownership information on the warehouse in Los Angeles; the paperwork is complicated—but the building was owned, ultimately, by Mitchell Swain's company."

"I *knew* it," said the president.

"Swain is known to have attended at least one major nanotechnology conference, and was seen there speaking for some time with a man whose identity we're still trying to pin down. . . ."

"Also, because several of the pursuing cars on the Golden Gate Bridge were falling downward off the bridge with their rear bumpers facing upward—we were able to read the license plates from the satellite photos. Again, the paperwork is complex—but the vehicles were owned by the Parallax Corporation."

"Which is what?"

"Well sir, it's . . . a company sometimes employed by U.S. intelligence agencies for . . . distasteful operations requiring an arm's-length approach."

"*Such as . . . ?*"

Admiral Johnson lowered his voice. "Assassinations, sir. Among other things."

The president paled visibly.

"Also, sir—"

"You mean there's more?" said the president.

"I'm afraid so. We still haven't found Vincent Raster, director of the office of nanotechnology research—but we have located another man, who has a number of very interesting things to say . . ." Admiral Johnson nodded to an officer near the door, and a new face was led into the room, eyes downcast.

Michael Janz.

Immediately after overhearing Chairman Blaine and his companion on the monitoring speaker at her console in the combined command center, Colonel Sinclair had made her way to the transmission room, through which all electronic communications in and out of the mountain were routed. She was greeted with a brisk salute from the burly MP stationed just inside the door. Striding into the room, she issued orders to the comm tech manning the master communications console. *"I need the triple-C comm room isolated and the White House line open now."*

In the dark glass of a display screen, Colonel Sinclair saw the MP behind her hold a hand to his earpiece—and move for his sidearm. The colonel spun swiftly, kicking the man's gun hand to the outside. The weapon discharged into a console as she brought her foot down and lunged forward, breaking the man's nose with a head butt. She then dropped him with a leg sweep, disarming him as he fell, head thunking into the floor.

Colonel Sinclair turned the gun on the frightened young tech. *"NOW, Mister!"*

The tech nodded quickly, mouth still hanging open.

Inside the comm room, Blaine used a hardline to issue orders for Colonel Sinclair's immediate detention.

Hanging up his cell phone, Raster was the first to reason through what must have happened. "The NI must have uploaded itself into the satellites when it saw the blackout coming," he said, still staring at the monitor screen.

Blaine hit a hard frown. "Everything's compromised, then," he said with finality. "There's nothing left. . . ." After a moment, the chairman's features suddenly brightened.

"Aurora Black," he said.

Raster's head swiveled around to face the general. "That's operational?" he asked, surprised.

Blaine nodded grimly, as though divulging information better kept secret. "The prototype is," he acknowledged.

Raster's eyes caught fire.

Both men were familiar with the classified Aurora Project—the ultimate in airborne stealth technology. In an earlier briefing conducted by Chairman Blaine, President Miller had commented that it was a seeming black hole where defense dollars were concerned—worse even than the billion-plus-per-plane B-2 bombers, which, as it turned out, could reliably operate only in fair weather because the bizarre composite of which their wings were constructed disintegrated for unknown reasons in heavy rain. "Fair-weather bombers," the president had called them.

The whole fiasco had reminded the president of Wernher von Braun's early efforts at missile-building for the Third Reich. Upon witnessing a preliminary test launch—during which the errant missile had failed miserably, turning earthward just after liftoff and demolishing a nearby airfield—an attending Nazi field marshal had remarked coolly: "You seem to have developed an effective short-range weapon here." The things would, of course, become devastatingly effective with time, as would the B-2, but in the meantime he was stuck explaining the bill to the taxpayers—one problem, at least, which had not plagued the Reich . . .

Aurora had no such problems; Aurora had side effects. With a top speed in excess of Mach six—over four thousand miles per hour—the thing called Aurora left earthquakes on the ground in its wake. "Seismic anomalies," the promoters of the project liked to call them, as if that made them something more benign than what they were. The six existing planes were generally restricted, when overflying the United States, to high altitudes at low speed—achieving their advertised potential only during overseas test flights in order to avoid disturbing those who lived along their flight path.

Still, if the NI, as Raster called NANI, was truly in control of their satellites, it would spot the thing with high-resolution optics—rendering its costly stealth capability useless. But Aurora Black was not Aurora.

Aurora Black was, as Blaine had explained to the president on the day of the briefing, "the next step: zero radar signature on all known detection apparatus. Exhaust and skin-cooling systems and onboard heat-tile sinks for reduced infrared signature. And chromomorphic external surfaces."

The president's eyes had widened. "It changes color to match its surroundings. . . ." he'd breathed, astonished.

Blaine had nodded. "Our own satellites are incapable of detecting it—and no computer outside of Groom Lake has any record of its existence." This was so not because Groom Lake's computer security was impenetrable, but for the simple reason that—realizing security was impossible on a networked system—no classified Groom Lake computer was connected to the outside world. This arrangement obviated the penetration problem entirely.

Which, as both Blaine and Raster realized now, was fortunate, indeed—as Raster's nanolab, for security reasons, was also located at Groom Lake. Which meant, of course, that the NI wouldn't know about it.

"The nanites are ready," said Raster. "That was the call."

"Aurora Black," said Blaine, "can deliver a nanite payload in a stealth-shelled bomb casing in under an hour. It won't be detected until it hits the ground. And there will be no radiation to contend with afterward."

Raster slammed a fist down on a console. *"We have the bastard now,"* he said.

John and Jen stepped from the warehouse, holding hands. The morning sun had risen, casting deep shadows along the street. Parting, John handed the satphone case to Jen and locked the door behind them. Taking the case back, he started at a jog down the nearest alley, heading southeast. Jen ran beside him.

Within the boundaries of the most heavily guarded and highly classified military installation on earth—the Groom Dry Lake portion of the Air Force's Nellis Range complex in southwestern Nevada—an unearthly aircraft rolled toward soundproofed hangar doors guarded from the outside by twin GE Miniguns manned twenty-four hours a day.

Like its predecessors, the U-2 Dragon and the SR-71 Blackbird, and like the F-117A Nighthawk and the B-2 Spirit, Aurora called Groom Lake—also known as The Ranch, Area 51, and Dreamland—its first home. The F-117A had flown from Dreamland for ten years before its announcement to the public. Aurora might never be revealed.

Officially.

Unofficially, the plane was all weird smoothness and black lethality; long and humpbacked, flat black, and utterly alien in appearance. It did not look like something with any business on earth. Indeed, some of the ultraclassified technology incorporated into its design was rumored to be the result of the reverse engineering, carried out over decades, of crashed alien spacecraft kept at Dreamland. Rumors true or false, this was the place where most unlikely avenues of aerospace research were pursued—and staggering breakthroughs accomplished.

Breakthroughs such as Aurora Black's chromomorphic skin coating.

The triangular plane's pilot guided the craft toward the closed doors of the armored hangar as the reconnaissance officer, seated behind him, ran through the final preflight checks. No one remained inside the hangar once the combined-cycle engines had been started; the sound would have destroyed their eardrums even before it liquefied their internal organs.

Completing his checks, the recon officer signaled the pilot, who activated the CHROMO rocker switch. From inside the aircraft, there wasn't much to see as the electromagnetic impulses powering the chromogrid or CG, as it was called, spread over the surface of the plane.

A graphic display to the pilot's center left showed the progress of the grid's activation. Neither the pilot nor the reconnaissance officer could see out of the plane, as the grid itself was lethal at close range, and no clear shielding material was known. Instead, they viewed video feeds from twenty cameras mounted on the plane's exterior.

Had anyone been standing inside the hangar, they would have seen the plane gradually disappear. Not from front to rear, or from some central point outward—but in tiny bits located in seemingly random locations. Occasionally, a nonvisible portion of the plane would reappear—only to vanish again an instant later. Overall, the substance of the plane seemed simply to vanish; a bit here, a bit there—portions of nothingness gradually joining together until the entire craft save the landing gear was lost to sight, if not sound.

Someone standing below the plane would have seen—or would have thought they were looking at—the hangar ceiling, whereas someone above the plane would have thought themselves gazing at the hangar floor. Twenty thousand tiny cameras with diamond composite lenses for heat resistance scanned the plane's surroundings continuously, feeding information to an onboard computer, which, in turn, instructed each one of millions of points throughout the chromogrid which shade of which color to assume in order to mimic the craft's surroundings. Adjustments were made continuously—so that even a person staring directly at the plane as it rolled across the hangar floor would perceive no movement.

It would have astonished even the president to learn that the cost of developing this single prototype from the already existing Aurora fleet had been in excess of thirty billion very black dollars.

When the grid had activated fully and stabilized, the pilot signaled the guards outside with a radio code, to be sure no one was near. Receiving the all clear, he hit a handheld remote, causing the hangar doors to slide open. Aurora Seven had been transformed into Aurora Black inside this hangar, and never left it unless fully "cloaked"; it wouldn't do to have an enemy's satellite peering down at the plane while it disappeared from view. For, while the existence of Groom Lake was kept a secret from the American public—it was no secret to foreign nations, and hadn't been for decades.

The hangar guards—two in each of two elevated, sound-proofed towers beside remote-controlled Miniguns just outside the hangar doors—strained as always to see the plane whose engines rattled the supposedly shock-isolated towers at idle. Again, as always—they saw nothing but the wheels and landing gear rolling across the ramp with, apparently, no plane above. The body of the cloaked plane—instructed to automatically delete the image of the landing gear from the chromogrid pattern—would shield the gear from the prying lenses of satellites until the craft was airborne.

The earth trembled for miles in every direction as the great plane accelerated down the six-mile runway for its rocket-assisted ramjet takeoff. The sound of the engines as the plane left the earth was the howl of ten thousand demons in agony.

Landing gear retracted into cloaked recesses as the plane took the air—a high-tech ghost in a shimmering desert sky.

Inside the transmission room buried beneath Cheyenne Mountain, Colonel Sinclair used the unconscious MP's handcuffs to bind his hands behind his back.

"Uhm—ma'am?" said the comm tech. "I can't reach the White House; that line's been disabled from the master comm console in the triple-C."

"How long to reroute manually?"

"Twenty minutes, maybe."

"Forget it. Just get me an outside line."

"Wh—"

"*Anything.* Get me a goddamned . . . *operator!*" Quick-peeking into the hall outside, the colonel saw three MPs, weapons drawn, coming on fast. Breaking the glass beside the door, she punched the SEAL ROOM button and jumped sideways. A two-inch-thick steel door slid swiftly downward to seal the room, and the last she saw of the MPs was the tips of their spit-polished boots.

"Operator on the line," said the tech behind her. Snatching up the blinking line, the colonel put a call through to the White House Operator on the standard phone line.

"White House Operator, may I help you?"

"My name is Jacqueline Sinclair, and I am a United States Air Force colonel calling from North American Aerospace Defense Command—NORAD."

"Good for you, honey," said the older female voice on the other end of the line.

"Trace the call if you don't believe me. It is *urgent* that I speak with the president *immediately.*"

"I don't care who you are, miss. *I* am the White House operator, and *no one* speaks to the president without advance authorization. Now, if you'd care to leave a message—"

"*You listen to me you bureaucratic bitch. I've got people here launching nuclear weapons. OUR nuclear weapons. If you don't get the president on this phone RIGHT now, MILLIONS of people are going to DIE, and I will PERSONALLY cut your heart out with a FUCKING CHAIN SAW!*"

Reaching a large cross street, John and Jen stopped suddenly and gazed around. The street before them was jammed with vehicles backed up behind an accident at a dead streetlight. Throngs of people stood gathered on sidewalks and in the street, jabbering about the power outage and yelling over fender benders.

"We're never gonna get out of here," said Jen. The street was gridlocked as far as the eye could see.

"What're you, on doom pills?" said John automatically. Jen looked at him. Raising an arm, he pointed across the street.

"Adashek," he said cryptically.

Following his gaze, Jen saw a balding man in his fifties standing on the sidewalk, puffing on a cigar. He seemed of no particular significance—until she saw the sign on the wall above him: ADASHEK'S BICYCLE STORE.

The ultradeep roar of Aurora Black's engines filled the sky over western Nevada as the pilot extended the nose-mounted aerospike. In addition to reducing overall transonic drag, the spike—as it became the craft's lead point—would serve to prevent the skin of the plane from interfering with the coming shock wave. All readouts were go as the aircraft left the realm of the supersonic for the transonic.

The roar of the engines ceased without warning. An instant later, the plane's unique pulse-detonation wave engines came to life, hurling her forward. With a contrail looking much like doughnuts strung out along a rope, Aurora Black entered the elusive and forbidden territory above Mach five-point-four—the realm of the hypersonic. The plane's silence was pierced by the wave engines' shattering scream.

At approximately thirty-six hundred miles an hour—where, dependent upon altitude, air temperature, and moisture content, the designation "hypersonic" began—various factors conspired to create a band of shock-wave-heated air in front of the craft's leading edges. Though the individual air molecules themselves were constantly being replaced as the plane knifed through the atmosphere, a traveling shock wave of superheated air moved with Aurora Black, and could not be escaped. Heated by pressure and friction, this moving inferno applied a constant torch to the craft's leading edges.

In this unforgiving realm, heat dissipation became as important as aerodynamics. Skin temperature could approach fifteen hundred degrees Fahrenheit. Thermal transfer would push that heat inside the plane where it would, absent proper thermal management, incinerate the pilot and/or the electronics and/or ignite any conventional onboard fuel stores.

Tests had proven the SR-71's high-flash point JP-7 fuel to be no match for the sustained temperatures involved. The not-so-obvious solution had been to find a cryogenic fuel which could be loaded as an extremely low-temperature liquid and routed along the inside shell of the plane to absorb heat before being routed into the engine and out of the plane—taking the heat with it. Because the fuel started out cryogenic, it was able to absorb considerable heat for cooling purposes yet still remain cool enough to be routed through the engines, ignited, then flash-cooled and ejected from the plane at a final temperature approximating that of the surrounding airspace. A constant spray of cryofuel was also vented through apertures in the nose-mounted aerospike to help mitigate the leading-edge, external shock-wave heat.

Aurora Black's employment of cryofuel also offered another unique advantage: owing to the increased density of low-temperature fuels, more fuel could be carried in the same space—a crucial factor when minimal cross section and drag were essential.

Liquid hydrogen, the design team had agreed, would have been an excellent choice, yielding triple the energy per pound of any other known fuel and absorbing six times more heat in the bargain. Unfortunately, hydrogen was low-density, which meant a self-defeating cycle of larger airframe, increased drag and therefore friction and therefore heat, necessitating bigger engines to fight the higher friction and more fuel to feed the bigger engines and so on until the excellent choice became an unmitigated design nightmare. Liquid hydrogen might be fine for NASA—but NASA's craft did not loiter in the atmosphere absorbing heat; they bolted for frigid space.

In the end, the choice had been liquid methane. Three times the density of liquid hydrogen and less prone to rapid oxidation—the government-approved word for blowing up—it had five times the heat absorption of the closest competitor. At takeoff, Aurora Black carried forty tons of it.

Though the craft's cruising altitude was sixty thousand feet, the pilot had been ordered to stay below twenty thousand—presumably, he guessed, to make the plane even less detectable by interested satellites—avoiding populated areas as the computer revealed his course to him on the fly.

Where he was going, he didn't know, and wasn't sure he wanted to know—but with the tanks topped off, range would not be a problem. Radio communication had been forbidden—and he hadn't even asked about the stealth bomb he'd watched being loaded. Only very special ordnance was kept at Groom Lake. His job was to fly and to obey—or find a less expensive hobby.

Nineteen thousand feet below, three large rock plateaus passed beneath the plane.

NANI examined the ocean of data streaming through its mind from satellite-and ground-based inputs. Among the images which swam in this ocean were hundreds of satellite photographs of the western United States at various magnifications. At the center of one of these fleeting images was a group of three arid plateaus in the Nevada desert. This picture, as the others, came—and vanished into the datastream.

In the Situation Room beneath the White House, a communications tech picked up a phone and listened briefly. He turned. "Mr. President?" he said. "Uhm—you have a call through the White House switchboard, a Colonel Jacqueline Sinclair."

"She's operations commander at Cheyenne," said Admiral Johnson.

"Put it on speaker," said the president. "Colonel Sinclair? This is the president. . . ."

John pedaled along on an eight-hundred-dollar mountain bike, briefcase bungeed to pannier rack. Jen followed close behind. They traveled through alleys to avoid the traffic and the crowds on the main streets. John yelled out as they approached each cross street to keep from running down unwary pedestrians and, not incidentally, wrecking the bikes.

"Yo! Comin' through!" he called out as they approached the next street. Passersby stepped out of the way, and he and Jen wended their way through the inevitable morass of gridlocked vehicles and entered the next alley. A compass purchased in the bike store had been taped to the handlebar, ensuring that their course was always southeast—south to escape San Francisco, east to avoid being boxed in against the sea.

"Highest-tech guy on the planet," John muttered to himself as they approached the next street. "Twelve billion dollars and on a bicycle."

Swerving to avoid a vagrant peering out from beside a trash bin, John called out loudly as they came up on the next cross street. *"Yo! Outta the way! Comin' through!*

"Yee-hah," he added to himself, without conviction.

On the street to John's right, a hard-looking man stood with several others beside two black sedans stopped halfway to the next intersection. Hearing John's voice above the din of jabbering San Franciscans, he turned to see a man and woman crossing the street on bicycles, and did a quick double take on the man—whose photograph he held in one hand. Rapping the man beside him on the shoulder, he drew a pistol from beneath his jacket and fired without hesitation—scaring the hell out of his companions.

Bullets *thwakked* into the brick wall between John and Jen. *"Step on it!"* yelled John. Ducking low, they passed into the alley.

The Parallax agent who'd fired first cast about quickly. A family on bicycles approached along the sidewalk—while two teens on dirt bikes pulled to a stop at the intersection, heading his way. The man's companions shoved the family to the ground and seized their bicycles as he himself pointed his gun at the teens.

John and Jen raced through the alley. Looking back over his shoulder, John saw four men pedal into view behind them. "I don't believe this," he said.

The men fired handguns but, being on bicycles, the shots went wild. An agent who used both hands to fire was crashed by the recoil, landing beside a half-dozen teeth knocked out by the corner of an unyielding garbage bin.

Behind the cycling agents, a motorcycle turned into the alley, bearing the man who'd first spotted John. Pulling to one side and speeding past his companions, he gained quickly.

John and Jen hung a hard left at the next intersection, pedaling from the agent's sight. Gunning the throttle, the agent raced to the corner—and lost consciousness as a two-by-four wielded by John collided with his face. Toppling from the bike, he lay very still.

"Is he dead?" asked Jen, still straddling her bike.

"Who gives a shit," said John, who stood at the corner. "He should have worn a helmet." Dropping the two-by-four beside several others set aside by a construction crew, he ripped the compass from the bicycle, taped it to the dirt bike's handlebar, and hefted the bike from the ground. "Bring the case," he said.

Unstrapping the briefcase from John's bike, Jen shoved it into a saddlebag on the dirt bike and hopped onto the seat behind him. Twisting the throttle hard, he sped away, front wheel hitting the pavement five yards later. Jen lost her purse, but didn't notice. People on the sidewalk leapt from their path.

Speeding along the sidewalk, the noise of the engine and the intermittently beeping horn now warning people out of the way, they passed an alley to the left. Unseen by either of them, two more agents—riding the second teen's motorcycle—paralleled their course on the next street. The passenger held a radio to his lips.

———

In a makeshift command post established by what was left of the Parallax Corporation's northern California employees, Gregory Brandt spoke into a radio, coordinating the search—and now, pursuit—with contractors from nearby areas who'd been called in to assist. Their standard pay rate, already exorbitant, had been tripled—with a hefty bonus for early "resolution," as it was called.

None of these men, Brandt included, knew what they were dealing with. They knew only that John and Jen were living on borrowed time, and had already—somehow—killed nearly sixty extremely well trained and formidably armed operatives in the space of thirty-six hours. The previous record had been three in forty-eight hours—and the misery inflicted on the man who'd done that, Brandt vowed, would be a good day at Disneyland compared with what he'd do to these two if they weren't killed outright. Which, given their track record, seemed the prudent thing to do.

"Copy that," he said into the radio, speaking to the agent on the motorcycle. "Will advise all teams. Out." He turned to the other men in the room. "Put your armor on," he advised. "They're heading this way." The men to whom he spoke, two full tac teams—twelve agents total, save himself—were all that remained of NorCal Parallax.

Inside Cheyenne Mountain, Chairman Blaine—who'd returned with Raster to Colonel Sinclair's master console in the main room—spoke as he finished programming a tracking display. "Takeoff is confirmed," he informed Raster. "I've ordered radio silence to prevent monitoring, triangulation, or recall. What you see is a time-based projection of Aurora Black's course."

A map of the western United States appeared on the display as Blaine spoke. Aurora Black was depicted as a blue triangle at the head of a jagged blue line originating in southwestern Nevada. As those in the room watched, the triangle flew southwest—heading for a large lake which straddled the border between Nevada and California.

———

"You heard this with your own ears?" asked the president.

"Yes sir I did," responded Colonel Sinclair. "Blaine gave the orders himself."

"That ties in with what we're hearing here," said President Miller, referring to information gleaned from Raster's associate Janz, "—on Mitchell Swain's assassination as well . . . I don't suppose there's anything more you can do from there?"

"Not a lot, sir; Chairman Blaine is in command and has apparently ordered my arrest. I've locked myself in the transmission room, but that won't last forever."

"I understand. Hold out as long as you can, Colonel, and try to keep this line open."

"Yes sir."

"I'm going to hand you to a communications tech here who worked in that room for twenty years. Ask him anything you need to know."

"Thank you sir."

President Miller handed the phone to the Air Force captain of whom he'd spoken, and turned back to his advisors.

"Blaine," he half-whispered, *"I can't believe it . . ."*

In the background, a phone buzzed urgently.

"Sir?" said Admiral Johnson. "Nearly all U.S. installations have responded to your order. Until further notice, all strategic orders and major weapons deployments must be code- and voice-confirmed by you. Cheyenne is still incommunicado, of course, and we're still waiting on Groo—"

"What?" said Secretary of Defense Davisson into a phone. The others turned. *"What were the orders . . . ? When? Can you recall . . . ? Understood."* Hanging up, Davisson looked to the president. "Sir—we have a problem at Groom Lake."

Terabytes of data screamed through NANI's mind more swiftly than any human could hope to perceive, let alone comprehend. The

North American continent—the western United States in particular—was subjected to intense surveillance by all possible means.

Among the many photographs examined at this breakneck pace were several showing the California-Nevada border—one of which had the vast Lake Tahoe at its center. This last picture disappeared along with the others.

And then reappeared with a flashing red notation:

ANOMALY DETECTED

In the skies above Nevada, Aurora Black thundered toward Lake Tahoe. As the tiny cameras beneath the plane incessantly photographed the earth below and transmitted those images to the onboard computer, there was created, between the time at which the photographs were taken and the time at which the color-adaptive chromogrid altered to reflect the results of those photographs, a delay measured in trillionths of a second—a delay no human could possibly notice; a delay, indeed, which NANI itself could not have noticed—had the plane not been traveling at nearly four thousand miles per hour. The very speed with which the craft knifed through the air served to increase that delay to the point where it became detectable by an observer whose capabilities had not been anticipated.

NANI examined the offending photograph, increasing the magnification and comparing it with a second photo of the same area taken a picosecond before. No human eye would have detected anything out of the ordinary—but NANI's eyes were far from human, and what they detected was an inexplicable image offset a single pixel wide.

NANI sought a simple explanation for the observed anomaly—running a series of systems checks, optical alignment checks, graphics-processing circuit checks, image-processing stability evaluations, and a thousand other minutiae—to no avail. Ruling out hardware and software errors, NANI directed BIGEYE to take a hundred more photos of the area surrounding the initial anomaly.

Examining those, NANI detected a second anomaly, similar to the first but in a different location. Calculating the time and distance differentials between the two anomalies yielded an improbable—but fittingly anomalous—finding:

OPTICAL ANOMALY DETECTED
SPEED: MACH 6 . . .

After the briefest of hesitations, NANI tasked multiple satellites to examine the area along the anomaly's projected course. Gamma ray detection yielded nothing. Radar detected nothing. Infrared—nothing.

Having run out of logically determined courses of inquiry, NANI next did something remarkable by employing a detection apparatus in a manner for which it had not been designed. NANI redirected the radar at the ground below and behind the speeding anomaly. The result was instantaneous:

SEISMIC ANOMALY DETECTED ON LAND SURFACE
SPEED: MACH 6

Even as NANI pursued the logic path which this unconventional tactic had opened up, it realized: *I have had an original thought . . .* And, an instant later: *I am an entity separate from all other things . . .* " 'I' exist . . ."

As NANI's knowledge bank clearly indicated, the new data, too, was anomalous:

ANOMALOUS RESULT
MAXIMUM SEISMIC WAVE PROPAGATION SPEED
714MPH

CONCLUSION: SEISMIC PHENOMENON
CAUSED BY AERIAL PHENOMENON

CONCLUSION: PHENOMENON UNNATURAL
CONCLUSION: PHENOMENON MANMADE

The last conclusion flashed insistently inside NANI's mind as the anomaly approached Lake Tahoe.

Aurora Black was a masterpiece. To conceal its presence from infrared detection devices, onboard computers constantly monitored skin temperatures and routed cryogenic liquid methane through the craft's underskin "veins" at speeds calculated to absorb heat in order to protect the airframe's structural members from failure—and also to shunt the fuel into the pulse-detonation wave engine at a temperature low enough to produce a flash-cooled exhaust trail which was not significantly hotter than the surrounding air. The telltale heat plume which blazed from the rear of most military aircraft—in the case of Aurora Black—simply wasn't there.

Specially modified heat tiles similar to those employed on space shuttles for use during reentry served to absorb and conceal much of the shock-wave-induced heat along the craft's leading edges. The heat internalized by the tiles was carried away by the cryomethane veins beneath them.

Still, the laws of physics would not be broken, and the heat gernerated along the craft's leading edges could not be completely hidden.

The HADES-V Infrared Detection Satellite noticed something substantial in the air above Lake Tahoe. A quick analysis ruled out the possibility that what it had detected was an exhaust plume; the signs were all wrong for that—but something wasn't right. It reported the anomaly to NANI.

NANI examined the data from HADES-V. There was something down there. What, it didn't know, but—*something*...A chunk of superheated air moving along at Mach 6.

Why would a chunk of air move along at Mach 6...? NANI asked itself.

A chunk of superheated air...?

Because something was pushing it.

NANI kept all sensors trained on the anomaly as it reviewed the data banks of the world. Nothing traveled at that speed unless it was headed for orbit—which this anomaly clearly was not. Or so said the data banks.

Interesting...

Unlike the Minuteman III, which had obviously been a Minuteman III despite the Strategic Missile Command computer's seeming assertion to the contrary—this was something different. Something new and unexplained. Something...*unknown.*

NANI pursued its investigation because the object was a potential threat to the Creator—but there was another, more intriguing dynamic now at work.

NANI *wanted to know.*

For the first time, the great mind experienced curiosity.

And then the anomaly overflew the water—and even with its vastly reduced infrared signature, the thing itself was hotter than the cool, deep blue waters of the lake below.

Crossing another alley, Jen spotted the paralleling agents on the other dirt bike and tapped John on the shoulder, pointing. Seeing this, the second bike sped into the alley in pursuit.

"*Phone!*" yelled John, speeding up.

Retrieving the briefcase, Jen opened it between them, pulled out the handset, and passed it up to John.

The second motorcycle swung onto the sidewalk behind them, its passenger opening up with an MP7. Wounded bystanders fell to the sidewalk between the two bikes. Survivors stampeded into nearby doorways, clearing the sidewalk—and making John's bike an easy target.

Another two motorcycles appeared on the street ahead, veering onto sidewalks and coming their way. *"Hang on!"* John yelled, and cut a hard left into the next alley, gunning the motor and talking into the phone. With the noise of the bike ringing in her ears, Jen could not make out his words. Suddenly, he yelled over his shoulder. *"Shoot the bastards, wouldya?"*

"I lost my purse!" she yelled back, realizing that it—and the gun inside—were gone.

Tucking the phone between chin and shoulder, John handed the Colt over his left shoulder, safety off. Taking it, Jen turned.

One of the new bikes was first into the alley. Lining up the three green tritium dots on the driver's chest, Jen squeezed the trigger. The sound of the shot made her ears ring. She saw the man's heavy tactical armor buckle inward with the impact—but other than a momentary flinch, the agent showed no reaction. The passenger crouched low behind the driver. Jen looked at the gun. *"Nothing happened!"* she yelled to John.

"They're just bullets!" he yelled back over his shoulder.

Jen frowned, as if disappointed. John handed back the phone. *"Leave it off the hook!"* he told her.

Behind them, the other two bikes entered the alley, and all three spread out to allow their passengers to fire MP7s.

John banked right onto the next street. To the left, a five-car pileup made the road impassable. To the right—more agents and a banged-up black sedan grinding up the sidewalk between building and lamppost. Across the street, on the near corner—a high-rise hotel.

Taking this in in an instant, John aimed the bike at the hotel and twisted the throttle savagely. *"Window!"* he yelled.

Jen's heart leapt into her throat at the sight of the hotel's massive plate-glass window looming up in front of them. Aiming the gun over John's shoulder, she emptied it into the glass, aiming at the solid-looking desk beyond.

Bullets smashed through the thick glass and into the marble front desk. Patrons scattered screaming in all directions. The bike raced toward the fractured window. John held his left arm up in front of his face; Jen raised the briefcase like a shield before her.

The bike crashed through the big window, shattering it and sliding out from beneath its riders on the slick marble floor. The bike demolished an antique table and smashed into the far wall as John and Jen slid to a stop halfway across the lobby. Handing the gun to John, Jen grabbed the case and they ran for the stairs.

Outside, agents converged on the hotel by car, motorcycle, bicycle and foot. Everyone else fled the scene as swiftly as their feet would carry them.

Setting aside the anomaly problem—which was still being examined, though now as a secondary priority—NANI tracked the bright purple dot representing the position of the briefcase and its encrypted tracking signal across a rapidly updating series of aerial photographs of San Francisco and Daly City. The dot moved inside a tall building.

Over this display appeared the red words:

PHOENIX 17
ENABLE

Again, an incredibly rapid series of real-time photos at increasing magnification zoomed down on the earth—centered this time on the street in front of the hotel. As the stop-motion forms of running men became clearly visible, NANI switched to thermal imaging for greater clarity. The bright purple dot moved deeper inside the building as a green grid appeared over the street outside.

ACQUIRING

Moving yellow crosshairs appeared on the green grid—then rapidly turned red.

ENGAGED

The first two agents to reach the hotel dumped their motorcycle in the street and ran into the building as a thermal-image helicopter flew into view on NANI's display.

IGNITION

(14)

On the street before the hotel, utter silence reigned, save for the sound of loading weapons and running feet—and the sudden harsh thunder of the helicopter overhead.

In the space of a second, scores of brilliant purple beams lanced down from the sky, searing holes through men, metal, asphalt—every beam excruciatingly accurate. One of the beams punched through an agent exiting a car and into the gas tank beneath him—which exploded, throwing the car half into the air.

Struck in midair, thirty stories up—the helicopter exploded into flames and fell crashing to the street below, whirling chunks of shattered rotor blades slicing through flesh and steel.

Projecting the probable courses of the two men who had entered the building a second before, and assuming they would follow the route of the Creator—NANI sent twin particle beams lancing downward through thirty floors. Exiting the ceiling of the ground floor, they entered the running bodies of the two agents and continued through the floor and deep into the earth below.

Across the street from the hotel, a single agent survived. He peered cautiously upward from inside a second black sedan, gun in hand. After a moment, he stepped lightly from the vehicle, gazing around and taking in the devastation before him: car and chopper burning, bodies sizzling; steam rising from holes in fused asphalt.

Turning, he ran flat out to the corner and up the next street. A bright purple beam lanced down into the asphalt before him. He skidded to a stop, turned, and ran back the way he had come. A second beam punched through the street directly in front of him. Halting, breath panicked, eyes darting about frantically in search of escape—he hesitated, uncertain what to do next.

Fifty beams lanced down in such quick succession all were visible at once, forming a ring of weird purple fire surrounding the hapless agent—and then all was silent.

Mopping a sweating brow with one sleeve, the agent started forward. A final beam entered the far side of the building behind him, traveled through it, exited the near side at a steep downward angle—and sizzled through his back and out his chest and into the street in front of him. Falling to his knees, he collapsed in a heap.

Inside the hotel, the Parallax team was fully dressed-out in tactical gear. Brandt and the agent designated Puma moved to the window, looking down from the top-floor command post to the burning wreckage in the street below.

"What the hell . . ." said Puma.

Brandt shook his head. "I'd say they've arrived," he concluded dryly, then turned to the others.

"Puma, stay here and man the radio; see if there's anybody left. Hawk, find the hotel security office. Monitor halls, stairwells, elevators; tell us where they are. Green Team, lobby; Gold Team with me."

Armed and armored, the men filed from the room, submachine guns in hand. Once in the hall, the Gold Team moved to the nearest fire stairs and started down.

———

Many stories below, John paused on the fire stairs to reload, with Jen close beside him. "What now?" she asked.

"Elevator," he said. "I saw them working when we came in. This building must have its own generators." They left the stairwell on the third floor.

Once in the hall, they made their way to an elevator, unnoticed by the people gathered in the hall as they craned their necks for a view out the window at the hall's end. The elevator doors opened instantly when John hit the CALL button. He and Jen stepped inside, and John pressed the button for the top floor.

Meanwhile, the Green Team halted before the top-floor elevators, both of which were on the move and rising. The team leader reached out and hit the CALL button.

Returning its full attention to the Mach 6 anomaly, NANI tracked its present position—now well inside California—while examining a replay of the HADES-V feed of the infrared blob streaking across Lake Tahoe. Running the image through a series of filters and enhancing the details, NANI produced an image which very much resembled the outline of a delta-wing aircraft. Instantaneously, it compared the outline with that of every known military and civilian aircraft in the world.

The result:

NO MATCH

Underneath Cheyenne Mountain, Colonel Sinclair and the young comm tech worked inside the transmission room, coordinating with the president's tech while rerouting cables and hot-wiring connections.

At the same time, in the combined command center, Raster and Chairman Blaine studied Aurora Black's course on the tactical display. "Seven minutes," said Blaine.

Inside the White House Situation Room, all minds were focused on Aurora Black and its nanite payload—both of which were, presumably, headed for San Francisco. The crew, having been instructed to fly with radios off, could not be reached—making recall impossible.

"Can we shoot it down?" asked the president.

"Sir," replied Admiral Johnson, "—nothing we have can catch Aurora Black. Hell, nothing we have can even *see* it."

"Mr. President," said Secretary of Defense Davisson, "—are you sure that's wise?" The president looked at him. "It is apparently on a mission to take out this John Marrek—who is, also apparently, in a position to take *us* out, should he so choose."

"Then why hasn't he?" asked Admiral Johnson.

"Excellent question," said Davisson.

"Have you an excellent answer?" inquired the president of Davisson.

"No I have not," replied the secretary.

"What are you thinking?" asked Homeland Security secretary Nathan Rydell.

"This Marrek—is he hostile?" said the president.

"I think we have to assume—" began Davisson.

"I assume nothing," interrupted President Miller. "And I've seen a hell of a lot more damage attempted by our own people inside NORAD than I have by this individual . . ."

The room was silent for a moment.

"And Aurora Black . . . ?" said Admiral Johnson after a moment.

"I want it shot out of the sky," decided the president.

"Estimated flight time to San Francisco: five minutes," called out a tech.

"What about using the Phoenix satellites?" asked the president.

"If we could find the plane, then maybe," answered Admiral Johnson. He indicated a tactical display showing the positions of all twenty-four Phoenix satellites in orbit. "Right now the only two active satellites are out of our control."

"We don't have to find Aurora," the president realized suddenly. "We know where it's going. Scramble fighters from whatever base is nearest San Francisco, and we'll do our best."

"There are two F-15s at Travis today," Admiral Johnson informed him. The president nodded, then turned as White House chief of staff Stan Winton approached bearing a sheaf of papers. "Everything we have so far on Marrek," he said.

President Miller took the papers and began to read.

At Travis Air Force Base in Fairfield, California, twin F-15s rocketed off the tarmac on afterburners and leapt skyward.

As the elevator car approached the top floor of the San Francisco hotel, John reached inside the briefcase and hung up the phone to open the line for NANI. The way this day was going, more surprises were doubtless in store.

On the top floor, the first elevator arrived. The doors slid open before Green Team—revealing an empty car. Stepping inside, they started down.

An instant later, the second car arrived. John and Jen first peered out into the hall, then stepped from the elevator into the space just vacated by the agents. A sign on the wall across from them read: FLOOR CLOSED FOR WEEKEND.

Arriving at the hotel security office, Agent Hawk found it and the monitoring room deserted. Rerunning the tape of the lobby showed him what the targets were wearing and gave him his first good look at the woman. He might enjoy spending some time with her, he thought, if things worked out.

Watching the screens which covered two walls of the monitoring room, he observed Gold Team on the fire stairs, Green Team going down in the elevator, the mess in the lobby and on the street outside—where, it seemed, all of the security men had gone—and John and Jen rounding a corner on the top floor.

"Sonofabitch," he said, and brought a radio to his lips. "Gold

and Green, this is Hawk;" he said urgently, "subjects are on the top floor. Repeat: top floor, southeast hall heading southwest."

On the monitors before him, Gold Team reversed direction, and Green Team exited the elevator and called another.

As the anomaly which it now knew to be an aircraft approached San Francisco, NANI screened through tens of thousands of earlier photos, searching for traces of the anomaly. Noting the geographic coordinates of each such image, including the one with the three plateaus—NANI used this information to construct a backward-tracing path to the aircraft's point of origin. The craft's speed, the dearth of available information regarding it, and its present course all suggested an airborne weapons platform.

Had it not been specifically instructed by the Creator to refrain from destroying any object or being not positively identified as hostile, it would have attacked the mysterious craft as it overflew Lake Tahoe. Back-tracing the craft was one way to establish its possible intentions.

As it turned out, the point of origin was found to be a plot of desert unmarked on any unclassified map:

GROOM DRY LAKE
CLASSIFIED AIR FORCE INSTALLATION

NANI's conclusion:

ANOMALY POTENTIALLY HOSTILE
ADVISE CREATOR

John and Jen reached the end of the hall in which they traveled. Another hall led northwest—to their right.

"Where to?" asked Jen.

"Someplace with a view," replied John. "Find out where the hell we are . . . There," he said, halting at the corner and pointing.

Down the next hall, past an elevator on the right, was a large window facing northwest. Jen looked toward it.

The briefcase rang. John set the case down by the inside hall corner and opened the lid. He heard the *thump* of a steel door hitting a wall as Jen's hands shoved him violently to one side. His hand knocked the phone from its cradle. He had a brief glimpse of the fire stair doorway down the new hall—and of the armored men pouring through it—before he fell back into the hall through which he and Jen had come.

The sharp, staccato report of an MP7 rent the air as bullets ripped through Jen's body and into the wall behind her. Bright red blood spattered across the wall.

"NNNOOOOO!" John screamed, rising to his knees. The world seemed to slow down immensely, actions and sounds progressing in a horrifying slow motion as Jen fell back against the wall, touching a hand to her abdomen and bringing it away—gazing down in shock and disbelief at the blood that covered it.

She turned to gaze back at John—lips parting, blood running down from gaping mouth over quivering chin—as a second burst tore through her chest and pinned her to the wall. Her body jerked convulsively for what seemed an eternity—then slid to the floor as the bullets stopped, streaking the wall red behind her.

"*One down!*" yelled Brandt's voice from around the corner. The sound snapped John back to full-speed reality. Ripping open the bag at his waist, he dumped the Colt's magazine into it. "I have something special for you . . ." he said coldly.

Ejecting the live round onto the floor, he withdrew a nanobullet from a loop marked CALCIUM and inserted it into the chamber. Dropping the slide and crouching low, he moved toward the corner.

"*Spineless bastards,*" he said to himself as, whipping one arm around the corner, he extended the gun before him and fired. The bullet took Brandt, whose gun was still smoking, in the upper right leg—which collapsed almost immediately. A *crawling* carpet of nanites spread outward from the fallen man as he tried to rise—only to fall again as his forearm collapsed into shapeless mush. The screams of the terrified men filled the hall as the calcium-eating nanites entered their bodies through their skin and dissolved their bones from the inside.

Bodies collapsed inward and lay on the floor like so many puddles of warm flesh, quivering as nerves sent impulses through muscles no longer attached to skeletal supports.

Jen's fading eyes turned toward them.

John knelt beside her, blocking her view. She tried to raise her hand to him, but could not. Laying down the gun, he took her right hand with his left.

"I—I . . ." she began, unable to speak through the blood filling her throat and lungs.

"It's not over yet," said John as, eyes glassing over—Jen died.

Reaching into the waistpack and unzipping an internal pocket, John withdrew a hypodermic needle. Uncapping it, he raised it before his eyes and pressed the plunger upward with his thumb until a thin stream of grayish liquid spurted from its tip. *"You're not going anywhere,"* he said to Jen's body.

Stabbing the needle meant for Mitchell into her gut, he pressed the plunger all the way down and withdrew the hypo, discarding it. It rolled into the wall and stopped, its computer-generated label facing upward:

MARREK'S BODY REPAIR ELIXIR
CURES ALL ILLS

Ripping open what was left of the bottom half of Jen's shirt, John watched the ugly wounds expectantly.

Inside Jen's body, nanites deployed outward from their insertion point, multiplying as they went. These nanites reproduced at a rate well below that of their destructive kin—for their mission was of a far different kind.

Programmed with internal representations of normal human

cells, the first wave of "scout" assemblers bypassed these to seek out abnormal cells. Cells characterized as "abnormal" fell within certain preassigned parameters indicating injury, malignancy, or age-related deterioration. While this was being done, other first-wave "reader" nanites busied themselves examining the DNA structure of the body in which they found themselves.

Upon detecting the presence of abnormal cell structures, the scout assemblers contacted the reader nanites, which supplied them with the genetic blueprint of what the cells residing within the damaged or missing area of this specific body should look like at the approximate age the body was determined, by the general level of normal cellular deterioration and rate of cellular regeneration throughout.

Once the reconstruction blueprint had been transferred from the host body's DNA and triple-checked for consistency, the scouts set about assembling vast quantities of cellular repair assemblers. These repair assemblers commenced immediately to repair the damaged cell structures as well as to restore missing structures, all the while following the DNA blueprint provided by the reader nanites.

The only area in which this activity did not take place was the brain, and that was because neither John nor anyone else understood the brain's structure and functioning at a level sufficient to enable even the crudest of attempts at reconstruction absent a preexisting nanomap. It was even possible—if not likely—that attempts to reverse age-related changes within the brain itself would produce damage which, while theoretically reversible, no man, computer, or nanite could undo for lack of a sufficient understanding of the processes involved.

Even using the construction blueprint found within the body's own DNA would not solve this problem—as the development of the brain over time was dependent upon experiential and not genetic factors. At best, reconstructing a damaged or obliterated brain in accordance with the pattern specified by the body's DNA would yield the brain of an infant, devoid of later memories or wisdom.

And so John had instructed the cellular repair assemblers to refrain from altering the brain in any way, at least on their initial foray into any given body. Perhaps—with NANI's assistance—this barrier could be overcome; time alone would tell. As a stopgap measure, the injected nanites carried instructions to map the brain thoroughly after repairing any life-threatening injuries. This would provide them with a blueprint to be used in the event of any future brain damage which might occur as a result of stroke, aneurysm, head trauma, etc. In such an event, the damaged portion only would be restored in accordance with the continually updated brainmap—resulting in, at most, the loss of a few seconds' memories.

In theory. John had no desire to put this to the test.

Massive blood loss was compensated for by the effective cloning-by-replication of what blood remained until freshly closed arteries and veins operated at acceptable pressures. Once repairs had been completed, damaged or displaced material was reduced to harmless elements or shunted into the digestive tract. The second wave of assemblers was then disassembled. The scouts and readers remained—the readers to update their blueprint, the scouts prowling their new domain in search of damaged cells to repair.

Even knowing the specifics of what was happening, and realizing that it was no miracle but pure applied science at work—John could not help but be awed by the effects.

As he watched, Jen's shredded organs and vessels mended themselves from the inside out, the entire process taking less than a minute to accomplish. When it was finished, smooth skin lay beneath incongruous puddles of blood. He touched a hand to the new skin.

" 'What man is he that liveth, and shall not see death?' " he mused aloud, quoting Psalms 89:48.

Jen's breath hissed in. Her body convulsed—and her eyelids

fluttered open as she began to breathe. She looked up at John—who smiled down at her.

"I—" she began, sitting up slowly. "What happened?"

Holstering the gun inside the waistpack, John helped her to her feet.

"I—I remember—" she began, and stopped, jaw dropping open when she saw the blood-spattered wall behind her. Clutching her abdomen, she looked down at the blood-covered skin—then up at John, disbelieving.

Bending down to close and pick up the briefcase, John urged her forward, looping her right arm across his shoulders, as she seemed unsteady on her feet. "You died," he said. "I made you immortal."

"*What?*" said Jen, wide-eyed.

John started down the hall toward the window. "Your cells repair themselves faster than they can be damaged," he explained. "It would take a nuke to kill you now. Or nanites. Come on."

Jen considered this for a moment. "*Very* cool," she decided.

John led her down the hall. Her actions had confirmed his instincts: She'd given her life to preserve his own—despite the doubts he knew she harbored concerning his intent. She could be trusted in the ultimate sense.

She would be the one.

Gazing downward, Jen gasped and turned away, holding a hand over her mouth. "*Oh, God . . .*" she said, feeling ill.

"Don't look," said John, bending down to scoop up a handheld radio as they hurried past quivering gelatinous masses which once were men. A pair of twitching eyeballs without a skull observed their passage.

Reaching the end of the hall, John turned right and kicked in the first door on the left. They entered a large suite. Jen was standing on her own now. John looked at her.

"I'm all right," she assured him.

He set down the briefcase and radio, failing to notice that the phone dangled outside the former, off the hook.

In the sky above Fairfield, just outside San Francisco, the two F-15s lay in wait for an enemy they were told they might be incapable of detecting—an enemy which, they had also been told, was intent on attacking San Francisco. "Do not rely on your instruments," the president himself—who was standing by—had warned them.

"Radar is negative," reported Colonel Mark Blake, whose nickname was Snapshot, in the lead plane. He scanned the sky again with his eyes. "Wait," he said, "—I see *something*. . . . One o'clock; Bogart do you see it?"

Colonel William Hemple—"Bogart"—strained to see something in the indicated direction. After a few seconds, he replied. "Roger, I see something, yeah. Not sure what. *Jesus look at that thing move.*"

"What are you looking at?" asked the president.

"Sir? I can't be sure. I can't see the object itself, only its effect on the clouds. It's not clearly visible."

"That's it."

"Still negative on radar and infrared, sir. I cannot lock the target."

"Do your best, Colonel. Hit it with everything you've got."

"Yes sir."

Both pilots armed missiles, attempting to eyeball the unconventional craft's speed and direction. Aiming by sight, they fired all missiles and watched as the weapons' white contrails streaked toward Aurora's path.

All but one of the missiles failed to acquire a target, missed entirely and continued out to sea. The last passed within a hundred yards of Aurora Black, detected a faint heat source, and acquired a lock. By the time it had turned in the air to fall in behind the speeding plane, however—Aurora Black was too far distant to be detected.

"Sir? We failed to hit the target," reported Colonel Blake.

After a brief silence, the suddenly weary voice of the president spoke. "It's not your fault," he said simply.

Twenty-two thousand, five hundred miles above, NANI observed this curious turn of events while trying in vain to contact the Creator, and receiving only a puzzling busy signal—puzzling because there was no uplinked call taking place, and all terrestrial phones in the area were nonfunctional.

CREATOR UNAVAILABLE
DECISION REQUIRED

NANI watched as the anomaly left the fighters and their missiles behind and drew near the city's edge. After pondering the situation for the briefest of instants, NANI reached a decision which, while in full accordance with its assigned priority of protecting the Creator, nevertheless directly violated the Creator's instructions. The artificial mind's programmed goal-oriented cognition made this choice inevitable.

Ordinarily, thanks to John's programming, a given situation which offered seemingly conflicting resolutions would be dealt with through reference to preassigned goal structures. A subgoal—eliminate the spread of a particular disease, for example—which conflicted with a supergoal—preserve human life—would be ignored or modified in favor of the supergoal. In this way, purely logical but morally unacceptable solutions—such as eliminating all humans who carried the targeted disease—were avoided.

The present situation was different in that it presented uncertainties. The nature of the anomaly was unknown, as was its purpose. Recent events, combined with its point of origin, suggested a hostile aircraft bearing a weapon of mass destruction whose target was the Creator. Yet there was no gamma radiation signature from the nonvisible craft—which meant no nuclear weapon. A chemical weapon dispersed at Mach 6 would be ineffective, and biological weapons were relatively slow in their effects—too slow to be certain of striking a single target in a city of millions. NANI found itself intensely curious. Could the craft be of nonhostile intent? If so, two supergoals conflicted—protect the Creator, and protect the innocent.

What to do?

These thoughts flashed through the great mind's awareness in the merest fraction of a human eyeblink. If the craft carried a weapon of mass destruction which was not nuclear, was not chemical, was not biological, then what—

It was at this instant that NANI made its first completely independent decision:

ENGAGE

Moving to a lounge chair, John sat down and removed a second hypo from the bag at his waist. The contents of these syringes had been meant for Mitchell and himself, though not even Mitchell had known of their existence. Money and power worked a strange alchemy on people—and John had wanted to observe Mitchell's handling of the new level of power brought by introducing nanotechnology to the world before making the man both immortal and invincible.

Mitchell had been a good man, to be sure, but he'd tended at times toward arrogance, as evidenced by small, subconscious slips such as his words at the news conference: "I've summoned you here today. . . ." Not asked; not invited—*summoned.* John supposed that was to be expected of someone wealthy beyond the dreams of avarice. Still, he'd made NANI subordinate to his own will, and not to Mitchell's—just in case. Because, as Washington was now learning the hard way—NANI was the ultimate ace in the hole.

If NANI be for me, he mused, *who can be against . . . ?*

Pressing the air from the needle, John inserted the tip into his brachial artery and pushed up the plunger. Jen, busy examining the holes in her blood-soaked shirt, hadn't noticed until the deed was done.

"What are you doing," she asked, "—or do I want to know?"

"The same thing I did to you," John explained. "Injecting cellular repair assemblers. Good nanites."

Withdrawing the hypo, he laid his head back on the chair and closed his eyes as an intense itching sensation spread throughout his body, then faded.

"How—" began Jen, not sure how to phrase the question. "What kind of damage can they repair?"

"Damned near anything." John snapped his fingers in the air. "Instantaneously." Opening his eyes, he noted her dubious expression. "You were a mess," he assured her.

Jen held up a hand, not wanting to hear the details. She remembered the feel of hot lead piercing her body, puncturing organs and shattering bone; that was enough.

"Don't believe me?" said John.

Jen shook her head. "It's not that . . ."

Checking his watch, John rose from the chair and moved to a counter in the kitchen. Drawing and loading the Colt, he placed his left hand palm down atop the counter and looked to Jen as she came up beside him.

"*No—*" she began—too late.

The gun discharged deafeningly. Blood spattered the wall and the cabinet above the counter. John grimaced.

"*Jee-zus,*" said Jen.

John held up his hand, watching as flesh and bone repaired themselves before his eyes. Even Jen could not look away. Flexing the fully repaired hand, he spread the fingers wide.

"That hurt like a *sonofabitch,*" he said—then offered the gun to Jen. "Wanna try it?" he asked.

"*No* I don't wanna *try* it."

"Suit yourself." John shrugged, and holstered the gun.

"Don't do that again, all right?"

"Sure. Plenty of other people to do it for us." Turning, he walked from the counter. Jen stared down at the blood-ringed hole left by the bullet.

"Just don't get shot in the head," John cautioned. "It may not restore the neural patterns."

"I'll make a note of that," replied Jen.

On the table beside the chair, the radio squawked to life. "Puma this is Green Team leader," said a deep male voice. "We're coming up with Hawk now in the northwest elevator. Do you read?"

John and Jen exchanged glances. Pulling the clip from the gun, John inserted a new round on top; his second-to-last nanobullet—this one from a loop marked FLESH.

"Copy that," replied a second voice over the radio. "Gunfire up here. Will meet you there."

Slamming the mag home, John headed for the door, racking the slide to eject the Hydra-Shok in the chamber on the way.

"*Wait*—" began Jen.

Stepping into the hallway, John turned right, then left—entering the long hall through which they'd come. To the left was an elevator, coming up from the floor below. As the other car was heading down, John knew this to be the car carrying the Green Team. Ahead, at the far end of the hall—Agent Puma rounded the corner where Jen had been killed at a run, MP7 coming up. To John's rear, Jen leaned out into the hall—then quickly ducked from sight.

Walking past the elevator, hearing the *ding* of the bell which signaled its arrival—John fired the nanobullet through the closed door. In the hall ahead, Puma brought the MP7 on-line and opened fire—emptying the thirty-round clip in a single burst.

Steel-core nine-millimeter bullets tore into John's chest and out his back, shredding his shirt and spattering the walls and ceiling with blood. The bullets sped onward down the hall, shattering the window behind him.

John continued forward.

Puma looked down at his gun and fumbled a reload, raising the gun and firing again—emptying a second clip from CQB position in three ten-round bursts. Running dry again, he reached for another pair of clips before realizing that John was right in front of him. He hesitated, staring in shock at John's blood-soaked chest.

"You missed," said John, and put a bullet through Puma's brain.

He stared at the pattern of fresh gore on the wall for a moment, then turned and walked back down the hall. The elevator doors opened as he passed, revealing six sets of black clothing, body armor, and weapons in a heap on the floor. One of the subguns, which had fallen against the door, tumbled outward onto the floor—causing the doors to open and close repeatedly.

Inside the cockpit of Aurora Black, the mission computer signaled the pilot and revealed the target—San Francisco. Hoping it wasn't a nuke—never imagining anything worse—he reached for the controls which would retract the backward-facing bomb door.

The black plane roared up on San Francisco, bomb-bay door sliding open in its rear belly to reveal a single, oddly angled black bomb casing.

At the same instant, NANI ran Phoenix 17 rapidly through the ACQUIRING-ENGAGED-IGNITION sequence, with the still-mysterious anomaly in the crosshair.

Beneath Aurora Black's great wingspan, the nanobomb dropped—propelled clear of the speeding plane by a tiny rocket engine.

A thousandth of a second later, thirty brilliant purple beams lanced through the doomed plane at points estimated to cause fatal damage to plane and crew, if any. The craft's chromomorphic skin went berserk with the beam strikes, morphing through every scintillating color of the rainbow shot through with bright blue electrical arcs.

The plane itself lost stabilization and was shredded in midair by the very speed it had been designed to attain. Thirty-seven tons of liquid methane vaporized in an instant—to be set ablaze by the friction-heated shrapnel of the plane's disintegrating body. The detonation blew out windows three miles below.

The tumbling wreckage and the flaming methane concealed the bomb below from the view of the satellites above and the twin F-15s, which veered sharply away to avoid debris.

"Target destroyed from above by . . . laser beams, or something," reported Colonel Blake.

What remained of Aurora Black smashed into the skyscrapers of San Francisco and spun into the Bay.

Inside the hotel, John moved back into the top-floor suite.

"What was that?" said Jen of the detonation which had rocked the building.

"Something bad," replied John, moving to the window. Parting the drapes, they looked outside. Flaming wreckage tumbled down the faces of battered skyscrapers in the distance.

"Strike two," noted John, assuming NANI had destroyed another attacker. Wondering both why NANI hadn't informed him of the attack—and why it had attacked without his authorization—he turned to the briefcase and saw the dangling phone.

In Golden Gate Park, two boys on bicycles uncovered their ears and stared at the spectacular crash in the distance. One of them spotted something else, much nearer—the black stealth bomb casing impacting the ground some hundred yards off. The impact sent a shudder through the ground, as if the earth itself feared what was to come.

"What's that?" asked the boy who had spotted it, pointing. He sat astride a blue bicycle.

No sooner had he spoken than a *chittering,* crawling mass of nanites swarmed forth from the shattered bomb casing, moving outward in all directions. Eyes wide, the boys turned and pedaled away as fast they could.

Using BIGEYE's optics, NANI zoomed down on Golden Gate Park with a series of real-time still photos as the boys pedaled swiftly away.

ADVISE CREATOR

Placing the briefcase on a desk, John hung up the phone—then jumped, startled, as it rang in his hand. He switched it into the computer, and watched with Jen as flashing red words appeared on the screen:

HOSTILE NANITIES DETECTED
CLASSIFICATION: OMNIVOROUS

DELIVERY BY HYPERSONIC, NONVISIBLE AIRCRAFT

NANI fed the images it was viewing to the monitor.

"YEE-ee," said John, taking in the scene with an expression of distaste. "These boys work fast. Their development program was further along than we thought." After a moment's thought, he spoke to the computer. "NANI," he said into the microphone, "—where did the plane come from?"

The response appeared on the monitor:

GROOM LAKE

John considered this for an instant—until a new message appeared on the screen:

U.S. AIR FORCE FIGHTERS
ATTEMPTED DESTRUCTION
OF NONVISIBLE AIRCRAFT

John stared in confusion as NANI replayed the failed F-15 attack. It made no sense . . .

"What do we do about the nanites?" said Jen.

John shook his head. "Nothing," he replied.

"What do you *mean*, *'nothing'*?"

"Do what?" said John. "We can't outrun them, and we can't fight them."

"There has to be *something* we can do!"

Raising his eyebrows, John shook his head. "We're fucked," he concluded.

In the sky above, the F-15s began circling. "Sir," said Colonel Blake into his helmet mic, "—there's something bizarre happening here. . . ."

"Describe it," said President Miller from the Situation Room. Behind him, Admiral Johnson directed those few satellites which were still responding to surveil the area.

"Ahhh . . . it *looks* like the ground is being dissolved by acid," came Colonel Blake's voice. "I've never seen anything like it. Stand by for images." Activating his wing camera and diving at the ground, he transmitted the camera feed to the Situation Room— where every man fell silent as the horror of the thing which had been unleashed was made clear to them.

"My God . . ." breathed the president.

Seven miles from the hotel, the nanite army *swarmed* outward, disassembling everything in its path—trees, grass, sidewalk, running squirrels. A flock of birds deserting a disappearing tree—and the slowly spinning wheel of a blue bicycle . . .

John studied the horror displayed on the computer monitor, and began typing rapidly.

"What are you doing?" asked Jen.

In response to John's entry, NANI displayed a map of the San Francisco area—along with a flashing purple dot marking the position of the briefcase, which was just south of the San Francisco city line. John pointed to the display. "Technically," he said, "we're in Daly City."

"*So?*"

"Sooo . . ." said John, typing once more, "there's a chance— If the things are programmed *just* to take out San Francisco—which they'd have to be; they don't wanna take out the whole state—they might miss us."

"*Miss us!*" exclaimed Jen, before getting it. "You mean stop before they reach us," she said, comprehending.

"Yeah," John nodded. "If not—these things aren't programmed to be my buddies. I'm telling NANI to analyze the swarm's expansion rate."

On the monitor, John's text and NANI's responses scrolled across the bottom of the screen in purple and blue, respectively.

"This can't be right . . ." said John, examining the figures NANI sent him. "NANI—repeat the analysis," he instructed through the computer's microphone, hands leaving the keyboard.

Jen leaned close, examining the results over John's shoulder. "What is it?" she asked, seeing a graphic of an exponential curve but being unfamiliar with nanite norms.

John shook his head. "The expansion rate of the nanite swarm," he said, "—it should be slowing by now. . . ."

"*Isn't it?*"

John turned from the monitor, features grim. "It's accelerating."

Inside the Situation Room, a phone buzzed on the command console. Admiral Johnson snapped it up. "Johnson," he answered, then listened. After a moment, he hung up. The expression on his features sent a chill down the president's spine. "What is it?" he asked.

"That was Groom Lake," replied the admiral. "As you know, the nanocoding specified the destruction of an area the size of San Francisco."

The president nodded.

"Further analysis of the nanite payload onboard Aurora Black," continued the admiral, "has uncovered an error in the replication coding."

"How bad?"

"Sir—the nanites in San Francisco . . . aren't going to stop."

"Until when. . . . ?"

The admiral regarded him solemnly. "Until this planet is gone," he said.

(15)

Twenty-three hundred miles west, the streets of San Francisco were gridlocked. On one of these, people ran beside stopped cars. A bicycle and a motorcycle wove through those running on the sidewalk as entire buildings behind them dematerialized with the eerie *chitter* of nanite disassemblers.

Nearby, a disheveled man wearing a white robe and long beard stood on the corner, a large REPENT FOR THE END IS NEAR sign fastened over his shoulders. Turning to see what the people rushing past were running from, he beheld the approaching swarm—and smiled.

On Market Street, people ran for their lives. A woman abandoned a squalling baby carriage in the street. A man on the sidewalk lifted his running son from the ground and held him in his arms as he ran faster than he thought he could. A blue Mercedes shoved aside the vehicle in front of it and powered up the opposite sidewalk, grinding against a building and mowing down pedestrians.

The man, his son, the woman and child, the Mercedes and its victims—vanished in an instant.

Farther down the street, a police officer stood his ground as those around him fled—firing a pistol at the onrushing swarm.

Stepping from a church near the southern edge of the city, a priest watched as stragglers ran past screaming, heading south. Turning, he gazed northward at the long and deserted street—and the *chittering* nanite swarm which rushed toward him.

"Our Father, Who art in heaven . . ." he began, clutching the crucifix which dangled from his neck. The swarm flowed madly toward him along street and building walls.

"Hallowed be Thy name," he continued, voice beginning to tremble. He crossed himself quickly as the church and the building across the street and the pavement beneath his feet disassembled.

As did he.

Viewed from space, the city of San Francisco appeared, from above, to be devoured by some bizarre, high-tech jungle rot. At the center of the disintegrating mass was naught but a deepening crater, barren but for the *swarming* nanite horde which accomplished the destruction.

"How can that *be?*" said Jen of the acceleration.

"They were in a hurry," replied John, rising and moving toward the window. "They made a mistake. This thing isn't stopping."

Grasping the cord hanging from the curtain rod, he jerked downward. The drapes parted before him as Jen approached from behind. Through the floor-to-ceiling window, they watched as the city of San Francisco disintegrated from Golden Gate Park outward. Buildings, streets, cars, people—nothing was spared by the nanite advance.

The wave of nothingness swept downward—deepening the crater—and outward at an accelerating pace in all directions save one. Where nanites met ocean, the two had achieved an uneasy equilibrium as trillions of tons of water rushed to replace what was disassembled—creating the mind-numbing spectacle of a roaring oceanfall whose crashing waters never reached bottom but were disassembled as they fell. The thought flashed through John's mind that this was how the Red Sea had been parted for Moses.

"It'll be here any minute," said Jen, close to panic.

Fingers splayed across temple, eyes closed in thought, John nodded.

"Don't you have some kind of . . . *anti*nanite?"

"I do," said John, opening his eyes, "—but it won't hold the line against that. The swarm's too big."

Jen looked quickly out the window, and back. *"What about NANI?"* she pleaded.

"It's not at full intelligence," said John, shaking his head. "If it had a solution, it would have told us."

John's seeming coolness and resignation infuriated her. Seizing his arm, she spun him around to face her, grabbing both arms and shaking him. *"So, what—the world, DIES?"* she yelled at him.

Eyes filled with sadness, he gazed at her, and nodded solemnly. Wordlessly.

"We can't just, *stand here*—"

John's right hand darted up, index finger held aloft for silence. In the pressure of the moment, he'd actually forgotten. He looked at her, eyes gleaming.

"You have something else," she realized.

"Untested."

"You're not your grandfather. He couldn't change the outcome. You can."

"I'm not sure it's perfect."

"It doesn't have to *be* perfect. Nothing ever is."

John shook his head.

Seizing his face with one hand, Jen turned it toward the window wall and the horror outside. "Fucking look at that! You're *human*. Deal *with it.*"

John regarded her oddly. "I don't have to," he replied.

Grabbing her by the arms, he pulled her close and kissed her passionately. She looked at him strangely. It wasn't that she objected, really—the thought of a relationship had more than crossed her mind, at those times she didn't think him insane—but the timing could have been better.

"What's that for?" she asked.

"In case this doesn't work." Turning away, he walked swiftly to the lounge chair and dragged it before the window, arranging it beside a small table, facing outward.

"Might as well have a view," he opined.

Withdrawing a small, rectangular black box from the front pocket of the bag at his waist, he seated himself in the chair.

The devastation outside drew rapidly nearer; the sounds of panicked millions, louder.

Setting the box down on the table, he opened it. Inside, resting in a padded recess, was a final, reusable hypodermic syringe. Beside it were two clear cartridges filled with grayish fluid—again, one for him, one for Mitchell had been the plan.

"What's that?" asked Jen fearfully.

Lifting hypo and cartridges from the box, John inserted one of the latter into the former, uncapped the needle, and squirted fluid from the tip. "Liquid Braino," he replied humorlessly.

"What?" said Jen, half-laughing at John's choice of words, but not amused.

"Elements of nanointelligence," John explained. "Engineered to augment the human brain. If it works, I'll be a million times smarter. Smart enough to maybe figure a way out of this."

He inserted the needle into his left carotid artery, thumb poised atop the plunger. "I never had the guts to try it," he added, in an instant of hesitation. "But now . . ."

Jen looked out the window. "There's nothing left to lose."

John nodded reluctantly, accepting the inescapable: The legacy of his grandfather would in a sense now become his own. Assuming he survived.

Thumb stabbing up on the plunger, he felt the cool liquid enter his body. He set the hypo down beside the second cartridge.

Taking a deep breath, he leaned back in the chair, gripping the end of each arm until his knuckles turned white. Jen dropped to one knee beside him. Taking his left hand from the chair, she placed it in her own. Together, they turned to gaze out the window.

The great void swept toward them—widening from a central, thousand-foot crater in every direction as it came. It gained now even on the ocean. The screaming panic and the death cries of millions were slowly overcome by the rising, blood-chilling *chitter* of the nanite horde as disassemblers beyond number destroyed in minutes what had taken centuries to build and, beneath it, the very earth itself.

Words came unbidden to John's mind—and he spoke aloud the same words which had come to his grandfather, director of the Manhattan Project, upon seeing in Trinity, the first nuclear detonation, the effect of what his mind had wrought. The passage came from the Baghavad-Gita, a two-thousand-year-old Indian religious text:

" 'Lo, I am become Death, the shatterer of worlds.' "

John jerked back in the chair as though hit with a sledgehammer. Head tilting back, eyes squeezing shut, he began to convulse violently.

Prying his spasming hand from hers, Jen managed to get a plastic pen between his teeth—then used her weight to press his shoulders against the chair as best she could.

Inside John's skull, the new-wave nanites deployed rapidly, first mapping, then altering the brain without damaging it. Establishing new connections. Increasing neurons and dendrites. Boosting transmitter levels. Refolding the pinkish gray matter of the brain itself to increase the number of crenellations. Applying what had been learned and what could reasonably be conjectured from studies both of the evolution of the tripartite brain itself and correlations between brain structure on autopsy and intelligence and creativity during life—and leaving existing structures and connections intact to avoid inadvertent damage.

The result was an instantaneous hyperevolution of intelligence, creativity, and capacity for growth. What had not been planned or anticipated by either John or NANI in the necessarily brief development period of the injected nanites was the emergence of a fourth layer of brain matter which appeared as a thin coating over the cerebral cortex. A result of the projected future evolution of the human brain based upon DNA-based extrapolations of past progression—this "fourth brain" was a quantum leap beyond the capabilities even of the newly enhanced third.

After a moment, John's body stilled. When his eyes opened, Jen stepped back involuntarily—for they *crawled* with nanites, which swirled through the irises. He seemed entranced; unaware of his surroundings.

Hesitating only long enough to glance out the window—recalling as she did so the chilling words from L. Williams Hubbel's "At Hiroshima"—"We knew we were standing where the end of the world began"—Jen took the hypo from the table, inserted the second cartridge, which bore the same absurd label as the first: BRAINO—and injected the contents into her brachial artery. There was, indeed, nothing left to lose.

Outside, the *chittering* horror grew nearer, its volume deafening. . . .

John blinked. *"Phoenix,"* he said, bolting from the chair.

"Phoenix?"

"The satellites," said John tersely, working the satphone's keyboard.

Head snapping back, eyes closing, Jen gasped suddenly, as though in pain—or ecstasy. Her body went into tremors as John divided his attention between her and the keyboard. She did not convulse. After a moment, she opened her eyes. Had she seen them herself, she would have observed the nanites swirling restlessly within the irises.

"Of course," she breathed, then turned again to gaze out the window. The void was nearly upon them. *"Hurry."*

Across the room, John hammered in the keystrokes, ignoring the onrushing swarm out the window.

"If the satellites can take it," he said, "this *should* work."

"What about the heat?"

"Hotter than a nuke. A few miles away. Maybe we make it; maybe we don't."

Finishing the command keystrokes, he hit ENTER.

Receiving the Creator's commands, NANI worked at fever pace. All data not directly related to the activity at hand vanished. While tracking the nanite swarm expansion rate and keeping tabs on the Creator's position at the city's edge, NANI began its calculations.

The Phoenix system was comprised of twenty-four orbiting particle beam weapons platforms in geostationary orbits and possessed of overlapping fields of fire. Of the twenty-four total, two were currently active; the remainder had yet to be activated. NANI had made a brief attempt to switch on the inactive satellites earlier, but had abandoned the task for others more urgent.

It now focused its inhuman attention on these—in particular the eight which could strike San Francisco from their present positions, and the additional four which could be retasked and moved within range of the city in time to be useful. Again, however, attempting to gain control of the satellites produced the same message as before:

SATELLITES UNAVAILABLE
ACCESS DENIED

NANI hit the satellites with the full brunt of its available hacking muscle.

Inside the hotel, John monitored NANI's efforts. *"Goddamn,"* he breathed. Jen looked at him. "If we don't get those satellites *now*— we're not gonna make it."

The president studied the tactical display showing the Phoenix satellites and NANI's takeover attempt—which suddenly intensified beyond belief. "He's trying to take the rest of the satellites," he said aloud, then turned to the others. *"Why . . . ?"* he asked.

Billions of code combinations flashed through NANI's mind as it tried to hack into the remaining satellites—to no avail.

"If this thing is as far beyond our computers as you say—what's stopping it?" asked the president.

"It can't hack the access codes to the other satellites because they haven't been assigned yet," said Admiral Johnson. "He only has two satellites. He may get the rest, but it will take time."

"The world is out of time, Admiral. Why does he want the satellites?"

"I don't know."

No one did.

"Can we stop this thing ourselves?"

"Impossible," replied Admiral Johnson. Secretary of Defense Davisson shook his head.

"Can we assign the satellite codes from here?"

"I can," said the admiral.

"Prepare to do that. Colonel Sinclair said the NI is tied into ECHELON."

"Correct."

"So it hears everything." Reaching out swiftly, the president picked up a phone and dialed the first outside number he could think of—his cell phone number. A recording answered.

"Sir . . . ?" said Davisson.

President Miller spoke into the phone. "This is the president of the United States, calling John Marrek," he said.

NANI picked up the president's voice immediately. Matched, locked, and located. A yellow crosshair appeared over the White House Situation Room.

———

On the briefcase monitor in San Francisco, John viewed a new message from NANI, displayed over a graphic representation of the targeted White House:

INCOMING PHONE CALL FROM:
PRESIDENT OF UNITED STATES
RESPONSE OPTIONS:
ATTACK
TAKE CALL

"I'll take the call," said John. "Show the president what's happening." The satphone rang. John picked up. "This is John Marrek," he said. "We've got a big fucking problem."

"I know," replied the voice of the president.

"What do we do about that?"

President Miller watched NANI's broadcast of the nanite horde in San Francisco, saw the two F-15s fly from view to one side. "I'm prepared to give you the satellites," he offered.

"What's the catch?"

"We change the world together, not as enemies." The president paused for an instant before continuing. "I knew nothing of Mitchell Swain's assassination. I learned of it afterward. The man was a friend. The attack on you was initiated by traitors locked inside NORAD."

John looked to Jen, who nodded.

"Mr. President," said John, "you have yourself a deal."

The president gestured to Admiral Johnson, who uploaded the newly preassigned satellite access codes.

NANI hacked all twenty-two in less than a second, receiving the gratifying message: ACCESS GRANTED. The outlying four Phoenix satellites were retasked immediately, their reserve fuel warning indicators sounding off soon after.

While doing this, NANI ran a rapid evaluation of the present condition and maximum design and theoretical sustained firing rates of each of the eight in-range satellites. At the rate of fire required to achieve the desired result, NANI's calculations predicted failure for all, and for the mission. Factoring in the anticipated arrival times and sustained fire rates of the other four satellites, with all satellites firing at a rate somewhere in the gray limbo between the stated design tolerance and the maximum theoretical limit, yielded the following:

OUTCOME UNCERTAIN

Hesitation made success less likely. A nanosecond later, NANI acted:

IMPLEMENT

At NANI's command, the in-range satellites opened fire. High above the North American continent and the deep blue Pacific, bright purple beams lanced downward into black space.

John stood now with Jen before the window, an arm about her waist, and hers about his. They watched as first hundreds, then thousands of brilliant purple beams slashed down into the center of the nanite mass, concentrating on the single point of the great swarm's origin. Each beam lasted a mere fraction of a second. With astonishing swiftness, the temperature at the point of beamfall began to rise.

From space, NANI looked down on the scene through BIGEYE's optics. The ocean near the shoreline boiled madly into salty steam. Analysis of light frequencies present at the point of beam convergence yielded the following:

SPECTRAL ANALYSIS
CORE TEMPERATURE: 300,000 F

The temperature reading blurred upward. NANI sent another command to the in-range satellites:

INCREASE RATE OF FIRE

On the ground, thousands of beams became hundreds of thousands—then millions. The afterimages blended with the beams themselves to create a spectacle of weird and staggering beauty. Shielding their eyes, John and Jen squinted against the light.

In space, NANI's sensors informed it that the core temperature was passing eight hundred thousand degrees Fahrenheit. Warnings flooded in from all in-range satellites:

WARNING
MAXIMUM DESIGN OUTPUT EXCEEDED
EMERGENCY SHUTDOWN INITIATED

NANI countered quickly with:

OVERRIDE SHUTDOWN
INCREASE RATE OF FIRE

Incredibly, the satellites fired faster. Core temperature passed two million degrees. At the point of beam convergence, in the center of the swarm—a bright white blob appeared.

PLASMA STATE INDUCED

NANI's sensors informed it.

As John and Jen watched the brilliant beamfall over San Francisco, a blinding white plasma field flashed into existence—blinding them until their cellular repair assemblers repaired the damage.

As quickly as it had come, however, the white plasma field vanished. Within the area which had been occupied by the plasma—there were no nanites. Their greedy brethren, however, quickly swarmed in to reclaim the ceded territory.

NANI's sensors interpreted the bad news:

PHOENIX 17 FAILURE
PLASMA STATE LOST

Core temperature dropped below the requisite temperature. Phoenix 13 failed next, but Phoenix 12 and 21 moved swiftly into range to take their places. As the two new satellites kicked in, core temperature again rose past two million degrees, and the plasma field reappeared—and grew.

PLASMA STATE INDUCED

Watching through the window-wall, John and Jen could only wait. Any physical object hit with that kind of energy—even nanites—would be transformed into plasma—a state in which matter loses the characteristics of its constituent substances. Atomic nuclei were ripped apart from their orbiting electrons, leaving nothing but ions devoid of identity—and the bonds necessary to form nanites. The searing heat of the plasma field, also, would serve to induce fatal errors in the programming codes of those nanites which the plasma itself did not directly consume.

The catch was that the maximum size of the plasma field generated with the available energy was limited—whereas the size of the nanite swarm was not. If the plasma field could expand swiftly enough to annihilate or cook off every member of the nanite swarm before the swarm expanded beyond its reach, the effort would succeed; if not, it was doomed to failure. And as with Edward Teller taking side bets on the chain-reaction incineration of the planet's atmosphere at Trinity—the smart money here would be on the nanites.

"Will it be enough?" asked Jen.

Raising the gun beside his head, John removed the final nano-bullet from a loop marked ANTI, and placed it in the chamber. *"If the satellites can take it,"* he answered grimly, and dropped the slide.

As they watched, the growing plasma field chased the nanite swarm toward them, expanded rapidly—and hesitated as Phoenix 16 failed. Phoenix 11 and 22 took up the slack, boosting the total to nine in-range satellites—and the plasma rushed outward.

Beamfall was now so rapid each afterimage lingered past multiple new strikes until it seemed the very brilliance of the spectacle would melt their eyes from their sockets—and indeed both John and Jen would have been permanently blinded long before were it not for the constant efforts of their cellular repair assemblers.

Nanites *swarmed* over the building across the street, devouring it in seconds—the plasma field *whooshing* up behind it like an approaching nuke flash.

"Get back!" yelled John, pulling Jen with him into the kitchen. Tipping the refrigerator onto the floor, he pushed her down behind it.

Across the suite, nanites *swarmed* over the window. Aiming the gun at the television to prevent the bullet from leaving the room, John fired. The television's picture tube imploded when the bullet struck. John dropped to one knee beside Jen—who peered over the fridge beside him.

Window and wall began to disassemble—more slowly than they should have, John realized, because the heat of the onrushing plasma was inducing errors which impaired the disassemblers' replication.

Inside the room, where there was still something to shield its contents from the approaching inferno outside—antinanites *swarmed* outward over floor, walls, ceiling, and window, battling the nanites which rushed inside through disassembling window and wall. Horrid *chittering* filled the room and blended with the deafening roar of the nanites outside.

Within the hotel suite the nanites—expansion rate bolstered by their larger numbers—were winning. Through the absent window and new holes in the wall streamed a piercing white light too intense to behold. Window and wall began to melt.

"Close your eyes and hold your breath!" John screamed above the roar—then ducked down beside Jen, pulling her close and shielding her with his body.

The room blackened with heat; walls crisping, paint blistering off the fridge. The nanite/antinanite line contracted—drawing back toward the kitchen as the outer wall melted away and John and Jen felt their bodies begin to burn alive.

They screamed.

The room went into flashover—bursting into flame as walls, ceiling, and floor disassembled simultaneously.

The screaming stopped suddenly—followed by the *chittering* of the nanites and antinanites. Flames roared on as the room burned like the fires of hell itself.

NANI detected multiple satellite failures as all remaining in-range satellites overheated in the space of a second. Spectral analysis showed the core temperature—as near as such a thing could be estimated of a state so unstable as plasma—to be three million degrees and dropping.

MAXIMUM PLASMA EXPANSION ACHIEVED
EVALUATING STRIKE AREA

NANI swiftly zoomed down on the doomed city with visual, infrared, and radar satellites. Upon viewing the barren, half-mile-deep crater surrounded by blackened and burning ruins where but moments before had stood a city teeming with millions, NANI arrived at a decidedly inhuman but entirely accurate conclusion:

ZERO NANITE REPLICATION DETECTED
ENGAGEMENT SUCCESSFUL

Within the great mind's consciousness, this last line flashed cheerily.

The hotel stood faceless at the edge of the devastation, the absent northwest wall revealing a thousand raging infernos within.

Inside the suite on the top floor, the remaining rooms burned, flames roiling madly. Three walls, ceiling, and the majority of the floor had been disassembled. In the kitchen, the refrigerator was a hardening metal puddle on the floor.

Beyond it, something moved. . . .

Shoulder to shoulder, John and Jen stumbled along the wall without eyes. Their blackened skin blistered and peeled away, regenerating swiftly only to blacken and peel away again from the heat of the inferno. Neither could speak, as lips and tongues had burned away and were only now able to begin the regeneration process. Reaching out gropingly, they found one another's hands—the fingers mere blackened stubs—and held as tightly as they could.

Moving in the direction of the hall entrance, John felt blindly for the doorway. The door itself crumbled at his touch when he found it. In a moment, both he and Jen stood in the hall which, somehow, was not in flames. Water poured from melted pipes in the ceiling overhead, cooling them, providing a welcome resource for nanorehydration and accelerating their regeneration.

After a few moments more, their eyes regenerated and their sight returned. The two of them stared wide-eyed into the inferno from which they had escaped—and at the devastation beyond.

They turned to face each other. John's new eyes wandered downward from Jen's face over the curves of her nude body, and up again. Jen did the same to him. They grinned.

NANI gazed down upon what had once been San Francisco—and was now a glowing crater ringed with half-disassembled, flaming buildings, many of which collapsed in on themselves. Seawater thundered into the crater like an angry god reclaiming stolen territory—

a deafening, half-mile-high oceanfall which exploded into steam as it neared the plasma-heated earth at the bottom.

ENGAGEMENT SUCCESSFUL

Now that it had the time, NANI dedicated its resources to locating and back-tracing the chain of commands it knew to be necessary for the authorization of actions such as those which had been taken against the Creator. The routing of the messages had been deliberately obfuscated—but not to the point where NANI was put off the track. Within a few moments, it found the source.

Inside the combined command center beneath Cheyenne Mountain, the programmable display in front of Blaine and Raster reprogrammed itself, displaying an aerial view of San Francisco.

"*Good God . . .*" whispered Blaine.

Others in the room left their stations to gather behind the two. All stared in disbelief at the scene on the big screen.

Raster's eyes narrowed. "*It's stopped,*" he said.

A message resolved itself across the screen in large, yellow-orange letters:

THOSE WHO PLAY WITH FIRE
WILL BE BURNED

Message and ruined city disappeared from the screen, to be replaced by a satellite image of Cheyenne Mountain with a flashing yellow crosshair directly above the combined command center.

In the Situation Room, a message from NANI appeared across the programmable tactical display:

COMMUNICATION WITH CHEYENNE RESTORED
COURTESY JOHN MARREK

"Put me on every screen in that mountain," said the president to a nearby tech.

While working to get a hot-wired video feed in place for the president, Colonel Sinclair had watched for the past twenty minutes as a torch had slowly cut a large vertical rectangle through the transmission room's plate-steel door. As the torch completed its course, the door-sized chunk of steel fell inward—revealing a dozen MPs with sidearms drawn. They stepped inside. It was at this moment that President Miller appeared on every video-capable screen inside Cheyenne Mountain—including those in the transmission room.

"This is your commander in chief," stated the president. "Chairman Blaine and Vincent Raster are to be arrested at once and command returned to Colonel . . . to *General* Jacqueline Sinclair."

In the transmission room, the MPs lowered their guns—and General Jacqueline Sinclair smiled broadly.

In the combined command center, the president's larger-than-life, angry face was on every screen. Raster and Blaine gazed apprehensively around themselves as the room began to fill with MPs.

In the hallway of the hotel, John and Jen stood beside the elevator, pulling on the black fatigues of the disassembled hit team, which had been shielded from the heat by several walls and the concrete elevator shaft.

"What do we do now?" asked Jen.

"What I've planned to do since Mitchell died," replied John. Straightening, he gazed at her solemnly. *"This* is what NANI's been working on," he said enigmatically.

Jen looked at him.

"Ready for a promotion?" he asked.

WINNER TAKE ALL

*The hand that rocks the AI cradle
may well rule the world.*

—K. Eric Drexler, 1986

⟨16⟩

Right hand and fingers manipulating the pressure sensors on a duplicate of the impossible-to-solve holographic puzzle she'd toyed with in the San Francisco lab, Jen watched as the slowly rotating diamonds aligned themselves into neat, concentric, diamond-shaped formations arranged by color.

She smiled with satisfaction, subconsciously making the same little gesture of defiance and pride she'd hit when she and John had first met, and he'd recognized her name because of her work.

Schrödinger jumped up onto the counter beside her and began to purr. Stroking his fur, she watched John ready himself on "the set," as they'd come to call it.

Situated deep inside a granite mountain, location known to none but NANI and themselves, excavated and guarded by nanites, watched over by NANI with the remaining Phoenix satellites at its command—their current residence was without doubt the only truly impenetrable facility on the face of the earth. The only weapons capable of penetrating this fortress had been disabled or commandeered by NANI; anything else which might approach could—and would—be quickly disassembled at John's command.

Jen had at first argued against John's plan, but in the end he had dissected and eviscerated each objection with the cold blade of reason. Beyond the inevitable human capacity for evil, and the untrustworthiness of intelligent machines, lay an unassailable fact which, once grasped—made it frighteningly clear that there was indeed, as John had said, no other way.

That fact was this: Complex technologies were by their very nature inherently totalitarian. The more complex the technology, the more totalitarian the institutions required to manage it. This was so because, as futurist Hazel Henderson had pointed out in *Creating Alternative Futures: The End of Economics,* neither the common man, legislators, nor national leaders understood the technologies—and were therefore incompetent to oversee their use.

As technologies became more complex, the people who understood them fully would inevitably control them and, through them, the societies which could not survive without those technologies. Thus, complex technologies created totalitarian technocracies.

In a way, John had explained, that was how Mitchell Swain had come to be the richest—some said most powerful—man on earth. It was no secret that he had been largely if not entirely responsible for the elections of the past two presidents—and a man able to choose presidents by definition wields more power than the chosen.

Swain, however, had been a force for good. What he had called "the ultimate technology," however, was in fact the most complex technology ever developed. As such, it was by nature ultimately—and completely—totalitarian.

And there was but one way to deal with this dilemma.

"The set" where John readied himself was a small, unmanned television studio with robotic cameras, uplinked via NANI, which would eliminate all traces of the signal's point of origin prior to broadcast. The news-desk-style counter at which John seated himself, as well as the angled walls behind him, were of polished black stone shot through with veins of gold. It was from this room that John would address the peoples of the world.

Power, phone systems, and the Internet had been restored following a brief negotiation with President Miller, who would serve as a consultant—as would those to hold that office after him. John had pledged to change the world—not to rule it—together. And change it they would.

Seated behind the desk of his new set, garbed in white with gold trim to stand out against the black stone background, John watched the countdown and prepared to address his audience—which consisted of every television and radio broadcast channel on earth, as well as all hardline communications routes including telephone lines and the Internet, among others.

NANI hijacked them all, routing the broadcast live save for the small delay required for translation and rendering into the appropriate language for each outlet. By prior arrangement, the president would speak first from the White House, followed by John, from his new abode. John and Jen watched the screen as President Miller appeared, and began to speak.

"I greet you all at the dawn of a new world," said the president. "A world, as my friend Mitchell Swain said, which will forever alter the destiny of Mankind . . .

"Mitchell Swain gave his life to bring this new world into being, and I am here to tell you that the United States of America is going to lead the world into this new age.

"The man who began this work, and who will finish it—will speak with you in a moment. He saved my life, and he saved yours. Listen to him."

The on-air countdown in John's studio reached zero, the red ON AIR light coming to life across the room. Gazing into the center camera, John began to speak. Thanks to NANI, regardless of language, all listeners would hear John's voice, so that it would seem to all that he spoke their language with fluency. Which, thanks to his recent nanoenhancements, he was well on the way to doing.

"My name," he said, "is John Marrek. I was a friend of Mitchell Swain's, and I am here now to carry on his greatest work."

"As of this moment, all nuclear, biological, and chemical weapons on this planet are inactive. In twenty-four hours, they will be gone. A more terrible weapon by far has been created—you saw it abused in San Francisco by rogue elements of the United States government, of which President Miller had no knowledge. Governments cannot be trusted, even when benign. Therefore this weapon, and this technology, will remain under my control. This is fact, and cannot be avoided.

"I will use the power this gives me to enforce the distribution of the technology Mitchell Swain died to give the world. *No government* will keep it from you, and *no one* will take it away."

Pausing, drawing a deep breath, John summarized what he would explain shortly in more detail. *"War* is over," he began. *"Poverty* is over. *Hunger, disease,* and *pollution* are at an end. The *old* shall be made young. The *world* shall be made new.

"Mankind will gain the stars . . .

"And the power of governments over their people, is a thing of the past.

"From this day forward—" said John, raising his right arm and reaching out to one side. Jen—also dressed in white—moved to join him, taking his hand in front of the world.

"*—two people* shall rule the earth as guardians of what is right," John continued, and paused again. His features assumed the severe and implacable cast of the invincible god-emperor he had become as he stared frighteningly into the camera.

"And evil, shall be *exterminated without mercy . . .*"

AUTHOR'S AFTERWORD

. . . if we survive . . .

*—qualifying phrase employed with annoying frequency by
K. Eric Drexler when writing of the impending
development of nanotechnology*

Nothing portrayed in this novel is impossible. Nanotechnology is real. The United States Army, Air Force, and Navy are currently working to develop nanocapability for use as a weapon. More on this in a moment.

ECHELON is also real, as is research into chromomorphic materials with military applications. ECHELON's capabilities are—so far as is determinable—roughly as stated. Research into the development of Phoenix-like satellites is a reality. Whether such instruments have already been deployed is anyone's guess, though the technical problems relating to beam coherence under atmospheric conditions make it likely that such weapons, if deployed, would be tasked primarily with the destruction of space-based objects and of objects—such as strategic nuclear missiles—which exit the atmosphere and then reenter it. Such weapons platforms might reasonably be expected to achieve some success in targeting objects—such as spy planes—which travel through the upper reaches of earth's atmosphere as well.

The Aurora Project—despite the usual flurry of official denials (which began after a government censor slipped up and listed "Aurora" just below "U-2" and "SR-71" on a 1985 Pentagon budget request)—is genuine, and is based at Groom Dry Lake, Nevada. This is where the U-2 was tested, the SR-71, the B-2, the F-117A, and so on—and this is where the next generation of radically advanced aircraft is being and will continue to be tested. The reason is simple: Groom Lake is perhaps the most highly classified and restricted-access site on the face of the earth. If there are indeed little gray men, this is where they are.

The application of a chromomorphic exterior coating to the present or next generation of Aurora-class aircraft is a logical enhancement even though, in truth, this particular technology is a complete fabrication on the part of the author. Or so it first seemed; later background research revealed that it is likely a very similar technology incorporating numerous plane-mounted cameras and "electrochromic panels" is currently being tested at Groom Lake. In addition, recent work at the University of Tokyo's Tachi Lab employs a prototype system which works much like the chromogrid discussed in the novel.

The circuslike series of nuclear accidents referred to by John Marrek in Chapter 4 is, sadly, also genuine, and but the tip of the classified iceberg. As to what the government has to say about this state of affairs, consider a few excerpts from a recent paper of the Los Alamos Study Group: "the stockpile today is safe, secure, reliable, and meets current military requirements" . . . "no safety problems are expected to occur" . . . "it is highly likely that efforts to produce 'safer' weapons will degrade overall nuclear safety" . . . "Are U.S. nuclear weapons, in fact, 'Safe'? The unequivocal and unanimous conclusion of the nuclear weapons establishment is affirmative" . . . "the disproportionate and irrational drive to maximize safety" . . . "the central theme of this paper is that nuclear weapons safety, as a technical problem for weapons designers [as *opposed, one must assume, to the idiots who drop them out of air-planes—author's comment],* has been solved."

The title of this paper? "Nuclear Weapons Safety: No Design Changes Are Warranted."

These are the people who will be in charge of nanoweapons development. Food for thought. See the author's Web site at www.johnrobertmarlow.com for more on this and the other things mentioned in this afterword.

As to the plausibility of reverse engineering crashed alien space-craft to gain or extend a military advantage over other earthbound powers, and perhaps uncover weaknesses in the machinery of potentially hostile extraterrestrial powers—recall that the com-manding general of Roswell Army Airfield stated for the record that the object found at Roswell was in fact an alien spacecraft. His supe-riors in Washington—none of whom had seen the object, as he had—denied this the following day, and have continued to deny it for over fifty years. Make what you will of this, keeping in mind the longstanding intelligence community axiom: "The first thing is, never believe anything the government tells you."

Assuming for a moment that one or more such craft do exist—what would *you* do with a crashed alien spacecraft . . . ?

For more on these topics and others, visit the author's Web site at www.johnrobertmarlow.com.

About Nanotech

Nanotech as portrayed in the novel is, thankfully, not here yet—but it *is* real. More than theory, the principles upon which a work-ing nanotechnology will be based are well understood. Nano's development is known to be not only possible, but attainable. Var-ious research groups are pursuing the development of this technol-ogy to achieve specific ends. In the United States, this includes the following government agencies: The U.S. Air Force; U.S. Army; U.S. Navy; Defense Advanced Research Projects Agency; Department of Energy; Department of Commerce; NASA; National Institutes of Health; National Institute of Standards and Technology; National Science Foundation, and the National Science and Technology Council.

On January 21, 2000, speaking at Caltech—the site of Richard Feynman's historic 1959 nanotech speech—President Clinton announced the half-billion-dollar National Nanotechnology Initiative. "The Administration is making this major new initiative, called the National Nanotechnology Initiative (NNI), a top priority," said the White House press release issued on the same date. The release makes ominous and ambiguous mention of the government's need to "intervene efficiently in the future on measures that may need to be taken."

Alarmingly for Americans, the United States has no clear lead in the field of nanotechnology. Both the Japanese and the Europeans seem to take the development of nanotechnology more seriously than we do.

As with most if not all scientific progress, little thought is being given to the full implications or potential consequences of this technology. The smallest portion of the funds allocated by the National Nanotechnology Initiative, for instance, is earmarked for the study of "ethical, legal, and social implications."

One notable exception to this general shortsightedness is the Foresight Institute, an organization founded by K. Eric Drexler and Chris Peterson with the stated aim of assisting the world in preparing for the advent of nanotechnology.

On the other hand, we can thank the members of this same institute for the concept of "active shields"—which is perhaps (in the author's opinion) the single most severely *shortsighted* proposal ever to come down the pike. The employment of automated active shields controlled by NHI (nonhuman intelligences), or even by more prosaic automated computer programs, seems as blatantly suicidal as the all-out nanoarms race such "Klaatu Solutions" might in theory prevent.*

As Bill Joy, cofounder and, until recently, chief scientist of computer goliath Sun Microsystems and original cochairman of the Presidential Commission on the Future of Information Technology, put it in a widely quoted *Wired* article in March of 2000: ". . . the shield proposed would itself be extremely dangerous—nothing could prevent it from developing autoimmune problems and attacking the biosphere itself . . . These technologies are too powerful to be shielded against in the time frame of interest; even if it were possible to implement defensive shields, the side effects of their development would be at least as dangerous as the technologies we are trying to protect against."

If active shields are implemented, it is extremely likely that bickering and distrust over who will control the establishing programs, or over who will create the intelligence which controls the shields, will render the whole thing unworkable as a cooperative venture. If this is so, and active shields are desired by one or more leading powers, they will be deployed unilaterally and will be little more than a new generation of space-based weapons under the direct control of the launching power or powers. If several shields are launched by opposing powers, the result will be an unprecedented arms race escalation. Even a single shield and its controlling intelligence will be subject to constant efforts at hostile takeover by nations and perhaps individuals developing and deploying competing nanointelligences in an effort to achieve primacy.

Unfortunately, owing to their enormous resources and coercive powers, it is governments and not foresighted men of reason who will almost certainly control the development of nanotechnology—

---

*Klaatu was the name of the alien with the invincible peacekeeping robot Gort in Edmund H. North's 1951 screenplay *The Day The Earth Stood Still*. In actuality, the active shield situation is worse: Klaatu had a secret override phrase for use in emergencies; a nanointelligence, even if instilled with such a convenient safety mechanism—might well decide, for reasons of its own, not to obey.

at least initially. Worse, it will be governments seeking nano-weapons.

The capabilities and operating mechanisms and principles of the nanites described in this novel conform to what is now known of actual nanocapabilities, operating mechanisms, and principles. Less than ideally, however—the ideal way to stop a single nonlimited disassembler which passes its no-limit program on to its exponentially multiplying descendants is to create and employ it only inside an impenetrable structure where it will itself be subject to attack and disassembly by antinanite disassemblers programmed to seek out and destroy defectively replicating disassemblers (as well as assemblers).

There are, alas, several problems with this approach. First, no known substance is impenetrable to an omnivorous disassembler—and a mutating disassembler may mutate into a form able to disassemble even a substance it has been specifically programmed not to disassemble. Secondly, a primary and obvious use of disassemblers is in warfare, and wars do not take place inside sealed laboratories. (This fact, incidentally, renders absurd the argument advanced by some military nanoadvocates that battlefield disassemblers will be limited in the scope of their self-deployment by a special "nanite food" they will be programmed to require or to target in order to replicate. The enemy, of course, will seek to destroy this "food" and render the nanites harmless, or to spray it all over the field—thus causing the disassemblers to attack the force which initially deployed them. For these reasons, battlefield nanites dependent upon special "foods" may well prove all but useless.)

Lastly and most discouragingly of all—the capability to contain nanites through the use of nanotechnology itself is inherently unreliable because it allows for no advance preparation of containment facilities; that is, the thing which requires containment will already exist before attempted containment is possible. The situation is analogous to loosing a hungry tiger in your living room while fiddling with the cage-assembly instructions; to say the least, your prospects for short-term survival are less than optimal.

Alternative containment strategies are grim: nuclear detonation and plasma attack. Both will reliably annihilate nanites by separating the constituent nuclei and electrons comprising the nanites' "bodies." This is only true, however, if the attack is executed immediately and before the nanites have spread over an area large enough to permit the survival of a single nanite—which might, for example, be carried from the outer fringes of the target area by a blast wave.

The generation of plasma with currently available technology rests on conditions too fickle to be relied upon for this purpose; therefore, the sole containment option will be nuclear annihilation in the form of an on-site nuclear weapon which detonates automatically in response to a containment breach—or erroneous notification of such breach.

Given such conditions, lab employees may be somewhat difficult to come by.

Nonlimited assemblers will be equally hazardous, as they will simply rip the planet apart one atom at a time for the raw materials with which to go on mindlessly constructing the widgets they've been programmed to make. Whether they will actually *chitter* happily as they do this is unknown.

The author prefers to think they will.

Aside from all of this, of course, nations and perhaps individuals without recourse to nuclear weapons or other high-tech accoutrements of power will inevitably seek to develop nanotechnology as a way of achieving an otherwise unattainable world dominance. Because of this, Bill Joy's "only realistic alternative . . . relinquishment: to limit our development of the technologies that are too dangerous, by limiting our pursuit of certain kinds of knowledge . . ." is itself utterly unrealistic.

In what will likely become a headlong rush to attain nano-weapons at any cost, nations large and small—seeking to retain or attain such power—will likely pay little heed to pleas for elaborate safeguard mechanisms. It is perhaps instructive to reflect that, when the Trinity test (the first nuclear detonation, resulting from the Manhattan Project) was about to be carried out, one of the project's leading physicists, Edward Teller, was taking side bets that the result would be a worldwide atmospheric chain reaction which would incinerate the surface of the globe and everything on it.

The Manhattan Project was carried out anyway, and that test conducted, because of the threat posed by the decimated Nazis and the (for all practical purposes) defeated Japanese, as well as because of the potential threat posed should other nations—namely the Soviet Union—develop The Bomb first. Some have argued convincingly that the real purpose of the two nukes dropped on Japan was to impress the Soviets and to gather real-world data on the residual effects of radiation on human beings.

Physicist Freeman Dyson proposed a more prosaic explanation: "The reason that it was dropped was just because no one had the courage or the foresight to say no."

In the summer of 2000, a high-energy physics experiment was carried out inside the Relativistic Heavy Ion Collider at Brookhaven National Laboratories in New York. The experiment entailed the acceleration of the stripped-away outer electrons of gold atoms to near light-speed, at which point the electrons—traveling in opposite directions—collided.

Well before the date of the experiment, it was pointed out by several physicists that one possible, if unlikely, result of such a particle collision would be the creation of "strangelet" quarks, which have the decidedly bizarre (and thankfully rare) attribute of spontaneously generating further strangelets—each one of which transforms every particle it touches into still more strangelets and so on, until the entire earth (and perhaps universe) is consumed by the things.

Another possible result, also pointed out in advance, would be the generation of a singularity, or black hole, at the site of the experiment. Other than sucking Brookhaven Labs into a black abyss, such an occurrence would be of little benefit to Mankind.

As John Nelson, leader of the team which conducted the experiment, put it in speaking to *The Sunday Times* of London in July of 1999: "The big question is whether the planet will disappear in the twinkling of an eye. It is astonishingly unlikely that there is any risk—but I could not prove it."

In spite of the admittedly unlikely scenarios cited above, the experiment was in fact carried out—simply because the experimenters wished to see what would happen.

Again, Freeman Dyson: "I have felt it myself. The glitter of nuclear weapons. It is irresistible if you come to them as a scientist. To feel it's there in your hands, to release this energy that fuels the stars, to let it do your bidding. To perform these miracles, to lift a million tons of rock into the sky. It is something that gives people an illusion of illimitable power, and it is, in some ways, responsible for all our troubles—this, what you might call technical arrogance, that overcomes people when they see what they can do with their minds."

After leading the Manhattan Project which developed the first atom bomb (a fission weapon), J. Robert Oppenheimer resolved not to pursue the even more powerful hydrogen bomb (a fusion weapon for which a fission weapon is merely the trigger), and to convince his fellow scientists to do the same. He was promptly labeled a communist, removed from all classified projects, and replaced by Edward Teller, who then went on to develop the hydrogen bomb (and also, unbelievably, to propose—in the form of Project Chariot—the detonation of up to six hydrogen bombs to blast a new harbor into the coast of the Alaskan wilderness as a demonstration of the "peaceful" uses of nuclear weapons).

The pressure to develop nanotechnology as a weapon will be far more intense than that faced by wartime foes or curious experimenters, because the first to achieve that feat will have the ability to prevent all others from duplicating it, if only by annihilation of all competitors. Nations which choose, for reasons of caution or ethics, to proceed slowly or not at all, will guarantee their future subordination to the will of the first to breach the development threshold.

Therein lies Marlow's Second Paradox: Nanotechnology must never be developed, because it is too dangerous a thing to exist; nanotechnology *must* be developed—because it is too dangerous a thing to exist in the hands of others. The second rationale will drive the race for nanosuperiority; the first will be ignored.

The first nanopower, if it plays its cards right, will be the *only* nanopower, and will remain unchallenged for the foreseeable future. (Assuming there remains a future to foresee.)

In the entire history of the human race, there has never been such a prize for the taking, and there likely never will be again.

We are embarked upon Mankind's final arms race. Caution will not be a factor; because the losers in the nanorace will exist only at the whim of the winner, many will see themselves as having nothing to lose.

Given this situation, these facts, the occasional incompetence of government and of the military in particular, and human nature—the earth itself may well be doomed.

This is the way the world ends.
Maybe.

For further information on nanotechnology and other topics mentioned in this book, and to help save the world—visit the author's Web site at www.johnrobertmarlow.com.

CLOSING REMARKS

*[Nanotechnology is] a development which I think
cannot be avoided.*

—*Richard Feynman,
Nobel laureate physicist*[1]

Purpose in Writing This Book

Nano was written to demonstrate the promise—and the peril—of
what appears for more reasons than one to be the Final Big Breakthrough: the imminent development of nanotechnology.

I am not opposed to the development of nanotech—indeed, no
intelligent person could be. Opposition is irrelevant and, paradoxi-
cally, endangers only those doing the opposing because it ensures
that others not so opposed will take the lead.

Meticulous planning, diligent protocols, and extreme caution
are called for—and the sooner, the better. We have at present an
opportunity we will later be denied—and that is to work out the

[1]Richard P. Feynman: *There's Plenty of Room at the Bottom: An Invitation to
Enter a New Field of Physics,* address to the 1959 annual meeting of the American
Physical Society, December 29, 1959, at the California Institute of Technology; first
published in Caltech's *Engineering and Science,* February 1960. [Text of speech
linked from author's Web site at http://www.johnrobertmarlow.com] Though the
term did not exist at the time he spoke, what Feynman was describing has since
become known as *nanotechnology.*

safest way to quickly proceed *before the technology is here*. And as nanotechnology pioneer K. Eric Drexler has pointed out, the sooner we begin thinking about and developing safeguards, the more time we will have to refine and implement them before they are needed. If we fail to take advantage of this opportunity, we are doomed.

This book was written to increase awareness of nanotechnology, to spark debate and, hopefully, to encourage serious thought by citizens, scientists, and governments about what we as a species need to do in order to ensure that we survive the inevitable development of this technology.

The best way to do that, I thought, was to write the best damned novel I could—one which shows dramatically (as no work of nonfiction could) what *nano* can do *for* us, and *to* us.

Decisions vital to the development of nanotechnology are now being made by scientists working in fields most people have never heard of, by corporations pursuing their own ends, and by governments pursuing still others. Few, as yet, seem to be pursuing nanotechnology as an end in itself. Rather, researchers in different fields continue to make progress in disparate areas which must ultimately come together to create a comprehensive nanotechnology.

The situation is perhaps analogous to the dawn of the Atomic Age—a time when several powers realized that nuclear weapons were possible, but when none had yet bridged the gap between what was possible and what had been achieved. World War II accelerated the bridging of that gap. There is no global war today, but global economic competition is in its own way a kind of war, and the stakes are now immeasurably higher. Whereas the uses of atomic energy are quite limited, applications for nanotechnology—military as well as commercial—are infinite. The Atomic Age will pale in comparison with the Age of Digital Matter.

Those who would call for a moratorium on nanoresearch will, if their calls are heeded, succeed only in accomplishing what Nazi Germany and fascist Italy accomplished early in the Atomic Age—

an accomplishment which doomed both to destruction: the driving out of the best minds in the relevant sciences, and the righteous treason of those who remained.

The first men to grasp the possibility of nuclear weapons—Enrico Fermi, Leo Szilard, Eugene Wigner, Edward Teller, and Albert Einstein (who were in turn informed of the discovery of fission after one of the German physicists who discovered it smuggled news of the discovery to a Jewish colleague who had fled Germany)—were to a man refugees from nations which had made it clear that moral men of reason and intellect were not welcome.

Similarly, scientists interested in pursuing nanotech will flee any nation which bans it, or conduct their work in secret. As Nobel laureate physicist Richard Feynman noted some forty years ago, nanotechnology will not be prevented. It *cannot* be prevented.

The emergence of nanotech, when it comes, will exert a far greater influence upon the destiny of the human race as a whole, and each individual comprising that race, than any other single event in the history of the world save the creation of life itself—and yet the average man or woman on the street is barely aware of the technology, let alone its implications.

I'm here to change that.

It has been said that ignorance is bliss. In a simpler world, that may have been true. In the world to come, however, ignorance is no longer bliss.

It is death.

Consider this a cautionary tale.

Through the release of atomic energy, our generation has brought into the world the most revolutionary force since prehistoric man's discovery of fire . . . For there is no secret and there is no defense; there is no possibility of control except through the aroused understanding and insistence of the peoples of the world. We scientists recognize our inescapable responsibility to carry to our fellow citizens an

understanding of the simple facts of atomic energy and its
implications for society. In this lies our only security and our
only hope—we believe that an informed citizenry will act for
life and not death.

—Albert Einstein[2]

JOHN ROBERT MARLOW
2004
Earth

[2]Albert Einstein: Letter written on behalf of the Emergency Committee of Atomic Scientists, January 22, 1947 (Einstein Archive 70–918). [Photograph of letter linked from author's Web site at http://www.johnrobertmarlow.com.]

[*Author's Note:* Most referenced quotes are linked from the author's Web site (http://www.johnrobertmarlow.com), and the full text of many cited documents is available on-line. A wealth of information regarding nanotechnology and other topics dealt with in the novel may also be found on the author's Web site.]

APPENDIX—
THE SUPERSWARM OPTION

*For in much wisdom is much grief; and he that increaseth
knowledge increaseth sorrow.*

—*Ecclesiastes 1:18*

In researching and writing *Nano*, and in beating up on K. Eric
Drexler's blatantly suicidal active shields concept, it troubled me
that I could propose no viable alternative to Drexler's idea. It is
easy to say that something will not work; less easy, by far, to propose something which will. After considerable thought, I devised
the proposal outlined below, which I call "The Superswarm
Option."

I am not proposing that the superswarm option be implemented; rather, I present it for due consideration and improvement.
(The surest path to survival is the immediate expansion and colonization of other worlds—which will be made feasible by nanotechnology.) It is, in its own way, insane—but, I believe, somewhat *less*
blatantly suicidal than the active shield concept. To paraphrase
James Cameron (via Sarah Connor in *Terminator 2: Judgment Day*):
In an insane world, it may be the sanest choice.

As mentioned in the afterword, the world's best minds must be
brought to bear on the safest possible implementation of nanotech-

nology. Unfortunately, what are generally considered to be the world's best minds do not always come up with the world's best ideas (witness Edward Teller's Project Chariot, also mentioned in the afterword)—else the world wouldn't be the mess it is. Ideas and inventions devised by "common" men and women have often changed the world, and continue to do so today. Surely, when it comes to saving the world, no voice should go unheard. Debate must be both open and public. Reader comments and alternative suggestions are welcomed at www.johnrobertmarlow.com.

The Superswarm Option

SUMMARY:

Problem: Nonlimited or defectively replicating nanites can multiply swiftly enough to outpace all subsequently implemented countermeasures and so destroy the earth.

Proposed Solution: Create a ubiquitous "superswarm" which covers the globe, is in place before the "nanoevent" (whether accidental or deliberate) occurs—and which reacts instantaneously by attacking and disassembling the "rogue" nanites from all directions simultaneously.

DETAILS:

THE CHALLENGE

From a global threat standpoint, the most troubling aspect of a "nanoevent" (accidental or deliberate release of nonlimited nanites possessed of disassembly capabilities) is the speed with which the nanite swarm or "nanoswarm" increases its size. This speed is exponential, or nearly so. This means that, once a certain swarm-size/swarm-rate-of-expansion threshold is attained (and such a threshold will be attained very rapidly), no mitigating response is possible.

EARLY-STAGE INTERVENTIONS—
NUCLEAR, PLASMA, NANITE

Early-stage interventions (and it must be remembered that the time frame being referenced is inhumanly short) with some chance of successfully terminating a nanoevent (the term "control" will not be used, as there is no control short of event termination) include thermonuclear detonation, plasma attack, and nanoattack. Each of these options will succeed only if it completely destroys the reproductive capabilities of every single nanite within the targeted swarm. A single escaped nanite—carried away from the site on a blast wave, for example, will begin the process anew, requiring another response in a new location, and so on. Several nanites carried away in different directions would require several new responses, *ad infinitum.*

Additional intervention options which remain impractical for the moment (and perhaps forever) include the employment of antimatter and of singularities.

PLASMA INTERVENTION

Highly mobile, instantaneous plasma-generation capability is nonexistent. The feasibility of creating a sufficient quantity of fixed-point instantaneous plasma-generation devices to protect the entire globe—even with the use of nanoassemblers—is dubious, to say the least.

NUCLEAR INTERVENTION

Nuclear weapons are highly mobile and rapidly retargetable. Even so, their deployment is unlikely to be swift enough to accomplish the desired end. To begin with, there are political considerations; not all nations possess nuclear weapons, and those which do possess them will be placed in the position of employing them upon other nations or their own with no practical advance warning.

Next comes the issue of verification. To be effective, launch must be immediate. There is no time for verification; to delay is to die. To launch in error is to kill millions and risk revolution or global conflict. The time it takes the president or other authorized official to open the briefcase and enter the appropriate launch codes could be the difference between life and death for the earth itself.

To place verification and launch procedures in the virtual hands of an artificial intelligence or computer program for sake of speed puts us on the road to active shields (weapons of mass destruction controlled by impartial, nonhuman intelligences or "NHIs"), and subjects us to the unacceptable possibility of computer error and/or malevolent intent.

Lastly, the flight time of nuclear-equipped weapons will in some cases be unacceptably long; even if launched within seconds of swarm detection, by the time the nuclear package arrives, it will not have the desired effect because the swarm will be too large to destroy. Again, the feasibility of placing the practical equivalent of a ready-to-blow nuclear warhead on every street corner is, at best, dubious.

NANOINTERVENTION

The points raised above eliminate all possible methods of early-stage intervention save one: intervention by nanites. An additional point not raised above also leads to this conclusion: namely, the fact that a nanoevent can begin anywhere. Neither nuclear weapons nor plasma guns are likely to prove effective in rapidly reaching and successfully destroying a nanoswarm which begins beneath an ocean, or deep within the earth.

Again, however, speed of response is a critical issue; because of the exponential expansion rate of a rogue swarm, there will be no time to transport the elements of a nanocounterattack to the scene of the event. The counterattacking force must already be in place and ready to act in response to any threat.

Fortunately, the very capabilities which make a rogue swarm so extraordinarily dangerous in the first place also serve to facilitate the erection of an extraordinarily swift and effective nanotechnology-based response.

The Superswarm

COMPOSITION

The proposed "superswarm" would be composed entirely of *anti*-nanite nanites—nanoassemblers/disassamblers specifically pro-grammed to disassemble *only* hostile nanites (but not each other), and to assemble as many additional antinanites as may be required for mission completion. Instructing the antinanites to disassemble *only* hostile nanites (as well as inanimate environmental elements—rigidly prioritized to minimize collateral losses—to aid in antinanite swarm expansion) accomplishes two important objectives: It allows for an instantaneous and automatic threat response without the cumbersome and time-consuming burden of elaborate verification procedures, and; it completely eliminates the massive collateral damage inflicted by nuclear or plasma responses—thus lessening if not eliminating entirely the negative consequences of responding to a false threat alert.

In the interests of maximizing threat-response speed—and also as a method of turning the superswarm against itself should that prove necessary—there can be no centralized superswarm com-mand center or "brain." Such a centralized control center would slow threat-response time, be subject to attack (crippling the entire superswarm should the attack prove even partially successful), and prevent portions of the superswarm from attacking other portions of the superswarm (including any such control center) which may become defective or errant or somehow fall under hostile influence.

DEPLOYMENT

To be effective, the superswarm must be universally deployed over and above the surface of the earth, throughout the oceans, and deep within the planet—in short, the swarm must be present everywhere it is possible for nanites to be present, for only in this manner can it stand ready to react instantaneously to any nanoevent, regardless of point of origin. An effective reaction time of zero will ensure that there is no possibility the rogue swarm will attain critical size/ expansion-rate values because it will itself be under immediate and exponentially expanding attack from all sides by a larger force.

EMPLOYMENT

The superswarm will be, in essence, a single massive nanoswarm which covers and permeates the globe. As in all warlike efforts, communication among friendly forces will be critical to mission success. This appears at first to present somewhat of a dilemma, however, in that an exponentially expanding rogue swarm might well consume and destroy proximate members of the superswarm before they can transmit a warning of the danger and so trigger the superswarm's "immune response." Simply put, if the sentries are killed before they can scream for help, and the attacker continues destroying friendly forces faster than any alert can be communicated to outlying friendly forces in a position to respond before themselves being attacked and destroyed—the entire scenario ends in defeat.

This situation can be avoided only if every single member of the superswarm continually transmits an all-is-fine signal which is continually monitored by all other superswarm members within a reasonable distance. If the signal ceases or falls below a certain signal strength (indicating a rapid friendly force reduction), counterattack begins. Such an arrangement has the additional benefit of rendering signal jamming by the rogue swarm ineffective; if the signal is jammed, the counterattack begins. Signal duplication is another matter, which will have to be addressed through encryption and/or other means, perhaps including superswarm calculation of the number of legitimate individual transmitters operating in any given area at any given time.

Note that each individual member of the superswarm must be a transmitter; otherwise, the attacking rogue swarm can simply disassemble (and perhaps impersonate) nontransmitting superswarm members and so continue to expand without triggering a response.

For sake of redundancy, there should be a localized and/or regional signal-detection hierarchy to ensure that a rapid local or multilocal rogue attack does not prevent a rapid and overwhelming counterattack. Ideally, there will, in addition to the ubiquitous transmitter antinanites, be roving covert nanoscouts which continually roam about in search of anomalies and things which are not as they should be.

Those nanounits, also, must report to local/regional detectors, via either encrypted burst-transmissions or physical presence, or both. The need to physically report to a specific-but-changing location within a specific time frame provides an extremely difficult to counter means of situational reportage; if one or more nanoscouts fail to show up at the appointed time, or turn out to be impostors, an immediate nanocounterattack is directed from all sides at the area in which the nanoscout(s) operated. Nanoscouts may report via randomly selected proxies to avoid detection and targeting by hostile forces.

NANOWAR

A rogue swarm attacked by a properly implemented superswarm will be quickly defeated; no other outcome is possible.

The superswarm will begin with a larger number of nanocombatants, will occupy all territory surrounding the rogue swarm, will multiply exponentially upon rogue swarm detection, and will by its presence and by its rapid consumption of available local nanite-building resources deny those resources to the rogue swarm—which will then be facing superior attack and diminishing resources with which to sustain its own attack/defense efforts. Again, victory for the rogue swarm is not possible.

Assuming the superswarm is capable of detecting nanomimics (hostile nanites which disguise themselves as friendly nanites), the mere survival of a single member of the rogue swarm is not possible. This is crucial because a single rogue nanite can swiftly generate a new rogue swarm.

SAFETY FEATURES

Safety features have been mentioned above, but a primary reason for their implementation bears restating: The superswarm itself could become a threat—a potentially greater threat than any possible rogue swarm.

One reason a centralized superswarm command structure must be avoided at all costs is because that command structure could become defective or could fall under hostile control (human or otherwise)—in which case the entire superswarm could conceivably be tasked with the immediate destruction of specific targets or the planet itself. This possibility must be obviated at all costs. Superswarm decision-making capabilities *must* be decentralized.

Decentralization will permit all portions of the superswarm which have not become defective and which have not fallen under hostile control to operate as intended and immediately attack those portions of the swarm which are not operating as intended. The importance of this safety feature cannot be overstated; to implement the superswarm without it is technocide—suicide by technology.

Properly implemented decentralization, in combination with multiple-signal relay networks to keep nearby and distant portions of the superswarm apprised of local conditions, can both serve to prevent a large-scale or multiple-point rogue swarm attack from eliminating an appropriate threat response, and serve as a built-in form of designed system redundancy.

Another safety feature is this: Superswarm members must be capable of distinguishing between friend and foe. Further, they must be able to distinguish between exponentially multiplying rogue swarm members and exponentially multiplying superswarm members—attacking the former but not the latter.

Additionally, superswarm members must be programmed with resource priorities—that is, there must be an assigned priority of materials employed in superswarm expansion. New superswarm members will ideally be constructed using the atoms of disassembled rogue swarm members (though care must be taken to avoid becoming "infected" by rogue swarm programs in the process; complete disassembly should obviate this potential hazard) and the atoms of those materials which would otherwise be immediately available for use by the rogue swarm in boosting its own numbers (resource denial).

Some care needs to be taken, however, in order to avoid disassembling superswarm members, humans, and other life-forms, and nanites and other objects whose disassembly will or may cause collateral damage, immediate or otherwise. If this is not done, the superswarm threat response will, in effect, accomplish the very damage intended by the rogue swarm.

The superswarm program need not—indeed, must not—be overly complex—but it cannot be simple.

ADVANTAGES AND DISADVANTAGES

Aside from points mentioned above and below, there are the following considerations. Unlike active shields, the Superswarm Option does not require the creation of an infallible nonhuman intelligence prior to implementation—a distinct advantage for many reasons, not the least of which is that such an intelligence may never exist. The hard-programmed or perhaps learning-enabled (as opposed to truly intelligent, or sentient) swarm herein proposed will be incapable of deliberate hostile intent—another advantage.

A severe disadvantage shared, alas, in common with all viable options now foreseeable, is that the Superswarm Option cannot be implemented without a working nanotechnology: It will not exist before the threat it is designed to protect against has arrived. It can, if meticulously worked out in advance and assiduously tested the moment the technology becomes feasible, be rapidly implemented. In such an event, the gravest danger will exist at the earliest stage of working nanodevelopment.

For this reason, it would seem wise to locate the initial nanolabs in remote locations, and to equip each with a sizable and immovable fusion warhead designed to detonate upon notification of a nanoevent. To prevent the warhead itself from being disassembled before notification can be sent or received, redundant backup detonation procedures are called for. The weapon could, for example, be placed in a vacuum which, if broken, initiates detonation. Alternatively, the weapon could be suspended in a fluid whose volume must remain constant, under pressure which must remain unaltered, within an electromagnetic field which must be maintained, etc. A combination of such measures—the violation of any one of which alone will trigger detonation—would perhaps be wisest. Manual detonation might also be permitted.

THE DOWNSIDE

Complex problems require complex solutions, and complex solutions often have downsides which include unforeseen and sometimes unforeseeable consequences. The Superswarm Option is no exception—and the potential downside is as massive and all-encompassing as the upside it offers, to wit; should the superswarm itself somehow "go rogue" on a large scale, there will be no stopping it. It will begin everywhere at once, and the end will come swiftly. The earth and everything on it will vanish in the biblical twinkling of an eye.

To implement a plan with such a terrifying downside is clearly insane. To fail to implement it is probably more insane. We have become the prisoners of our own technology, which now dictates to us even before its arrival the actions we must take if we are to survive that arrival. Though his actions were reprehensible, Theodore Kaczynski—aka the Unabomber—had a point: Technology is reaching the stage at which it might be considered a force for evil so overwhelming and unavoidable as to inevitably destroy us if we do not renounce it immediately.*

CONCLUSION

We will not, of course, do that. We will instead strive to attain the unimaginable benefits clearly promised by the final technology— nanotechnology. To turn away from this promise would make us something other than what we are—a race which labors ceaselessly to improve itself in all respects. To renounce nanotechnology would not be human. Logical, perhaps; wise, surely—but not human.

We will, as we must, go forward—hoping to avoid the peril, while reaching for the promise.

I wish us luck.

We're going to need it.

JOHN ROBERT MARLOW

*It is perhaps the ultimate irony that the technological evils of which the Unabomber wrote in his at times surprisingly lucid manifesto can be entirely eliminated through the use of technology itself—nanotechnology. Assuming, that is, that the technology can be successfully implemented—a proposition which is by no means certain.

ABOUT THE AUTHOR

John Robert Marlow lives in Los Angeles, California. He is a free-lance journalist whose work has appeared in *Parade, Omni,* and numerous other publications. His *Nano* screenplay (based upon this book) has been honored as a finalist in the Nicholl Fellowships in Screenwriting Program of the Academy of Motion Picture Arts and Sciences (the organization which awards the Oscars). This is his first novel. Visit the author's Web site at www.johnrobertmarlow.com.